To Kill A Unicorn

by DC Palter

pandamoon
publishing

www.pandamoonpublishing.com

Jacket design and illustrations © Pandamoon Publishing
Art Direction by Don Kramer: Pandamoon Publishing
Editing by Zara Kramer, Rachel Schoenbauer, and Kathleen Bosman: Pandamoon Publishing

Pandamoon Publishing and the portrayal of a panda and a moon are registered trademarks of Pandamoon Publishing.

Library of Congress Cataloging-in-Publication Data is on file at the Library of Congress, Washington, DC

Edition: 1, Version 1.00
ISBN 13: 978-1-950627-65-3

Reviews

"A deftly-crafted, funny, scintillating, and down-to-earth mystery set in the atmospheric and chaotic, high stakes world of Silicon Valley... *To Kill a Unicorn* could only be written by DC Palter, who lives and breathes the Silicon Valley venture capitalist life... Readers will revel... and demand the second book in what will inevitably be a series." — **J. Carson Black, NY Times best-selling author of** *The Laura Cardinal Novel*

"*To Kill a Unicorn* is a spirited, fast-paced mystery that quickly engages the reader in a universe of corruption, greed, and high-stakes betrayal...Author DC Palter skillfully provides the needed elements for a grand story and exploration of dangerous competition in the tech world, of friendship, of the need for strong, personal ethics, as well as of deep cultural ties - and love. Get ready for a heart-pounding read." — **Jule Selbo, author of the award-winning** *Dee Rommel Mystery Series, Find Me in Florence,* **and historical fiction for the** *Mentoris Project.*

"Palter's wildly entertaining debut delves into hardboiled crime in the world of high-tech start-ups via Tatsu a.k.a Ted a.k.a Teddybear Hara, a sake-sipping, bunny-slipper-wearing IT employee with hacking skills. When ex-girlfriend Sumire shows up begging him to find her missing brother, Ted becomes a reluctant cyber-sleuth and gets sucked into the evil doings of a nefarious unicorn. Oh, and there are elephants! Prepare to have your mind blown." — **Suzanne Kamata, author of** *The Baseball Widow*

"The original plot, featuring a smart-mouthed coder-turned-hacker/sleuth with predilections for fine Japanese sake and pure mathematics, makes *To Kill a Unicorn* a highly entertaining mystery. A great read with colorful atmospherics and an intriguing premise.**" — **Christina Hoag, author of** *Skin of Tattoos* **and** *Law of the Jungle*

"In this fast-paced cyber thriller, *To Kill a Unicorn*, DC Palter carries readers along on this quest through the glittering and increasingly menacing urban landscape of Northern California. We careen through a maze of hidden hurts and private dreams chasing a menagerie of cryptic characters from unicorns and elephants to geeks, beauties, and Japanese Nisei." — **Rebecca Copeland, Professor of Japanese literature and author of** *The Kimono Tattoo*

"*To Kill a Unicorn* is a modern cautionary tale disguised as a high-tech thriller. A combination of a hero's journey and detective story, Palter accurately captures the greed and desperation of Silicon Valley founders, executives, and venture capitalists in search of the next great thing. Palter also weaves in life in the Valley as the son of a Japanese immigrant, pursuing the American dream while trying not to abandon the history and teachings his mother and her country. A fun ride!" — **Tony Ollivier, author of** *The Amsterdam Deception*

"DC Palter's well written thriller is a masterpiece that contains everything I love in a novel. The main character seemed like an old friend that I was cheering on from the moment I learned his name; Hara Tatsu (literally "angry" in Japanese). I never wanted to put it down, and when I did, I couldn't wait to pick it back up again." — **Joe Palermo, author of** *No Pianos, Pets or Foreigners!*

"Culturally fragmented in a world outlined by the sense of millennial, intriguing, hyper realistic writing, this novel, pulls you right into its cinematic vaults…Amidst the turmoil, his novel points out the importance of shared narratives, even if only evoked… by a bowl of green tea, for they bring the illusory feeling of a steady continuity, and a kind of kintsugi (a golden repairing of the cracks) back into life." — **Alejandra Olivera, author of** *Here be Dragons*

"DC Palter's *To Kill a Unicorn* reads like a Dashiell Hammett hard-boiled detective novel, except the part of Sam Spade—the quintessential private detective—is portrayed by an unwilling Japanese-American mathematician/ computer hacker who goes by the name of Ted…To Kill A Unicorn is a masterfully written story introducing readers to Japanese-American culture…A real page-turner that spurs the reader on to keep reading to find out what happens next." — **Kristine Ohkubo, author of** *The Sun Will Rise Again,* **and** *Talking About Rakugo*

"*To Kill a Unicorn* is the cyberpunk dystopia to worry about waking up in; not next century, but next week. A book for readers centered in the Venn diagram of Tom Robbins and Douglas Adams. Step right up and get your heart broken by an elephant." — **Rachel Sharp, author of** *Phaethon Series*

"This book is a real page-turner. Kind of like climbing a mountain, you can see more and enjoy more as you climb higher. Aside from the mystery that keeps you guessing, the author throws in so many Easter eggs to unwrap that the reader will begin to look for them. Specific locations, Japanese terms, tech insider words, and more all make this a book you'll surely talk about to your friends." — **Dave Berkus, author of** *Starting Up!, Extending the Runway,* **and** *Berkonomic*

"DC Palter's fresh take on a classic genre brings a detective story to Silicon Valley, in which our hard-boiled detective, Ted, happens to be a lackadaisical hacker forced into action when his former best friend goes missing. Although peppered with sly jabs at Valley institutions, Palter's plot never slows, with a gripping, page-turning mystery that will leave you wondering which unicorn is going to be axed." — **Jessica Powell, author of** *The Big Disruption: A Totally Fictional but Essentially True Silicon Valley Story*

"A William Gibson-esque cyberthriller for a new generation… A wild ride with teleportation, ramen, and elephants. *To Kill a Unicorn* kept me guessing… Palter is reminiscent of Blake Crouch, but with an absurdist twist." — **Amber Logan, author of** *The Secret Garden of Yanagi Inn*

Dedication

For everyone in Silicon Valley, in person and in spirit.
May your craziest dreams come true.

To Kill A Unicorn

Chapter 1
Japantown

The door rattled open and Sumire walked in as if it had been hours instead of years. "Hello, Teddybear," she whispered, her wide, brown eyes still sparkling, just like long ago.

My mouth hung open, my mind in a panic, a strange mixture of emotions swirling—the old guilt roaring back, a blur of pain, a hint of sweetness underneath. I jumped to my feet in my bunny slippers, nearly knocking over the sake bottle, and stood like an idiot not knowing whether to kiss like long-lost lovers, hug like childhood friends, or bow like our Japanese parents. But she only waved a shy greeting as her chamomile scent spread through the room.

"Hello, Sumire," I said, raising my sake cup.

Her shiny, black hair swished back and forth as she shook her head in disappointment. "Still drinking, Ted?"

I fought the urge to tell her to leave and saluted her with the cup. "*Kanpai*," I said, downing the clear elixir.

She clenched her jaw, her only reply, reminding me of the sullen silence when I'd told her to leave me in peace after my father's accident.

She glanced around the tiny studio, the last of Japantown's creaking apartments, wrinkling her nose at the mildewed carpets and scuffed walls, the flakes of paint sitting in the windowsills. "What the frick, Ted?"

I didn't need her disapproval; I had my mother for that. "Why are you here, Sumire?" I asked. "Just dropped by for a drink?"

Her long ponytail had been shorn away to a shoulder-length bob, halter top and shorts replaced with a lawyer's blouse and skirt. The Converses she'd worn in high school—manga of her friends drawn on the canvas sides and people she hated on the soles to be stepped on—traded for the black flats now lined up beside the door.

Then I noticed her slumped shoulders, the patched mascara on her cheeks, and felt guilty again. The fierce, playful girl I'd once loved was gone; before me stood a sad, troubled woman.

"Sorry," I said. "It's good to see you."

I didn't expect her to tell me she missed me, but she didn't even ask how I'd been. "Ryu is missing," she said, head bowed. "Can you help me find him?"

Though I didn't understand why she'd come to me looking for her brother, I was glad that after all these years, and everything that had happened between us, she knew I was the one person she could count on.

I stroked the wisps on my chin like a detective. "What makes you think he's missing?"

"He was supposed to have lunch with Mom on Sunday and he never showed up. No call, no message, nothing. You know Ryu's not like that. And now his phone is disconnected." She held up her MeCan 5XL, the list of unanswered calls filling her screen with angry red.

It had only been three days, I pointed out. "He's probably just hanging with a girlfriend in Cabo." At least that's what I'd be doing if I wasn't busy with work. And had a girlfriend to take to Cabo. I imagined sipping a margarita on the beach beside Sumire once I found her brother, her bare skin glistening under the tropical sun. "I'll bet the last thing on his mind right now is talking to you and your mom."

"No," she said, certain as always. "I'm sure something happened to him."

I was just as sure Ryu was fine but knew there was no point arguing. "Did you call his office?" I asked. "They must know where he is."

"He joined a startup. I can't find any way to contact them."

A startup? I wondered what a physicist like Ryu was doing at a startup. Probably wasting his life writing JavaScript, the same as all the other dopes. Everyone was quitting their jobs to join startups, expecting them to magically morph into glorious unicorns and rain riches over them like candy from a piñata. I pulled up Ryu's profile on LinkedIn. "Look," I said, pointing at the page. "Says he's still at Intel."

"He didn't tell anyone he left. Not even Mom or me."

"Then how did you find out?"

"I got Kenta to spill the tea. He said Ryu joined some company called SüprDüpr but had to keep it secret."

I'd never heard of a job where you couldn't tell your family what you were doing, not even the stealthiest stealth-mode startup. "I'll bet he was afraid to tell your mother he'd left a steady paycheck for some startup that'll be gone in a month. I know what *my* mother would've said."

She rolled her eyes. "Thank goodness my mother isn't like yours."

Half-expecting the ground to rumble and lightning to shoot forth, I bowed a hasty apology to Kaa-chan's ashes in the white urn atop her tea ceremony cabinet.

On the computer, I pulled up the SüprDüpr website to look up their contact info. I was surprised to find nothing but a cartoon elephant filling the page. Below it was the only text: "Stay tuned for a revolution in transportation!" No links, no email, not even a contact form. Total sus, for sure, but nothing to do with Ryu going MIA. If he wasn't at the beach or a Christian retreat somewhere, I told Sumire, he was probably in a hospital.

"Already checked," she said.

"Nervous breakdown? Drug addiction?"

"No way."

"How about Kenta—they're still close, aren't they? He must know what's going on."

"He's busy with the restaurant and the baby. He didn't have a clue."

"Did you try the cops?"

"Just came from there. Filled out a missing persons report. They told me not to hold my breath. That's why I came here."

I still didn't understand—if Ryu's sister and his best buddy didn't know where to find him, there was no reason I would. "Nothing I can do." I pointed at the stack trace of a bug glowing malevolently on the screen. "And I'm kind of busy." My boss had ordered me to fix the urgent bug tonight.

Instead of leaving me to my solitary bug hunting, she placed her hands on the table. No rings, I noticed. No nail polish either. "You work in mapping at MeCan, don't you?"

Like any good lawyer, she already knew the answer to her question. I was surprised she'd kept tabs on me but I shouldn't have been—in Japantown, everybody knew everyone else's grandparents. "Navigation, actually," I corrected her. "Need directions home?"

She glared at me through black frame glasses that magnified her wide, round eyes. "No, Ted. I need you to track his phone."

Ah, now it made sense why she'd come to me of all people. It wasn't that I was the one person she could count on, or even that I was the best hacker in town. And it certainly wasn't because she wanted to see me again. No, I was the one person she knew who worked at MeCan, the king of mobile phones. Like the rest of the 89.6% of the population that wasn't an Apple zealot, Ryu used a MeCan phone and a MeCan email address. As a programmer at MeCan, Sumire assumed I could look up the GPS coordinates of his phone to track him. That was a reasonable assumption if you didn't know how security worked inside the company. My pride deflated, the knot in my stomach burned.

"Do you have his phone?" I asked.

She shook her head.

"Do you know his password?"

"Come on, Ted, I'm not stupid. Do you think I'd come here if I could get into his account myself?"

Yeah, I shouldn't have been surprised she wasn't thrilled to see me. "Can't help you."

"Why not?"

"Because I'd lose my job, that's why. Believe it or not, MeCan takes privacy seriously. The second I try to look at any user personal data, the security team will be at my desk with boxes to pack up my belongings."

"Please, Teddybear, can't you do something? I'm sure Ryu's in trouble."

Her old nickname for me only made me cringe. "I'm not a stuffed animal," I reminded her.

"Okay, Ted," she said, the dreamy girl gone, the lawyer negotiating now. "Just do me this one favor and I swear I'll never bother you again."

I sipped at my sake as I tried to think of how to tell her no. But when the chocolate-brown eyes that used to dance with playfulness stared at me sad and puffy, I couldn't refuse. "Alright," I relented. "I'll see what I can do."

It wouldn't take long to shoot Ryu an email and hope he'd reply to me. If that didn't work, with a little poking around, I ought to be able to find someone at SüprDüpr. It wasn't much, but it would have to do.

She kissed me on my stubbly cheek and hugged me tight, the touch of her arms through the thin fabric reigniting memories of our long-ago fumbles in the dark. "Thanks, Teddybear," she whispered in my ear. Despite cringing at the nickname again, somewhere inside that knot in my stomach, I knew it was more than just the flush of the sake that made me feel warm now.

She smiled sadly once more before turning for the door. "Call me first thing in the morning," she ordered, "and let me know what you find."

I stood there, not knowing what to say, the heat of her body draining from my hands, the memory of her skin on my fingers. Then the door rattled open and she walked back out as if she'd never walked back in, leaving behind nothing but the scent of chamomile lingering in my empty apartment.

I returned the frosted blue bottle of Mu to the fridge; I needed something stronger now. Carrying the Yamazaki single malt to the window, I poured two fingers of honey-colored fire and peeked out through the metal blinds to Jackson Street below. Japantown was deserted, all the shops and restaurants shuttered, only the neon of the ramen joints and izakaya bars still shining their beacons through the fog.

As the cool burn slid down my throat, its tendrils spreading into my veins, I recalled growing up with Ryu. He'd been my best friend since we were toddlers playing in the sandbox together under the watchful eyes of our Japanese mothers. Growing up, we'd battled each other at video games in his room every night, my escape from the brooding that filled my own home with gloomy silence. Until suddenly he grew tall and became the star of the baseball team while I stayed short and taught myself to program. He was handsome and sociable and all the girls crushed on him, the same girls who called me shrimp or *chibi* or four eyes when they acknowledged my existence at all.

Then his parents divorced and his sister, the little pest with a crooked tooth and sticking out ears who'd begged to join our games, grew into a sullen teen who loved to draw and for some reason still wanted to hang with me. The more I saw of Sumire, the more awkward Ryu and I became. A strangled hello when we passed each other in the school hallway or he caught me sneaking out of her room. When the screaming baseball shattered his jaw, crushing his major league dreams, I should have rushed to the emergency room, but by then, my own world was in chaos, and anyway, the church girls got to him before I ever had the chance. I swallowed the last drops of liquid gold and vowed that when I found Ryu, I'd renew our friendship and become best-ish buds again.

Setting the glass on the windowsill, I returned to the computer to contact him. I shot him an email, but within seconds, my inbox dinged with an error: *account does not exist.* I stared at the screen, not comprehending. Sumire had said he wasn't replying, not that his account was gone, and that was a completely different kettle of koi. I tried calling. A robotic woman's voice droned: "The number you've dialed is out of service. Please hang up and try again."

It made no sense. Even if Ryu was dead in a ditch, his email would live on until the silicon in the SSD drive crumbled into sand. This was no private time in Cabo, not even a lost phone. If his account was deleted, something had gone horribly wrong. It was time to panic.

Sumire was right—the best way to find Ryu was to hack into his MeCan account. The company was required to keep records of every GPS coordinate, every phone call, every text for years in case the FBI demanded to see them. If I could access the data, I could track where he'd been until the moment his phone was disconnected. But I couldn't do it from my own VPN into the office where the IP address would point straight back at me. I'd have to make it look like any other untraceable hacker, and that would take most of the night to navigate through the layers of security designed to prevent anyone from doing exactly what I intended to do. As for the bug I was supposed to fix tonight, my bosses would just have to wait until morning.

But when I cracked my fingers to get started, my stomach growled in complaint. It would be a long night and the refrigerator was empty except for a wrinkled daikon and the remaining half a bottle of Mu. It was time to visit Kenta for a bowl of ramen while squeezing out whatever else Ryu's confidant hadn't wanted to tell his sister.

Chapter 2
The Dandy Lion

The weather-beaten sign hanging over the Dandy Lion's narrow entrance creaked as it swayed in the breeze, every trace of the yellow dandelions that had once bracketed the name flaked away. As the wooden door rolled open on its metal rail, the scent of simmering broth, pig fat, and moldering wood greeted me with the smell of home. Inside, the joint was empty except for a few stragglers and the golf farts, as always, in the corner booth laughing over their whiskey ices.

"Sorry, we're closed," called a woman, her voice barely audible over the television blaring the wrap-up of a Giants game.

I spied Kenta's wife in the back, her sturdy body hunched over sweeping the floor. "Hello, Yukiko," I called.

She squinted in my direction. "Ted? Is that you?" she asked in a welcoming voice, as if she didn't hate me. "Come back tomorrow, okay?"

When I said I was here to see Kenta, she gave me a look that made clear she wanted to close up and go home. I promised I wouldn't stay long.

Kenta, though, was happy to see me. "Tatsu!" he hollered from the counter. The wall of steam rising from the steel cauldrons in front of him turned him into a shimmering ghost.

We'd always been Kenta and Tatsu to each other, our Japanese names, never Ken and Ted, ever since we'd played together on the jungle gyms. Despite telling him I just wanted to chat for a sec, Kenta insisted on cooking.

I sat at one of the lacquered tables and listened to the hiss and pop of the frying pan. Behind him, a long row of sake bottles filled the back wall—the cheap crap for customers who didn't know any better. Kenta hid the good stuff in the refrigerator under the counter to drink with friends. "Got any Dassai?" I shouted across the restaurant.

Yukiko flashed her annoyance but brought over a fist-sized bottle and a plate of sizzling gyoza. "*Arigatou*," I thanked her with an exaggerated bow. She replied with a dismissive head bob and strode away without saying a word. She was best friends with Sumire and even though our breakup was ancient history, history lived in these broth-soaked walls forever.

The green bottle of Dassai was fogged with condensation, kanji characters flowing across the front of the cottony white label. I filled the small cup and sipped the liquid, felt it slide down my throat, clean as water, a touch of sweetness, a faint shadow of alcohol at the tail. Heaven.

The steam rising off the gyoza carried a tang of ginger that made my mouth water. I mixed a saucer of soy sauce and vinegar and added a few drops of chili oil, then dipped a dumpling and took a bite. Hot juice squirted out, burning my tongue. Kenta laughed as I grabbed a napkin to wipe my face.

He plopped onto the chair across from me, shoulders hunched with fatigue. I filled his cup and saluted him with mine. He must have been hungry working all evening—he hardly looked up as he shoveled rice into his mouth. He scarfed down half a bowl before I dropped the bomb.

"I just saw Sumire," I said.

Kenta stopped mid-bite and raised his eyebrows, his mouth a surprised O. "Bruh! You guys finally getting back together?" he said through a mouthful of food. "It's about time."

I grimaced. News of her visit to my apartment would be all over the neighborhood tomorrow—Kenta was the worst gossip in town. "She still hates me," I insisted. "She thinks Ryu is missing. She asked me to find him."

He said nothing and returned to snarfing the gyoza off the plate in the center of the table.

"You got any idea where he went?"

"No," he said, avoiding looking at me. Even I could tell he was lying.

"What is it?"

His eyes darted to the side of the room where Yukiko was topping up the soy sauce dispensers. We sipped at the sake and grumbled about the Giants until she disappeared into the stockroom.

"Spill the tea," I said, waiting to hear all the secrets Ryu couldn't share with his sister.

"Nothing." Kenta shook his head. "Not a damn thing."

"Jeez. You couldn't tell me that before?"

He leaned towards me and whispered, "You don't get it, bruh. He tells me everything."

I missed the camaraderie between Ryu and Kenta that I'd once been part of, listening to tunes together or playing Legends of Emperors. "Any idea what Ryu wasn't telling you?"

"Nope," he said, shaking his head. "But lately he's been acting weird."

"Weird?" I repeated, a little too loudly, prompting Kenta to shush me again.

"What's weird, honey?" Yukiko called from the back.

"Giants' relief pitching," he hollered. "Total disaster this year."

"Oh, that." She slipped into the stockroom again. We pulled our chairs closer.

"Last week, Ryu was acting kind of…I don't know—nervous? Came in, ate, drank, drank some more, wouldn't talk, went home. Every night. And he's never been a drinker, not like, well…not like some people."

I didn't appreciate the dig, even if he didn't say it. I had enough people already telling me how to live my life. "Ryu was drinking. Big deal." I emptied the remainder of the bottle into our cups. "What happened—did he lose his faith in God?"

At least that got Kenta to laugh—Ryu was a true believer.

I expected a long story. But all Kenta said was, "Don't know. Haven't seen him since then. I didn't think anything of it until Sumire showed up and gave me the third degree. Maybe something did happen to him."

"Like what?"

"Like…you know…"

I motioned for him to continue, waiting for reality to smack a screaming line drive at my face.

He ducked his head as he said, "Like, well…like your father."

I closed my eyes. Could the same thing have happened to Ryu? Sumire said she'd already checked around. If Ryu had turned up dead by the roadside, the police would've called her mother, the same as they'd called Kaa-chan at 2 a.m. and I had to hold her screaming, shaking body when they pointed at the crumpled hood of the Mustang under the cone of light still shining down from the bent light pole.

I blinked away the vision and instead pictured Ryu sitting at this table night after night, until one night his chair went empty. "When was the last time he came in here?"

"Must have been Saturday—it was super loud, a bunch of frat boys ordering sake bombs. Ryu was sitting over there by himself." He pointed at the table in the corner behind the entrance. "Said he had to talk to me. I should've made time, but…you know how it is—the orders were backing up. So I told him to chill 'til we closed. He took off anyway. I thought he'd come back when it was quieter, but I haven't seen him since. That was only a few days ago, so I didn't think anything of it until Sumire showed up. And now you. What's going on?"

"Did he say what he wanted to talk about?"

Kenta shook his head.

"Did he say anything? Girlfriend? Work? He must have at least complained about the Giants."

Kenta stroked the tufts on his chin that he called a goatee. "Well…this probably doesn't mean anything, but he asked if I thought elephants have a soul."

I would have told him no, and neither did humans, which is why we had so little to say to each other once the church became his life. "What did you answer?"

"I said I've got no clue. Then he mumbled that he was sure they did, and that he had to save them."

"Save the elephants?"

"Yeah, something like that."

"So he packed up and moved to India to go save elephants? Or did the elephant mafia get wind of it and knock him off?"

My sarcasm always made Kenta uncomfortable. "Sorry, bruh, just telling you what he said. I thought maybe he was talking about a new video game or something."

There weren't any new games I knew of with elephants, and I knew every game worth playing. The only place I'd seen elephants lately was the cartoon elephant on the SüprDüpr website. "What did Ryu tell you about this new job?"

"Not much."

"How much is 'not much'?"

"Come on, dude. He made me swear not to tell anyone, not even Yukiko."

"And yet you told Sumire."

"She's his sister."

"And I'm his friend."

Kenta raised his hands in surrender. "All I know is he started working there a couple months ago. He was all excited at first, said they were developing some new technology that was going to change the world. Told me they were going to be incredibly rich by the end of the year."

The usual startup blather. "What else?"

"Well…the head of the company was this genius lady named Katie—Ryu said she was the smartest, most beautiful woman ever."

Right. If there was a man in trouble, and Ryu sounded like a mess, there had to be a woman involved. But Ryu never chased after girls—they came to him. "Didn't he have a girlfriend?"

I waited for Kenta to answer. And waited. "Maybe," he finally said.

"What do you mean 'maybe'?"

"Chill, bruh."

"Ryu's missing. Did he have a girlfriend or not?"

"There was Grace—"

"Grace who?"

"Grace Kim."

"When was the last time you saw her?"

"Been a while. Must've been before he started the new job."

"Jeez," I said. It sounded like Ryu quit his job and joined some secret startup to chase after the company's president. My money was on a personal crisis. When things didn't work out with her, he probably left for a camp in the desert or took off to India to save some smelly elephants.

There wasn't much more to be learned here and I had work to do. I drained my cup, gave Kenta a fist-bump, and shouted goodnight to Yukiko. Then I tramped the three blocks up the deserted street, past the shuttered shops, back to my grungy apartment.

The computer was raring to go, Octa-core CPU overclocked to 135%, the fastest graphics card on the market purring inside, able to solve millions of parallel calculations for artificial intelligence or BiteCoin mining or just kicking butt at the latest MMORPG. Serious overkill for basic hacking, but like a Ferrari stuck in traffic on the 101, it was nice to know you could outrace anyone if you had to.

All the lights off, I cracked my knuckles and started by searching for Ryu's girlfriend. If there was anyone who knew what Ryu was doing at SüprDüpr, it wasn't Sumire, it wasn't Kenta—it was Grace. If there was anyone who might have a reason to kill him—maybe a baby he refused to acknowledge or just a woman scorned with a grudge and a knife, that would be Grace, too.

Based on her name, Grace Kim had to be Korean, and that must have been awkward for both of them. A Korean girlfriend would have launched Kaa-chan into a never-ending fit, which is why I never told her about anyone I was dating after Sumire, none of them Japanese.

I was surprised to find how many Grace Kims lived in the Bay Area. But poking around on LinkedIn, one Grace jumped out—a volunteer at the same church Ryu attended. I was sure that was her. Just my luck she worked at the Spaceship—Apple's headquarters in Cupertino—the one place in this world I could never enter. I sent her a connection request with a note, asking to jump onto a Zoom tomorrow to talk about Ryu. That done, it was time to start hacking.

Waiting for the computer to reboot into Linux, I sipped at the Yamazaki to focus my mind. Once the cursor blinked back at me, I fired up a Tor browser and headed down into the depths of the dark web to build an untraceable tunnel to Romania. From there, my connection to the MeCan servers only a few miles away would appear to come from some script kiddie in his parent's basement in Râmnicu Vâlcea. That was the easy part. Tougher was getting inside the account servers.

I browsed through the hacker forums for security holes for sale looking for a zero-day that MeCan hadn't patched yet. Then it hit me—the bug I was supposed to be fixing tonight—I could use it to trigger a software crash and get administrator access. The chance to break into my own office using my own security hole was too ironic to pass up. Plus, it wouldn't cost me anything. That worked perfectly to get me onto the company network, but I still had to worm my way into the account servers, and that was the tricky part.

Half a bottle of whiskey, six coffee pods, and four hours later, I succeeded in crashing a billing daemon. I was so proud of my handiwork I typed the gamer's triumph into the crash log: "All your base are belong to us!" Stupid, for sure, but as a loyal MeCan employee, it was my duty to point out the attack vector if the security team ever bothered checking.

Though my head was spinning and my fingers ached, my eyelids drooped and I craved sleep, there was no stopping now. I stepped into the bathroom to splash cold water on my face. When I returned, I drained the last dregs of coffee and cracked my knuckles once more. I was ready.

I logged into the user database and grepped for Ryu's account. The cursor replied: `no account found.`

Oh, shit, I thought and searched again using wildcards to make sure I didn't miss anything. There was nothing. The account was gone—all his emails, phone records, voicemails, texts, GPS coordinates, and photo archives, even his shopping history and YouTube videos. All the electronic ephemera of Ryu's life, disappeared into the void. Everything that would tell me where Ryu had been and what he'd been doing— every byte of it wiped away.

This was no accident, no oops I lost my password. The whole account was gone, as if it never existed. That had required clicking through warning after warning of "Are you sure you really want to do this?" There was no recovering a deleted account. Either Ryu had deleted his account himself, or somebody had deleted him. Undoubtedly, a backup survived somewhere in case the FBI came calling, but we'd need a search warrant to access that.

I needed to tell Sumire but didn't want to frighten her, not before I knew more myself. We'd have to bring this to the cops, but I couldn't tell them about Ryu's deleted account without exposing my hacking. That would certainly get me fired, maybe even thrown in jail. I wracked my brain, but it was after 4 a.m. and my head was spinning. I had no idea what to do next. I fell into a sweaty, fitful sleep to dream about elephants.

STOP ACTING LIKE A MONKEY, TATSU-KUN!

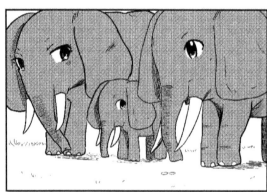

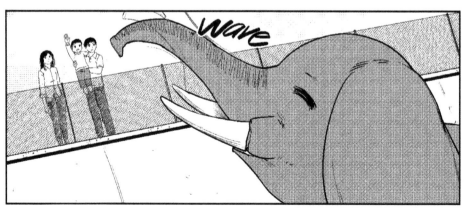

Chapter 3
Center of the Universe Centre

I awoke to the buzz of a slack from my boss demanding to know why the bug wasn't fixed yet. My eyes narrowed against the light, my head throbbing, I was tempted to ask how late he'd worked last night but replied instead with a promise to get it done right away this morning.

As I fumbled to my feet, a wave of nausea washed over me, knocking me back to the couch. I wished I could call in sick to sleep off the hangover before getting back to tracking Ryu, but there was no avoiding the office now. I stumbled into the kitchenette where I popped a fresh pod in the knockoff Keurig and followed it with an aspirin chaser.

In the bathroom, the pair of bloodshot eyes staring back at me from the fogged-up mirror were disappointed with what they saw—a square face on a short, scrawny body, wide nose holding up geeky, wire-frame glasses. Shaggy hair hung down to my eyes while my chin was dotted with stubbly shoots that would never grow into a tech-bro beard. I wondered what Sumire had seen in me years ago, and what she'd see now. I resolved once more to work out with weights. And eat a healthy diet. And drink less. Soon.

After a shower washed away the residue of the night and the caffeine cleared out the cobwebs, I donned my sunglasses and pulled my red remembrance cap low to head out into the burning sunshine.

The McQueen-green '69 Mustang galloped up Winchester Blvd. towards the forty-four-story tower of orange-tinted steel, its iconic dome atop the conical building visible throughout the Valley. MeCan's headquarters was officially named the Center of the Universe Centre, but known less pretentiously as the Tangerine Tower and referred to by competitors and teens alike as Mobile Dick because we were the kings of cell phones.

Passing the Winchester Mystery House, I turned left onto the MeCan campus built atop the rubble of a dead shopping mall. Along the access road were the employee diversions—gyms, restaurants, cinemas, laundromat, community center, culture center, conference center, even an Olympic bobsled track with artificial snow. I passed the enormous data center, painted white on blue to resemble the puffy cumulus clouds that sashayed over the low hills, a reminder that "the cloud" where everyone stored their email, GPS data, and nude photographs was simply this windowless building and fifty others like it dotting the globe. Somewhere among the countless racks of servers inside was a backup of Ryu's data. I had no idea how to navigate past the three layers of physical security to get into the building much less where to find the one hard drive that held a copy of his data.

In the parking lot, I was relegated to the purgatory for hulking pickup trucks, monster SUVs, and classic muscle cars like mine nearly a quarter mile away, past the crossovers, the family sedans, and the econocars arranged by fuel efficiency, past acres of hybrids and electric vehicles all plugged into the free charging. More Teslas here than at the Tesla factory across the bay. As I hiked to the tower, I considered trading in my father's pony, as he always called his Mustang, for a tricked-out racing scooter, transforming my reputation from unrepentant reprobate to quirky nonconformist. But there was no way I could ever give up my father's baby, not after Tou-san and I had spent so many Saturday mornings buffing its paint to the waxy green shine of a freshly unfurled tea leaf.

Once I reached the fourteenth floor and settled into my cubicle, it would have been impossible to concentrate even without the fading headache. On one side of me, Amol banged away at his keyboard while on the other, MeiLi yelled into her Bluetooth. Across the partition, Twitter-Dee tossed Cheetos at Twitter-Dumb, raining dayglow orange crumbs over my desk.

At the top of my inbox was an urgent notice for my own security breach. The I.T. department chief, head of escalations, and some flunky in security were all slacking me, asking when I'd have a patch ready. I cracked my knuckles and dove in.

First, I checked the incident report to make sure there was nothing tracing the breach back to me. The suspected origin was skiddies in Romania, as I'd intended. It didn't take long to discover the cause of the bug—corrupted input from someone else's routine. That code turned out to be a giant mess of spaghetti that would take at least a week to refactor. Though I was tempted to take the easy solution like everyone else and simply add error checking to my code, that would only kick the bug down the stack where it would crash somewhere else. Instead, I opened a ticket to log the bug, entering a completion date of next week. I half-expected the entire

Tangerine Tower to explode in fury, but the world continued on the same as before, air conditioners humming, Cheetos dust raining down.

Before getting started on the project, I went to the breakroom to brew tea. Avoiding the stupid scrubs gathered around the kombucha tap gabbing about some new TikTok star, I texted Sumire: "*any news?*" I was hoping Ryu had turned up overnight so I wouldn't have to tell her about his deleted account.

Within seconds my phone buzzed back: "☹ *nothing* ☹"

I stared at the screen, my eyes fuzzing out, the frowny face emojis morphing into angry baseballs. Before wasting time trying to figure out how to hack into a backup of Ryu's account, it was worth checking if anyone in Ryu's office knew how to reach him.

At my desk, I mecaned for a phone number or an email for SüprDüpr. I was surprised I couldn't find anything. There was no shortage of articles about the company, from *TechCrunch* to *Forbes* to the *Wall Street Journal,* all raving about the company's billion-dollar valuation in its initial seed round, declaring it the first virgin unicorn ever. They gushed over the founder and CEO, Dr. Katherine Deauville, or Katie D as they called her, a Ph.D. in particle physics from the unicorn factory of Stanford. The accompanying photos showed long auburn hair over a sculpted face lit up by a pixie grin. Brilliant and beautiful, a hint of geekiness, the perfect woman of Silicon Valley. I could understand why Ryu had ditched Intel.

I decided to contact this Katie D directly to ask about Ryu. But she had no LinkedIn profile, no Insta, not even a Facebook page, a shocking lapse for the CEO of the hottest unicorn in town. She'd posted nothing on Twitter but a single message retweeted a million times: "SüprDüpr is about to unleash a revolution in transportation that will transform the world." Typical unicorn blather. Reddit was full of speculation about what this startup was building, everything from another taxi app, to an electric airplane, to a time machine, guessing from the jobs the company had open.

I followed the link to the job postings. The company was hiring a chief financial officer, a chief marketing officer, a chief revenue officer, a chief personnel officer, a chief physics officer, an architect, and a construction foreman. And like every startup, a gaggle of web programmers and backend programmers and full stack programmers, along with a giggle of office assistants and anyone willing to intern for free. And there at the bottom, I was surprised to find a job for a mathematician, a specialist in Riemannian geometry. Nobody hired mathematicians, had no idea what we did, thought we were nothing but programmers since computers handled all the calculations.

But despite having a master's degree in mathematics, I'd only heard of Riemannian geometry in passing. It was far from my specialty. After changing my master's thesis to a problem in Riemannian manifolds I dug up online, I submitted my resume to the HR portal, hoping the automated response would include some way to reach the company. I waited and waited but nothing dropped into my inbox, not even the usual form letter stating they received too many applications to respond to each individually.

For a company with no customers or even a product yet, I wondered how they could afford to hire so many people. A quick glance at Crunchbase made that obvious. Of course they had venture capital funding. Two hundred fifty million dollars of it. But what made me groan was that most of the money came from BiteCoin Investments, the venture arm of the blockchain company created by Satoshi Nakamoto. Before becoming one of the richest men on earth, his wealth rivaling Musk and Bezos, Satoshi had been a gawky Stanford postdoc from Kyoto, and my mother's most devoted tea ceremony student.

As awkward as it would be to ping Satoshi now, he'd know how to reach SüprDüpr. Although I hadn't seen Satoshi since Kaa-chan's funeral and it was unlikely he'd remember me, it was worth a try. At least I had an excuse to contact him since I was supposedly applying for a job.

I didn't expect a response, certainly not right away. The eleventh richest man in the world had to be too busy running his empire to bother with a peon like me. So I was surprised when only a couple of minutes later, my inbox buzzed with a reply.

"Tatsu-kun, so good to hear from you. You will be perfect for this job. It's quite urgent. Katie-chan will be at the San Jose City Council meeting today. Can you meet her there?"

It was strange how Satoshi referred to her so familiarly—like a daughter. Or a girlfriend. But I didn't want to think about that. I checked the city's website. The council meeting started in less than twenty minutes. I slacked my boss that I was taking an early lunch and made a dash for the door.

Chapter 4
Another Downtown Revitalization Plan

From the double doors at the back of the room, I scanned the hall for the red hair of Dr. Deauville but didn't see her inside. The sparse audience consisted of a few cottonball heads and a smattering of middle-aged suits. On the stage, a stern-looking woman stood at the podium while behind her, a dozen council members sat around a curved dais of blonde wood. Slipping into the back row, I awaited the coming of Dr. Deauville.

Despite my family farming many of the prune orchards that had defined San Jose for nearly a century until the tech invasion, I'd never been to a council meeting, barely knew the council existed. The third largest city in California and the epicenter of Silicon Valley was shaped like a Rorschach inkblot; few residents knew where its borders ended and where Cupertino or Sunnyvale or Milpitas began. And as long as its schools delivered its graduates to Harvard and Stanford, nobody much cared, either.

Playing a game on my phone until a bitter smell of onions pricked my nose, I looked up to see the long, red hair breezing past. The photos online didn't do her justice. In a hunter-green dress with narrow straps exposing milky white shoulders, she was as radiant as any movie star. The entire room stopped to watch Dr. Deauville glide down the aisle cradling a small dog in her bare arms, the hum of the microphone the only accompaniment to the clack of her heels on the tile.

For the founder of a company already worth a billion dollars, she was surprisingly young—under thirty, I guessed, probably not more than a couple years older than me. I thought how little I would accomplish before thirty except writing a pile of code that nobody needed, and maybe, possibly, cracking the top ten in a Legends of Emperors tournament. It was depressing.

When Dr. Deauville reached the front, she waved to a man seated alone in the middle of the first row, the bald dome of his head sticking up out of a gray sports jacket. As he turned to bow in her direction, I caught a glimpse of the cold fish eyes and taut jaw that reminded me of a Buddhist monk—Satoshi. She sat beside him and kissed his cheek, a pang of jealousy stabbing my chest. Were the two of them lovers? If so, was Ryu a third variable in the equation? I wondered if something had happened between her and Ryu. Had he bowed out to the richer man and bailed out of town, or had Satoshi found out and paid his younger rival to depart the scene? Knowing Ryu, it would take a lot of coin to convince him to disappear without a word to his family. But Satoshi had billions of BiteCoins to spend.

Before he became the lord of the blockchain—the BiteCoin exchange rate quoted alongside the Dow Jones index—Satoshi had taken tea ceremony classes from my mother every week in the makeshift tea house in our living room. Even after BiteCoin became the exclusive medium of exchange for drug deals, cybercrime, and child porn, his personal wallet swollen to $17 billion, he still came to our house every Thursday morning carrying a plate of *manju* cakes from Shuei-Do. When he left the house two hours later, he bowed deep in appreciation for the brown paper sack I'd hand him, overflowing with the tangerines or kumquats or loquats or persimmons Kaa-chan and I had collected from our yard. Tea ceremony suited him perfectly—he was a man of logic and rules, a disciple of Zen. What was he doing with this woman young enough to be his daughter?

I snuck down to sit a few rows behind the pair, my head ducked low to watch them. While the speaker droned on about yet another plan to revitalize the downtown district, a commotion began in the back. Shouting and stamping grew louder and louder until the doors to the lobby banged open. Protesters burst into the hall dressed in matching t-shirts that declared in bold letters: "Unsheltered People Are Human Too!"

The t-shirts marched down the aisle with fists pumping, chanting their slogan in unison, led by a woman with short-cropped blue hair and a gold ring dangling from her nose. The other protestors looked like college kids in ripped jeans or spandex leggings and bright-white Nikes. Behind them a handful of homeless people followed in a haphazard column, pushed forward by another group of t-shirts marching in behind them. At the base of the stage, the t-shirts continued shouting, ignoring the chairwoman's demands for order, exhorting the homeless people to join in.

The homeless people were a motley bunch, white and black, men and women, sad children holding hands with vacant-eyed mothers, a stringy-haired man in a faded army jacket, a rail-thin teen girl in mismatched clothing. Some were confused, others laughing for no reason; one man waved a cell phone, panhandling for BiteCoin donations.

I couldn't help imagining my mother's indignation at this disorder. "Why do Americans coddle them?" she'd shriek. "Put them on a bus and send them to the desert!" When Tou-san once lifted his head after a few too many Johnnies and mumbled that his own grandparents had been bussed to an internment camp in the desolation of Wyoming, she'd flown into a rage about everything wrong with this country. "*Baka*," she'd yelled—*stupid* in Japanese—though it wasn't clear if she was insulting Tou-san or the country or the entire *baka* world.

The shouting continued nonstop while the chairperson banged her gavel to no effect and other council members attempted to mediate. It was hard to tell what the t-shirts wanted other than to make a spectacle. A pair of security guards stood on the stage, hands on their guns, but made no move to clear the room.

After a few minutes of nonstop shouting and stamping, a squad of San Jose blueboys burst through the side entrance and charged at the noisy protestors. Uncowed, the t-shirts raised their phones, their cameras recording, daring the police to attack. The two sides glowered at each other, the protestors defiant, the cops a brooding wall of blue.

Dr. Deauville rose from her seat, handed her dog to Satoshi, and walked into the crowd of t-shirts. She gathered three of them, including the woman with the nose ring, around her. After a few minutes huddled in the middle while the protesting continued unabated around them, a small cheer added to the cacophony. The chanting stuttered to a stop as excited whispering spread through the t-shirts.

Standing below the stage, the now silent protestors a circle behind her, Dr. Deauville waved the chairwoman over. The chairwoman stepped to the front of the stage, flanked by the other members of the city council.

As they spoke, the chairwoman's eyes grew large, her tweezed eyebrows arched towards her hairline, and her jaw fell down to her chest. "We will adjourn for a short break," she announced into the microphone to titters around the room, then led Dr. Deauville to join her at the back of the stage.

The t-shirts waited. The police waited. The cottonballs and suits waited while the chairwoman and Dr. Deauville held a private conversation beside the row of flags. Aides streamed in with donuts and coffee for grateful homeless men, women, and children. A murmur grew louder, gradually filling the hall, until the chairwoman suddenly reached out to hug a surprised Dr. Deauville. Together they returned to the podium where the chairwoman tapped the microphone before speaking.

"I have the great pleasure today to announce that in support of our downtown revitalization, SüprDüpr has offered to donate $100 million to build and operate a homeless shelter for the unhoused residents of San Jose."

A collective gasp was followed by a huge cheer, as if the Giants had slugged a walk-off home run. Even the suits clapped and fist-bumped the grannies. The t-shirts hugged each other, then hugged the cops, then hugged their homeless friends. The entire city council lined up at the podium to thank Dr. Deauville and shake her hand.

I seemed to be the only person who wasn't cheering. I couldn't help wondering how a startup without any customers could afford to give away $100 million? Something didn't add up.

After the t-shirts led the homeless people out the side exit and the cops left, the doors banged shut and a hush descended over the hall. Someone sneezed. Nervous laughter spread through the room.

The councilwoman banged her gavel once more. "Before we can celebrate," she started, "SüprDüpr has placed two conditions on their donation that require council approval."

Aha, I thought, now we'll find out what this is really about. It was hard to fathom anyone giving away $100 million for free.

"First, SüprDüpr is requesting immediate authorization to convert the vacant apartment building at the corner of St. James and 3rd Street into a homeless shelter. Second, they've asked for ownership of the city's Corinthian property to be used as their headquarters and technology center."

Not as enlightening as I'd expected. Certainly, SüprDüpr was getting something for their $100 million, but it wasn't obvious what. The Corinthian Grand Ballroom was a San Jose landmark; its white marble blocks and fluted ionic columns made it the most handsome building in town. Constructed a century ago as a Masonic Temple, it now sat vacant except for a low-impact exercise class in the basement that once hosted weird sacred rites.

The white building was nothing but a white elephant, the chairwoman declared—the meagre rentals it generated from an occasional wedding or corporate gathering didn't even cover the cost of maintenance. When she opened the floor for debate, there was not a hint of opposition. Not from any of the council members, nor from the cottonballs who came to the meetings for the purpose of objecting to everything. A motion was made, seconded, and approved unanimously. I smelled a rat somewhere.

When the chairwoman gaveled the meeting adjourned, applause accompanied Dr. Deauville's exit from the hall, the little dog strutting behind. By the time I reached the lobby, a mob of reporters and cameramen were already surrounding her, microphones and tape recorders thrust in her face. There was no way news crews from as far away as San Francisco could have arrived in the few minutes since the announcement—the supposedly spontaneous donation must have been carefully managed, the media alerted beforehand. I wondered if she'd paid the protestors, too, or if that was just a lucky coincidence.

Security guards cleared a space through the crowd for Dr. Deauville to reach the stand already prepped for a press conference. On the front of the podium was an S with umlauts atop a cartoon elephant—the SüprDüpr logo. Sunlight streamed in through the floor-to-ceiling windows behind her, setting her hair aglow.

I was stuck in the back where I could only catch glimpses of her red hair and green dress through the gaps in front of me. Her voice rained down from speakers in the ceiling like a goddess, but with the flattened vowels of a Midwestern farmhand.

Before she could finish her prepared statement, a reporter up front shouted at her, "Why is a tech startup building a homeless shelter?"

"Because it's the right thing to do," she answered, training a megawatt smile on the news cameras. "As members of this community, it's our responsibility to help those most in need."

Another reporter shouted, "Where did the hundred million dollars come from?"

"Our investors are very generous."

I had to call bullshit on that one. Venture capitalists invested in startups to make money and for no other reason. I wanted to hear what Satoshi had to say, but the bashful billionaire was nowhere to be found. The rat was starting to stink.

"When will the shelter open?"

She seemed surprised by that question. "Right away, of course," she said, as if there could be no other answer. She fingered a silver cross that sparkled around her long, elegant neck. "These people need our help now."

Even as questions continued bombarding her, she waved and stepped away from the podium. The cameras switched off and the reporters hurried outside, dictating into their recorders. Two security guards escorted her through the thinning crowd to the parking elevators, muscled arms barring me from entering. I ran down the stairwell and in the dim light, tracked the tinkling of the dog's tags to see her walking towards the row of parked cars.

"Dr. Deauville?" I called. "Can I talk to you for a sec?"

She walked away faster.

"Satoshi told me to come here," I shouted across the garage. "About a job?"

That worked like magic. She stopped. Turned around. And focused her megawatt smile on me.

She waited for me at her red Porsche with a license plate that read HIGGS. When I caught up to her, the little chihuahua raised its ratty tail and growled a warning at my ankle. Saliva glistened on sharp, crooked teeth that resembled vampire fangs.

"Shh, Higgsy," she cooed, lifting the dog in her arms, a silver cross with rubies dangling from her neck, matching the studs in her ears. Petting the dog's head, she turned back to me. "Satoshi mentioned a math whiz to work on our mapping. Is that you?"

Math whiz wasn't the term I'd use, but I told her I had a master's degree in mathematics.

"Stanford?"

"MIT."

"Marvelous," she said, more impressed than I expected. My *alma mater* rarely got much respect in Silicon Valley where the only schools that counted were Stanford and Harvard. She dropped the dog into the passenger seat and held out a hand. "Call me Katie. And this here is Higgs. How soon could you start?"

"As soon as you need me," I offered. "I can come in for an interview today."

"Did you bring a resume?"

When I told her I applied through the HR portal, she grinned, exposing high cheekbones and a prominent jaw. "Oh, I stopped looking at those ages ago. I'll dig it up as soon as I get back. Look, I'm late for a critical demo for our investors and then have to meet Mayor Gadh—but you sound like a great fit."

"If you give me your number, I can text you my resume right now."

She only threw me a quick smile as she climbed into the car.

"What's the job?" I asked, but she didn't hear me over the engine that vroomed to life. The car lurched backwards, forcing me to jump out of the way. Then the tires squealed and she zoomed off, leaving me breathing her exhaust.

I knew I should get back to the office before my boss went on the warpath, especially since the bug I was supposed to fix last night was still open, but the Corinthian was only a few blocks away. I decided to make a quick detour to see if there were any clues about why a mysterious startup was spending millions of dollars fixing up an old building.

Chapter 5
Home in Saint Jimmy's

Although it was only three blocks away from the postmodern abomination of steel and glass that was San Jose's City Hall, St. Jimmy's Park was a different world. The sidewalks around it were filled with shopping carts overflowing with the detritus of the city, the alleys strewn with dirty cardboard, empty bottles, and broken glass. Used syringes littered the gutters.

The two blocks of the park itself were ground zero: the old Spanish-style plaza that was once a bucolic town square filled with grass and trees had been invaded by an army of homeless people, permanently bivouacked in soiled tents scattered pell-mell over the lawn. The smell of piss and pot and rotting garbage hung thick in the air, making me want to gag.

Kaa-chan would have shrieked that the police should get rid of them, all of them, they were dangerous, they were useless, they were a burden on society. To me, they mostly looked sad. I wished there was a way to fix whatever was wrong with them. I felt grateful that Katie was doing something, anything, to alleviate this disaster.

A man on crutches, one leg missing, hobbled towards me holding out a cup. I dropped in a dollar, feeling guilty for not giving him more, feeling guilty for giving him anything. Kaa-chan would've slapped my hand and said it would only buy drugs.

A memory came flooding back of a frigid Christmas morning at a small park near my dorm in Cambridge. An old man wrapped in dirty blankets had sat shivering in a wheelchair on the corner, the cardboard sign on the sidewalk at his feet: "Help a Vet?" He'd looked up at me with eyes rimmed in crimson and rattled a blue Mr. Peanut can. Away from Kaa-chan for the first time in my life, I'd dropped a full Jackson in his cup.

"Merry Christmas," he'd mumbled as he'd smiled with surprise. "And God bless you, brother."

Proud of my good deed, I'd watched as he wheeled himself across the street to the 7-Eleven where he'd left his wheelchair beside the door and walked inside without a limp. When he strode out, a bottle of vodka clenched high in his hand, he'd shouted to me, "Jesus loves you!" Pushing the wheelchair down the sidewalk until he reached the next corner, he'd laid his sign on the concrete, wrapped the blankets around himself and sipped at the bottle while awaiting the coming of the next sucker.

Here in St. Jimmy's, the man on crutches looked in the cup, disappointed, and waved it at me demanding more. "That's all I've got," I lied, and walked away, keeping my distance from a woman screaming at unseen voices and a man prone on the ground. Sitting on a boulder, a younger man strummed a Beatles tune on a guitar surprisingly well; beside him an older man banged on a paint can with a stick.

Two cops ambled along the sidewalk surveying the chaos all around. A muscled Viking glowered at the homeless while his partner, a round doughboy, warned away the tourists stepping off the light rail thinking they'd arrived at the center of the tech universe.

I leaned against a tree, the bark rough against my back, and surveyed the scene. Most of the old buildings arrayed around the square were vacant now. The churches had erected tall fences to hold back the unwashed tide. But there amidst the desolation all around, stood the Corinthian Ballroom, gleaming like a palace in the sun.

A man wearing an army jacket, its olive green faded to drab brown, placed his hand on the tree beside me. "Azaz!" he yelled, startling me with an order I couldn't comprehend. "Azaz!" he repeated to my confusion. "My name, man! And this here's Azaz's tree."

I edged away. I wasn't about to get into a fight with a homeless man over an elm.

"Wait, man," he said. "It's okay, I'll share it with ya. Just give me a little something." He thrust his palm out at me, every crease encrusted with grime.

As I backed up, Azaz grabbed my sleeve. "Anything to help, man. Anything would be 'preciated."

I ripped my arm free and walked away until indignation curdled into guilt. But I couldn't give him money. "Come with me," I said, waving him towards the gas station to buy him a case of granola bars and the biggest jug of Gatorade they sold. His empty palm remained outstretched as he followed a step behind. When we reached the sidewalk at the edge of the park, he stopped and would go no further.

"Can't can't can't leave," he said, panicky, his feet unable to cross the concrete border. "Just give me cash. I need cash."

His pupils the size of pinpricks, I was sure any money I handed him would go straight to meth or heroin. "I'm not paying for your drugs."

"No, man, it ain't that, it ain't. Listen, I gotta tell you something." His hand reached across the sidewalk, but Azaz would come no closer.

I was tempted to walk away and pay a guilt-absolving indulgence to the Red Cross, but instead I stepped back over the sidewalk into his side of the world. A crow high up in an oak tree squawked at us. Azaz shook his fist at the bird, his face contorted, then he squatted low to hide from its gaze. "You see them, man?" He pointed up at the bird. "They're spying on us."

I couldn't resist asking who.

"All of them—police, FBI, CIA, NSA, Mossad. Especially Mossad. They're all listening, man, they have to make sure we're not on to them, but we are, that's what I'm saying. So we gotta be careful or the bird—the bird's got microwave eyes that'll fry your brains and you'll twitch and scream and then you'll fall over dead. I seen it, man, truly."

There was no question he was off his meds. They didn't need a fake bird in a tree to spy on us—the real spies had our own phones listening 24/7 to do it better. "Come on," I said, waving him forward. "Let's get you some food."

But he still wouldn't step over the sidewalk. "Can't man, they're watching us, won't let us out."

He stood scared, his eyes darting to the two cops patrolling the periphery. The Viking and Doughboy were chatting to themselves, ignoring the drugs being bought and sold, smoked and injected all around them.

"They're not looking at us," I said.

Azaz stamped his feet and shouted, "Everybody knows you step over the line and the cops take you away. My buddy Job is gone. Pretty Paddy, too. Ain't nobody seen them for days."

With Azaz's commotion, the two blueboys glanced over at us before returning to their lattes.

I wondered if Azaz's buddies actually existed or had disappeared long ago in 'Nam. Still, it wouldn't be surprising if the cops were clearing people out of the park or taking them to a shelter. With my own friend missing, I had to ask, "Any idea where they went?"

"You won't tell nobody, you swear? Because this shit's gotta stay secret. Otherwise, the cops will take you away, too, and then you'll have to meet Jesus, and you don't want that, believe me, man, anything but that."

I nodded my assent. I wouldn't be able to describe this conversation anyway, not coherently.

"They're cooking them and drying them and grinding them up into that protein powder that all the techies drink—soiled ant or something. That's what's going on here, you'll see. We'll all be gone and they'll be making their powder."

I laughed. I couldn't help it. Some crazy rumor must have started that Soylent, the meal replacement powder that had become as popular as double IPAs among the sandals crowd, was made from human remains, just like in the old Charlton Heston movie. But that was absurd.

He thrust his hand out again. "You gotta gimme money, man, cash, not that BiteCoin crap they can trace. I gotta get out of here, get to Santy Cruz or Mexico before it's too late. The other Chinaman, he gave me a hundred bucks."

My antenna went up. My dander, too. I hated being mistaken for Chinese. "Was another *Japanese* guy here?"

"Yeah, that's what I said. Another Chinese kid, just like you, 'cept he weren't so short. Said his company was gonna build us a shelter over there." I held my tongue as Azaz stabbed a finger towards the derelict building Katie's company was taking over. "But I wasn't born yesterday, man. I know they's building a factory there to make more protein powder."

Could that've been Ryu? "Did he have a scar?" I asked, pointing at the spot where his jaw had been stitched together after the baseball accident.

"Yeah, man, that's him. Oh shit. Shit shit shit. You're with them, too, ain't you? I shoulda known. All you Chinamen building a Chinese factory here." His pupils grew large and his breath quickened.

"Don't worry—we're not Chinese," I said, trying to calm Azaz. "And there's no Chinese factory. The man you met is my friend, Ryu. I'm looking for him. He's missing."

Azaz's body shook. "You ain't turning me into powder. Uh-uh." He swung his arms, whacking me across the chest before I could jump away. He lunged at me, screaming, as I twisted out of his reach.

The doughy cop blew his whistle, ordering Azaz to stop. He looked up to see the cop racing towards us and took off, stumbling across the lawn. When he reached the edge, he hurdled the sidewalk and landed awkwardly, careening face first onto the asphalt. I rushed over, worried he was injured, but before I could reach him, he jumped up and dashed into the middle of the street. A car sideswiped him, knocking him to the pavement.

Azaz lay on the ground unmoving. I was afraid he was dead. When the Viking reached him, he poked at the inert body and barked into his radio. An arm moved, then his body shuddered. I sighed with relief. The Viking grabbed him in a chokehold while Doughboy slapped on the handcuffs. Azaz screamed until the Viking jammed a taser into his side, causing him to twitch on the ground. Doughboy stood over him while the Viking tased him a second time for no apparent reason.

If he hadn't been wearing a gun, I would have tried to push the Viking off Azaz. And then gotten clobbered myself. Because the Viking was well over six feet tall, with short-cropped blond hair and bulging Skeletor muscles, the likes of which were rarely seen this far north of Los Angeles. All I could do was yell at him to stop. The Viking sneered and ordered me to stand back, waving the taser at me.

I stood in the street, wielding my camera to prevent him from zapping Azaz again. Some residents of the park gathered at the edge of the sidewalk shouting encouragement. A few jumped over the sidewalk to escape in the opposite direction.

Instead of calling an ambulance, the Viking lifted Azaz's limp body and dragged him down the street. His toes scraped the ground as the cop carried him past the filthy tents, past the Corinthian, past the churches, all the way to the tow-away zone where their patrol car awaited. I chased after them, but they pushed him onto the back seat and sped away.

Something weird was happening in this park and it was more than just the weed in the air. I was sure Ryu and SüprDüpr were somehow involved. Exactly how wasn't clear.

Chapter 6
Tears Like Whiskey

That evening, I stretched out on the old leather couch that doubled as my bed, thinking about Ryu. Why was his account deleted? And what did that have to do with SüprDüpr? I'd learned nothing about the company except it was donating gobs of investors' money to house the homeless. As I sipped at the Mu, I replayed everything Katie had said at the council meeting, every word she spoke in the garage, watched her long hair cascading over bare, white shoulders, green eyes sparkling when she looked at me. I imagined her lips drawing close as she told me how perfect I was for the job. Long fingers reached out to brush my chest, nails drawing a line of red on my skin, reaching down, further down, until they wrapped around...the doorknob that rattled open as Sumire stepped into the room.

I scrambled upright, wishing it had been anyone other than Sumire who'd walked in on me now. "How about some sake?" I choked out, holding the blue bottle in front of me to try to hide my embarrassment.

"Is that all you can think about?" she said, frowning her disapproval while I flopped around zipping up my jeans. Waddling into the kitchen, I made a big display of picking a sake cup for her while waiting for my hard-on to subside. Glass or ceramic or lacquerware or wood, I asked, holding each up for her to choose.

"Sit down already, Ted."

I grabbed my favorite—a brown ceramic cup lined with gold leaf—the only one I'd succeeded in rescuing when Kaa-chan had smashed all the others after the accident. I set it on the desk in front of Sumire, clear liquid inside sparkling gold. She said nothing as I sipped at my own cup, the Mu tasting of freshly squeezed clouds and the purest snowmelt. Sumire pushed hers aside. "Haven't you had enough already?"

She sounded exactly like Kaa-chan admonishing Tou-san. So I did exactly what Tou-san would do when my mother ordered him to stop drinking—I downed my cup in a single gulp and poured another.

"Stop acting like an idiot," she said.

I answered by grabbing her cup off the table and downing it, too. She ripped the bottle from my hand and marched into the kitchen to upend it into the sink.

"That's expensive," I muttered.

"Mu?" she scoffed as the frosted bottle clanked against the other dead soldiers in the recycling bin. "Thirty dollars at Nijiya." She opened her purse and banged a ten and a twenty onto the counter. "There's your money back." I must have flinched in surprise. "Believe me, you're not the only alcoholic around here."

"It's just sake," I protested.

But she didn't care. She rooted through the kitchen cabinets and rummaged through the drawers. Afraid she'd discover the emergency Johnnie in the cabinet over the refrigerator or the cheap hooligans cavorting with the cleaning chemicals under the sink, I hummed a Britney Spears song she used to sing at karaoke to distract her. One glance from her strangled the hum in my throat. "Where's the tea?" she demanded.

Ugh. Tea—the answer to everything, if only I knew the question. There was no tea that didn't come wrapped in its own baggage. "If you're going to be my mother," I said, "there's only one way to make tea."

Sumire sighed. "I don't want to be your mother, Ted, though God knows you need one."

I fought back the urge to tell her to leave again. I remembered the days when it had been the two of us together against the world. I wondered if she ever thought about those times, too; that somewhere inside the hard-boiled shell of an apprentice lawyer still lived the shy, angry girl who'd hid out with me along the banks of the Guadalupe, reading manga and laughing together.

But there was no arguing with her now, or laughing either, so I stepped to the back corner where my mother sat perched in her white urn atop her tea cabinet. Unlike the rest of the Ikea cast-offs that decorated the apartment, the cabinet was a family heirloom, a Meiji-era antique that Kaa-chan had brought with her from Kyoto. Inside were all the tools of tea ceremony: ceramic bowls, bamboo whisks, silk cloths for purification, a full shelf of lacquered tea caddies, each depicting in bas-relief one of the twenty-four seasons of the tea year.

I took out my bowl, smooth *arita-yaki* porcelain, cobalt blue base grading to white at the lip like a snow-covered Mt. Fuji jutting into the sky. Kaa-chan hated that one, thought it too gaudy American in its bright colors. For Sumire, I reached all the way to the back to grab Kaa-chan's favorite, hand thrown and unsymmetrical, adorned with a single maple leaf in mottled red on the front. A gift from Kaa-chan's beloved student, I turned it over to see his signature etched into the clay, a single character of ten strokes—悟—meaning *enlightenment*. Satoshi.

I didn't have the patience now, or ever, for a real tea ceremony, an ordeal that lasts for four hours through a meal and both thin and thick teas, with a complex script that changes for each of the tea ceremony seasons. Though Kaa-chan would've had a fit, I focused on the one thing I thought actually mattered—sharing a bowl of tea. So I boiled water in the kettle on the stove instead of a cast iron pot over *binchotan* charcoal and skipped the purification process entirely. Using an ancient bamboo *chashaku* darkened with the oil of a thousand fingers, I scooped out the matcha—a tiny tin costing as much as a full bottle of Mu—and measured out a cone of powder like the sands of an hourglass into the bottom of Sumire's bowl.

When the kettle hissed, I filled the bowl halfway with steaming water and whisked the tea to a frothy foam. Sumire kneeled on a mat on the floor and I set the bowl in front of her. She placed it in the palm of her left hand, gripping it with her right, and turned it around to face away before lifting it to her mouth. I prepared a second bowl for myself and took a small taste, sweetness on the tip of my tongue, bitterness behind, warm foam tingling the sides, as thick and creamy as a matcha smoothie.

She started to speak, but I put a finger to my lips. We drank in silence, the liquid warming deep in my chest. The heat coursed through my veins as the tick tock of the universe's clock slowed and there was nothing in the world but the two of us. When we were done, she turned her bowl to the front and set it back on the mat.

"Wasn't that nice?" she whispered.

"Real nice," I agreed. But the Mu would have been nicer.

Dispensing with the cleaning ritual my mother claimed was the most important part of the ceremony, I carried the bowls to the kitchen and simply left them on the counter. When I returned to the living room, Sumire was combing through my collection of *One Piece* manga jumbled up on the bookshelf. She pulled out Volume 1 from the bottom of a pile and, smiling through thin lips, thumbed through the dog-eared copy. I remembered the cherry taste of her lip gloss when we sat side-by-side under the jacaranda trees on the banks of the Guadalupe River, laughing as we read that manga together.

"I can't believe you still have this," she said.

As if I could throw it away. "I'm not allowed to read manga without you?"

"Not *One Piece*. That was ours. And this was my copy." She opened the cover to show me the schoolgirl signature in glittery gel ink. As if I didn't know it was there.

"You can have it back," I said. "You can have all of them." I didn't know why I'd kept them, the only thing other than Kaa-chan's tea ceremony cabinet and her beloved vacuums I hadn't tossed when I'd packed up my parents' home.

She slipped the manga back onto the shelf and straightened the entire row. "Thanks, but you can keep it. I was never into your pirate stories, Ted. I just enjoyed being out by the river with you."

Yeah. The fantasy world was great while it lasted. Until the real world of death and misery arrived with a vengeance. I flopped onto the sofa. She sat beside me like we were at the river again. It felt awkward now.

"What did you find?" she asked. I didn't know what to say. I wanted to impress her with how I'd cracked MeCan's security last night, but then I'd have to tell her someone had deleted Ryu's account. She'd understand what that meant. So I said I was sorry I hadn't found anything yet. I braced myself for her to rip into me for not helping more. Instead, she placed her fingers on my hand. I felt the heat of the tea, the warmth of her touch. "You're a lousy liar, Teddybear. Always have been."

I bowed my head. It was true.

"I know you mean well, but don't lie to me. Just tell me what you found. Even if it's bad, I need to know."

I couldn't. I hummed the old Beatles tune, *Norwegian Wood*, that popped into my head. From her tightening grip on my wrist, I realized I'd given away more than if I'd spoken. "Is it really that awful?" she sniffed. I was afraid she was about to cry and I wasn't ready for that. Would never be ready for that.

"I met the CEO of SüprDüpr today," I said, attempting to sound triumphant.

"And? What did she say about Ryu? Does she know where he is?"

"Did you see their big announcement?" I showed her the headline on the Mercury news about SüprDüpr's super-donation.

She waved it away. "What did she say about Ryu?"

"She said she'd review my resume. I'm trying to get into their office."

"What did she say about Ryu?"

I couldn't do this now. Not without help. Sumire's gaze followed me as I climbed on a chair to reach the cabinet over the refrigerator. When I returned with the emergency Johnnie, she put out a hand and said no. I filled two shot glasses anyway and downed one in a single gulp.

"Drink," I ordered, though I was surprised when she knocked it back. I refilled her cup and she held it in front of her eyes, staring into the liquid while I told her everything—the deleted account, meeting Katie in the garage, the weird homeless guy who saw Ryu in the park.

When I was done, she said nothing. She grabbed the bottle out of my hand, marched into the kitchen, and poured it down the drain. Once it all glugged away, she smashed the bottle against the side of the sink. Drops of amber splattered the tile and rolled down the backsplash like the tears streaming down her face.

I stood frozen, not knowing how to help as she leaned against the counter sobbing. "What can I do?" I asked softly, wanting to put my hands around her but afraid to touch her.

"Nothing!" she screamed. "Don't you understand?"

I wished I did understand, but I didn't, not the times my mother had screamed the same thing at me and not now. When I was young, I'd thought it was my fault. I'd knocked on the bedroom door and when there was no answer, I turned the knob and slipped into the darkness. Kaa-chan was in bed, sobbing the lyrics of *Norwegian Wood*.

"I'm sorry, mommy," I'd said, though I wasn't sure what I was sorry for. There were a hundred things she told me I did wrong every day, and it was hard to know which was making her sad.

When I reached out to hug her, she'd slapped me. "Get out!" she'd screamed. "Leave me alone!"

I ran out of the room, ran out of the house, ran down the street to Ryu's house where I hid the rest of the evening, playing video games for hours until Tou-san arrived and took me to the Dandy Lion, where he gave me my first taste of whiskey. Holding my hand as we walked through the darkness, he'd told me, "Your mother is a difficult woman. But she loves you. Just be patient and when she wants to be alone, let her be." He started whistling the Beatles tune, *Let it Be*, and I hummed along the whole way home.

Standing behind Sumire now, I didn't know what to do or say. I tried to say something reassuring. "Don't worry," I told her. "We'll find Ryu. I'm sure he's fine."

"You're an idiot," she sniffed. "Don't you understand anything?"

"No," I said, shaking my head. I could solve the most difficult differential equations but couldn't differentiate emotions.

"I need you to hold me, you idiot," she yelled. "Can't you see I'm all alone?"

I really was an idiot, I realized. I reached out to pet her hair.

She grabbed my hand and wrapped it around her waist, then buried her head in my shoulder, her body trembling as hot tears rolled down my neck.

When the storm passed, Sumire wiped her eyes with the back of her hand. Ignoring the silk purification cloth I held out, she carried a box of tissues to the couch. She blew her nose and threw the tissue to the floor, then dabbed at her streaked mascara with another.

Looking up at me, her nose red, hair disheveled, she wore a crooked frown. She looked messy. But also beautiful, the tough lawyer gone, the sad, passionate girl I once loved returned, the tips of her ears poking out through the curtain of shiny, black hair. I sat beside her and tried to cheer her up by humming the frolicky White Stripes tune we used to sing together at karaoke until she started to hum along. When we were done, she snuggled close and rested her head against me, the peaty smell of the whiskey mixing with the chamomile cloud around her. It felt as if we'd been sitting on this couch together for years, the same contours meshing into the same places.

"Teddy?" she whispered.

"Yes, Bunny-chan?" I mumbled, my old nickname for her.

"I don't understand."

I thought she meant the breakup, or my mother's suicide, or my father's accident, or all the other things I didn't want to talk about. "Me, neither."

She slapped my arm playfully. "Come on, Ted," she said. "Why is that woman giving away so much money to the unhoused?"

I described the ruby cross she wore around her neck. "Souls for Jesus, I guess."

"Christian charity is one thing, but a hundred million dollars? From a startup? There has to be something else going on."

I told her about the gleaming palace that would become the company's headquarters, the disaster zone all around.

"Yeah," she said, nodding, "that's a pretty good scheme."

Whatever Sumire had figured out escaped me.

"You don't have a clue how the world works, do you?" she said.

There seemed no point in admitting she was right.

"Isn't it weird how she wants the Corinthian? Why not move into a regular office like everyone else? That would be a whole lot easier."

"Is the building worth $100 million?"

"In the current condition, no way. Not even $10 million."

"How do you know so much about property?"

"You forgot about my father?"

Right. Her father, the big shot commercial realtor, owner of Yamashita Realty. How could I have forgotten the never-ending arguments when he'd brokered the sale of the Hara family orchards for my father and his brothers.

"So why the Corinthian?" I asked.

"You're not thinking like a developer."

That was true. I hated the developers who'd bought up the last of the Japanese farmland to build yet more office parks and luxury condos.

"Just imagine St. James Park with all the unhoused gone."

I pictured the plaza returned to its historic splendor, replanted with flowering cherry trees and rows of rose bushes, neighbors greeting each other as they passed on the sidewalk, dogs sniffing each other's butts on the lawn. "That would be nice," I said.

"Nice? Forget nice—it's two blocks from City Hall. One block from the center of downtown. What do you think will happen to property values after the park is cleaned up?"

"It'll go up in value?"

"It'll go to the fricking moon, Ted. Like all the other real estate around here."

"And then the building will be worth $100 million?"

"You have to think bigger. Think sneakier. Think like a developer. Where's the money?"

I was good at math, but money was nothing but numbers on a spreadsheet. "In the bank?"

She elbowed me. "I'll bet you a hundred million dollars that woman bought up every piece of property around the park she could get her hands on. Then she'll tear them all down and put up a bunch of office towers."

"Oh," I said, finally understanding—the homeless shelter was nothing but a way to make money. That would explain the investors' interest in corporate philanthropy. And even more cynical than I could've imagined.

"It's brilliant," Sumire said. "And legal, too. She gets the unhoused out of the park so she can redevelop the area. And she gets her hands on the most primo piece of property, the only one she couldn't buy."

It made sense. But I was disappointed. "What about revolutionizing transportation?"

"Isn't it strange the company is so secretive about whatever they've invented? Have you ever heard a tech startup be coy? Ever?"

"No," I had to agree. The only quiet unicorn was a dead unicorn. Maybe Sumire was right. "If I can get a job interview, I can find what's going on inside."

"How long will that take?"

There used to be a rule among my MIT classmates that if an employer didn't call within seven and a half minutes of submitting a resume, they weren't desperate enough to bother with. But those feeding frenzy days were done. "A few days, hopefully. Depends on how busy they are."

"We're going to find out what's going on tomorrow." She jumped up from the couch. "Meet me at the Hall of Records in the morning."

After I messaged my boss saying I'd be in late, she leaned over and whispered sweetly, "Teddybear?"

When she said it like that, I didn't mind the old nickname. "Yes, Bunny-chan?"

She kissed me on the cheek. "See you tomorrow."

Chapter 7
Hall of Mirrors

Sumire was waiting for me, hands on her hips, in front of the county municipal building. I skidded to a halt, jumped off the Bird and dumped it with all the other scooters littering the sidewalk.

She scowled. "You're late."

It was three minutes before 9 a.m., which by Japanese rules, made me two minutes late. "Sorry," I said.

"And where's your helmet?"

Only dorks wear helmets, I wanted to protest, though when I said that once to Kaa-chan about skateboarding, she sawed my board in half. "This will protect me," I told Sumire, tipping my remembrance cap. She turned and headed into the mirrored menagerie without saying a word, leaving me behind on the sidewalk. I rushed to catch up.

Though the tinted mirrors that covered the building must have looked modern in the 1970's, they were now out of place amidst the gas stations, Mexican restaurants, and concrete parking structures that filled the neighborhood. I followed her through the hissing door and into the Clerk-Recorder's Office. Rather than a dusty library filled with shelves of plat maps bound into moldering books, the room resembled nothing so much as the horror of the DMV.

After ordering the ownership records for every parcel in a two-block radius around St. Jimmy's, we avoided the rows of uncomfortable plastic chairs and retreated to the back to wait. Soft morning sunlight streamed through the mirrored glass, casting a golden glow on Sumire's face. She stood beside me as we watched beaming couples registering for their marriage licenses until finally our number was called.

At the counter, the clerk handed us document after document, stamping each on the back with the county seal. We took them downstairs to the café and sipped at insipid coffee while arranging the papers around the table like pieces of a puzzle.

"Look!" Sumire said, tapping her finger on a page. She pointed at another, and then another. Three properties had changed hands in the past thirty days: two on 4th Street just behind the Corinthian, one more a block north of the park. All three had been purchased by a company named Higgs Transport, LLC.

"That's Katie," I said. "Her dog, actually."

"I knew it! It all makes sense now."

To her, maybe; not to me.

"Look, Ted, it's simple—the venture capitalists invested in a technology business, right? They gave SüprDüpr hundreds of millions of dollars to develop some great new product, not buy up apartment buildings. She hired a few engineers like Ryu to make the company look legit, but she's using most of the money to clear the unhoused people out of the park. Meanwhile, she sets up this Higgs shell company she owns personally to buy up property nearby. At some point, she'll admit whatever technology she was supposedly inventing doesn't work and SüprDüpr goes belly-up. The investors lose their money, but that's no big deal—investors expect most startups to fail, right? But now she personally owns these buildings that have doubled or tripled in value. She'll sell them to developers and walk off with tens of millions of dollars. Not bad for a day's work."

It seemed like a complicated way to turn company money into personal riches, but it fit the evidence. Still, it didn't explain everything, or even the most important thing. "What's this got to do with Ryu?"

"I don't know," she said. "Maybe Ryu found out what she was doing and she killed him?"

I wouldn't be surprised if beneath the megawatt smile and sculpted face, Katie was a tough businesswoman. But a cold-blooded killer—no way. "I can't picture her shooting Ryu and then what, hiding his body somewhere?" There was something else that didn't add up. "If she wanted to keep this secret, why would she use the name of her dog?"

"Because it doesn't matter, Ted. I'll bet you this Higgs Transport is owned by another corporation which is owned by one in the Caymans. Our law office sets up these nested shell companies all the time. They're impossible to trace."

Satoshi, though, would recognize the name of her dog, and it was his money she was playing with. Still, the real estate purchases were suspicious. "Can we take this to the cops and get them to look into Ryu's disappearance?" If we could convince them to issue a search warrant for Ryu's email and phone records without having to divulge my illicit hacking, I'd be off the hook. I could return to my video games and a fresh bottle of Mu without Sumire's scolding. But the thought of climbing the steps back to my solitary apartment suddenly made me feel lonely.

"No way," she said. "There's nothing that's actually illegal. Or ties it to Ryu. But we're on the right track, I'm sure of it. I'll see if I can dig up any financial records for Higgs Transport. But, Ted, can you do me one more favor?"

I cringed, knowing I was in for trouble. "What?"

"Can you snoop around the Corinthian and find out what's going on?"

It had only been a day since the council meeting; there couldn't be anything there yet beside the same sad sea of homelessness. It was easy enough to drop by later, though, if that's what she wanted. "Sure. I'll check it out after work."

"Now?" she pleaded, squeezing my hand. "Please, Teddybear?"

I sighed. My manager would not be happy.

Although it was only a few blocks away, Sumire refused to allow me to bird over to Saint Jimmy's without a helmet and insisted on driving me instead. Inside her lemon-colored Prius, the smell of chamomile prickled my nose. When we arrived, I was surprised to find the streets around the park had turned overnight into a giant construction zone. She weaved past the backhoes prowling the pavement like fire-breathing dragons and pulled to a stop beside a row of moving vans. I could barely hear the honking of the outraged drivers behind us over the percussion of jackhammers.

The Corinthian stood on raised ground, making it look even grander, its colonnaded front entrance up a flight of stairs. Sumire pointed to a woman standing at the top. "Is that her?"

Katie looked like a princess in front of her white marble castle, long hair fluttering in the breeze. She wore a simple, mustard-colored sundress, its skirt flaring high up bare legs, the dress so carefully designed to look flouncy and fun that it had to be outrageously expensive.

"What a fake," Sumire huffed. I waved as the car rolled silently away.

I started up the steps intending to ask Katie about Ryu, but it was impossible to break through the phalanx of ties and hardhats that surrounded her. Instead, I headed over to the Corinthian's elaborate entranceway to see what she was building inside. I followed a crew of burly movers, six of them lugging a large wooden crate hiding me from Katie's view. I was nearly through the doorway when a meaty hand grabbed my shoulder and jerked me aside. The foreman, his belly hanging out from under a stained undershirt, bellowed, "Who the hell are you?"

I flashed my office badge. "MeCan," I said. "Here to configure your network." There was no way he'd know the difference between a C/C++ programmer and a lowly network technician.

He pointed at my feet. "Uh-uh. No flip-flops. This is a construction site."

I held up my phone, hoping he thought it meant something. "Just doing a quick site survey. Only take a couple minutes."

"Beat it, kid," he said, blocking my way with his belly.

I muttered, "I'm not a kid, Blob-butt."

The mini-blobs holding the crate whooped in anticipation. The foreman snorted like a bull as he reared up over me with fists balled. "You're not no man, neither."

As we stood glaring at each other, a woman hollered from the distance, "Hara! Is that you?"

I squinted to see Katie waving at me, the sun behind her setting her hair aglow. Blob-butt ducked his head to hide from the boss and retreated inside the doorway. I couldn't help smirking.

"Wait there," she yelled. I leaned against the marble balustrade until she left the hardhats behind and strode over to meet me, the ugly chihuahua nearly skewered by a stiletto heel with every step. When she reached me, the smell of onions a fog around her, she smiled. "Come for the office tour?"

She'd seen me trying to sneak into the building. "Sorry," I replied sheepishly.

If she was annoyed, she didn't show it. "I'm glad you're here, Hara. I was meaning to call you. Your resume is quite impressive. I spoke with Satoshi this morning and we think you may be just the person we need."

I was surprised a billionaire and a busy CEO had talked about me. That was probably due less being the top of my class at MIT, the winner of every coding contest I'd ever entered, and more about the fake master's thesis I'd added to the resume. I hoped she didn't ask for details.

"I noticed you're in the navigation group at MeCan." When I nodded, she said, "Marvelous. We've got a complication with our mapping that I need solved urgently. Satoshi says you're the man for the job, and he knows better than anyone. Are you ready for an exciting new career?"

"Doing what?" I asked, my chance to find out what Ryu was working on.

"We're building the future, Hara," she said, switching on the megawatt smile. "We're doing well by doing good—we're solving a critical problem while fixing the homelessness crisis. And getting rich in the process."

The same Unicorn Valley blather I'd heard a million times. "What does that actually mean?"

An indulgent laugh. "We're reinventing transportation. And that will change everything."

Which told me nothing. "Can you be more specific?"

"Not without an NDA. But I guarantee it's like nothing you've ever seen."

After all the ride-hailing apps and scooter startups and electric cars and self-driving vehicles and delivery autobots and flying taxis and a million kinds of drones, it was hard to believe her startup wasn't the same as the thousands of other startups reinventing transportation. Was it even anything other than a shell company buying property as Sumire suspected? I pointed at the huge crate the movers were lugging past and asked what they were building inside.

"That's equipment for the operations center."

"What kind of operations?"

She waved off the question by pointing at the top of the building. "Our offices will be upstairs. How would you like your own office with a window view? That has to beat fighting over a hot desk at MeCan."

The windows overlooked the tents and shopping carts and heaps of trash covering St. Jimmy's. "Not much of a view."

"Oh, this park will be magnificent as soon as we move everyone to the treatment center we're building next door." She pointed at the derelict apartment building where workers were busy erecting scaffolding.

It was looking like Sumire was right. "That'll help the value of all of your buildings."

Katie's face froze for an instant. "What buildings?"

There was no backing down now. I pointed at the three buildings Sumire had discovered. "All bought by Higgs Transport. That's you, isn't it? Or is your dog buying up all the real estate around here?"

I braced myself for a hot denial, but she only bent over to pick up the ugly dog. "You've been a busy little bee, haven't you, Hara? Well, good—I need employees like that."

"Sorry, I'm not into real estate."

"Real estate?" she said, laughing. "Really, Hara? How much do you think those buildings are worth?"

"Millions?"

"Exactly." She waved it away as if I'd said acorns. "Millions don't matter. SüprDüpr is out to make billions. Hundreds of billions. Real estate isn't even a rounding error."

"Then why buy those buildings?"

She pointed a finger up St. James Street, following a trench that ran the length of the road before curving around behind us. "Do you see where that goes?"

"Past your buildings?"

"*Under* the buildings, actually."

I still didn't understand. "Fiber optic cables?"

"Close. We're building an underground loop."

I saw it now, the gash in the earth that made a circle around the park, the Corinthian at the center.

"The parking garages in those buildings were in our way. So we bought them."

I couldn't imagine buying my own home, much less three hulking apartment buildings for no other reason than to run a metal tube beneath them. "Seems like an expensive way to install some cable."

"It was the quickest way to get what we needed."

"What's that?"

"A particle accelerator," she said proudly. "A cyclotron. To generate Higgs bosons."

I nearly fell over. My jaw hung open while Katie laughed. "I told you this is revolutionary. Interested now, Hara?"

That explained why a physicist like Ryu was working at her company. He must have been in the park supervising the ring construction.

"Here's the best part," she continued. "Our IPO is already in process. When we go public, your stock options will be worth millions. Imagine driving a Ferrari to work. Or flying a G5 to your own private island. What do you say to joining us? I need a mathematician who understands mapping."

She had the pitch down, but I wasn't swinging. Anyone offering to make me a millionaire in short order was either lying or deluded or facing imminent arrest. "Why are you making Higgs particles?"

"Imagine being in Paris at the snap of your fingers instead of flying an entire day. Can you understand how that changes everything? It'll be magnificent, Hara. We'll bring the world closer together. This is your chance to make a real difference. Are you getting that at MeCan?"

"Nope," I had to admit. I hated my work. Toiling to produce yet another set of features that nobody would ever use.

She zeroed in for the kill. "Tell me, Hara, what are you getting from MeCan other than a salary?"

But I refused to take the bait. "Health insurance," I answered.

"Fully paid medical and dental. Vision, too." She pointed at my cheap wire-frames. "Get yourself some new glasses."

"Same-day dry cleaning."

She looked at my Sharks t-shirt and crinkled her perfect nose. "I'll sign you up for Stitch Fix. Send you a new wardrobe every month."

"Free pizza."

She laughed. "All the pizza you can eat."

"Gianni's?" It wasn't exactly gourmet—in fact it was cheap and crappy, but their ramen-top pizza beat the foo-foo junk with kale and tempeh toppings in the MeCan café any day.

"I'll put a Gianni's franchise right in the basement. How about that? What do you say—ready to join us?"

There was nobody at MeCan who would plead for me to stay, not my manager, not the engineering manager, not the program manager, not the product owner, not MeiLi or Amol or the Twit Twins, certainly not Evgeni or any of the other balding turtleheads on the 44th floor who had no idea I existed. To work on real mathematics and maybe make a difference in the world and buy a GT to drive the preening fashion models around my private tropical island? With Gianni's pizza on top?

It was tempting. Except I didn't know anything about Riemannian geometry. I'd get fired on the first day. I reminded myself I was here to find Ryu. All I needed to do was get into the office. "When should I come in for the interview?"

She licked her lips and smiled through perfect teeth. "No need. This is it. How soon can you start?"

Never? I needed another way to get inside. "Can I meet the team first?"

"Absolutely!" she said. "I'll text you over an NDA as soon as I'm done here. But our requirement is urgent—I need you to start right away. So let's get you in here tomorrow. Now if you'll excuse me, I have people waiting."

With that, she turned to hike up the steps to the waiting hardhats, the ugly mutt close on her heels.

Thrilled at my progress—I'd get to meet the team tomorrow—I knew I ought to head back to the office, but I wanted to talk to Azaz first. I had to find out what happened after the cops had taken him away and try again to decipher what Ryu had told him last week. Or maybe I was procrastinating, aware now how little I wanted to climb back up the Tangerine Tower, how pointless my job really was. If I waited long enough, my boss would be at the cafe munching on his kale frosted, gluten-free pizza when I returned, giving me time to hack together something to show progress before he berated me in front of the team. Katie's offer was growing more tempting by the minute, even if I still had no idea what the company did.

At the corner, a large man staggered towards me, filthy blanket wrapped around his shoulders. He stopped in front of me, hands raised high in the air. "Lord, save this child," he called to the sky, his voice booming like a prophet.

I wanted to yell that I wasn't a child, but that would only rile him further. "Any chance you know a guy named Azaz?" I asked, though it was unlikely he even knew his own name. The Prophet reached out to lay his grimy hands on my head. I ducked out of reach. "Just looking for Azaz."

"Aren't we all," he said, staring up at heaven. He stumbled across the sidewalk and lurched into the street, hands reaching up to God. Cars honked, drivers yelling to get the fuck out of the way. The cops rushed over, the same Viking and Doughboy who'd taken Azaz away. The Viking slapped on a pair of handcuffs and pushed the Prophet towards the patrol car.

I ran over to them. "Why are you taking him in?"

"Drugs," the Viking sneered. "Can't you see he's on chinatown? We need to get him out of here for his own safety. Yours, too. So back away."

I asked about Azaz, but they ignored me as they shoved the Prophet down the street. "You picked him up yesterday," I yelled, chasing after them. "Gray hair, green army jacket. What did that guy do?"

"Buzz off, twerp," the Viking grunted. "Can't you see we're busy?"

I tried Doughboy instead, hoping he'd be more helpful.

He shrugged. "We brought a bunch of them in yesterday. Most of them are right back here today."

The Viking opened the door of the cruiser and pushed the Prophet inside. I stepped in front of Doughboy before he could get into the car. "Where did you take him?"

"What do you want with him anyway?"

"He's a friend of mine."

"Then get him off drugs and get him off the street. That's your job, not ours."

The Viking yelled from the passenger side, "Lock 'em up or kick 'em out, that's what I say."

"Did you arrest him? Is there a record?"

Doughboy shook his head. The Viking slapped the hood and hollered at him to get in. From the back seat, the Prophet rained down heavenly commandments vowing plagues unless his people were freed.

"Shut up!" the Viking yelled.

"Check at the station," Doughboy told me. "If he's not there, try the underpasses. Or the other parks. Or the encampment by the river. Or maybe he went to San Francisco. There's thousands of them everywhere. No way we can keep track of them all."

The cops got into the car and slammed the doors, the engine revving to life. I started to walk away when the Doughboy rolled down his window and whistled to me. "Hey, kid," he called, "if you're really his friend, get him the hell out of here before it's too late."

I asked what he meant, but the Doughboy switched on the siren and the car sped away.

I looked at the mess all around me, the overpowering smell of weed. Expensive bicycles poked out from under blue tarps. One group was fighting while another was pissing against a rock. There was no shortage of reasons to arrest anybody here. Still, it didn't require advanced mathematics to calculate that something wasn't adding up.

Chapter 8
Called to Jesus

The flood of missed messages when I un-DND'ed my phone was overwhelming. Richard, my manager, had given up slacking me and was now texting me instead. *"Get ur ass in here ASAP!!!"* was repeated with minor variations *ad nauseam*, the frequency increasing along with the number of capital letters and exclamation points.

After hissing through the doors of the Tangerine Tower, the elevator scanned my badge and whooshed me up to my home base on the 14th floor. Like every other floor in this giant steel cylinder, the managers had offices along the curved wall of windows that looked out over the Valley, their position in the corporate pecking order evident by whether their view overlooked the industrial blight of the highway or the serenity of the mountains. Grunts like me populated the rows of narrow desks in the middle sharing a view of the elevator shaft.

When I reached my desk, I was surprised to find Dick's shaven head sticking up from my chair, his grubby fingers on my keyboard, scrolling through my email. That was an egregious breach of etiquette—managers were supposed to snoop on us hunched over in the secrecy of their own offices. I was about to tell him to get lost when I noticed the rent-a-cop beside him in a wrinkled uniform, mustard stains on his collar.

When Dick noticed me approaching, he grunted, "Figures it had to be you. The only one around here who's any good."

I had no idea what he was talking about. "That's my chair," I said.

"Then you should've been in it." He swiveled around to face me, his eyes focused like daggers straight at my throat. Mustard, the guard, reached for the holster, ready to whip out his radio to call for help.

Twitter-Dee popped up from his cubicle to see the commotion, so Twitter-Dumb followed, like two moles needing whacking, arguing over nacho cheese vs. cool ranch while pretending not to watch.

When Dick stood up, I thought he was leaving me in peace, but he handed me a folded cardboard box. "Start packing, Hara. And don't touch that computer. Or any other company property."

Was I being fired? Really? I motioned my total bewilderment.

He turned to Mustard. "Take him down to HR for his exit interview." The guard's face contorted trying to hide his glee.

"Just because I was late?" I asked, baffled. "Didn't you get my message that I had a personal emergency this morning?" Given the number of weekends I'd worked and the number of holidays I'd sacrificed to meet his impossible deadlines, he owed me a few hours to help out Sumire this morning.

"I don't give two shits about your being late! Everyone here is always late!"

The Twitters scurried off to continue their argument elsewhere. MeiLi clicked off her phone and started working for the first time ever. Dick glared at me like I was a dolt. "Come on, Hara," he said. "Do you honestly think we wouldn't find that backdoor you added to the code?"

Now I was even more confused. "What backdoor?" There were rumors that someone in the company was leaving security holes to sell to the NSA or the Russians or the North Koreans so they could spy on our customers. But that wasn't me.

"Cut the bullshit!" Dick yelled, his face turning bright purple all the way to the top of his shaven head. "Now I understand why you've been taking forever to fix that bug—you were selling access to the Russians, weren't you? We've got the evidence, Hara, so don't fucking deny it. I don't know what shit you're mixed up in, but you should've picked your accomplices better. Your stupid friends left a note in the log file, something about stealing all our bases." Dick banged his fist against the desk so hard, MeiLi's collection of framed photos fell over. The entire floor popped up from their desks to check out the excitement. "I just finished filing out the police report. We've got the FBI combing our code worried there's an impending terrorist attack on our military bases. I sure hope for your sake they're wrong because I really thought you were a smart guy, even if you can be a pretentious prick."

I flopped down into my chair. This was stupid. There were no hackers in Russia; there was only me. I wasn't concerned about the FBI—I was sure they had someone who played video games who could clear up the misunderstanding, even if it meant descending down into the depths of the subbasement of the Hoover Building to find the I.T. hobbit in his lair. But getting fired for a security breach was worse than being convicted for armed robbery—no company would ever hire me again. My life would be ruined. I'd be stuck working as a cashier at Nijiya or worse, selling my soul as a contractor on Upwork doing HTML coding forever.

"It was me," I tried to explain. "I broke into the server. I was tracing a missing account. I left that message as a flag for security. It's a joke."

"You're full of shit, Hara. What kind of lame joke says you're taking over military bases?"

The drunken kind, I didn't want to admit. "Look it up on Wikipedia," I said, reaching for the computer to show him the meme.

"Don't touch!" Dick yelled. "That's evidence!"

Mustard grabbed my collar, jerking me away from my desk.

I tried to explain about Ryu and why I'd hacked into the system, but Dick wasn't listening, because Dick was a dick. "Tell that to the police, if you want, but I'm done with you! It'll take weeks to clean up your mess." He motioned to Mustard to take me away and stomped back to his office overlooking the highway where he slammed the door.

At friendly, soothing HR World that sprawled across the 3rd floor, a place where employees could go for dog therapy or rabbit therapy or a chat with a personal motivator whenever they were feeling stressed, I tried again to explain what happened, but the stupid scrub there only cared about getting rid of me without a lawsuit. When I begged to be allowed to talk to the security team, hoping the I.T. guys would understand, they called in Mustard instead to sift through my meagre belongings to make sure I wasn't walking off with any company property. At least they allowed me to keep my employee MePhone, dropping it ungraciously back into the box.

After the VP of HR arrived to strip me of my badge, my stock options, my health insurance, and my dignity, MeCan was done with me. Mustard escorted me through the lobby, hushed snickers following us as he led me towards the glass doors. We were almost to the exit when, from inside the box, my phone rang.

Mustard craned his neck to check. "You gonna get that?"

I continued walking. I wanted to escape the tower and get home as quick as possible to crawl into bed with Johnnie Red, the worst shit they made, and figure out where I could live. Even a cheap apartment in San Jose wasn't cheap and student loans never slept. I'd have to find a job somehow if I didn't want to end up sharing a tent with Azaz.

Mustard reached over to grab the phone. "Maybe you ought to get this." He held it up to show me the caller ID: "SJ Police Dpt." Shit. Mustard contorted his face trying not to grin as he turned on the speaker so the entire lobby could hear.

A woman's voice, old and rough, boomed through the room. "Theodore Tatsu Hara?" asked the voice of doom like a summons from the underworld.

I set the box down and ripped the phone out of Mustard's hands. "Yeah?" I answered.

"This is the office of the Chief of Police." Even after shutting off the speaker, her voice still echoed off the walls. "Jesus would like to speak with you."

The HR interrogation had been frustrating, but at least they didn't have guns. Or prisons. If MeCan staff didn't know the difference between legitimate bugs and intentional backdoors, what was the likelihood that the cops would understand?

"Sorry, ma'am," I replied to the lady of doom. "I'm already late for a meeting with Commissioner Gordon."

Doom wasn't amused. It was unlikely she'd ever been amused. "Your GPS shows you currently at MeCan Tower. We're sending a cruiser to pick you up."

It was bad enough being escorted through the lobby by a guard with a gun and a mustard stain. I didn't need cops out front, too, their strobing red and blue lights drawing the entire tower to the windows. I thought of making a dash straight to Mexico or Tahiti where I could live cheaply while I cleared my name. But I couldn't survive anywhere without good Wi-Fi. Or a Nijiya market for good sake and salmon bento. So I begged her to allow me to drive myself to the police station and was surprised when she agreed.

Passing one final time through the hissing doors, a combination of sadness and shame threatened my equilibrium. I thought of Dick, thought of HR with their lying smiles, thought of the Cheetos dust covering my desk, thought of the entire stupid company firing me until I regained my righteous fury. On the other side of the thin wall of glass that separated the evil from the damned, Mustard waved a friendly goodbye, a crooked grin still plastered on his face. I flipped him off and dumped the entire box into the trashcan. And with that, I was done with MeCan. Then I called Sumire—I needed a lawyer. Fast.

She didn't answer her phone. Annoyed, I called her firm's switchboard. After five minutes waiting on hold, imagining the police cruiser screaming up the driveway and the cops jumping out with guns drawn, a voice politely informed me that Ms. Yamashita was tied up in an important meeting.

I told her far less politely that I was Satoshi Nakamoto, the firm's biggest client and yelled at her in Japanese, random phrases I remembered from tea ceremony. Sumire was pulled out of her meeting and on the phone to me within seconds. When I explained why I was standing beside the trashcan outside the front entrance of MeCan, she was beyond apologetic.

"Of course, I'll help," she said. "But you need a criminal defense attorney with experience, Ted, not an associate in intellectual property. Let me get a referral from one of our partners. Just wait there a minute. I'll call you back."

But I didn't have time to find anyone else, so I told her to meet me at the police station. She owed me that at least.

Chapter 9
Impending Doom

Unlike the mirrored menagerie where we'd started the morning, the police headquarters a block away was traditional butt-gov ugly—two stories of brownish concrete with wide, tinted windows hidden behind a row of shaggy oaks. Sumire stood beside the yellow Prius in the parking lot, frowning at the low burble of the Mustang.

When I stepped out of the car, she hugged me tight, guilt etched into the downward turn of her lips. After informing the desk sergeant that Jesus was expecting me, we retreated to a corner to wait. I was nervous and nauseous and wanted to get this over with so I could go home and commiserate with Johnny. I prayed Jesus didn't march me straight to the jail around back.

A dozen different languages filled the room, all of them angry or scared. Sumire stood in front of me like a bodyguard protecting me until the door to the back swung open. A hunched over woman emerged, older and smaller than I'd expected. "Theee-o-dooore Haaaaraa," summoned the woman who'd called me—the voice of doom. Her face was as gnarled as the angel of death without his mischievous grin.

Sumire and I followed her down the corridor to the interrogation room. Doom raised a heavy key ring that looked like it could unlock all seven gates of hell. "Wait inside," she ordered before banging the door shut behind us, rattling the window in its frame. We sat on the uncomfortable plastic chairs bolted to the floor inside the narrow room. The four walls painted in industrial gray felt like they were closing in.

"Don't worry, Ted," Sumire soothed. "It'll be okay."

"I'm not worried," I said, trying not to sound worried. Like any son of a Japanese mother, I knew how to *gaman*—endure hardship without complaint. Kaa-chan had instilled it in me, insisted it was what made us different from Americans who whined about every little thing. She told me to *gaman* every time I got beat up at school, chanted *gaman* to herself the nights Tou-san didn't come home.

Sumire stared down at the floor, looking more anxious than me. "This is all my fault," she said. "I should never have gotten you into this."

I stroked her hair as I assured her it was my own damn fault—I should have been more careful—and if anyone was to blame, it was Ryu, for whatever stupidity he'd gotten himself into. "Just get me through this," I said.

She placed a hand on my back, her touch still familiar after so many years. "I'll find you a good lawyer," she offered. "Let me pay for it. That's the least I can do."

"No way," I said. I'd never be desperate enough to accept her money to pay for yet more baggage. The interest rate on pity compounded even faster than student loans.

"My family can afford it, you know."

Yeah, I knew that too well. Another reason for Kaa-chan's distaste for *that girl*, as she'd always called Sumire, resentful at Sumire's rough-mannered mother in her big house and designer clothes, thinking she was equal to Kaa-chan's aristocratic lineage because her husband made gobs of money buying and selling other people's property.

"Consider it a loan. You can pay me back as soon as you find a new job."

"I have a job," I said.

"Come on, Ted. Do you really think MeCan is going to take you back?"

When I told her I found a new job, she looked incredulous. "How? It's been less than an hour."

"Meet the new sake sommelier at the Dandy Lion," I said, trying to maintain a poker face.

I could see her searching for the words to tell me this was a bad idea—in fact, the worst possible thing I could do. When I broke out in a grin, she realized I was joking and slapped me playfully across the arm. Suddenly we could both breathe again.

"What's the job?"

"SüprDüpr," I said, her gasp giving me a small thrill.

I told her about meeting Katie at the Corinthian. It was hard to believe that was only a few hours ago; it felt like another lifetime, one where I worked for a big, respected company and hadn't been publicly shamed, wasn't sitting in an airless police interrogation room waiting for the inquisition to arrive. I'd called Katie from the car on the way over, told her I'd been fired for hacking without mentioning why and asked if she still wanted to hire me if I wasn't in jail.

"Absolutely!" Katie had said. "Let me see if I can help out. I need you to start right away."

Sumire's face brightened. "You'd do that for me?"

"For Ryu," I corrected her. I didn't bother mentioning the Gianni's Pizza Katie had promised to put in the Corinthian basement. Or the attraction of her long legs.

Or that I was looking forward to working on something useful for once, though I still had no idea what that was.

Sumire hugged me. "Just promise me you'll be careful," she whispered. "I'm sure that woman is up to something."

I wasn't worried about Katie. Despite her warm smile, I knew she'd be a hard-nosed boss. But she was super-smart and I was sure we'd get along well, so long as I crammed a couple of semesters of Riemannian geometry into the weekend before I showed up for work.

Sumire was still hugging me when the door swung open. Two cops filed into the room: a tall one, dressed in a crisp blue uniform decorated with braided gold aiguillettes and an older man in a dusty herringbone sports coat and wrinkled slacks, a folder in his gnarled hands.

"No fornicating in here," the uniform said, throwing Sumire a leery smile. His hair was razor cut where he wasn't bald on top, his face dark with stubble around a goatee. I waited for old Herringbone to admonish him, but he just smiled and snickered a throaty cough.

Sumire and I jumped to our feet to face Herringbone. The uniform laughed at us. He banged his spit-shined shoes onto the table as he leaned back. "I'm Jesus," he said. "Chief of Police. Thank you for coming in."

Herringbone smiled weakly and lowered himself onto a chair.

"This is a misunderstanding," I said to Jesus, launching into an explanation of why I'd been hacking.

Sumire kicked me under the table. "Let me do the talking."

Jesus turned to Sumire. "And who are you, sweetheart?" He looked her over like she was something the vice squad had picked up off the street. I hated him intensely.

"His lawyer."

"His lawyer?" Jesus raised his eyebrows. "Aren't you a bit young for the job?"

Small and athletic, despite the conservative blouse and skirt, Sumire looked like she could still be in high school. "Berkeley Law," she answered. "Order of the Coif," she added proudly. "California Bar #256568."

"Cal, eh? People's Republic of Berkeley," he added with a condescending grunt. He gave Sumire the once over again, at least three more times. "Chinese *and* female— they must've loved you. And a Coifer, too. Well good for you, young lady. Your parents must be really proud of their little girl. You know where I went to school?" He didn't wait for an answer. "Anderson University. Ever heard of it?"

We both shook our heads. Herringbone looked bored digging the dirt out of his nails. He'd heard this before. "Church of God. Divinity School," Jesus announced proudly. "That was before I realized the best way to serve God was to put all the sinners in jail. Let 'em taste hell on earth and repent while they still can. Or not, and fuck 'em. Graduated San Jose Police Academy 55th out of 58, Order of the Quaff." He stopped to chuckle at his own joke. "And yet here I am." He pulled on his gold aiguillettes. "And there you are." He pointed at Sumire standing at attention across the table. "You know why, sweetheart?"

We shook our heads again. Jesus turned to Old Herringbone. "Tell 'em, Joe."

"SAT scores," Herringbone declared.

Was this doofus a secret genius with a perfect score on his SATs? Seemed hard to believe, or that it would get him promoted through the police department.

"You see, kids," Jesus continued, "the only thing the mayor cares about are SAT scores. You know why?" He stopped and waited for us to shake our heads. "Tell 'em, Joe."

"Sure, Chief." Herringbone cleared his phlegmy throat. "Why do all the Chinese live in Cupertino?" He waited for us to contemplate his riddle. "Because the Cupertino schools have the highest SAT scores in the Valley."

"Exactly," Jesus said. "So I explained to the mayor that if we got our SAT scores up in San Jose, all the Asian families would start moving here. SAT scores go up, property values go up—simple as that. Developers build more fancy apartments and condos. Companies like MeCan build their giant penises here instead of San Francisco or Mountain View. Tax revenues go up, the budget goes up, and the mayor gets a fancy new City Hall."

Herringbone nodded wisely.

"You see, kids," Jesus continued, "everyone is happy—the city is successful. Mayor Gadh gets appointed Secretary of Commerce by a president who understands that a successful Indian can be a vote winner. And I'm the one who explained this to the mayor."

N.V.V. Gadh was the perfect mayor for San Jose—he'd started as an I.T. outsourcing tycoon in Bangalore before remaking himself into a Silicon Valley venture capitalist, then promised to apply the Valley's brains, technology, and capital to solving San Jose's problems. I wondered why he trusted this goon.

"When the mayor appointed me chief of police, he gave me one job: get the SAT scores up. You follow?"

I nodded though I had no idea what this had to do with my hacking, or if this meant I was being charged with a crime.

"You know what happened last year?" Jesus asked. We shook our heads. "Tell 'em, Joe," he ordered Herringbone.

"SAT scores went down."

Sumire and I looked at each other. "You want us to set up a test prep class?" I asked.

Sumire shushed me. Jesus grunted, "Tell 'em why, Joe."

"The transients, Chief."

"Damn straight. Those homeless have invaded our city from God knows where. They're taking over the parks, sleeping on the sidewalks, pissing all over the alleys. This used to be a boring town and that's how we like it here. Joe used to spend his days fielding calls for cats stuck in trees and stupid kids playing their music too loud. Now we've got serious problems—burglary, drugs, vandalism, assault—you name it. All because of those damn homeless. People who can afford to are moving away—the Chinese, the Indians, even the fucking Afghanis. The only people left are singles and dink dorks like you. The mayor is clear—he wants something done. Immediately."

"What's this have to do with my client?" Sumire asked.

"Your client?"

Sumire pointed at me.

"Oh, him. Right. Yeah, I got a call from Katie D—Dr. Deauville. Said Mr. Hara is her new Chief Mathematics Officer."

I beamed at my impressive new title. It sure beat Staff Engineer at MeCan, though the inflated title hardly made up for a salary that would barely cover my rent.

"Dr. Deauville is an important person around here who's helping us clean up downtown. The mayor told me just yesterday he's so thrilled, he offered to marry her if his wife will agree. I'm all for making an example to teach you little snots that unauthorized computer access is a crime we take seriously. But Dr. Deauville insists she needs you and convinced Evgeni not to press charges. So Mr. Hara, you're a lucky man— you're getting off easy thanks to her. But I warn you, there'd better not be a next time because she won't be able to help you again. If we get any more reports of hacking, we've got enough evidence to put you away for ten years. And you've been added to the FBI watch list of hackers with potential terrorist connections. So I'd advise you to keep your nose clean and your hands off other people's computers. *Capisce?*"

I capisce'ed. Katie had set me free. I was so relieved, I couldn't speak until Sumire kicked me under the table. "No more hacking," I swore. I wouldn't need to break into MeCan's computers now that I was inside SüprDüpr.

"Then you're free to go," Jesus said and stood to leave. Sumire squeezed my hand. She tried to pull me up from the chair, but I didn't move.

"There's just one thing," I said.

"Let's go, Ted."

"I was hacking into MeCan for a reason. Sumire's brother is missing. If you can get a search warrant for his phone records, you'll be able to find him in minutes."

"Sure, kid," Jesus said. "We'll get on it right away for you. Anything else you need?"

Herringbone turned to Sumire. "How long's he been missing?"

"Since last weekend. Sunday."

Jesus threw up his hands. "Not even a week? I guarantee he's shacked up somewhere. Girl, guy, coke, Jim Beam, whatever his preference."

"In my experience," Herringbone croaked, "he's likely to resurface any day. They always do."

"Can't you get a court order to see his phone records?" I asked. "Then we'll know right now."

"Look, kid, I don't think you understand. We've got serious problems here. I don't have the manpower to deal with all the shit going on downtown much less chase after every Tom, Dick, and Pussy with a personal crisis."

"It's all those homeless," Herringbone added.

"My brother did not run away," Sumire insisted.

Jesus raised his hand. "Stop." He pointed at her chair. "Sit."

"But Ryu wouldn't—"

"Not another word." We both fell silent. "Have you filed a missing persons report?"

"Yes, but—"

"Here's what I'll do, sweetheart. Joe will submit the report to the FBI and we'll see if anything turns up. There's a chance they'll find his name on a flight manifest or a border crossing. But don't hold your breath. If he hasn't contacted you yet, he doesn't want to be found. Other than that, all you can do is sit tight and wait for him to reach out to you. Or his body to turn up somewhere."

"But I'm sure he'll resurface soon," Herringbone reassured us. "They always do."

Jesus pulled open the door, a burst of cool air rushing into the room. "Now if you'll excuse me, I've got a powwow with the mayor to figure out how to move all those homeless into the new shelter."

After Jesus left, Herringbone turned to me. "A word of caution, son." He looked over my folder again. "If you don't want to be back here, I strongly advise you not to take matters into your own hands again. I guarantee the chief won't be so forgiving next time."

Sumire marched me back to the lobby, hurrying straight for the exit. I stopped at the front desk where the Doom woman was sitting on a tall chair, daring anyone to approach.

I stood on tiptoes to look over the raised counter. "I'd like to check on someone."

A cockroach scurried away to hide in the corner. Doom stared straight into me, her eyes the deep blue of the coldest glacier. Goosebumps ran down my spine. I told her I was looking for a man picked up in St. James Park yesterday named Azaz.

She didn't even check the computer in front of her. "Vagrant?" she grunted. When I nodded, she snorted. "Not here."

Azaz probably wasn't his real name. "Do you have a list of people who were arrested yesterday?" I asked. "Maybe mug shots I could look at?" That's the way it worked on TV.

"No," she answered, eyes unblinking.

"Is there someone else I can talk to?"

"No," she repeated.

"Is he in jail?" I asked, my voice rising in frustration.

"No," she said again.

"Where do your officers take the homeless people they arrest?"

She said nothing. I waited. She stared. I stared back.

Sumire tapped me on the shoulder. "Come on, Ted, let's go." She pulled my arm, but I didn't budge. "Don't do this, Ted."

"I have to do this," I said.

"Stop being pigheaded," she demanded. I was surprised she understood me so poorly. I was pigheaded and I could never stop. "Let's get out of here already." She waved me towards the door.

But I stayed, staring straight back at Doom for what seemed like eternity, but I'd never stare her down, not in million years. So I started humming the most insipid, earworming Justin Bieber song. She ground her teeth. Then I started dancing. Badly.

She closed her eyes in pain. "Stop!" she bellowed.

"Where do the homeless go?" I asked again.

"To hell," she sneered, her voice dripping with hatred. A chill draft blew through the room.

"Help me find my friend," I begged.

Doom leaned forward on her high chair and wiggled a bony, arthritic finger at me.

"A word of advice, boy," she said in a hoarse whisper. "You know what happens to nosy fellows?" Her crooked finger drew a sharp line down my face. "They lose their noses."

Then she cackled through brown teeth loud enough to terrify the prisoners in the jail a block away.

Chapter 10
Spotless

That evening, I waited for Sumire at the Dandy Lion and this time I was even early. Yukiko set the steaming bowl of noodles in front of me just as Sumire walked through the door. After they hugged, Sumire sat down across from me. I thought she'd be thrilled I had my freedom, but when she looked at the table, she snapped, "Already?"

I saluted her with my cup. "A toast to your great legal victory."

She grabbed the bottle off the table and handed it to Yukiko, telling her to take it away.

"Wait!" I rescued the Dassai from Yukiko's tray and gulped the last drops straight from the bottle. Not the best way to enjoy Dassai's fruity aroma and silky finish, but better than not enjoying it at all.

Sumire's nose flared, her small hands balled into fists, and I saw the rage submerged.

"What? It's almost dark," I said. Outside, the sky was fading to gray, a red glow on the horizon. Though I made it a point never to drink during the day, in the lingering evening of early autumn, this was close enough. "Have a drink with me to celebrate. It's just sake. Same as a glass of wine."

"There's nothing to celebrate," she snapped. "And you, of all people, don't need a drink."

When Yukiko returned with Sumire's miso ramen, I held off ordering a refill of Dassai. I'd have to stop by the Nijiya on the way home to restock the Mu for my weekend crash course in mathematics.

We slurped our ramen in noisy silence, both staring down at our bowls, filling our mouths with chewy noodles and meaty slices of chashu. As I drank the rich broth tingling of ginger, I pondered Doom's warning. Did she quote from the movie Chinatown to everyone she hated or was that a special message for me? And what was that message—stop looking for Ryu? Or stop nosing about the homeless encampment at St. Jimmy's?

The wooden door slid open and a hulking figure in blue ducked his head to squeeze through the narrow frame. He tipped his cap to Yukiko who was rushing over to him in a panic. I wondered why a cop had her in such a fluster until I saw it wasn't any cop—it was Mayeda.

Michael Mayeda had attended the same high school as Sumire and me. He'd been the rock star on the offensive line of our pathetic football team while I'd held up the defensive line of our nationally ranked Math Olympiad club. He'd been a bully, singling me out for torment until Sumire had put an end to that. It figured he'd become a cop; wearing a uniform and badge, he now had the legal right to bully me and everyone else. With his short-cropped raven hair, moon face, and wispy moustache, he could be taken for a native on the train in Kyoto, but that's where the resemblance stopped. Despite the Japanese name, the rest of him looked pure Hawaiian. Which wasn't unusual here. There were so many Japanese-Hawaiians in Japantown that they even had their own supermarket a block away where we went for real Hawaiian *poke*—fresh ahi and pickled seaweed instead of the weird, new-agey vegan crap.

As Yukiko led him towards a booth in the back, I warned Sumire, "Don't look behind you." I pulled down my baseball cap and ducked my head close to the bowl of ramen.

Passing our table, the cop said under his breath, "Hiya, shrimp."

"*Bakayaro,*" I muttered in reply, the worst insult in Japanese.

Sumire wagged an admonishing finger at me; the jackbooted footsteps stopped and turned around. He stood in front of our table, his football player's body blocking the light. I cringed, waiting for his attack.

"Hiya, Sumire," he said affably, still pronouncing her name like the stupid *gaijin* that he was—"Sue Mary" instead of "Sue-me-ray." I looked up to see a wide, dumbass smile across his wide, dumbass face.

"Hello, Mike," she replied. "It's nice to see you." She sounded friendly, as if she was actually glad to see him.

He turned to me and chuckled. "Too bad about getting fired, shrimp." I wondered how he heard the news already since he surely didn't read Recode or Reddit. There had to be a rumor about me floating around the station. "How ya been, Sumire? How's the lawyer life?"

"No complaints," she answered, as if they'd hung out just last week.

"How's your mother?"

"Okay, I guess. Considering everything."

"Oh?" he said, concern on his face. "Is something wrong?"

Before Sumire could answer, Yukiko tapped him on the shoulder and pointed to the waiting booth. He tipped his hat to Sumire and followed Yukiko to the back.

I exhaled in relief. "You act like you know him."

"I do know Mike."

"Not since high school. Not since you beat him up."

"That was ages ago, Ted."

It still felt like yesterday to me, the day Mayeda said he'd be waiting for me after school when I'd made some snarky remark in class. Sumire begged me to take a different route home. She couldn't understand that because I was short and scrawny and couldn't fight, running away was the worst thing I could do, would leave me shamed forever, a fate far worse than a black eye.

True to his word, that afternoon he'd stood on the corner, the entire offensive line blocking our way. As the others jeered, Mayeda loomed over me, poking a fat finger in my chest, calling me shrimp or sissy or something equally juvenile and said he was going to pound my *haole* ass. Little Sumire, dressed in a pink t-shirt with a bow in her hair, whipped around with an aikido move that dropped him to the ground. He landed on his face, blood spurting out, his nose dislocated.

For weeks afterwards, his friends made fun of him for getting beaten up by a girl. But the whole school laughed at me forever—the boy who had to be defended by Hello Kitty. Mayeda and I avoided each other after that. I asked Sumire why she was so friendly with him now.

"What's the big deal?"

"He's a dipshit. And a bully."

"Maybe he's different now. People change, you know."

"I haven't."

"Maybe that's your problem, Teddybear."

I said nothing more. I wasn't going to win this argument. Or any other. I picked up my chopsticks and returned to fishing for the remaining bits of chashu at the bottom of the murky broth. When there was nothing left, I had an idea. "Come with me." I led her over to Mayeda's booth.

His cap was on the table, its outline still visible on his hair. While he slurped a mouthful of noodles, spraying gobs of broth and fat all around, I slid over the red vinyl bench across from him. Sumire sat down beside me.

"You mind?" I asked.

"Sure, *Teddybear*," he chuckled. Sumire laughed along. I wanted to slug him myself. I would have left right then if Sumire wasn't blocking my way out.

He looked back and forth between us. "You two back together or what?"

"No," we replied in unison.

"That's good," he said, though I didn't see why he'd care. "Never understood why you let a girl stick up for you, shrimp. Especially someone as nice as Sumire."

Though she was small and cute, I was surprised he still didn't understand how fierce she was underneath.

"Got a favor to ask," I told Mayeda. He ignored me and returned to his noodles. "It's for Sumire," I added. "She needs your help."

He put down his chopsticks and grinned at her like a clown. "At your service." But when she explained that Ryu was missing, his goofy smile fell into a frown. "Sorry, Sumire. I'm not a detective." Then his face lit up. "Hey, why don't you come with me to the station? I'll help you fill out a missing persons report."

"Already done," I told him.

"Thanks, Mike," she said. "It's great seeing you again." She stood and motioned me to follow.

I stayed in the booth facing Mayeda who returned to slurping his noodles. I banged the table. "Come with us to Ryu's apartment," I demanded.

He took his time chewing a mouthful of noodles before answering, "I told you, shrimp, I'm not a detective."

I was planning to check Ryu's computer and we needed him to take it to the actual detectives if we found anything. "Come on, Mayeda, are you going to help her? Or are you going to be a dipshit?"

Sumire pulled on my arm. "There's nothing there, Ted. I already looked."

"You didn't check the computer," I said. "Or maybe Mayeda will use his special sleuthing skills to notice something you missed. Right, Mike?"

With the chance to play the hero, Mayeda changed his mind. "Well…I guess I can join you. But only for a few minutes. I gotta get back to patrol."

"Great. Let's go!" I slid out of the booth and started for the door.

"Can you at least let me finish my dinner?"

Sumire and I stood on the sidewalk, waiting for the cop. "I'll get the car," I said. The pony was in my garage, only a couple blocks away.

Sumire frowned her disapproval. Kaa-chan had hated Tou-san's car, too, complaining it was noisy and hot and smelled of engine oil, so we always took her Camry whenever we went out together as a family.

"You shouldn't be driving," Sumire said, and pointed at her lemon Prius parked down the street. I couldn't let Mayeda see me driven around by a girl, much less Sumire. I'd only downed a mini-bottle of sake—the equivalent of less than a couple of glasses of wine.

"I'm not even a little buzzed," I assured her, and went to retrieve my car. Idling in front of the shop, the ground vibrating from the rumble of the engine, I rolled down the window and told Sumire to get in.

"No way," she said. "I can't believe you still have that monstrosity."

The Mustang was the only thing I had left of Tou-san, the real love of his life, a hand-me-down from my grandfather. He'd restored it into a gleaming show car that I'd secretly rebuilt from scrap after the accident. Kaa-chan thought I was out with Sumire every evening for half a year while I worked in a rented garage to resurrect the pony. She would have screamed and cried and grounded me forever if she'd found me with the car that killed my father. I finished it just in time to drive across the country to college without ever telling her.

Mayeda squeezed through the door of the Dandy Lion and donned his flattop. "Nice car, shrimp," he said when he saw me. "1968?"

I didn't bother replying. Anyone who didn't know the difference between the '68 and '69 Mustang didn't know shit. "Hop in," I told him. "I'll drive you over."

"Nah," he said. "Gotta take the cruiser." He pointed to the corner where the cop car was parked in a red zone. "Come on, Sumire, I'll give you a ride."

"Tell Ted he can't drive now."

The cop peered through the window at me. I wasn't about to let Mayeda tell me what to do, cop or not. I slipped the car into gear and rolled a block down the street to wait. Sumire shook her head angrily. I watched through the mirror as she walked off with Mayeda who looked glad to have her alone. I hated seeing him beside her, two heads taller and twice as wide. He opened the door and helped her into the car.

Without Ryu's address, I had to follow behind the police car, its lights flashing and siren screaming as it ran through the red lights at high speed, my pony in hot pursuit down 3rd Street. To everyone we passed, we must have looked like a weird, backwards car chase. Probably not the smartest thing to be doing, even with the buzz nearly gone, but there was no way I could let Mayeda leave me in his dust.

The cruiser screeched to a halt in a no-parking zone in front of a modern apartment complex a few blocks from the SJSU campus. Mayeda dashed around to the passenger side to help Sumire out. The closest parking I could find was three blocks away. By the time I arrived, the pair were already inside the lobby chatting. I had to bang on the window before they noticed me. I regretted bringing Mayeda with us.

When he finally opened the door, I asked, "What did Sumire think of the ride?" I waited to hear how she'd screamed at him the entire way to slow down. Maybe now he understood.

"That was fun," Sumire laughed. "And you really shouldn't be driving."

Mayeda beamed at me. "Yeah, Teddybear."

I decided not to ask any more questions.

Sumire led the way to Ryu's apartment while Mayeda acted like he was in charge. "Don't touch anything inside," he warned us. "In case we need forensics."

"That's strange," Sumire said as she unlocked the door. "I'm sure I bolted it last time." Then her expression cleared. "Ah, it must have been the housekeeper. Have to remind her to lock up next time."

Inside, the narrow apartment was tidy, with no furniture other than a cheap Ikea dining table, desk, and bookshelf against the wall. I spotted the computer monitor on the desk and beside it, a photo—the family at Disneyland. Sumire was wearing the Minnie Mouse ears we teased her about forever, Ryu smiling through braces, parents on either side of them looking harried and unhappy, a portent of the divorce that came a few months later.

The bookshelf was filled with quantum physics textbooks from the SJSU bookstore and newer books on Higgs particles that had to be for SüprDüpr. I pulled one off the shelf and thumbed through it, but there were no notes inside, not even any highlighting, just page after page of formulas and explanations that I couldn't understand. When Mayeda noticed me grabbing a couple books to take home to study later, he rushed over to reprimand me. "I told you not to touch the evidence," he said, putting his own fingerprints all over them as he returned them to the shelf.

On the top shelf was a row of zoology books about pachyderms beside a well-worn Bible and a bunch of pop religion books about rediscovering God. I never understood how someone with an advanced degree in physics could believe in ancient superstitions. I wondered again if Ryu was holed up in the desert somewhere trying to circle that square. Had whatever he was doing with Higgs particles—the "God Particle"—caused him to question his faith in a fairytale afterlife? Had he finally realized the universe was every bit the cold and unforgiving place it really was? It made you want to kill yourself if you thought about it too long.

The only solution I'd ever found was to start drinking and stop thinking about it. Which might explain Ryu's recent drinking at the Dandy Lion. I worried he'd taken that leap into the void; it was as likely as anything else. I asked Sumire to see if she could find any clues in his Bible while I went to check the bedroom.

Tacked to the wall above the bed was a blue and gold SJSU pennant beside a simple wooden cross. His clothes hung neatly inside the mirrored closet. The room was spotless, the sheets without a wrinkle. Not a speck of dust anywhere.

Mayeda said there wasn't anything interesting in the bathroom. I checked anyway. The usual soaps and shampoos, shaving implements, Tylenol and cold medicines, a hemorrhoid cream. The box of condoms was half empty, I noted jealously. No opioids or narcotics to hint at addiction, no sleeping pills to kill himself, no cancer medications or antidepressants to expose a secret he hadn't told his family. Not a single thing out of place.

There was nothing out of place in the kitchen, either—the sink was empty, all the dishes stacked in the cabinet. The refrigerator held a few days of food. Even the trashcan was spotless. Sumire was right—nothing here but an empty apartment. Had he scrubbed his place clean before leaving town?

"It's too neat," I told her.

"So?"

"Doesn't that seem strange to you?"

Sumire laughed. "Ryu's a pig, just like you. That's why he has a housekeeper come twice a week. I'll give you her number—your apartment could use a good cleaning."

I ignored the gibe at the state of my apartment. I was comfortable there, and that was the only thing that mattered. Besides, nobody but me was allowed to touch Kaa-chan's vacuums or dust her tea ceremony cabinet.

Sitting down at Ryu's desk, the monitor stared out at me, its face blank. The keyboard and mouse were beside a brand-new game controller. When I touched the keyboard, nothing happened—it was powered off. I followed the HDMI cable out the back of the monitor as it snaked behind the desk. The other end was lying on the ground, unconnected to anything. The computer was gone.

Sumire and I hunted through the apartment while Mayeda admonished us not to touch anything. I rifled through the linen closet, throwing all the towels into the hallway. In the back was the vacuum cleaner, a sleek, expensive Dyson, but no computer hiding anywhere that we could find.

"He must have taken it with him," Sumire said. "Can you find out where it is?"

Phones were easy to trace—each had a unique SIM to identify it and GPS to record its location. Computers were different—they only had an IP address that changed whenever they connected to a different network. If I could find a website Ryu accessed regularly and break into its server, it would show me the IP address he'd used to login. Then I could run a traceroute which would tell me his location within a few miles. That would be a major undertaking. It would require a lot of guesswork. And more than a little luck. And days of work. I started explaining this to Sumire, but her eyes glazed over.

Mayeda scoffed. "Did you check the building's security tapes? Maybe we can see when he took it."

Sumire jumped up. "That's a great idea, Mike!"

Beaming with pride, the cop hitched up his pants and raised himself to his full height. Leading the way to the front desk, Sumire walked beside him, the tap of her sandals on the carpet in lockstep with the thump of his heavy boots. I shuffled behind, annoyed at my own stupidity.

Instead of a wireless fob or an electronic entry system, all this building had for security were old-school cameras tacked up around the complex. The concierge at the front desk was a Chinese kid as skinny as a pole, with thick, bristly hair gelled into spikes that made him look like the end of a broom. After Mayeda flashed his SJPD badge, Broomhead showed him the security monitor. But when the cop asked to review the recordings, Broomhead asked if he had a warrant. Mayeda shook his head sheepishly, defeated by a single shot.

I stepped up to the desk. "Look, kid," I said.

"I'm not a kid," he mumbled.

"Look, sir," I said, though he looked like a college kid, "one of your residents is missing. We'd be grateful if you'd assist us in checking the last time he left his apartment."

Broomhead pulled a binder from the drawer and flipped through the pages. "Says here, 'Only employees of the management company are authorized to access or view the security system'."

"May I see that?" Sumire asked, taking the binder from his hands.

While Sumire was reviewing the regulations, I asked Mayeda how long it would take to get a warrant. "No idea. Gotta put in a request through CID." I should've known he'd be useless.

Sumire handed the binder back to Broomhead. "What's your name?" she asked. When he mumbled Bobby Zhang, she placed a hand on his shoulder. "Listen, Bobby, I need your help," she started. "The resident in unit 207 is my brother. You can check his name in your records. It's the same as mine—Yamashita." She placed a business card on the desk in front of him. "I'm a lawyer, Bobby, and I have power of attorney to represent my brother. As a tenant of this facility, my brother, and by extension myself, have the right to review all records that include his image. So, Bobby, will you help us? Or do I have to get a subpoena and haul your ass into court?"

Broomhead jumped back in panic and flipped through the binder again. "'Any threat of litigation,'" he recited, "'must be recorded and the legal department notified immediately.'"

"Give me that number," Sumire demanded. Over the phone, she pleaded and threatened a succession of neckties until she handed her phone to Broomhead. "They want to talk to you."

He nodded and bowed and said okay a half dozen times before handing it back to Sumire. She clicked the phone off, triumphant. "Let's start with the garage on Saturday."

We fast forwarded through the video, searching for Ryu's gray SUV. "There he is!" Sumire exclaimed.

His car left the garage just after ten on Saturday morning according to the timestamp. We could see a lone driver inside. He didn't return again until evening. His murky, grainy, black and white face staring out through the windshield was like a ghost. He left again on Sunday morning just before 9:30 a.m. Though we spent an hour searching the rest of the video, neither Ryu nor his car ever returned.

"Gimme the license plate," Mayeda said. "I'll call it in. We'll see if the vehicle turned up anywhere."

While Mayeda radioed the dispatcher, Sumire steadied herself against my shoulder. "I didn't want to believe it," she said. "It's strange seeing his face staring out the window. It's like he drove away and never came back."

Outside the lobby, a pair of college girls in tight shorts walked up to the door and pressed buttons on the security panel outside. The intercom rang, then a tinny "*Wei?*" could be heard though the speaker. "Hey, this Lixia," one girl yelled into the intercom. When the door buzzed open, the girls strutted through the lobby, waving to Broomhead and giggling at the cop.

The security system seemed particularly old-school for the capital of the tech world. But it had to keep a record of all the calls from the front door. Sumire convinced Broomhead to scroll through the entries on Saturday evening after Ryu returned home. There was one call to Ryu's phone at 8:57 p.m. We pulled up the video of the front door again.

It was a Saturday night with a steady stream of visitors, mostly college kids, girls dressed to kill, boys dressed to die. At 8:57, two frat boys were standing at the door, twelve packs of crappy beer in hand, waiting to be buzzed in. A woman's voice came through the intercom. We turned up the volume as loud as it would go, trying to catch what she said over the shouting and music behind her.

"Sounds like a party," Mayeda commented from the other side of the lobby, proving his detective skills.

"Is that his girlfriend?" I asked Sumire. She didn't know. I wondered if the voice was Grace Kim, who might or might not be his girlfriend. I still hadn't heard back from her. Or maybe it was her replacement. I was sure, though, it wasn't Katie's Midwestern accent.

"Any idea who those guys are?" I pointed at the screen.

Sumire didn't recognize them, said it didn't look like Ryu's church friends.

"Hey, Mayeda," I called to the cop, "you got any way to identify these two?"

He offered to get a friend in Investigations to run a screenshot through the FBI database. "Can't promise nothing, but if either of them have a record, we'll know in a few days."

There was no reason we had to wait. I could use Google's Face Match to identify them within seconds, whether they had a criminal record or not. I took a snap of the screen. "Let's go," I said to Sumire. I told her to come with me to upload the photo and find out who they were.

Sumire waited for Mayeda to join us, but he stepped over to Broomhead and asked, "This building got any other entrances?"

"Sure. There's the side entrance on Virginia and the one around back on Martha."

Mayeda beamed at Sumire as if he'd just won the Nobel Prize for police work. Broomhead pulled up the video for the Martha St. entrance. And there, at exactly 20:57:15 according to the timestamp in the lower corner, clear as day in the middle of the night, was the dead fish eyes and shaven head of Satoshi, the eleventh richest man in the world. The call to Ryu's phone had come from Satoshi from a side entrance. The frat boys at the front lobby were going to a party somewhere else in the building.

Sumire turned to the big cop. "You're brilliant, Mike!"

He stood even taller, basking in her praise. With his phone he took a snap of Satoshi standing at the gate. "I'll shoot this over to CID right away." Sumire stood on tiptoes to kiss him on the cheek.

I mumbled to Broomhead, "I was going to check that, too."

Walking back to my car, I heard stomping behind me. When I turned around, I was surprised to see Sumire standing alone at the patrol car while Mayeda was waving at me to stop. I walked faster, head ducked, and cringed when he shouted my name.

He pulled up beside me. "Hey, Hara, wanna grab a drink? For old times' sake. Maybe we can catch up or something."

I told him the only catching up I was doing tonight was a textbook on Riemannian geometry. He looked at me confused. "Come on, shrimp, don't be like that. I know a place with a late happy hour."

I shook my head. "Nobody's happy but you."

"How about a raincheck then?"

"Sure," I said. "Next time it rains." In the current drought, that probably wouldn't be for months.

I left him there and took off toward my car. This time he didn't follow. I didn't understand what Mayeda was after, but I didn't want to drink with him. We'd stayed clear of each other after the Sumire incident, and that was one tradition worth keeping. Besides, I could hear the frosted blue bottles of Mu calling from the Nijiya refrigerator case, offering their help preparing for Monday when I'd start work at SüprDüpr. One way or another, everything would be revealed then.

Chapter 11
Schrödinger's Elephant

When I awoke to the clattering of rain against the window, my fingers still twitching after playing Legends of Emperors long into the night, I tried to clear my pounding head to dive into Riemannian geometry. I brewed a mug of Earl Grey, the crinkled leaves spreading their perfume of bergamot, and stood at the window watching the rain dancing on the street below. I pictured Sumire at her window, too, staring out into the gloom, fleece robe over flannel pajamas, cup of milky tea in hand, and wondered if she was alone.

My phone buzzed. A message. *"Where are u?"*

For a moment, I thought it was from Sumire, but that wasn't her number. Could it be Ryu? My heart skipped a beat as I checked the messages that had arrived overnight. From Katie, all of them, with instructions to meet at 8 a.m. at the MeWork on 3rd Street.

I shot back a thumbs up. *"cya monday"* I replied. I was excited to tell Sumire I finally knew where the SüprDüpr office was. We could drop by this afternoon while the place was empty and look for Ryu's computer.

My phone buzzed immediately. *"Today!"* came the reply from Katie. *"See u NOW!"*

Even Dick, who demanded I work through the night, never expected me to report to the office at 8 a.m. on a weekend. Life at a startup would take adjustment. I dumped the tea and gulped down a quick cure from the CureRig Keurig clone, then headed into the bathroom to shave my face clean. Once I'd scrubbed the sweat from every pore, I felt alert, ready to start a new life. I picked out a fresh Giants t-shirt and found a pair of brand-new ripped jeans hiding in the back of the closet behind the row of vacuums. Already an hour late for my first day of work, I donned my remembrance cap and rushed out into the rain.

"Sign this," Katie said as soon as I squeezed in beside her in the phone booth-sized privacy stall at the back of our unmarked office. Her laptop cast an eerie blue glow through the darkened cubbyhole. She dumped the remains of a half-eaten salad back into the Heavenly's bag. Seated hip-to-hip, her bare arm brushed mine as she turned the DocuSign to me. It would have felt cozy together in the tiny room if not for the dog clawing at my ankles and the reek of onions.

Outside our privacy box, the small SüprDüpr team was huddled around a set of blueprints tacked up on the wall. Our office in the back of the MeWork coworking space that filled the 4th floor was hidden behind shaded windows and could only be entered through a separately locked door. Katie took security seriously. Other than us, the MeWork was empty this early on a Saturday morning, the tech-bros still sleeping, reception desk deserted, even the kombucha taps turned off.

I squinted as I scrolled through the documents on the screen—stock options, non-disclosure agreement, company regulations—all the usual crap. I asked Katie if I could have my lawyer review them first.

"It's all standard boilerplate," Katie said impatiently. "Just sign it so we can get cracking."

I affixed my full miserable legal name—Theodore Tatsu Hara—in a million places until I reached the last page and instead of signing, drew a little cartoon of my goofy face. Sumire would have laughed before replacing it with a much better version with bug eyes behind Doctor Who glasses, but Katie wasn't amused. She erased the drawing and made me sign again.

Once the paperwork was out of the way, she threw me her megawatt smile. "I'm really glad you joined us, Hara—you're absolutely critical to our success. Your first project is to write a program to calculate the distance between any two points on the earth, and the exact spot in the opposite direction. Understand?"

I shook my head. "Not really."

"Let's say I want to go from the Corinthian in San Jose to the Hoover Tower at Stanford. You can calculate that distance, right?"

"Driving distance?" Were we optimizing the route to reduce carbon emissions? If that's what "reinventing transportation" meant, we were doomed—there were already a dozen startups developing something similar.

"Distance through the earth. In a straight line. Not curved."

Ah, so we were building loop transit tubes—Elon Musk's idea. Shooting people in capsules at supersonic speeds along a tunnel bored through the earth.

"Let's say the Hoover Tower is 16.2 miles north of the Corinthian, okay? Then you need to find the opposite point 16.2 miles south of the Corinthian. Understand?"

I understood what she was asking but not why.

"Call it ballast," she said, which wasn't enlightening, either. She opened a MeMap to show me. "If you follow the actual line between the Corinthian and the Hoover Tower, the opposite location is somewhere around here." She pointed at a spot in the Diablo Mountains south-east of San Jose.

"You want me to go out there?" I wondered why she needed a mathematician instead of a surveyor.

"You're not getting it, Hara. The Hoover Tower was just an example. It can be anywhere. We need to identify the opposite location between the Corinthian and anywhere in the world."

I didn't understand the point, but it didn't matter. The math was trivial and the hard work already done by my former employer. No wonder Katie was so determined to hire me when she found out I worked for MeCan. I could whip up an API call to MeMaps to grab the coordinates, then do the trigonometry to adjust for the curvature of the earth. "Easy-peasy," I declared. "I can have it ready before noon."

"I don't think you understand," Katie said sharply. "The coordinates need to be accurate to the millimeter."

"Millimeter?" I choked out. MeMaps were accurate to a few feet at best, which was as good as the GPS signals allowed. Close enough to know what road you were on, not good enough to know which lane, and a thousand times from being able to discern one leg of an ant from another.

"Yes, millimeter. It's a difficult problem. That's why I hired you. Can you figure out a way to do it?"

The simple answer was hell no. I felt a lump in my stomach, the air going out of my lungs. My train had pulled into crazytown. I could guess what happened to Ryu—he ran away screaming, the same thing I ought to do. I wanted to tell her what she was asking was impossible, but I needed to find Ryu first. So I tried to sound like any other startup acolyte when I declared, "You can count on me!"

"Marvelous," she said. "Then let's get cracking. There's only ten days before our big demo."

"What demo?"

She looked at me proudly. "Get ready, Hara, for an event the world will never forget. Picture a parade down 3rd Street, right out there in front of the Corinthian. The park packed with spectators. Millions of people all over the world watching the livestream. At the strike of noon, at the front of the parade, an elephant will materialize out of nowhere to lead the marching band down the street and into history. Everyone will remember that moment for the rest of their lives. Steve Jobs will roll over in his grave in envy. The whole world will be clamoring to get in on our IPO because after that demo, everyone will understand that teleportation changes everything."

"Teleportation?" She couldn't have said teleportation, could she?

"Yes, Hara," she said, a glint in her eye. "We're building a teleporter. But you can't tell anyone, not yet. Not until after the demo."

"But…" I stammered. "That's impossible." I looked at Katie to see if she was joking. "Isn't it? It's a magic trick, right?"

"It's not magic, Hara—it's quantum mechanics. Using Higgs bosons. The Schrödinger Effect."

I'd heard of Schrödinger's Cat, the Zen-like paradox about the meaning of reality argued over endlessly by the stoners in the dorm lounge but didn't know anything about the Schrödinger Effect. That was physics and I studied math, which was all theory, never anything connected to the real world. Katie pulled up a document filled with page after page of partial differential equations and pointed to a set at the bottom. "You'll need this equation for your calculations. It's how we use the quantum entanglement of a stream of paired Higgs doublets to transport anything with probabilistic states at the speed of light."

I had no idea what that meant. "This actually works?" I asked. "Have you tested it?" Equations on a page were one thing, moving an elephant as big as a house through spacetime was something else.

"Of course it works," she insisted. "Why do you think we're all here?" She pointed at the group outside our telephone booth marking notes on a whiteboard. "Here, I'll show you."

She set a video playing on the computer. It wasn't professional or even well-edited. It'd been shot with a phone—the image shaky, the focus uncertain. Katie was holding a cage, a white lab rat scampering inside, standing in front of a large metal dome that looked like the front of a submarine. The camera zoomed in to show 08 marked in black on the side of the rat like the number on a racecar.

"This is the prototype we're using for testing," she said. "It's very primitive—just a proof of concept. We're building the first SüprPorter now inside the Corinthian. The larger ring and superconducting cryomagnets under the street will give us better beamline control. We'll use the money from the IPO to build SüprPorters all over the world."

The video followed Katie hanging the cage on a hook inside the metal dome. She closed the hatch, locking the rat inside. After pressing a button on a keyboard attached to a rack of equipment, a bright white light began glowing inside an empty cage across the room. The light burst outward in a ring, then came a pop and the light imploded back into a ball. Once the light dissipated, a white rat marked 08 scurried about inside the previously empty cage on the other side of the room. An unseen audience broke out into an exuberant cheer. A man shouted bravo in a thick Japanese accent—that had to be Satoshi.

"Holy shit," I mumbled, my jaw hanging open. It worked. Teleportation. For real. The company would be worth billions no doubt, maybe trillions, just as Katie claimed. And I was the company's Chief Mathematics Officer. And soon to be billionaire. Assuming she hadn't faked the video.

"Do you understand how this changes everything, Hara? No more airplanes. No more driving cross-country. Just walk into a SüprPorter and step out seconds later wherever you want to go. This will revolutionize transportation, but it doesn't stop there. It's the end of warfare as we know it. The military will be able to send soldiers into bin Laden's cave or Putin's palace at the press of a button—think how many lives this will save. Not everyone will be thrilled about it, though, that I can guarantee. There are powerful companies that will do anything to stop us—airlines, car manufacturers, defense contractors—there's a long list. And you'd be naïve to think that every government in the world isn't desperate to steal our plans. So you need to stay on your guard at all times. You can't even tell anyone you work here. Understand?"

Still dumbstruck, unable to say anything, I just nodded.

"Then get going, Hara—we need your software to make sure customers materialize at the right spot, and only ten days before our unveiling."

"Ten days?" I choked out. Software isn't built in ten days.

"I said it was urgent, didn't I? Look, it's only a demo. We know the origin and destination locations for the parade so we won't need the mapping data yet. Just throw together a working algorithm for now. Don't worry—you'll have plenty of time for the final version. Actual customer trials aren't for another two months when we start the IPO roadshow."

"Two months?" At MeCan, changing a button on the interface took two months. Adding a new layer took a year.

"Welcome to startup life," she said. "I told you it would be exciting." She snapped her laptop shut and stood to go. The door accordioned open, fresh air rushing into the booth.

"Wait!"

"What?" she said tapping her heel on the carpet.

"There's something I need to ask. It's about one of the other employees."

She looked at me through narrowed eyes before glancing at her Fitbit. "I've got to run."

"It'll only take a sec."

"Look, Hara, you were an hour late getting here, and I've got a critical meeting with our bankers to discuss the IPO. We can talk next time. For now, have Evelyn set you up with whatever you need. And send me an outline of your algorithm tonight. We're all counting on you. So let's get cracking."

She waved to the team at the whiteboard before striding out through the security door, the dog yapping at her ankles, her pointed heels leaving a trail of exclamation points deep in the carpet pile.

Chapter 12
Chief Elephant Officer

I found the office manager at a desk in the corner wearing a pink Victoria's Secret t-shirt. She had blue hair, a tattoo of a horse on the side of her neck, and a huge gold nose ring that hung down to her lip. It took a moment to realize why she looked familiar—she'd led the protestors at City Hall. A setup for SüprDüpr. Arranged by Katie and Satoshi.

I braced myself for Nose Ring to mock my lack of any piercings or ridicule not having a single tattoo. But she turned out to be pleasant. "It's great you've joined us," she said. "It's kind of crazy here. We need all the help we can get. Dr. Katie said you're going to fix our mapping problem."

I asked if anyone else was working on the math. It seemed strange that the company was hiring someone for a critical problem only ten days before the demo.

"We did," Nose Ring said. "But she quit."

That was totally sus. "When?"

"A few weeks ago. We've been trying to find a replacement since then."

I wanted to speak with her. "Do you know how I can reach her?"

"You'd have to ask Dr. Katie."

It took only a few minutes to setup my payroll, my insurance, and my Slack account. I asked about the pizza benefits, but she only pointed at the cabinet. "If you get hungry, there's plenty of Soylent. And twenty kinds of cereal. If you want anything else, tell me. But just so you know, the office is strictly vegan."

I asked where the liquor cart was hiding. I was looking forward to perusing the selection of fine Napa wines and craft beers that startups shared for team bonding.

"Yeah, no time for that. Too busy."

"Then I might as well work from home," I joked.

Instead of laughing, she said, "That's right." Except for her, she told me, everyone worked from home, coming into the MeWork only for meetings. "It'll be different when the new office is ready. I'll make sure we have a liquor cart for you."

Then she recited the company regulations, which mostly involved security—no tweets, no Reddit posts, no telling anyone I worked here. "I tell my parents I work at Uber. That's about as much as they can understand. Some people tell their families they work at a stealth startup named Higgs Transport. My girlfriend thinks I work at Victoria's Secret since I meet her at the mall after work. She finds that a turn-on, so hey, whatever floats your boat."

That wouldn't be a problem for me. "My parents are dead. And I don't have a girlfriend." I didn't mention I'd already told Sumire—she wasn't my girlfriend anyway.

When we finished the paperwork, she introduced me to the group arguing at the whiteboard. One wore a Pittsburgh Steelers t-shirt, another an Oxford button-down. There were two women, one in shorts, the other in ripped jeans. They said hi, shook my hand, and returned to whatever they were discussing.

"Is that the whole team? Other than Katie?"

"Oh no," Nose Ring said. "That's just the mechanical design group. "Everyone else is working remotely. We have people all over. India, Poland, a team in China. One guy in Costa Rica—that was kind of a mistake, we didn't realize he was in the other San Jose."

And that was the end of my orientation. "Well, it's great having you aboard. Do you have any other questions?"

I asked about a badge or security code to get into the suite.

"When you arrive at the front desk, have them message me. I'll buzz you in."

"What if I need to come in at night or over the weekend?"

"There's really nothing here except, you know, some cereal. It's just a meeting room. But if you need to get in for some reason, Dr. Katie can always unlock the door remotely."

So much for my plan to return with Sumire tonight when everyone else was gone. But it didn't matter. Nose Ring was right—there was nothing here but a bunch of tables and white boards. No photos, no desk toys, not even a filing cabinet. Ryu's computer wasn't here.

As the office manager, Nose Ring would have to know Ryu. But after the two lectures on the importance of security, I needed to find a way to ask without sounding suspicious. "This is kind of a crazy coincidence," I said, "but one of my friends mentioned he worked at Higgs Transport. He must be here. Any chance you know a guy named Ryu Yamashita?"

Her face lit up. "Oh, you mean Ray?"

The name Ryu, which meant dragon, was hard to pronounce for Americans—it usually came out as Ri-yu which meant something else. I'd never heard him called

Ray, but I hadn't hung out with him for years. "Japanese guy, kind of tall, scar here?" I said, pointing at my chin.

"That's Ray! Oh, wow, how amazing. It's great you two know each other already."

"Any chance you've seen him recently?"

"To tell the truth, I've only met him once, for orientation, like now. But he was so nice. I had this idea to set him up with a friend of mine. I thought they'd make a great couple. But he said he already had a girlfriend."

I wondered again if something was happening between Katie and Ryu, and where Grace Kim fit into that story. "Any chance he told you who?"

She shook her head, the nose ring jiggling. "But next time you see Ray, ask if he's interested in meeting my friend." She showed me a photo of an Asian woman with a stud on her cheek and black eye liner that made her look like a raccoon. "Don't you think they'd make the cutest couple?"

"Absolutely," I agreed. "Do you know how I can reach him?"

"Oh, just message him on Slack."

Of course. I opened the Slack app and found someone named Ray, one of forty-two members in the all-staff channel. He was offline, but at least he wasn't deleted. I shot him a message saying hi and asking to DM me right away. "What does Ryu do here?"

"Whatever Dr. Deauville wants him to do. Mostly physics stuff, I guess. I wouldn't know."

"Does he have a title?"

"Ha-ha, yeah. He's the CEO."

I almost fell off my chair. "Ryu? He's head of the company?"

"Ha-ha. No. Sorry. Dr. Katie's little joke. She calls him the Chief Elephant Officer. She put him in charge of finding a pair of elephants for the demo."

"Ryu? He's a physicist, not a zoologist."

"Yeah, we're a startup here—we all wear lots of hats. Whatever needs to get done."

"Why a pair of elephants?"

"Don't ask me. I'm not a physicist. Or a zoologist. You should ask Ray. Or Dr. Katie."

"Any idea where he went? Did Katie send him to Africa or Thailand hunting for elephants?"

"Oh, nothing like that. I think it was a zoo or something. You should ask Ray."

Chapter 13
The Elephant of My Eye

With Katie demanding an outline of the algo tonight, I had to start on her impossible mapping problem right away. But as I birded home over the slick streets, I thought instead of elephants, wondering if Ryu had found them. Though Nose Ring had said he was checking the zoos, I couldn't imagine any self-respecting zoo letting us borrow their elephants, not even if we promised to bring them back cleaner than when we took them.

San Jose's zoo, Happy Hollow, was little more than a petting zoo, its main attraction a red panda which wasn't even a panda but a big, brown raccoon. It had a few monkeys and a jaguar and lots of snakes and birds, but no elephants, not even a beanie baby with a trunk in the gift shop.

As I rode along Jackson Street back to Japantown, I thought about the last time I'd seen an elephant in the flesh nearly two decades ago. That was at the San Francisco Zoo—our family's annual pilgrimage up the peninsula into the big city. I remembered a day swinging between my parents' arms, Kaa-chan slapping me on the arm, admonishing me to quit aping the chimps. The smell of dung and hay mingled with Tou-san's aftershave when he lifted me onto his shoulders to toss peanuts into the elephant pen.

I skidded to a stop on the corner in front of my apartment and pulled out my phone to check if the zoo still had elephants. Its website listed red-rumped agoutis and Chacoan peccaries, guanacos and bongos, mandrils, meerkats, siamangs, sifakas and even a greater kudu, not to mention seven different species of lemur. But no elephants. Had the elephants died? Or been traded to Oakland for an outfield full of lemurs and a draft pick to be named later?

A quick search found an article from years ago about the last two elephants at the S.F. Zoo. They had escaped the cramped confines of San Francisco and its high cost of living to retire at a home for senior elephants in the Sierra foothills, a pachyderm sanctuary with grass and trees and lakes and a wide expanse for them to roam, even a hot tub to relax in after a hard day romping in the mud. It had everything an old elephant desired except a nine-hole golf course. I hurried home to ride the pony into the void beyond the Bay; I had a couple of retired elephants to interrogate.

Galloping up the East Bay, I roared past the Ferraris and Porsches before turning inland, through Unpleasanton and Liverworst and over the browning hills. Soon I was into a world of mud-spackled Ford pick-ups and sunburned Corollas patched together with duct tape. As I sped deep into the flatlands, past Stockton and Lodi, mile after boring mile of nothing but cows and scrub, the air dry, the sun unrelenting, I tried to figure out a solution to the impossible mapping problem but couldn't get my mind off the teleporter.

Katie's video showed a rat zapped ten feet across a room. Amazing, certainly, but only an experiment with rats under carefully controlled conditions. That was a long way from zapping customers around the globe. If it worked, really worked—if it was reliable and safe and affordable—there was no doubt it would rock the world. But even then, would big companies really do anything to stop us as Katie feared? Airline executives conspiring to hire a hit man to kill Ryu, or North Korean spies whisking him to their worker's paradise to torture him into building their own teleporter felt like a crazy manga—too absurd to be true.

Had the teleporter been tested on anything other than rats? I wasn't convinced that even a demonstration with hulking elephants would get customers to step inside. We'd need to prove it was absolutely safe and that required more than testing on rodents. With a public demo ten days away and the company's IPO within months, we had to be testing now. Someone had to be eating the dogfood. Would Katie step inside herself? Or would she get someone else to do it, someone expendable, someone like Ryu?

Ryu had always craved the limelight. He'd been the star of the baseball squad and claimed to be the leader of our three-man gaming team though I did all the work. Being the first man in a teleporter and transported straight to a profile in Wikipedia would appeal to him despite the danger. One small step through spacetime for Ryu, one giant leap for a unicorn. But what if something had gone horribly wrong—what if he'd been teleported straight into a tree? Katie made a point of saying the new teleporter at the Corinthian was more accurate than the prototype, which meant the prototype had accuracy problems. What if the coordinates were off and Ryu was teleported to the wrong place, or worse?

If Ryu had been killed during testing, what would Katie have done—gone to the police? Called his next of kin? An accident would have destroyed the company. There'd be no more funding, no billion-dollar IPO, nothing but a failed experiment and one more dead unicorn, a footnote in Crunchbase, and a tax write-off for investors. Katie wouldn't submit to failure so easily, I was certain, not if she could hide the body. And an accident while testing the prototype would explain why Katie was desperate to build an impossible map of every millimeter on earth at the last minute.

If she'd recorded a teleporting rat on her phone, she surely would have videoed the first human test, too. Even if something had gone wrong and she'd deleted the file to cover her tracks, if I could get my hands on Katie's phone, there were ways to recover the video. A big if. The cops could do it easily—a search warrant was all they'd need. I couldn't ask Jesus and Herringbone, so we'd need Mayeda to ask the detectives. Sumire would have to convince him to help. But the thought of him puffing himself up to her made me want to gag—it would be better to see what I could do myself first.

I was daydreaming of a dramatic Mission Impossible plan to steal Katie's phone when MapLady ordered me off the highway. After a few miles down a narrow, winding road, the blacktop turned to gravel. Dirt and rocks crunched under the tires and dust flew up around the car until I arrived at a parking lot, a chain drawn across the entrance. I pulled to a stop on a strip of tall weeds and walked across the deserted asphalt.

At the trailer that acted as the management office, the ticket window was shuttered. I hopped over the locked gate and climbed to the top of a ridge. From there, I could see for miles over a vast, tree-covered savannah. Down below, staring up at me with sad, black eyes as they munched on hay in the shimmering heat— elephants. Two of them. One raised his trunk and trumpeted a happy greeting. The other stomped a heavy foot and lumbered away to splash angrily in the pond. Something about them reminded me of my parents.

"We're closed," called a scratchy voice from behind me. A thin woman in a white lab coat waved from the door of the trailer. "You have to leave."

When I didn't come down, she tramped up to meet me, shouting at me to come down. At the top, she strode over and said, "If you don't leave right now, I'm calling the police."

I smiled as pleasantly as I could. "Who's in charge of corporate sponsorships?"

She eyed me suspiciously, but I fished out a leftover MeCan business card from my wallet. Her eyes grew wide when she spotted the familiar tangerine logo. Her scowl turned into a hint of a smile. She had curly black hair streaked with white and ice blue eyes behind oversized glasses. She introduced herself as Angelica. "Just to be clear, we do not rent out our animals, if that's why you're here."

I wondered why she felt the need to make that point, and whether Ryu or Katie had been asking. "Nothing like that," I said to put her at ease. "We just want to do good for all creatures." I almost gagged at my own bullshit.

"Then come, let's take a look," she said, leading me down the hill to the elephants. "I want you to see what these animals mean to us all and what your donation to our foundation can accomplish."

At the base of the hill, she reached an arm between the steel cables of the fence to pet the wrinkled gray skin of the elephant's trunk. He seemed to be smiling at us, droopy eyes as large as Angelica's hand. He had a soft, gentle bearing and a quiet equanimity just like Tou-san. He poked his trunk through the fence to touch Angelica's shoulder.

"They're like family here," she said. "That one over there is Apple." She pointed at the angry elephant spitting water at us from the pond, the spitting image of Kaa-chan. "She's a little skittish. She's had a tough life. But this guy here is real friendly." She caressed his trunk. "Say hello to Google."

Apple and Google. The mention of Apple kind of made me sick. And Saint Steven would have been aghast that his namesake was mated to the one competitor he loathed. But it was fitting that the two elephants were named after a pair of companies once magical unicorns now grown into lumbering giants.

Google flapped his floppy ears and reached out to feel my face with the pink tip of his trunk. It was mucousy and weird, yet somehow felt like the caress of an affectionate father. I ran my hand over his wrinkled hide, dusty and rough, covered with thick hairs, and felt the warmth coursing underneath. "Why's he named Google?" I asked. "Isn't he older than the company?"

Angelica laughed. "Oh, that's not their original names. They leave those names behind when they come here. We rechristen them in honor of the companies that sponsor their freedom. Perhaps MeCan would be interested in a tax-deductible donation? We recently rescued a magnificent lion. He's still available for sponsorship."

"Elephants," I said.

"Take a look over there." She pointed at a speck beyond the next ridge that might have been anything, even a red-rumped agouti, for all I could see from here. "Isn't he the most magnificent lion ever? For $2 million to defray the cost of his upkeep, you can name him 'MeCan the Lion.'"

For $2 million, I'd rename myself—Dassai Hara had a nice ring. It beat the weird stares I got as Hara Tatsu from everyone who spoke Japanese and understood what Kaa-chan had named me. Or I could keep walking as Johnnie Walker Hara—the perfect way to honor my father and piss off the spirit of my mother. For an extra million, I'd even tattoo a square bottle on my butt, even if that meant Sumire would never speak to me again.

"Talk to Disney," I said. "We're interested in elephants. Anybody recently asked to borrow them for a parade?"

She turned to me, the scowl returned double-fold. "Just what I thought. Nothing but another entitled jerk. Let me tell you, there's someone asking about them every day. A rich kid's birthday. Fourth of July parade. Magic show in Las Vegas. A scientific demonstration. All you can think about is how wonderful it would be for you and your friends to play with the elephants. You never consider what it's like for them. Well, you can forget it. I'll tell you the same thing I tell everyone—we appreciate your donations, but the elephants don't leave. Ever."

My ears perked up. "What scientific demonstration?"

She glared at me. "Some jerk from Intel said they needed a pair of elephants to use in a demonstration."

"Japanese guy? Tall, thirtyish, scar on his chin?"

She nodded. Bingo. Ryu—he'd been here. "When?" I asked.

She narrowed her eyes and backed away. "Last week. Saturday. Same as you, barging in while the preserve was closed."

Ryu was here a week ago. On Saturday, before meeting Satoshi that evening. The day before he disappeared. He'd found the elephants Katie wanted for her demo. "What did you tell him?"

"Same thing I'm telling you—no way, no how. But at least he was a good fellow. He called the next morning to apologize and promised to protect the elephants."

The same morning he drove away, never to return. That was too much of a coincidence. "Did he say anything else?"

"He said be careful if a red-headed woman tried to take the elephants away. But it doesn't matter who asks, these elephants are never leaving."

Ryu was afraid something would happen if Katie used these elephants in the demo. The elephants were still here, but something had happened to Ryu.

Chapter 14
Saratoga Zen Zen

The biggest problem with the pony—besides the atrocious gas mileage, lack of air conditioning, sticky vinyl seats, and frequent repairs—was the radio, an original eight-track without Bluetooth, useless for anything other than checking traffic. To dial Sumire as I drove back over the dry, brown hills, I had to fiddle with the phone wedged into the ashtray. She took forever to answer.

"Busy?" I asked.

"Yeah, super busy."

My stomach churned as I imagined her out with friends or preparing for date night. It was none of my business, but I couldn't resist asking if she was going out somewhere.

"Huh? Are you kidding? I have so much work to catch up on. With everything going on, I've gotten behind, which, believe me, is not a good thing for a first-year associate at a big law firm."

I felt like a jerk. Again. "Want me to bring over some dinner?"

"Thanks, but I'll get takeout later."

I offered to pick up Gianni's, singing their nonsensical jingle we used to laugh over together, "It ain't pizza if it ain't got ramen on top..."

"Ugh. Don't you know that crap will kill you?"

I reminded her we used to eat there regularly and both of us were still alive.

"Yeah, well, we were stupid then. At least one of us is wiser now."

There was nothing I could say to that. After a painful silence, I asked, "Did Ryu ever mention anything about looking for elephants?"

"Not that I remember. Why?"

It was impossible to tell her anything without breaking the vows of my NDA on my very first day. "Sorry, can't tell you."

"Ted..."

"I found out he had a job, I can't say where. He was Chief Elephant Officer."

Sumire laughed. "That's a new one. What does a Chief Elephant Officer do?"

"I can't tell you that either."

"Come on, Teddybear. What was Ryu doing?"

"I don't actually know."

"Hypothetically, let's say there's a job posting for a Chief Elephant Officer. What would the responsibilities be?"

That was an interesting way to frame it. I told her a Chief Elephant Officer might have to find elephants for a company demonstration. That didn't seem confidential.

"Demonstration of what?"

That I couldn't say. Instead of answering, I hummed the Gianni's jingle again, hoping she'd take the hint.

"Come on, Ted. It's me."

I told her I'd started work this morning at a company I wasn't allowed to name and after signing an NDA, endured a lecture on secrecy from an office manager with a nose ring as well as one from the company president. I should have expected Sumire wouldn't be deterred by that.

"Don't forget—I'm your lawyer. We can discuss anything under attorney-client privilege. What did you find out about Ryu?"

I decided it was okay to tell her what little I'd learned about Ryu so long as I didn't mention teleportation. "There's a chance there could have been an accident that Katie's covering up," I whispered into the phone. "Or maybe not. I don't know." I told her about Ryu visiting the elephant preserve right before meeting Satoshi, then vowing to save the elephants the next morning before disappearing. When she pushed for more details I wasn't ready to discuss, I asked her if the police had questioned Satoshi yet.

She made a gagging sound. "Mike said forget it—the detectives aren't interested in interrogating a billionaire about a missing person, especially one outside their jurisdiction."

If there had been an accident with the teleporter, Katie might have told Satoshi. There was a chance he'd even witnessed it himself, just as he'd seen the teleporting rat. But I couldn't tell the cops without losing my job on my very first day. Someone needed to question Satoshi, and that left only me.

I hung up without telling Sumire what I planned; she'd demand to come along and I needed to talk to him alone, *mano a mano*. I had to find a way to get him to confide in me. As a family friend. As a confidant. As a drinking buddy. But first I had to convince him to meet me at all. I pulled over to the side of the road, the engine burbling, and shot him a quick email, thanking him for helping me get the job at SüprDüpr and asking for his advice. As my *senpai*, a kind of mentor, he'd have no choice but to see me. I was surprised, though, when a reply popped into my inbox before I reached the next traffic light.

"*Come to tea house*" was all it said, but that was enough for me. Although there were tea houses in parks and gardens dotted across the Valley, I knew he meant the *chashitsu* at Hakone Estate, the Japanese garden adjacent to his palace in the woods, the place where my mother once taught classes every Sunday afternoon, Satoshi along as her assistant. I alerted MapLady that I was headed to the little city of Saratoga and gunned the engine, tires squealing as I sped on my way.

Galloping up the highway, I wondered again why Satoshi had come to Ryu's apartment—were they friends? Business partners? Lovers? I had no idea. Had Satoshi videoed a tragic accident or helped Ryu disappear? Was it possible they were rivals for Katie's affection and Satoshi had him killed? Although he'd come to our house for years, I didn't really know him—he was my mother's friend, not mine. Other than the City Council meeting, I hadn't seen him since Kaa-chan's funeral.

Every week growing up, Satoshi had arrived at our house for tea ceremony class carrying a tray of sweets. Not chocolate or ice cream for me, but the *manju* or *higashi* that accompanied the tea. That reminded me it was a serious breach of Japanese etiquette to arrive empty-handed; even from the other world, Kaa-chan would have a fit. I thought about picking up a box of Ghirardelli's, but that didn't seem appropriate. Then I noticed the sign for the Mitsuwa along the side of the highway and swerved across four lanes of traffic to reach the exit. Inside, I made a beeline for the refrigerator case in the back. The biggest Japanese supermarket in the Valley, it had the best selection of sake, rows of bowling pin-sized bottles of crap on the bottom shelf, hundred-dollar *daiginjo,* as smooth as silk, on top. When I saw the matte black bottle adorned with elegant calligraphy and a cap spangled with a gold tassel, I remembered the rich taste, juicy with hints of honeydew and a yeasty smell like freshly baked bread. My mouth watered just looking at the bottle of Mizubasho. I stood on tiptoes to grab the last one.

Driving through suburban San Jose, I headed towards the western hills, passing mile after mile of single-story homes, gas stations, and fast-food stands as the low-slung mountains drew closer. After crossing the 85, the road narrowed, traffic lights disappeared, and the houses spread farther apart. From the base of the furred mountains, the road snaked into the wooded canyons where oaks and eucalyptus hugged the road and civilization sputtered to an end.

At a tight bend, I found the familiar sign carved into a granite pillar marking the hidden turnoff. I followed the steep, winding path into the forest until it dead-ended at a parking lot in front of an old Japanese house. I was back.

Although I hadn't been here for many years, nothing had changed, not even the old lady who sold tickets behind the window of the wooden hut that doubled as a gift shop. Kaa-chan had always greeted the ticket seller warmly, hiding her scorn for anyone who sat all day. I tried to recall her name—Kyoko or Chieko or Kumiko or something like that, but Kaa-chan referred to her only as Ticket-san.

"*Hisashiburi*," I greeted Ticket-san.

She lifted her half-moon glasses from her nose to squint through the window at me. Her face lit up. "Tatsu? Is that really you? How's your mother? We haven't seen her for ages."

"Better," I answered, not wanting to rehash how she'd quit in a huff when they'd allowed another teacher to hold classes in *her* tea house during the week, and never set foot again in this garden. Or that she was dead now. Although it was clear that Ticket-san wanted to reminisce, I cut the conversation short. "I'm here to see Satoshi."

"Good luck," she chuckled, then thrust a bony hand through the opening for my $10 admission, not even giving me the local resident discount. "We close in an hour," she called after me as I pushed through the ancient green turnstile.

Sunlight filtered through the leaves of the oak and fell on the humped vermillion bridge over the pond, igniting long forgotten memories from days standing on these banks alone. While Kaa-chan taught tea ceremony in the pavilion at the other end of the park, Satoshi by her side, I killed the afternoons feeding the koi, peeved to be stuck in this boring place instead of watching the Giants game on TV with Tou-san. Once Satoshi's cryptocurrency had exploded into a huge new industry helping drug dealers and cyber criminals keep their transactions secret, he decided to buy this park, offering the City of Saratoga a billion dollars to take the money-losing white elephant off their hands. I'd heard the news from across the continent where I was sure it was a gift for Kaa-chan, giving her not only the best tea house in all of California, but the one thing she'd appreciate most—revenge for the humiliation she insisted she'd suffered here. I imagined coming back from college to visit her in her private estate, the three of us, Kaa-chan, Satoshi, and I standing at the edge of this pond, watching the koi together.

But the nationwide outcry against selling off the picturesque garden to a tech billionaire, even a garden few people had ever heard of and nobody ever visited, had forced the city to reconsider. Instead, it took his billion dollars and deeded him the entire mountainside adjacent to the park. From the privacy of the palace he built on the hill above, he could gaze down on the tea garden, the wisteria arbor, the fireworks of cherry blossoms. I turned my head and squinted into the sun to try to spot him on his balcony but could see nothing but trees all around. I scanned the ridge, covered with spruce and sequoias, their canopies scraping the leaden bottoms of the clouds pushing inland from the sea, and realized how simple it would be to bury a body there in his own private forest under a bed of dead leaves and nettles. I shivered at the thought that Ryu might be there somewhere, his body disintegrating in the muck, and worried that if I wasn't careful, I might join him. I was glad we were meeting in the public space of the park and set out along the concrete path to find Satoshi.

When I reached the tea house, the *shoji* doors were shut. I tried to slide the door open on its wooden track, but it was locked from inside. I sent Satoshi a quick selfie in front of the door to tell him I'd arrived, then sat on the wooden bench to wait, staring at the Zen rock garden, granite boulders floating like islands in a sea of raked gravel. The trees swayed in the strengthening wind as the sun dipped behind the mountains, yellow and brown leaves swirling to the ground as the air took on a chill. I wrapped my bare arms around myself to keep warm until the scratchy speakers hanging from the roof blared that the gates were closing. A guard sauntered over to tell me to leave.

I checked my phone once more. There was nothing from Satoshi. I read his message again to see if I had the wrong time or date. All it said was "come to tea house." I told the guard I was waiting for Satoshi and asked if he knew where I was supposed to meet him.

"Ha," he snorted. "You and everyone else. Like the second coming of Jesus. Sorry to disappoint you, boss, but he's not coming."

When I pointed to the message from Satoshi, he jerked me to my feet. "No drinking in here," he yelled, grabbing the brown paper bag of Mizubasho out of my hand and shoving me toward the gate.

I was about to give up when I heard the shush of polished wood sliding on a wooden track. I turned to see Satoshi kneeling on the tatami inside the tea house and wondered how he came in without me seeing him. He was dressed in a black kimono, his bald head gleaming. "Tat-chan," he called to me.

The guard tightened his grip my arm. "Don't worry, Mr. Nakamoto, I'll get rid of him."

"That's okay, Javier," Satoshi said, the thick Japanese accent unchanged. "He's come for *ocha*. Would you mind waiting outside until we're done?"

The guard saluted and stood at attention. I stepped up to the teahouse. Inside the eight-tatami room behind Satoshi, charcoal was burning in the firepit cut into the floor.

Other than a few lines around his eyes and his head shaven completely bald, Satoshi still looked like the gawky postdoc of computer science who came to our house every week for years. But something in his posture, or his intense, confident focus, or just maybe an aura that surrounded him, left no doubt that I was in the presence of one of the new masters of the universe.

"Welcome," he said as if he owned the teahouse, owned the park, owned the entire city, beckoning me into the room. "Let us share a bowl together," he recited in Japanese, the opening of every tea ceremony, the tea equivalent of *Play ball!*

Although he'd invited me to the tea house, I hadn't expected an actual tea ceremony; I wasn't dressed for it and hadn't memorized the script, a different one for every season—more akin to a religious ceremony than sipping tea with friends. Embarrassed, I kneeled in my jeans on the tatami floor and offered my ritualistic thanks. Handing him the bottle, I realized my mistake—presentation was far more important than the contents; it would have been better to bring crappy sake in a beautiful box than the Mizubasho in a crinkled paper sack.

Satoshi peeked inside the bag and frowned. "I am saddened you have taken your father's bad habits instead of your mother's tea."

My chest burned with anger. When I started to protest, he cut me off and summoned the guard from outside. I thought he was kicking me out, but instead Satoshi handed him the bottle. "Very good sake," he said. "You will enjoy."

The guard glanced at me, confused, then thanked both of us profusely. Satoshi waved him away. "You are not dressed," he said, making me feel ashamed for entering a tea house in a Giants t-shirt and jeans. At least I was wearing socks. He pulled a phone out of the baggy sleeve of his kimono. "Chikako-san, can you bring a *hakama* for our guest?"

A few minutes later, Ticket-san arrived out of breath, a stack of folded fabrics reaching nearly to her head. "Is this okay, Mr. Nakamoto?"

While he set the cast iron pot over the fire and purified the utensils, Chikako stripped me down to my undies to dress me in proper tea attire. The clothing was complicated—black kimono underneath, wide *obi* belt wound tight around my waist, stiff purple skirt on top attached with a set of straps. The starched silk felt like layer upon layer of tradition wrapped so tight I could barely breathe. Chikako beamed at me. "Ah, such a handsome boy," she said, admiring her handiwork. The purple skirt scraped the tatami floor as I bowed my thanks to her.

"Shall we begin?" Satoshi said, continuing the tea ceremony script.

After admiring the toad lily flower in a wicker vase in the alcove below a hanging scroll of calligraphy, I returned to the center of the room and sat on the cushion with folded knees. Satoshi purified the tea bowl with choreographed hand movements, then warmed it with steaming water. He measured six scoops of matcha powder into the bowl, ladled in hot water, and whisked it to a thick froth of *koicha*.

Setting the bowl on the tatami at my knees, he sat on a cushion to face me. After the candy in the shape of a flower dissolved on my tongue, I apologized for drinking first. I picked up the bowl, placing it in the palm of my left hand, and gripped it with my right. Glazed a pinkish hue, it felt surprisingly heavy. It looked handmade, unlike the bowls that filled Kaa-chan's cabinet imported from all over Japan, except for the one made by Satoshi. I assumed he made this one himself, too.

I rotated the bowl 180 degrees to avoid drinking from its face, then took a deep sip, the tea warm and bitter, tasting of Kaa-chan and home and everything I did and didn't want to remember. After drinking half, I placed it back on the tatami. Satoshi drank the remainder with a final slurp of the last drops and set the bowl down on the floor between us.

Bending over to examine the bowl, I admired the handicraft of the molded clay, the thick glaze, the intricate design. When I asked who made it as the script required, Satoshi's expressionless face turned to an inscrutable grin. "This one is special," he said. "Can you guess?"

Could this be a priceless historical treasure made in the 16th century by the great tea master, Sen-no-Rikyu, himself? Certainly, Satoshi could afford such baubles.

He laughed. "You must examine more closely."

When I lifted the bowl up to look at the unglazed bottom, I gasped and dropped it on the tatami. The perfect brushwork of two kanji flowing one into the next would have been impossible to decipher if I didn't recognize them immediately—flower and picture—Hanae. My mother's name. After righting the tea bowl and wiping up the green drops staining the tatami, I looked up at Satoshi. "She made pottery?"

"Only once," Satoshi said, his gaze elsewhere. "She was a craftsman—very careful, very precise. But no interest, unfortunately. She said too messy."

That sounded like Kaa-chan; everything was too messy for her. He smiled sadly and I pictured them together at the potter's wheel, entwined in a sweaty embrace. Whatever happened between them after I'd escaped to the snowy land at the end of the highway, leaving Kaa-chan in San Jose, I didn't know except she'd leapt into the void alone. I wanted to believe it had something to do with Satoshi because otherwise it was all on me. I'd never know, though, because she failed to leave anything behind on the mountaintop other than her shoes and a rose-colored Apple iPod playing the Beatles' *Norwegian Wood* in an infinite loop.

"I am sorry I upset you, Tat-chan. Your mother is gone." Satoshi took the bowl in his hands. "This is only a piece of clay to remember her. I want to give this to you. She was a great woman, your mother. She was my teacher, my *sensei*. She taught me how to understand this world. We shared a bowl of tea together every week, drank from the same cup like the two of us today. We listened to each other's *kokoro*—our hearts, our spirits, our minds. There is a part of her that lives in me now, still speaks within me, and I know she still lives within you."

I didn't want to hear any more. She was my mother. My neurotic, depressed mother. I struggled to my feet, my legs unsteady after kneeling too long.

"Sit," he ordered, his voice no louder than a whisper, but a command nevertheless. I rubbed my legs to draw the circulation as I sat on the cushion again.

Something cold in Satoshi's expression sent goosebumps down my spine. "Did she ever tell you the story of *Ubasute-yama*?"

"Many times," I answered, wondering why he was bringing up this old Japanese fable.

The slightest hint of a grin peeked through the mask of his face. "Yes, I expected so."

Long ago, when Japan was a poor farming country, the specter of famine always haunted the population. If the rice harvest failed, villagers were left bartering away their life savings to buy a handful of potatoes to make a thin gruel. There was hardly enough food for the three generations living under the same roof. The old women, too frail to work, begged their sons to carry them into the mountains so the rest of the family could survive. Kaa-chan insisted the old fable showed everything that made Japanese society strong—a willingness to sacrifice our own needs for the greater good, where Americans thought only about themselves.

"That is why I am sure you are perfect for SüprDüpr," he said, a cold smile radiating towards me.

I didn't understand what this old story about sacrifice and death had to do with my suitability for a tech startup. But it was something I'd have to contemplate later. As this abbreviated *koicha* tea ceremony was drawing to a close, I needed to find out about Ryu.

"Do you mind if I ask something?"

"Of course, Tat-chan. What's on your mind?"

"Do you know Ryu Yamashita?"

I waited for him to deny ever hearing Ryu's name so I could watch his reaction when I informed him that the cops were examining the security tapes of Ryu's apartment. But he stood, expressionless, and stepped to the back of the room where he poured himself a cup of cold barley tea out of a thermos. "You are aware, Tat-chan, that I am SüprDüpr's chairman, yes?"

It was my own expression that registered surprise. "I thought it was Dr. Deauville's company."

"Oh, it is. Katie-chan is the CEO. The company is her vision. But she is a scientist. No business experience. So Sam Hill Ventures insisted I be company chairman before they agreed to invest. Fortunately, it doesn't take so much time. I give some advice and help make sure the business runs smoothly."

"And does it?"

Satoshi slurped at his tea. "SüprDüpr is a startup. There are always struggles."

"Is that what Ryu wanted to talk about?"

"In a way."

"In what way?" I pressed.

His cold fish eyes focused on mine, a carefully drawn blank stare. "The teleportation system has some technical complications that Katie-chan expected to solve by now."

Were those "technical complications" the mapping problem I'd been hired to fix? Or something worse—like an accident where someone working on the teleporter was injured or killed? "What complications?" I asked.

He waved off the question. "It is no matter. With my guidance, and some inspiration from your mother, Tat-chan, Katie could find some good solution."

I tried again. "Is the teleporter dangerous?"

"No, no, nothing like that. It is perfectly safe."

"Then why was Ryu so concerned he had to meet you?"

"Aah, Ryu-kun," he said, staring into the distance. "A very difficult boy. Very…how to say, *insistent*. He insisted the company must postpone our demonstration until everything is perfect. I had to explain that would mean the end of SüprDüpr. We must have the teleporter working now, even if there are some compromises. We can improve it later. That is the way of a startup, no?"

"And was Ryu satisfied?"

"No. Unfortunately, engineers are never satisfied. They don't understand business."

"Maybe I don't either."

"It's quite simple, Tat-chan. When Katie showed me her plan for a teleporter, of course, I didn't believe it. At that time, it was only theory. Some equations. But I checked the physics and couldn't find any error. So I thought maybe there's a small chance it could actually work. I offered to invest a few million dollars to try some experiments. I was surprised when Katie said no. She said she needed to hire a team, apply for patents, build a prototype, and so on. She said the only choice was all in or nothing. She can be very persuasive, you know. So I convinced Sam Hill and some other investors to put in $250 million to build the first teleporter. Quite a gamble, eh, for such a crazy idea? But we spend a trillion dollars every year on airplane travel alone. So the opportunity is big. Very big. If it works, our investment will go up in value at least a thousand times. Katie will be the richest person in the world. Even your share options, Tat-chan, will be worth hundreds of millions. What will you do with all that money?"

One thing I wouldn't do is buy a tea house just because Kaa-chan used to teach here. I'd tear down all the ugly apartments that had sprouted around Japantown and replant the prune orchards that belonged on the land.

"But it is still a crazy idea, no? With a big chance of failure. So we invested enough to build one teleporter to prove if it works or not. No blank check to waste money forever. We won't be another SoftBank. Katie must prove it works and go public to finance the rest. If the company doesn't start the IPO process right away, it will run out of money. The clock is always ticking. Ryu-kun couldn't understand that. He insisted to Katie-chan that the demo must wait until the technology is perfect. She said no, of course, so he demanded to talk to me. Quite an annoyance, as you can imagine. I had to explain that as long as the teleporter works and customers are safe, that is good enough."

I asked why, if the company had only enough money to build the first teleporter, it was spending so much building a homeless shelter now.

"You must think of the lesson of *Ubasute-yama*, Tat-chan. Ryu could never understand, but I am sure you can."

"Ryu is missing," I pressed. "You were the last person to talk to him. Do you have any idea where he went?"

Satoshi cocked his head. "What do you mean?"

"You met him last Saturday night. Sunday morning, he left his apartment and never returned. Nobody knows where he is."

He picked up his cup and slurped noisily. "That is most unfortunate. I am sure he will return soon. There is much work to be done. He is a very responsible boy."

"Was there an accident with the teleporter?"

"No, Tat-chan. Not that I am aware. Is that all?"

I started to ask another question, but Satoshi set down his cup. "Thank you for joining me in a harmonious bowl of tea," he recited, signifying the end of the tea ceremony. "I know you will do your utmost, Tat-chan, to make the company a big success." He snapped his fingers. "Javier," he called to the guard outside. "Please escort Mr. Hara to the exit."

I wasn't finished with my questions. "What compromises were made with the teleporter?" But Satoshi was finished with me. Like an emperor, he motioned for the guard to take me away. At least Satoshi didn't order him to chop off my head.

Javier grabbed my arm with one hand, clutching the bottle of Mizubasho in the other. "Grab your clothes, boss, it's time to go."

Satoshi handed me the tea bowl Kaa-chan had made, then stood bowing as the guard marched me away still dressed in the *hakama*. He called from the doorway, "Don't forget the story of *Ubasute-yama*, Tat-chan. It was your mother's favorite."

As we neared the exit, I told the guard I had to change my clothes. When he let go of my arm, I dashed back to the tea house as fast as I could, leaving him behind. Peeking through the window, I saw a tatami mat in the middle of the floor turned on its side, revealing a hole below. Just like in the old samurai castles, Satoshi had built a secret underground passage from the tea house to his palace. As the guard pulled me away by the collar, I saw a hand reach up from inside the hidden stairwell to drop the tatami back into place.

I was sure Satoshi was hiding something, but I was no closer to finding out what. My trip had been a failure. And I had no doubt he'd tell Katie everything we'd discussed. The entire ride home I waited for the phone to buzz with the news of my firing. But all that popped up on the screen was a warning to avoid a big backup on the 880.

Arriving back in Japantown, I stopped at the Nijiya to pick up dinner. From the snowcapped peaks of the refrigerator case, a bottle of Hakkaisan called my name, comforting me for the Mizubasho that would likely be sacrificed in sake bombs.

While nibbling at the unagi bowl, discouraged and confused over Satoshi and his fairy tales, I gulped cup after cup of Hakkaisan until the world started spinning. I fell onto the couch where I rejoined the elephants, Apple, Google, this time with grandmother Baa-zo, around a campfire.

Chapter 15
The Mountain of Old Elephants

THIS IS NOT ENOUGH FOOD FOR ALL OF US.

THE THREE OF YOU MUST EAT. I WILL LEAVE TOMORROW TO FIND MORE FOOD.

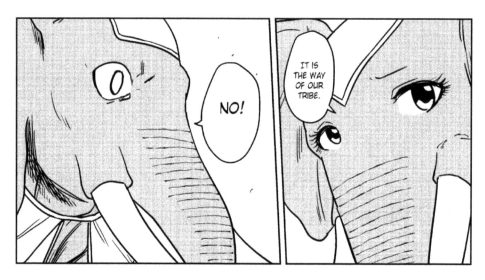

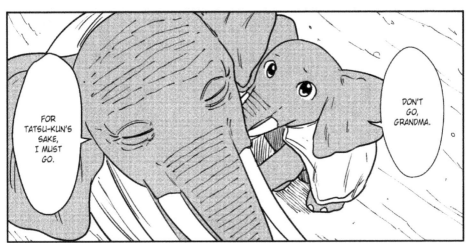

LET ME REST MY BONES HERE, SON. GANESH WILL WATCH OVER ME.

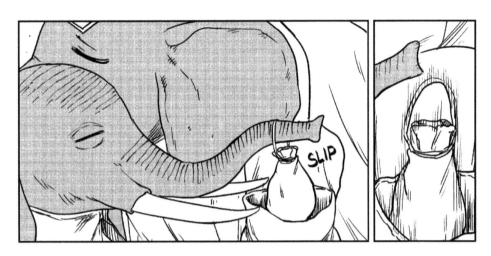

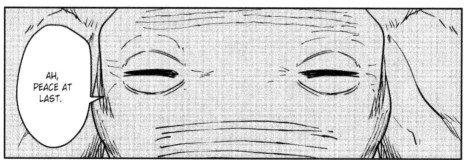

Chapter 16
Trendy Cats Salad Surprise

Sunday morning broke with a chill, a stiff breeze carrying the scent of pine through the open windows, rattling the blinds. Stray clouds swished overhead on the blue dome of the sky, the first whispers of the approaching autumn in the rustling of the maple trees. I yawned and tried to clear away the weird dream of elephants in *Ubasute-yama.*

On the phone was a text from Katie, the one I'd been dreading. I was sure I'd have to start looking for a job and another way to find Ryu. But instead of firing me, all it said was, *"Send outline of algo now."* No hint Satoshi had said anything about my visit. If I wanted to keep access to Ryu's colleagues, my health insurance, and stock options worth hundreds of millions if the teleporter worked, it was time to get serious about figuring out a mapping algorithm. I flopped onto the couch to contemplate how to map the entire world to the millimeter. But I couldn't stop thinking of Ryu at his desk pondering the same problem, Ryu in the park talking with Azaz, Ryu at the elephant preserve petting Google's trunk. I thought about his missing computer that might hold clues to his disappearance and wondered again what Satoshi wasn't saying.

Trawling through the company's Slack, I saw Ryu hadn't posted anything for weeks. Working at SüprDüpr was turning out to be less useful than I'd expected. With all the security rules, questioning my new coworkers would get nowhere unless Katie told them to help. Which meant there was no choice but to start at the top. I tried dialing Katie to see if she'd meet me at the MeWork today, but my call went straight to voicemail. When I tried DM'ing her, the reply came hours later: *"Send algo plan. NOW!"*

A fresh attempt to create an algorithm for the mapping problem hit the same wall as before. To clear my head, I walked down to the new coffee shop on the edge of Japantown. Inside, the bearded hipsters and tattooed hipsterinas jabbering about their startup business plans made the place as noisy as any sports bar. And the coffee was worse than Starbucks, something I didn't think possible.

I dumped my cup in one of the seven different recycling bins and headed home, stopping at Shuei-Do to pick out an assortment of *mochi* in case Sumire dropped by that evening, then crossed the street to the Nijiya for a fresh bottle of Mu in case she didn't.

Back at the apartment, after accomplishing nothing for a couple more hours, I debated cracking open the Mu early for inspiration. I drew the blinds to darken the room and pretend it was already evening. The room was dark but it wasn't the same—the world felt different, the air too light. I wasn't an alcoholic—I didn't drink during the day. I returned the bottle to the fridge unopened.

Staring at the blank wall again, I wondered why I was spending my weekend trying to solve an impossible problem. Was it the riches Katie promised as soon as our stock went public? Not really, though it would be nice to pay off my student loans. And buy a house. And plant a prune orchard where my apartment building stood. Was it Katie—had she mesmerized me with her confidence and her beauty? No, she wasn't my type, and I certainly wasn't hers. But the math problem—that was interesting. A real challenge. One the company was counting on me to solve. Me. Nobody had ever counted on me for anything. Not even my parents. But then I thought of Sumire—she was counting on me to help her find her brother. And that was the only thing that mattered. That's what I needed to be working on. Instead of spending all day solving Katie's problem, it was time to confront her with ours.

I texted: "*need 2 meet today*"

A few minutes later, my phone buzzed back: "*Busy. Make appt.*"

If Katie wouldn't come to me, I'd have to go to her. But first I had to find her.

When I searched again for Dr. Katherine Deauville's address, the same stupid ads popped up. "Find any address instantly – money back guaranteed!" This time, I picked the one that looked the least sus and used a prepaid card just in case. Still, I was surprised when it spat out an address in Palo Alto. That seemed totally Katie. I was ready to zip up the King's Highway to the enchanted land of organic rBST-free milk and orange blossom honey until I checked the map and saw the blue pin spearing the physics building on the Stanford campus. My request for my money back from the address scammers bounced.

Wherever she was living, it wasn't under her own name. It was hard to imagine Katie living with doddery parents in a small house out in the flatlands, but could she be shacked up with Satoshi at his estate? The only way to find out was to trail her home from the office. Or hack into Bergdorf Goodman to look up her shipping address. There had to be an easier way, one that wouldn't land me in the confession room with Jesus and Herringbone again. I phoned Sumire, hoping she'd have a better idea.

"I need to question Katie," I said. "I want to ambush her at home."

"Good. I'm coming with you."

I was sure Katie wouldn't tell me anything with an outsider present, especially not a lawyer. "Sorry, Bunny-chan. Got to do this alone."

"No way. It's not safe. What if she's involved with whatever happened to Ryu?"

"It's fine," I assured her. I wasn't afraid of Katie doing something crazy. I asked Sumire if she had access to any legal databases that would have Katie's address.

Sumire laughed at me. "Not much of a hacker, are you?"

That felt like a jab to the chest. I explained how secretive Katie was, but Sumire wasn't impressed. I listened to the clacking of her keyboard over the line. "Hmmm," she said, then yet more clacking. As much as I wanted to know where Katie lived, at least Sumire couldn't find her either. "Do you want me to call Mikey?" she asked. "Maybe he can check her driver's license."

When did Mayeda become Mikey? No, I didn't want her calling *Mikey*. I said I'd call him myself. When she read me his phone number, I wondered why she had it. And if she'd ever used it. I hung up and dialed Mayeda.

"Whaddaya want, shrimp?"

I had to remind myself I was doing this for Sumire or I would have hung up right then. I told him I needed Katie's address.

"Look up an address for a civ? Uh-uh. I'd get in trouble for sure."

When I told him it was for Sumire, he suddenly became more accommodating. He took down the name and promised to get back to me within three days. I should have known he'd be useless. It was time to get serious myself.

I could hack into MeCan's servers the same way as before and damn Jesus' warning; I'd just have to be more careful this time. If I could get into her account, I'd see not only her GPS coordinates, but all her email, text, and phone calls. It had been less than forty-eight hours since I'd been fired for not fixing the bug and there was no way Twitter-Dee or Twitter-Dumb were working on it over the weekend. But when I tried to get in, my VPN connection from Stara Zagora hit a solid brick firewall. I was locked out. The bug had been patched in record time. I wondered if the FBI helped out.

Time for plan B. I cracked my knuckles and opened an email from Katie to check the SMTP headers. A `whois` lookup on the IP address confirmed she'd sent it from home. A `traceroute` over the VPN sent packets hopping across the backbone: Stara Zagora, Paris, London, Boston, Chicago, and San Jose, finally terminating in Los Gatos. That fit. She had to be there, in the City of Cats, in the hills south of San Jose.

Los Gatos had always been a trendy place, even before Netflix moved half of Hollywood there. It was more exclusive than the techie hotspots of Cupertino and Mountain View, more fashionable than staid enclaves of Atherton and Los Altos

Hills. The SAT scores of the local schools were off the charts, at least until the Hollywood crowd arrived. It was a Katie Kat kind of place.

Unfortunately, it was impossible to trace her IP address any closer than the local cable office. She could be anywhere within a five-mile radius of that windowless building near the center of town. Finding her there would be hopeless. But I had to try. I put the computer to sleep and headed out to visit the trendy cats.

As I drove towards the hills, the remaining vestiges of fiery red on the underbelly of the thickening clouds faded to a bruised purple. By the time I reached the town, it was already dark. Sodium streetlights cast an orange glow over the crowds in the quaint downtown.

Where would Katie be? Living in one of the boxy apartments above the hipster coffee shops that dotted every corner? Or in a gigantic mansion that overlooked the town from a precipice on the rocky hillside? Neither seemed quite Katie.

I parked the car and walked the streets, past a million yoga studios, jewelry stores, and art galleries, an old theatre remodeled retro hip. The Apple and MeCan stores, glowing in white and tangerine, glowered at each other across a narrow street. I couldn't imagine Katie inside any of them. Out of the corner of my eye, I spotted a flouncy yellow sundress and thought that was Katie standing inside a shop. But when I walked towards her, I was disappointed to discover it was only a mannequin in a boutique window. She must have bought the dress here.

The bell jangled as I pushed through the door. A pair of high school girls glanced up from the counter without even pausing their conversation. I cleared my throat to get their attention. "Does Katie Deauville shop here?"

They looked at each other. "Who?"

"The CEO of SüprDüpr."

"What's that?"

I flashed the photo of Katie from the press conference. "She ever been here?"

"Wouldn't know," one said and turned back to her friend.

This was hopeless, I realized, and headed for the door. As I walked back to my car, passing one gourmet pizza parlor and sustainable coffee roaster after another, I had to squeeze through a boisterous crowd blocking the sidewalk. Bright lights spilled out through plate glass windows. It was so crowded, I thought the place had to be a nightclub, but the sign above the door said Heavenly Salads. This was it. Katie didn't walk the aisles of Safeway pushing a shopping cart, and she didn't sit alone on the hard chairs at Poky Poke poking fish cubes with a plastic fork either. I took out my phone and ordered delivery.

"Address?"

I read off Katie's phone number. "You got my address on file?"

"Dr. Katherine Higgs?"

Higgs? "Yeah," I stammered. "My wife."

She'd used the name Higgs. That's why I hadn't been able to trace her. Higgs had to be a fake name, the name of her dog, and her Porsche, but what about Deauville—was that fake too? That would explain why I couldn't track her anywhere.

"Be there in twenty to thirty."

I pulled my car around and watched the door until a lanky kid in a Gianni's baseball cap walked out toting a brown bag. I followed his tricked-out white Civic up the hill until he stopped in front of a stone complex that looked like an edifice from ancient Rome. I parked across the street and trailed him up the walkway.

"That delivery for Higgs?" I asked before we reached the security gate. He tossed me the bag and grabbed the twenty out of my fingers without even thanking me for the huge tip. I ripped off the receipt, glad to find her unit number written on the top. When the gate swung open and an older couple shuffled out, I slipped into the building and rode the elevator to the penthouse, then followed the hallway to the end of the corridor where it dead-ended at her door. I took a deep breath before knocking.

From inside I heard the muffled bark of her ugly mutt, the jangling of tags as it padded to the door. "Who's there?" came a voice, pleasant and brusque at the same time—unmistakably Katie.

I rang the doorbell. Footsteps this time, an angry clip clop that halted in front of the peephole. "Christ, Hara. I told you to make an appointment."

I held up the bag beside my grinning face. "Brought you dinner."

"Go away."

I dangled the salad. "Can't leave until the delivery is complete. Otherwise, your account will be stuck in limbo forever. Plus you owe me a tip, Miss Higgs." I couldn't help smirking.

When the door cracked open, I pushed it ajar and squeezed through, dropping the bag in her hands. The dog dug his teeth into my ankle, causing me to yelp in pain. I pushed him aside, trying not to hurt the runt and piss off Katie further. Dashing across to the living room, I fell into the buttery depths of the sofa. The dog jumped up onto the glass table and snarled at my face awaiting attack orders.

Katie stood at the doorway, hands on her hips, furious. She was wearing a faded Escher t-shirt and pink sweatpants; not what I expected. She looked different—cute, despite the killer laser beams of her eyes; less intimidating, despite the anger. Or maybe because of it. Without the clothes and makeup, she looked almost like a regular person.

Once I was sure the dog wouldn't lunge at my throat despite the constant yapping, I relaxed and looked around. Chrome and white leather furniture was arranged around a black bearskin rug, windows rising up two stories to the ceiling behind me. A pair of vague, abstract paintings hung on the opposite wall; I wondered if they were original Rothkos or Crate & Barrel specials.

Katie dug a can of pepper spray from her bag and held it in front of her. "Go home," she ordered.

I didn't move. "I texted you," I said. "You didn't reply. I called you, you didn't answer. I get it—you're busy. So here I am. We need to talk."

"No, we don't. Go home. Or I'm calling security." The pepper spray still in one hand, she picked up her phone with the other. "Now!"

I didn't move. "I've got questions. A lot of questions. If I leave without answers, I'm not coming back. You'll have to find someone else to solve your mapping problem."

I stared at her, my eyes burning from the stink of onions that permeated the room. "Well?" I asked.

She lowered the phone. The pepper spray remained trained in my direction. "What?"

"Did Satoshi happen to mention the two of us had a little tea party yesterday?"

"No."

"It's quite an amazing coincidence, but it turns out my friend Ryu also works at SüprDüpr. Chief Elephant Officer."

"So?"

"Seems Ryu also had a chat with Satoshi. The day before he disappeared."

She cocked her head. "What do you mean 'disappeared'?"

"His family hasn't heard from him in a week."

Her expression turned to annoyance. "Christ, Hara, is that what this is all about? Ray hasn't disappeared. He's busy, just like me. Just like you're supposed to be. Just like everyone at SüprDüpr. We've got nine days left until our demo. None of us have time for anything else, including this pointless conversation. Have you solved the mapping yet?"

I ignored her question and asked my own. "Have you heard from Ryu since last Sunday?"

"He sends me daily updates. Just like you're supposed to be doing."

"Can I see one?"

"They're confidential."

"I signed an NDA."

She grumbled but put the pepper spray down. "See?" She thrust her phone in my face, then pulled it away quickly. I saw a slack from Ray Yamashita but wasn't able to catch the date. "Satisfied now?"

"Not really. Do you know where he is?"

"I don't care where he is as long as he gets his work done."

"What's he working on?"

"He's refining the SüprPorter design. Okay? Are you satisfied?"

"That brings up another question."

"What?"

"Satoshi told me Ryu had some concerns about the teleporter."

"And?"

"He said you made some compromises. Suggested I talk to you about it. So let's talk. Or you can fire me. Your choice."

Katie's nostrils flared, her eyes burned, and her face turned red in anger. Instead of firing me though, she stomped down the hallway, the dog trotting after her. A door slammed in the back. Echoes of anger seeped through the walls. I thought she was yelling at the dog until I realized she was on the phone with Satoshi. I tried to listen, but all I could hear through the wall was a final curse, then silence.

Through the tall window overlooking Lexington Reservoir, I watched joggers looping around the park. Behind the lighted trail, civilization ended in the darkness of the redwood forest that covered the hillside, split by a narrow red ribbon of taillights snaking over the mountains towards the sea.

I wondered how she could afford to live in such luxury. Was she paying herself a generous salary out of investors' money, did she come from a wealthy family, or was someone else footing the bill? Now that I knew the address, I could look up the owner, but I had a hunch that this property, too, had been purchased by Higgs, the doggy real estate tycoon.

A door opened in the back, the clack of heels on tile. When she returned, she was wearing a maroon Stanford sweatshirt and skinny jeans. In the kitchen, she poured herself a glass of sparkling water, not even offering me any.

"Any chance I could get a scotch?" I asked, hoping her expensive tastes extended to the bar. It was dark now. And I needed a drink.

"Alcohol turns your brain to shit, Hara. You've seen what it's done to the winos."

Her cavalier tone surprised me. "I thought you were all about helping the homeless people."

"Most of them would be better off dead. Don't you think?"

That's certainly what Kaa-chan thought, but I wasn't sure I agreed. "Then why are you building a shelter?"

"Because we need them to work for us."

So much for Christian charity. I shouldn't have been surprised it was about business after all. But sitting in a cubicle farm with Twitter-Dee and Twitter-Dumb was bad enough; I wasn't ready to share an office with Azaz and his pals. "What can they do?"

Katie sat on the chair across from me and leaned across the table. "Listen, Hara. There are too many stupid people who will say what we're doing is heartless. They'd rather hand out rotten food and free syringes to keep the homeless on the streets. So this has to remain absolutely confidential. Understand?"

I raised my hand and swore an oath and waited to hear SüprDüpr's super secret.

"We're using them to solve our complication with conservation of mass in teleportation discontinuities."

I had no idea what that meant. "Sorry," I said, "I'm a mathematician, not a physicist."

"Conservation of mass and energy requires pairs of Higgs doublets to materialize in opposite locations. There's no free rides in the universe, Hara, there's only balance and symmetry."

That was too much to unpack. "Can you be more concrete?"

"Look, it's simple—if one person goes one way, another must go the opposite way. For someone to be teleported from here to San Jose, someone else has to be teleported to Santa Cruz. For every paying customer to go where they want, a second traveler has to be sent in the opposite direction. Think of it as ballast for teleportation."

"Can't we just use weights? How about recycled plastic? That would be better for sustainability."

"Doesn't work."

"Why not?"

"You'll have to talk to Deepak, our Chief Philosophy Officer, but it comes back to entanglement. There's a reason they're Schrödinger's cats, not plastic bottles."

"Then why use homeless people? There's plenty of retirees who'd be happy to travel to random places. I'll bet they'd even pay."

"Look, we need them at a moment's notice. The military only has a few minutes to teleport a squad into bin Laden's cave once they get a fix on a location. It's perfect for transients. We house them in shelters next to the SüprPorters. We get them off the streets, we give them food, even medical care. And a job with no skills required. They don't even need to be sober."

I imagined Azaz suddenly materializing at the top of a snowy mountain. If he thought the CIA was watching him with fake birds, materializing in a forest a thousand miles from home would really explode his brain. "How will they get back?"

"With your maps, we'll know exactly where they materialize. To the millimeter. We'll arrange for them to be picked up and brought to the nearest teleporter for the next trip."

"Is it safe?"

"Absolutely. Completely. 100% safe. That is, once your mapping is working so they don't materialize into a tree. When will you have that ready?"

I couldn't admit I'd spent all of yesterday visiting an elephant preserve and most of today hunting for Katie. "Soon," I promised.

"Then get going already. We don't have time to waste. I'm counting on you, Hara."

I was proud that the greatest invention in history—and that's clearly what the teleporter was—depended on me. I felt the immense weight of its success bearing down my narrow shoulders. Katie stood and walked to the door. But I wasn't done with my questions. "Can I ask one more thing?"

She crossed her arms over her chest. "Make it quick."

"Has Ryu tested the teleporter himself?"

A flash of anger. "We're testing with rats. You saw the video. Now go—I've got a thousand things to finish today. And you need to work out the algorithm."

But I remained on the couch. "You really have no idea where he is?"

She stomped back to where I was sitting. "Okay, Hara. I'm going to let you in on something. But you can't tell anyone. For Ray's own safety. If someone finds out where he is, there's a serious risk he'll be kidnapped by the Russians. Or the Chinese. Or North Koreans. Understand?"

I swore not to tell anyone, not even my dead parents.

"I sent Ray overseas to meet with cyclotron experts to refine the teleporter design. And he's not communicating with anyone but me until he gets back. For his sake and ours."

If what Katie was saying was true, Sumire would be thrilled. And furious—why hadn't Ryu let her know he was okay? But I still had my doubts. I knew Katie wouldn't show me his progress reports, but maybe there was another way. "Can you ask him to message me? Tell him his mother and sister are worried sick."

She grumbled but sent a message. "Satisfied?"

I knew that was all I'd get today. She pointed at the door. "Get cracking. Now. Go home and figure out how to do the mapping. We don't have much time left."

Chapter 17
All Your Base Are Belong to Bear

When I arrived home, I wanted to forget about SüprDüpr and relax after a tough first weekend at the new job, but I knew if I wanted to stay on Katie's good side, I'd better get started on the project. I broke out a fresh bottle of Mu and sipped at the drink. But no matter how hard I stared into the cobalt blue bullseye at the bottom of the white ceramic cup, I couldn't come up with a solution to an impossible problem.

Getting within a few feet was easy—that was simple math. Adjusting for the curvature of the earth and surface non-linearities was messy, but nothing MeCan's DeepThought cloud computers couldn't handle without batting an LED. It was the last meter that was the killer. How to know if there was a tree at that spot or a rock or something else? Even the highest resolution images from the NSA's spy satellites weren't nearly good enough. The only way was to send someone to survey each site prior to teleportation.

Unless…what if someone had already been there? And taken photos. Then it hit me—the solution was simple: there were billions upon billions of snapshots covering nearly every spot on the globe, from the summit of Mt. Everest to the base of the South Pole, already sitting on people's phones or uploaded to the cloud. We didn't need to map the entire world, everyone had done it for us, twelve megapixels at a time, so much detail that you could make out individual blades of grass if you zoomed in all the way. All we needed was for the world to share their photos with us, and that was easy—we'd pay them. If Katie could plunk down a hundred million to park the homeless next door to the teleporter, we could cough up a few bucks at a time to make the system work.

But building a database of billions of photographs and paying for the ones we used was a huge project that would take years to complete. Then I realized I didn't have to do any of that—blockchain already did it for me. Using the BiteCoin infrastructure would make it simple to access photographs anonymously right off people's phones and PCs. All the computers in the blockchain voted on whether a result was correct. A distributed application would vote on the best photographs to use based on location and resolution, use proof-of-stake to validate that the GPS coordinates were legit, then deposit BiteCoin payments for the ones we used right into the owner's wallet. To start making money, people only needed to give us permission to connect their BiteCoin wallet to their photos archive. The idea was totally slick.

Katie would be concerned about security, though, and for good reason. A hack could cause serious problems, potentially even kill a customer. But the public blockchain didn't need to be connected directly to the teleporter. I'd run the complex number crunching on dedicated DeepThought cloud servers and pass the GPS coordinates to the teleporter at the Corinthian over a VPN. Despite the blockchain wrinkle, this was nothing but a standard client-server architecture, no different from the way every bank ATM handed out money in one place and deducted it from the customer's account on their servers.

Excited, I spent the night teaching myself how to build a blockchain smart contract application until my head dropped onto the keyboard. When a thin strip of sunlight seeped through the blinds, burning a line across my face, I fired up the Keurig clone and set to work again.

The coding required intense concentration, but I felt like an artist at a grand canvas creating a masterpiece—sketching out the routine and painting in the details, watching it take shape function by function. Deep down in the guts of the code, my fingers gritty with variables, the outside world faded to a distant consciousness. I felt invigorated in a way that video games and hackathons only hinted at. This was real, this was me—alone.

Once my blockchain DApp was unleashed, other coders would look at it and marvel, so I left a comment in each function, not my name, not my hash key, but a silly Easter egg, just to make people think. And at the top of the root directory instead of my signing my name, I typed, "All your base are belong to me!" Then I backspaced over "me" and replaced it with "Teddy Bear."

While the light dimmed to darkness, the fog rolled back in, and the crickets chirped their lonely songs, I kept working non-stop until the first results popped up on the screen, exactly as they were supposed to. I pumped my fist in excitement, a grand slam home run. Proud of the best thing I'd ever created, I wanted to call Sumire to share my triumph, but I knew she'd only tell me to stop helping SüprDüpr. Katie, though, would be thrilled.

"*mapping solved*" I messaged Katie, then poured a Mu to celebrate.

Staring out the window, I sipped the sake as I let my mind go blank. The red and green glow of the traffic lights pierced the darkness. A lone car raced down the street, its headlights illuminating the mist. The touristy shops were closed, their storefronts dark, the hair salons, real estate agents, dentist offices, and optometrists that filled the three blocks of Japantown all shuttered. Only the ramen joints and sushi bars were still open, the reflection of their neon signs smeared across the wet asphalt.

I was surprised to see a solitary figure galumphing up the sidewalk. I pushed open the slats of the blinds to watch as he passed under the cone of a streetlight. When I saw the blue uniform and the peaked cap, I realized it had to be Mayeda.

He stopped to chat with Mrs. Ogawa locking up the tempura shack on the corner, then waited with a drunk for an Uber to pull up to the curb. When he reached the conveyor belt sushi bar, a Mayeda kind of place, where Filipino chefs and white college-girl waitresses mispronounced *irasshaimase*, I expected him to step inside, but he only waved to the hostess with dayglow pink hair and continued up the street to duck through the narrow entrance of the Dandy Lion.

I'd ignored him when he'd offered to buy me a drink a couple of days ago, but now was the time to redeem that raincheck and push the cops to investigate Katie and Satoshi. I put on a windbreaker against the damp, grabbed my red remembrance cap, and trudged down the creaking stairs to the street.

Mayeda's head was down in his bowl, slurping a spoonful of broth. I sat in front of him, cringing as he stabbed at the chashu with his chopsticks like a barbarian.

"Hiya, shrimp," he muttered without looking up, his wispy moustache glistening with oil.

"*Bakayaro*," I shot back.

"Glad you're here," he said. "Got something I wanna ask you." He waved Yukiko over. "Bring us a bottle of sake."

Yukiko glanced at me in panic, confused by the two enemies seated across from each other. "Kikusui," I told her. If I had to drink with Mayeda, at least the sake would be easy to swallow.

As soon as she dropped the order on the counter, Kenta looked up. I was one of the few people who knew about his stash of Kikusui hidden in the refrigerator.

"*Oi*, Tatsu!" he yelled, and waved for me to join him in the back.

When I walked in the stockroom, Kenta shut the door behind us. "Hey, bruh, what's going on with Ryu?"

I couldn't tell him Ryu might have died in a teleporter accident or run away somewhere. Or perhaps he really was working incognito as Katie claimed, though he hadn't messaged me back yet. But I had to be careful what I said to Kenta. Nobody was supposed to know I worked at SüprDüpr. Or that we were building a teleporter. Kenta was better than the free local rag at spreading gossip around Japantown. As he pressed me for details, all I could say was that I didn't know anything yet. He knew was I lying, but only asked how he could help.

Ever since we were kids our roles had remained unchanged. I'd been the know-it-all who'd tutored Kenta and Ryu with their homework and solved all the video game puzzles. Even hacked into Legends of Emperors to pilfer the unbreakable Sword of Muramasa that wasn't supposed to exist. Ryu had been the golden boy, tall and handsome, his quick reactions making him the best zombie slayer this side of the 101. Kenta had been the worker, willing to do anything for the team, but was stuck most evenings cleaning dishes here at what was then his father's restaurant. I didn't see how Kenta could help—he couldn't even set up a VPN—though he did know everyone in the neighborhood.

"Start asking around," I told him. "The golf farts, the college kids, see if anybody knows anything."

"Yeah, bruh, already did that. As soon as Sumire told me."

"And?"

"Nothing," he said. "Nobody's seen him."

"Try posting signs around the neighborhood. Can you include a reward?"

Though I was sure nothing would come of plastering Ryu's face on light poles up and down Jackson Street like a missing cat, Kenta was excited to help.

When I returned to the table, the cornflower blue bottle of Kikusui was waiting, beads of condensation running down the corn flour yellow label. I filled the two ceramic cups and pushed one across to Mayeda. He picked it up and knocked it back like a shot of whiskey. I couldn't help wincing.

"Wow," he said, his eyes bugged open. "This is some good shit."

Personally, I liked Dassai better, and Mu, too, but Kikusui wasn't bad. "It's even better if you drink it right," I said and sipped at the cup to demonstrate. Just a few drops on the tongue was enough to savor the clean, slightly sweet taste of Niigata snowmelt, of rice grown in the thin strip of egret-filled paddies between a cold, dark sea and the jagged, snow-capped mountains. I refilled both cups. Again Mayeda downed his in a single shot. At least he didn't add sugar or ice like a true barbarian or mix it with beer in a sake bomb that would've made me explode. I only sighed and poured him another, topping off my own.

When I cleared my throat and started to ask about Ryu, he buried his head in the bowl. I cleared my throat again. He slurped at the broth without looking up. When I cleared my throat a third time, more annoyance than phlegm, he mumbled, "Not here."

"Why not?"

I waited, staring at him until he slurped down the entire bowl one spoonful at a time. Then he belched and tapped his chest as he knocked back another cup of sake.

"Why not?" I repeated. I didn't know what he was allowed to say, but anything he couldn't tell me about the investigation was something I wanted to hear. I waited for him to speak, but still he ignored me, picking at the remaining bits of noodles and moyashi stuck to the side of the bowl. "Come on, Mayeda," I pleaded. The cop reached for his cup. I pulled it away. "What the hell's going on with the investigation?"

He glared at me. "This ain't the place for it, shrimp."

"I don't give a shit where we are. Why haven't your buddies paid a visit to Satoshi yet?"

"Christ, Hara, keep your damn mouth shut. Can't we just enjoy a drink together?"

"I can drink by myself. I came here to talk about getting a search warrant for Satoshi." I downed my own cup in one gulp. "Well?" I pressed.

"You wanna know about Satoshi, you gotta talk to Jesus."

"Went to church yesterday. Didn't see him there."

"Maybe you went to the wrong church, pal."

Pal? I wasn't his pal, didn't want to be his pal. I almost preferred it when he called me shrimp.

Mayeda donned his flattop and raised his arm to flag Yukiko. "About time for me to get going." He stood and adjusted his jacket before pointing his thumb toward the door. "Maybe you ought to get some fresh air, too."

When Yukiko arrived, the cop handed her a twenty.

I remained seated. "What's your hurry?" I poured the last drops into our cups. "Can't let good sake go to waste."

"Holy fuck, you're dense." He pulled the bodycam out of the pouch on his chest. "Jesus is everywhere," he said, the LED blinking in front of my eyes.

I dropped a Benji on the table for the bottle and followed him out the door.

Chapter 18
Jesus and the Five Golden Buddhas

The cop strode up 5th Street through the strengthening rain, nearly leaving me behind. When he reached Betsuin, the Buddhist temple that was by definition the center of Japantown, he trudged through the front gardens and past the stone lanterns aglow in stark white light. I caught up to him on the wooden veranda sheltering beneath the eaves where we both brushed the beads of water from our caps.

When Mayeda raised himself to his full height, he towered over me, nearly a foot taller, more than a foot wider, looking like a giant version in blue of the squat stone lanterns behind us on the lawn. "Sanctuary," he said, pushing a button on his bodycam. The red LED went dark. "No video here."

"Now you can shoot me?"

A sour expression filled his moon face. "Do you hate all cops, Hara? Or you still got something against me?"

He'd bullied me in high school, and despite what Sumire thought, I doubted much had changed. "Those aren't mutually exclusive," I pointed out.

"Why not let bygones be bygones?"

"Because they're not gone."

"Come on, shrimp, this is a small town. We went to high school together. My father worked on your family's orchard. Why can't we be friends?"

"Why do you care?"

Mayeda said nothing as we listened to the pitter-patter of the rain all around.

After what felt like forever, Mayeda cleared his throat. "What's with you and Sumire?" he asked, calling her Sue Mary again.

I froze. "Nothing," I said, wary of where this was headed. I was here because I wanted him to get his buddies to investigate Satoshi, not to analyze what was and wasn't happening with Sumire. "I'm helping find her brother, that's all."

He looked at me with a dreamy, dumbass smile. "So..." he started, drawing it out forever, "if you guys aren't together...I wouldn't want to get in the way..." He stuttered a few more times before blurting out, "Maybe I'm sweet on her. Sue Mary. Always have been."

Oh, Jesus. The pathetic cop had a thing for my former girlfriend. Is that why we were outside a Buddhist temple in the middle of the night in the rain? God save me from idiots and people in love. I wasn't surprised he liked her now. That couldn't have been plainer if he'd tattooed her mispronounced name on his forehead. But that he'd picked on me in high school because he liked her rather than because he got off on bullying short, scrawny kids like me—I'd never had a clue. It was impossible to imagine him interested in Sumire instead of a cheerleader or volleyball girl or someone who could at least speak sportsball. She was too smart for him—not that that had ever stopped the girls I liked from chasing after dumb guys who could bench-press twice my weight.

"Is she *sweet* on you, too?" I said, mocking his expression. "The two of you share a cherry *kakigori* together? Split a peanut butter *monaka*?" It came pouring out of my mouth like I was vomiting up the ghosts of all the desserts Sumire and I had ever shared. I had no right to be jealous, but as I heard my taunts echo into the rain, it sounded like I was.

The cop raised his hands in surrender. "Hey, just checking."

It's not like it was up to me anyway. "Talk to Sumire, not me. She makes her own decisions on who she dates. And everything else, too. In case you haven't noticed."

Neither of us said anything as we listened to the steady dripping. I wished I had a teleporter to zap me somewhere far away.

Mayeda pointed with his chin at the door. "Inside." He opened the ornate wooden door and disappeared into the darkness. I should have left him there and headed home. But I still needed to find out what was going on.

At the doorway I hesitated. The last time I'd been inside was my mother's funeral. I had to remind myself this was just an empty hall, but held my breath anyway as I stepped over the threshold that separated the spiritual world from the profane, careful not to show disrespect by touching the raised beam with dirty feet.

The chapel was lit only by narrow spotlights illuminating the five golden Buddhas behind the altar. We didn't need much light—we'd both spent countless hours here, the temple in the front and the classrooms in the back, summer Obon festival and New Year's celebrations in the courtyard, little league and boy scouts, calligraphy class on the floor of the gym. Every wedding and funeral in town. The entire community gathered here, including the half that prayed at the Methodist Church a block away, the chapels nearly identical: the same industrial, blue-gray carpet, the same musty smell of dust and decay, and the same dingy yellow lighting that left me feeling trapped. But instead of a giant cross on the wall behind the pulpit, five shiny Buddhas sat beaming beneath their spotlights.

The cop removed his dripping cap, hung it on the edge of a pew, and walked up the aisle to the altar. He stood before the row of Buddhas and put his palms together to clap three times, then crossed himself and bowed. Had to be some weird Hawaiian thing. When he returned to where I was standing, he slipped into a bench. I slid down the row to join him.

"What do you want from me?" I asked.

Mayeda looked at me with an embarrassed grin. "Got a favor to ask. Think you can help out a pal?"

Why was everyone asking for my help—first Sumire and now Mayeda? Sumire I owed a debt of gratitude and guilt; Mayeda I didn't owe shit. I wasn't his pal, didn't like him now that he was pretending to be nice any more than when he'd bullied me. But we needed his connections, and his badge. "What?" I asked, bracing myself.

"Any chance you could put in a good word for me with Sumire?"

I'd prefer getting zapped with the taser hanging from his belt—at least I'd know what to do with that. "I hate to break it to you, *pal*. I'm pretty sure she's not into you."

"How do you know? Come on, Hara, just talk to her. She'll listen to you."

"Ha!" I was pretty sure she had no interest in dating advice from me. "Why are you asking me? Call her yourself!"

"And have you talk shit about me behind my back? Uh-uh. I want you on my side. You gonna do me this favor, or are you gonna be a simp?"

I got up to leave.

He grabbed the back of my windbreaker. "Sorry, Hara. I didn't mean that. Really." He looked at me with big, sad eyes that reminded me of the elephants. "Be a pal, Hara. I'll owe you big time."

Finally, he was acting Japanese, understood that with every favor came an equivalent debt. And I was better off talking to Sumire about him than have him whining to her about me. "Fine," I grumbled. "I'll warn her you'll be calling."

"And you won't sabotage me?"

I hummed a few bars. "Dumb dumb de dumb." The bridal march. For idiots.

"You're really annoying, shrimp."

"Good thing we're best buds, dipshit."

The cop laughed. "Really wish I knew what Sumire saw in you."

"Yeah, me too." Because for some reason I never understood, she really did love me once. Could she love this Hawaiian instead? It seemed unlikely, even if he wasn't all that bad. Just lonely like the rest of us, growing up in a town that had transformed into something unrecognizable, stranded without a college degree in a place where everyone had at least a master's, stuck in a job that he expected to command respect but only brought contempt. I was sure he wasn't Sumire's type, but she could do worse—like me, for example. At least he wasn't one of the slick-talking white assholes in their BMWs that all the girls in J-town ended up with. "Next time I see her, I'll tell her you're the most wonderful person ever."

Somehow, he missed my sarcasm and clapped a beefy hand on my shoulder. "Thanks, pal." As if I was his pal.

I wasn't sure what I'd agreed to, but I felt vaguely dirty, like I'd slept with someone I wasn't really into. A golden Buddha gave me the side-eye from the third eye in the middle of its forehead. I pulled the baseball cap down low over my face to hide.

"So what's it you want to know?" Mayeda asked.

I had to remember what I'd come for. "Anybody going out to question Satoshi?"

"Nope. Wouldn't hold your breath, either."

"Why not? He was the last person to see Ryu."

Mayeda said nothing.

"Why not?" I repeated.

"Because that's the orders."

"Orders? Not to talk to a witness? Whose orders?"

Mayeda shook his head.

"Whose orders?"

"Don't know."

I was sure he did. "Guess!" He didn't answer. "You really my pal, Mayeda?" I hissed. "Cause pals don't keep secrets from each other, especially when we're looking for the brother of your future bride."

The cop sighed, then whispered, barely loud enough to hear, "Maybe Jesus ain't no angel."

"The chief of police?"

"Shhhh," he said. "Just saying. You didn't hear it from me, but maybe Jesus takes his orders from a higher power."

Who would be above the police chief? "The mayor?"

"Nah. He takes orders, too, if he wants to get reelected."

"Then who?"

"That's the $17 billion question, isn't it? Who's the big man upstairs, pulling the strings?"

There was only one person I knew with $17 billion in his crypto wallet. "Satoshi?"

Mayeda shrugged. "Make your own conclusions. Cause I didn't say nothing."

"Fuck," I muttered. The entire row of abstemious Buddhas scowled at my profanity. "Is anyone even looking for Ryu?"

"Sure, Hara, they're looking all right. Maybe just not anywhere he's likely to be found."

"Meaning?"

"Meaning they're covering their asses. Someone called the hotels and clinics around town, checked out the homeless encampments, that sort of thing. You think he's turned into a meth head?"

"No."

"Then they aren't going to find him, are they?"

That reminded me of Azaz. "How about a homeless guy your buddies hauled away from St. Jimmy's the other day? Any idea where he is?"

"What do you care about some vagrant?"

"Ryu talked with him. Now he's gone, too."

"He isn't in your shelter?"

"Our shelter? The one across from St. Jimmy's?" I was confused. "It's not even built yet." And how did he know I worked at SüprDüpr?

Mayeda coughed. "You sure that's the only one?"

Katie had explained we'd employ homeless people as the ballast in the teleporter. I hadn't asked if she'd already started.

"Let me give you a piece of friendly advice, Hara. Just between us pals. If I was you, I wouldn't go poking my nose into those homeless camps. Word out there is to keep an eye on you."

"On me? Why me?" I doubted anyone cared about what I did, much less the cops.

"Katie D has a lot of fans on the force."

"Fans? Of a tech startup?" That was hard to believe. "I'll bet you're all just fantasizing about her legs."

"Look, Hara, people may not think much of us, but we're trying to keep this town safe. And we're sick of dealing with the transients. It takes up all our time, watching over them. The assaults and petty crime, burglaries and stolen bicycles, needles all over the sidewalks. Our phones ringing nonstop with people begging us to do something. We bring them in for drugs or whatever, only to have them back on the streets the same day. Something's got to be done. At least she's got a plan, even if it isn't by the book. So, yeah, she's got a few friends willing to help with whatever she wants."

"Like following me?"

"Not following. Just keeping an eye out."

"That include you?" Then I got it. "Fuck. You were at the ramen joint to watch me! That's your job, isn't it?"

He chuckled. "Yeah, I was figuring you might be there. But not because of that. I wanted to talk to you about…well, you know."

His face went dreamy, but I hardly noticed I was so pissed. The idea of the cops watching me on Katie's behalf was almost as bad as being predictable enough to be found at the Dandy Lion. "Is that what happened to Ryu, too? Were you following him? Did your cop friends haul him away never to be seen again?"

"I'm telling you, Hara, I don't know nothing about that."

"And how would those goons even recognize me? 'Be on the lookout for a short Asian guy in a t-shirt and flip-flops?' Ha! Good luck with that. Bet your goons couldn't tell the difference between a Japanese and Chinese person if I bit them on the ass."

Mayeda smirked, making me even angrier. "What?"

"Hate to break it to you, pal, but everyone can spot you from a mile away." He tapped his head. I thought he meant he was smart which made me laugh sarcastically, but then he yanked the brim of my cap.

I took the red Asahi hat off. "This?"

"Yup. Complete giveaway."

I stared at the hat. It was a reminder of everything I wanted to remember. A San Jose Asahi baseball cap. Tou-san had given it to me when I was a kid. He showed me the family scrapbook of black-and-white photos of my great-grandfather playing third base for Asahi, the local Japanese-league team that had once, in an event that everyone in the neighborhood still talked about, beaten a team of all-stars touring from Japan.

My great-grandfather's team had been farmhands working in the orchards all day, practicing in the summer twilight until it was too dark to see the ball, playing on the weekends against the other Japantowns up and down the coast, before the war, when the professional leagues were for whites only, before 42 became the answer to everything. Before my great-grandfather and the entire team and the entire town was uprooted and bussed to the Heart Mountain internment camp in the barrenness of Wyoming, where he suited up in his red and white uniform again and kept playing until he was shipped off to fight and die in Germany.

That clapped-out old cap was long gone, tossed in the dumpster with the rest of my childhood junk when I took Tou-san's car and left his ashes behind for a new life as a Giant in Red Sox land. And it was the first thing I'd bought, a knockoff on eBay, when I returned six years later to join my mother's ashes and her tea bowls and vacuum cleaners back home in San Jose.

I reminded myself one last time of everything I shouldn't forget. "Like I said, pal," I told Mayeda as I placed the cap atop the cop's thick skull, "that could be just about anyone around here."

I slid out from the pew, saluted my new pal, and strode up the musty blue-gray carpet, all fifteen eyes of the five golden Buddhas burning a hole in my back.

Chapter 19
Journey to Junior U

The next morning, a slack was waiting on my phone.

"Hey Ted. Sorry to scare everyone. I'm working overseas. Tell my sister and my mother I'm absolutely fine. Not sure when I will return. Ray."

I should have been relieved that Ryu was okay, busy working for SüprDüpr, but I wasn't. We'd always been Tatsu and Ryu with each other, used Dragon Boy and Hulking Bear as our game monikers, called each other Debeso and Chibi when we wanted to piss each other off. Never Ted and Ray. Nor would Ryu ever use punctuation, not in a slack—this message was totally sus. If it had come from Ryu's account, but hadn't come from Ryu, there was only one person who could have sent it.

I messaged back, *"hey debeso where the fuck are u???"* There was no reply.

If he really was overseas working with cyclotron experts, where exactly would that be? The most obvious place was CERN, the lab in Geneva where the Higgs was first observed, but that was far from the only possibility. There were research centers in all the major countries, and dozens of universities, far too many places to check them all and rule out Ryu wasn't there.

Although I didn't know where he was now, I knew where he must have started, the place where Katie earned her Ph.D., the tree on her sweatshirt, the place where all roads in Unicorn Valley led. After a shower and a double dose of caffeine to chase away the ghost of Mayeda, I headed up to Palo Alto to see if there was anything to learn at Leland Stanford Junior University—Junior U as everyone at MIT called the training school for train robber barons.

🐘   🐘

On the manicured lawn, girls in crop tops lounged in packs, paging through their ochem textbooks together while flirting with the shirtless boys leaping after frisbees like show dogs. As I strolled past the Mission Revival buildings of adobe brick searching for the physics hall, I wondered what my life would have been like if I'd studied here as Kaa-chan had insisted. Satoshi had paved the way, the application I never submitted already accepted, the prerogative of a billion-dollar endowment to establish the school's blockchain program. Would Kaa-chan still be alive if I'd stayed nearby instead of decamping to the shores of the frozen Charles River? Even now it felt weird standing on the mall, the setting of an alter-life where my mother still made my decisions.

On the second floor of the Very Berry Ann Building, I found the Hansen Laboratory for Experimental Physics. The entrance was locked. When I rang the buzzer, the door cracked open. A man with a long, scraggly beard blocked my way in. His threadbare red t-shirt read: "If this shirt looks blue, you're going too fast."

"Who are you?" asked Blueshift.

Though I wasn't afraid of being kidnapped by North Korean agents, I didn't want to tip off Katie about my visit. "Murakami," I blurted out. "Camus Murakami," I introduced myself, combining two of Kaa-chan's obsessions. I liked that better than my real name anyway.

Blueshift looked me over. "Any relation?"

I never shared my mother's enthusiasm for the Murakami novels she foisted on me whenever she caught me reading manga. I wondered if she would have jumped from a mountain if she hadn't read *Norwegian Wood*, an angst-ridden story of forbidden love and suicide, so many times the spine had to be taped together. His surreal novels of parallel universes and vanishing elephants probably appealed to physicists more than mathematicians. "He's my cousin," I lied, hoping that would get me inside.

Blueshift's eyes lit up. "Murakami will win the Nobel," he claimed with the certainty of a solved equation. "His research on the Spin Hall Effect opened a whole new approach to the wave-nature of particles."

I had no idea what he was talking about. Or who. "Yeah, that sure was some sick research."

He looked at me like the clueless noob I was. Behind him was chaos: messy lab stations and racks of equipment in a dimly lit room, the air heavy with the smell of unwashed postdoc. A dozen beards stopped working to stare in my direction; the single woman glanced up before looking back at her computer. I wished I'd brought a pizza—that would have gotten me in. I pointed at the woman. At least she didn't look hostile. "I'm here to see her."

Blueshift eyed me suspiciously, then hollered across the room, "Hey, Lady Dave—you know this guy?"

Lady Dave peered out from behind her monitor. "Never see him before," she answered with a thick Mandarin accent.

"Better luck next time." Blueshift pushed me back with his hairy forearm, closing the door in my face.

"Ryu Yamashita sent me," I tried. I was surprised when the door opened again.

I darted into the room before he could change his mind. When I reached the woman, her face washed by the green glow of the monitor, I felt the cosmic rays of twelve beards trained on my back. The only person who wasn't looking at me was Lady Dave herself, even when I planted a chair and sat down beside her.

"*Ni hao*," I greeted her, the only Chinese I knew. She continued typing without acknowledging me. I cleared my throat to prove I existed. Apparently, I didn't. "Mind if I ask a couple questions?"

Apparently, she did. Bips and wiffs and zapps shot across her screen like the old school Asteroids game.

"Busy," she declared when I refused to go away. I waited. "Busy," she insisted. I waited harder. It wasn't until I started humming the Star Trek theme that she turned to me, annoyed. "What do you want?"

"Do you know Ryu Yamashita?"

"You mean Ray-ray?" Her expression turned dreamy. It was obvious why girls liked Ryu—tall and athletic, a winning smile, just nerdy enough to sound intelligent. I wished women had the same reaction when they heard my name.

"I'm Ray-ray's friend," I whispered, choking over his nickname. "Nobody has seen him lately. Do you have any idea where I can find him?"

"Ha!" she yelled, surprising the entire room of postdocs pretending not to be listening. "If he still works for that Katie D., I think he must run away."

"You know Katie Deauville?"

"Dr. Katie D.," she said with a sour face. "She used to run this lab. Until she left to start her company."

Even if Ryu wasn't here, at least I'd come to the right place. I was about to ask what she had against Katie when a gawky postdoc sauntered over like John Wayne playing a physicist. "This guy bothering you, L.D.?"

I felt sorry for the geek trying to be the hero in front of this woman, so I did him a solid by raising my hands in surrender.

"It's okay, Donny," she soothed. "Go back to work. Nobel Prizes don't win themselves."

He returned to his stool and continued eyeing me like a gunslinger in the physics saloon.

"Don't worry," she said. "Donny doesn't bite."

"Katie's not so bad, either."

"Ha!" she cried, then had to tell John Wayne to sit down again. "You like her because she's pretty."

It wasn't just her looks, I insisted; she was smart and capable, the founder of the highest-flying unicorn in town.

"Of course she's smart," Lady Dave said. "Everyone here's smart. But nobody crazy like her. Always thinks she's right. If you smart, you take my advice—stay away from Dr. Katie."

"Ryu is supposed to be meeting with cyclotron experts. Any idea who that might be?"

She pointed to the back corner of the lab where a balding Indian man with a wispy beard ducked his head behind an enormous monitor. "Ray-ray always meets R2D2 when he comes here."

Finally, a person who might know something about Ryu. I thanked Lady Dave and dragged the chair across the floor to R2D2. "Parents big fans of Star Wars?" I asked. The dome of his head attached to his squat body did look a bit like the robot.

He tapped the nameplate glued to the cinderblock wall behind him, the name Ramesh Rishabh Damodaran in block letters. "Parents didn't have a clue."

I sympathized. "Wish I could say the same."

"What's wrong with your name?"

How could he understand when even my father didn't realize what Kaa-chan meant when she declared that the annoying bump in her belly was to be named Tatsu—a common name in Japan. The only words of Japanese that Tou-san knew related to food and drink. He had no idea that Hara Tatsu, the family name first in Japanese, meant *pissed off*. Pissed off at being stranded in a land she hated, pissed off at being trapped in a marriage to a man who didn't understand her, pissed off that despite her aristocratic heritage, she was stuck in a provincial farming family, a failing farm at that. I wanted to think she was joking; even sober it was impossible for Tou-san to understand her unsmiling, deadpan humor. Sitting at the dining table as he always did after dinner, lost in his Johnnie and careful not to say anything that might provoke his easily angered wife, I imagined him nodding at her suggestion and innocently offering the English name of Theodore to match, pissing her off even further.

"Call me Ted," I said.

"Ramesh." He reached out to shake my hand. "Did I hear you talking about Dr. Deauville?"

I was afraid of this conversation getting back to Katie, but there was no choice but to take the chance. I leaned close and said, "I work at SüprDüpr."

His sleepy eyes bulged as he glanced around the room. "Poppycock," he whispered. "You wouldn't say anything if you really worked there."

"Chief Mathematics Officer," I declared. I thought that would impress him, but he waved it off like an elephant shooing away a fly. "Went to MIT," I added, incanting the three magic letters that should have brought respect, at least here in a particle physics lab.

He shrugged as if I'd said De Anza College. "Saw your team lost to Bridgewater State in soccer yesterday."

I couldn't let that go unanswered. "Yeah, but we annihilated Stanford at this year's NCAA coding championship." I was sure he wouldn't know there was no such tournament, though there ought to be.

He chuckled. "Everyone at MIT as bullshit as you?"

I laughed. "No, most people are way too serious."

"Same here," he said. We both sighed. "What brings you to our lab, young man?"

Ramesh looked older than the others in the room. I pointed back at Lady Dave. "She said you work with Ryu."

"So?"

"I'm Ryu's replacement."

"He quit? Good for him. I suggest you do the same."

"He's missing."

"Missing?" His eyebrows shot up. "Teleporter?"

I'd come to the right place. But all the beards were staring at us. All disapproving. The room felt like it was closing in. John Wayne hitched up his big boy pants and moseyed over. "Time for you to go," he declared, thrusting his scrawny frame in my face, and giving me a big whiff of his musty t-shirt. So much for doing him a solid.

I could hold my own against a single postdoc, even one who thought he was a drunken cowboy, but from the hard expressions that surrounded me, it was looking like twelve on one. "Yep, getting hungry," I said to John Wayne, patting my belly and trying to sound like a TV cowboy. "Anywhere to grab some chow 'round here?"

John Wayne jerked me to my feet and shoved me towards the door.

"Hey," Ramesh called from his desk. "You forgot something."

He was holding up a phone that looked like every other MeCan phone. I patted my pants, relieved to find the familiar bulge there. I was about to tell Ramesh that it wasn't mine when he hurried over and dropped the phone into my palm. I was about to hand it back to him when I noticed the message on the screen: "Wait for my call."

"Thank you," I said, raising the phone in thanks.

"Now get the hell out of here," Ramesh ordered as a dozen beards and a single ponytail all wagged their good riddance.

Chapter 20
Kätie's Käts

A wall of oaks, their leaves showing the first tinges of yellow, created a private space isolated from the bustle of students rushing past on the mall. Dappled light filtered into the shade as I sat on a bench waiting for Ramesh's phone to ring. The longer it stayed silent, the more I worried that this was a trick to keep me here until Katie could arrive with the fire of a thousand suns blazing from her eyes to incinerate me. I was considering giving up when the phone finally buzzed with a text ordering me to room 303 of Jacks Hall.

I walked past all the weird sculptures on the lawn and through a stone archway that looked like an old train station. After clumping up the worn marble staircase, I found the darkened classroom. I thought it was empty until I noticed Ramesh hiding in the back corner.

"What's with the secrecy?" I asked.

"It's SüprDüpr."

"So?"

"We're under NDA. I'm not supposed to be talking to you."

"But you talked to Ryu."

"Dr. Deauville's orders."

"What did you talk about?"

Ramesh shook his head. "Sorry. NDA."

There had to be something he wanted to tell me to drag me to a darkened classroom halfway across campus. "What could Katie do if she found out you were talking with me?"

"I'd lose my stock options. Maybe get booted out of the lab."

I ought to read my own NDA and find out what would happen to me. But Ramesh didn't even work for SüprDüpr. I asked why he had stock options in the company.

"Because my team discovered teleportation, not Dr. Deauville." I caught an undercurrent of irritation in his voice. "I was ready to publish the results of our Higgs tunneling experiments until Dr. Deauville insisted on commercializing it. 'Build a teleporter,' she said. We all laughed. I told her that was impossible. But she convinced that blockchain guy, Satoshi-ji, to give her barrels of money. Said we'd all become billionaires but we had to keep everything secret so competitors couldn't steal it."

That sounded like Katie. "Did she promise you a Ferrari, too?"

Ramesh laughed. "What do I want with a Ferrari? Research money and lab equipment—that I could use. Do you know how much the Europeans spent building CERN—five billion dollars. Americans are so short-sighted. No funding unless there's commercial benefit. Instead of doing research, we spend all day writing grant proposals to scrape together a few thousand dollars. With a billion dollars, we could increase the collider's energy level to measure the mass of the W boson accurately and disprove the Standard Model. That would win a Nobel Prize for sure. So everyone agreed with Dr. Deauville. Except me. I was the only holdout. I said teleportation could never work so there was no billion dollars and why were we doing this? Then Satoshi-ji offered a huge grant to fund research into blockchain for high-energy physics. What could I say? It was pure poppycock—there's no uses of blockchain in physics. But money is money, so that was that. Now we have stock options instead of research papers. And an NDA."

I pointed around the empty room. "Then why did you bring me here?"

"Curiosity, mostly. Wanted to find out why you're poking around our lab. I have a theory you're actually a spy for Dr. Deauville."

I insisted I was looking for my friend and told him about growing up with Ryu, our fathers drinking buddies, our mothers immigrants from the same region in Japan. "That was until I started dating his sister."

"Ah, the woman, of course. Boys in love and all that rigmarole. Now the truth becomes clear."

"Except the truth about where Ryu has gone."

"Is he truly missing?"

"Nobody's seen him for over a week. His sister is worried as hell."

Ramesh bowed his head. "That is most unfortunate. Maybe she is right to be worried. Ryu is quite naïve, eh? Too easy to become excited. I watch Katie spin him around her finger, just like her little puppy dog."

Was that a hint of jealousy? "Do you think there's something going on between them?"

"He's smitten with her, hundred percent certainty of that. And not the only one, eh? When she first came here, I would've given my life for her. That was before I saw what was inside. Anything to succeed. Only thinking of money. But everyone loves Katie-ji hundred percent. I suggest you stay out of her way if you don't want to get run over like me."

"Is that what happened to Ryu?"

He shrugged. "No idea. Haven't seen him in donkey's ages."

"Any chance there was a problem with the teleporter? An accident, maybe?"

"No chance he would get into that contraption. Too ludicrous to consider."

"Why not?"

"With a fifty-fifty probability of coming out alive?"

I didn't understand. "Because it's a prototype?"

He cocked his head as he looked at me. "You don't know anything, do you?"

"No," I had to admit. "That's why I'm here."

"You've seen the experiments with the rats, yes?"

"Sure. That was pretty slick."

"Then you understand why teleportation is impossible."

I told him I saw a rat being teleported. "It looked like it worked to me."

"You saw what happened to the second rat?"

"What second rat?"

"The dead one."

I only saw one rat on the video, but there could have been another hidden somewhere. "How do you know there's a dead rat?"

"Why should I trust you?"

I offered him the only collateral I had—I told him I'd lied to get the job at SüprDüpr so I could search for Ryu. "If you tell Katie, she'll make sure I never work in this town again. My life will be finished. I'll have to move to Lodi and do web maintenance." A fate worse than death.

Ramesh pursed his fingers over his lips. "It's so simple even a mathematician can understand," he teased. "I created a kind of a thought experiment, same as Schrödinger's cat. The thing you must know about Higgs bosons is that they pop in and out of existence in pairs. Instead of one Schrödinger's cat, you have two Katie's cats, I call them." He stopped to laugh at his joke. "Instead of a fifty-fifty probability Schrödinger's cat will be dead or alive when you open the box, one of Katie's cats will be alive, so the other must be dead. Which one is alive and which is dead is purely random. God doesn't play dice, but Schrödinger does, that much is proven. If my thinking is correct, the teleporter is completely useless. Except for teleporting cats. That is, if you hate cats."

Katie hadn't mentioned anything about half her customers arriving dead. Something they might want to know before getting inside. "You think the teleporter killed Ryu?"

Ramesh shrugged. "Dr. Deauville claimed she discovered a solution but had to keep it secret from competitors. Even Ryu said he didn't know how it worked."

"And you don't believe her?"

"Do you think I'd risk a billion dollars if I thought there was a chance that contraption could actually work?"

"Then why is she spending hundreds of millions building a teleporter?"

"I have a theory," he said. "More like a guess, actually. Dr. Deauville doesn't need the teleporter to work to become a billionaire, yes? She just needs the world to believe it will work someday so they buy SüprDüpr stock now."

A kind of scam after all—stock rather than real estate. "A teleporter that only works for rats?"

"Exactly. Nobody cares about a dead rat or two."

But Ryu cared about a pair of elephants. If Ramesh was right, one of the pair would end up dead in the company's demo. The mysterious phone call to Angela at the elephant preserve was starting to make sense. So was the meeting with Satoshi. But it didn't explain where he went. "Any idea where I can find Ryu?"

"Have you checked Slack?"

"Did he message you?" I asked, excited. Even if he wasn't active on SüprDüpr's account where Katie was watching, could he have slacked Ramesh directly?

Ramesh chuckled. "Sorry, you misunderstand." He repeated it, spelling out the letters: S.L.A.C. "Stanford Linear Accelerator," he said, pointing off in the distance. "Up there on Sand Hill Road. Where Ryu was helping Katie-ji build the prototype teleporter. Maybe you should see what your company's up to."

Chapter 21
Inside the Apple Core

To avoid any chance of running into Katie at SLAC when I was supposed to be busy on the mapping, I decided to come back late at night to reconnoiter. As I sped south on the 280, heading for home, the Spaceship—Apple's headquarters building—gleamed from the side of the highway, reminding me that I hadn't heard back from Ryu's girlfriend. Grace Kim hadn't accepted my LinkedIn connection and ignored repeated invites to follow each other on Insta. That alone made me suspicious. I needed to talk to her and the sooner the better. Even if they'd broken up, she'd have the best idea what was happening in his life and where he might have gone. Though the half-eaten Apple logo made me shiver, I turned off the highway at Stevens Creek and steered the pony into the neo-future.

Arriving at the Apple mothership hidden behind the identikit buildings of Cupertino was like entering a science fiction world, a four-story ring of glass and steel that had landed in the middle of an artificial nature preserve. I strode into a lobby lit with bright white lights to find a row of women in white uniforms preening behind a white counter. I needed to speak with Grace Kim in Wearables, I said when one finally deigned to glance up from her iPhone.

"Is she expecting you?"

"Nope."

"You'll have to make an appointment." She turned to the woman next to her and they laughed at the absurdity of my request.

I slapped my last MeCan business card onto the counter and waited for her surprise—MeCan and Apple were real enemies, not frenemies, and we did not fraternize. Everyone knew that Mobile Dick, MeCan's tangerine tower, was built to the exact width of the open core in the middle of the Apple ring, making it clear who wore the pants on the 280. She raised her eyebrows as she looked me over before pressing a button to call Grace.

"Tell her it's about Ryu," I said when she announced my presence.

"She says she's busy."

"Tell her I'm a programmer from MeCan looking for a job."

"She'll meet you in the cafe in ten minutes."

The Apple core was airy and bright, the pond in the middle of the technicolor lawn shimmering like a Pixar movie brought to life. As I sipped my single estate coffee at a picnic bench of varnished blond wood, I tried to avoid looking at the Apple logos all around.

I'd been an Apple fanboy once, taught myself how to program on a Mac, its blue translucent case glowing in my darkened room like a lava lamp for geeks. But then came the iPod Mini I'd bought for Kaa-chan, the worst birthday present ever. She'd listened to it all day locked in her bedroom, the sad Beatle's tune, *Norwegian Wood*, playing in an infinite loop, even took it on her final trip to Kyoto, carried with her in her purse as she hiked up the mountain path at daybreak. The sad sitar riffs played in her ears while she swept the graves of her parents and her parent's parents and countless other ancestors spending their eternity together on Mt. Arashiyama.

After cleaning grass and dirt off the stones, she laid incense and rice atop each. While the monks inside the temple chanted their morning incantations, she hung her purse around the neck of a golden Buddha glowing in the clear light of dawn. Dressed in a funeral kimono of black silk, she climbed the steep trail through a forest of spruce and pine to the summit. There she clambered over the guardrail to reach the granite outcropping overlooking the gorge. She slipped off her shoes, hung her sunhat on a branch, and leapt through the mists hugging the craggy slopes to smash feet-first into the boulder-strewn river far below.

When I'd arrived to claim the ashes of her already cremated body, the priests bowed deeply as they handed me the purse she'd left with the Buddha. Inside I found no note, no letter, not even a photo of Tou-san or me, nothing but her wallet, passport, and the wedding ring she carried in a brocade pouch. The side pocket contained no note, no explanation, only a pink lipstick and the rose-colored iPod I'd given her long ago, earbuds wrapped tight around it.

Through broken English, the po-faced priests explained that the Buddha taught life was nothing but suffering and pain. If that was meant to assuage my guilt for leaving her alone and lessen my misery, it accomplished neither. I was angry at myself, angry at the stoic statues that had done nothing to stop her, nor had a single word of comfort for me now. I explained to the priests in my pidgin Japanese my own Zen koan: in mathematics, the derivative of one plus one plus one is zero. I left them that mystery to ponder forever and walked out to follow Kaa-chan's final footsteps.

I'd climbed the path that switchbacked up the mountainside while a raven gawked at me from overhead. When I reached the summit, I sat on the ledge where my mother had exited from this world and passed into the next. As I looked down into the rocky gorge, the raven fluttered onto a nearby branch to watch me through an unblinking black eye. In the distance, where the wild mountains gave way to the flats of the valley and the turbid river calmed, I could see the Togetsukyo Bridge like a Lego toy joining the two halves of the town. Her smashed and broken body had been discovered bobbing towards the reedy shore by a tourist standing on that bridge.

I was tempted to jump, too, and join my parents, the granite ledge a bridge to reach them. There was nothing keeping me on this side—no family, no job, not even friends who cared. In my rush to escape from Kaa-chan, I'd left San Jose, left Japantown, left Sumire, left my grandmother and aunts and uncles who'd been banished from my life, left everything that mattered. I could give up now, call it game over, but the river below looked as cold and uncaring as the universe itself. As much as I wanted to put an end to my anguish, I didn't understand how Kaa-chan could leap into that void without even saying goodbye. I had no choice but to drag her ashes back to the San Jose she hated and start my life over from level 1.

I'd grasped the stupid iPod in my hand, wishing I'd never bought it, wishing Steve Jobs had never invented it, wishing Apple had never existed. I stood up and chucked it as far as I could throw, watched it arc over the empty space and fall into the raging river to join my mother's spirit on the rocky river bottom.

Since then, I'd never touched another Apple product. My mother's depression wasn't Apple's fault; it was my own stupidity for not understanding, for skipping town instead of sticking by her when she needed me. But that never stopped my gut from churning every time I saw an Apple logo. So when MeCan, the Apple fucker, offered me a job out of college, I accepted without even thinking how little difference I would make, how Apple would continue to thrive despite my efforts. Even sponsor an elephant. Surrounding me now were Apple logos glowing on the MacBook on every picnic table, the iPhone in every hand, the Apple Watch strapped to every wrist, the white AirPods hanging from every ear. My stomach churned as I fidgeted with the lone MePhone at the center of the Apple universe.

"Ted Hara?" a voice asked, startling me.

I blinked and looked up. The woman in front of me was tall and athletic, with the stretched legs and powerful shoulders of a volleyball player. Not what I was expecting, but a perfect fit for Ryu. Then I saw it, hanging from her neck, a silver cross with three red rubies, identical to Katie's. I offered to buy her a coffee or an iCoffee or whatever they called caffeine here in Appleland. She remained standing. "Sorry, I'm busy cat herding. Give me your resume. I'll pass it to HR."

I pointed at the bench across from me. "I just need five minutes," I said. "I need to ask you about Ryu."

She turned on her heels to leave.

"He's missing," I said as she headed away.

"Good." She glared at me over her shoulder. "I never want to see that worm again." That answered my question about whether they'd broken up.

As she strode for the exit, I jumped up from the table, spilling my coffee over the varnished wood. "I think he may be dead," I shouted across the room. Everyone was so absorbed in their AirPods that not a single person noticed.

But Grace stopped, turned around. "What did you say?"

When I repeated it, she returned to the table and sat on the end of a bench, looking shaken. I asked, "Did Ryu ever say anything about looking for elephants?"

She shook her head. "He didn't tell me anything except he joined some startup and convinced them to help the unhoused population."

"That was his idea?"

She shrugged. "He didn't tell me much. We were both super busy."

"Did Ryu give you that necklace?"

She rubbed the cross between her fingers and pressed it to her lips. "When he dumped me, I almost threw it away. Then I realized what matters is not Ryu—it's my personal relationship with Jesus." She set the cross back on her chest, touching it to her heart. "How did you know?"

"Katie D has an identical one."

Her eyes grew round and her jaw thrust out. "That worm! I knew it. I knew he was a liar. He said he loved me." She ripped the chain over her neck and slammed it down. "What a miserable slime. He's your friend?"

I grimaced, embarrassed for Ryu. "Kind of. A long time ago. It's complicated."

She stood over me, hands on her hips, looking like a dragon breathing fire. "If he sent you to say he's sorry, tell him to take a flying leap."

I grabbed her hand before she could leave. "Wait," I pleaded.

She ripped her arm away. "Why?"

"Because something happened to him."

"Good. He deserves whatever he gets."

"He's missing. Nobody knows where he went."

"Why are you asking me? He dumped me. Said he was too busy with work. The liar—he was lusting after that Jezebel."

Had I got it wrong—was Katie sleeping with Ryu and not Satoshi? Had Satoshi found out and eliminated his rival? Or had Ryu left to find himself when things with Katie went south? The only person who might have a clue was Grace. "I'm sorry to ask this, but do you know if anything actually happened between Ryu and Katie?"

A sharp intake of breath. She turned away and rubbed her eyes. "Do you think he really loved me?"

Her reaction seemed overly dramatic. Was this bad acting? Had she killed him in revenge? Or was something else going on? Then it hit me. "You're not pregnant, are you?"

She ran to the bathroom. I cleaned up the coffee mess while waiting for her to return. When she finally come out, she made a beeline for the exit. I jumped in front of her just as she reached the employee gate.

"I really need to know what happened between you and Ryu and Katie."

"Pray to God for guidance," she told me. "Then take a flying leap."

She shoved me aside and beeped her badge through the entrance. When I hopped over the gate to follow her, two large men in black jackets rushed over to escort me back out. There was nothing to do now except get away from the half-eaten Apple logo and head home, unsure of what I'd learned.

Chapter 22
The Impossible Sword of Muramasa

Late at night, the roads nearly deserted, the pony pulled off the highway. Headlights cut a hole into the darkness as I navigated up the steep hill, illuminating the signs for one venture capitalist firm after another: Sequoia, Kleiner Perkins, Draper, a16z. From up here the lords of the Sand Hill in their stone and steel office buildings looked down over the fertile valley where startups grew like weeds and watched over their stables of prancing young unicorns being fattened for the IPO. Then the road went dark until the headlights landed on the sign for SLAC National Laboratory in raised black letters on an ugly concrete slab.

I turned into the entranceway and drove to the squat guard shack where a lowered arm blocked the way. The little hut glowed with yellowish light punctuated with flashes of blue and green. While the pony puttered, a window slid open, a guard shoved out his hand. "Badge?" he demanded without even looking at me.

Though he had the buzz-cut of ex-military, tattooed muscles bulging from a starched sleeve, his fingers twitched so badly I hoped he didn't have a gun. My ears perked up when I heard the familiar cry of an animated falcon screeching from inside the shack. Peering over the row of Red Bull cans that lined the window, I saw the Legends of Emperors battle unfolding on a laptop perched on the counter. I was jealous—he'd found the perfect job—getting paid to sit in this deserted place playing video games all night.

I made a show of rummaging through my wallet, checking my pockets, and searching all around the car. "Drat," I finally yelled over the shrieks of an angry kraken. "I left my badge in the office."

"Authorized personnel only," he shouted as he battled the monster with both hands, stunning it with a photon bomb before dispatching it to Niraya with a stab of a sword through the neck.

"You're really good," I said, and I wasn't even lying. Not as good as me, of course, but he'd give me a solid battle.

He craned his neck to glance through the window. "Nice 'Stang," he said, and was nearly killed when a wyvern popped onto the screen breathing fire.

While he was busy fighting the monster with a flame thrower, I yelled over the screeching, "I need to get into the lab." He ignored me, his attention focused on the unfolding battle. "It's an emergency," I pleaded. "I need to get in to help."

When he turned to look at me, he was hit by a plume of flame. The horrible screams of his character catching fire blasted out of the shack. He could only watch as his avatar burned from the head like a candle and melted into a puddle. Then the familiar message filled the screen:

```
Would you like to be reincarnated?
1] to return as a scout,
2] for ninja,
5] for samurai, or return to Level 1 as an
interstellar insect.
```

He glowered at me. "No badge, no entry. No Chinese spies allowed."

I cringed. "I'm a Japanese spy," I said. Buzzcut didn't smile. Why had I thought I'd be able to get in without a badge?

He looked at me again. "You Stanford or DOE?"

When I said I was with SüprDüpr, he held out his arm. "Why didn't you fucking say so? Give me your driver's license."

I placed my license in his twitching hand. He typed my name into the computer. I could only hope Katie never looked at the security logs or I'd have some explaining to do.

He picked up an ancient pushbutton phone next to the computer. "Gotta call Dr. Deauville for authorization."

"Wait!" I couldn't let him call Katie. "She's sleeping. Can't you just let me in?"

"Federal lab. No entrance without proper authorization."

"You could authorize me. Just escort me over there."

His eyes sharpened in suspicion. "Why would I do that?"

Yeah, why would he? "I'll give you a Herod's Deathcrown," I offered. "Would've saved you from that wyvern."

"Got two Herods already. Would have used one if you hadn't distracted me."

"How about an Apple of Njord?"

He looked at my driver's license again. "I'd better call this in."

"Muramasa," I blurted out. My prized possession. "I'll give you my Muramasa."

He stopped, set the phone back on the cradle. "You have a Muramasa?" He looked me over. "Don't fuck with me—there's no such thing as a Muramasa."

A Muramasa was a mythical sword that couldn't be broken and never ran out of power. It also wasn't supposed to exist. Although it couldn't be bought in the in-game store and there was no way to earn one, rumors of its existence persisted. I obtained mine in classic Kobayashi Maru style—when I overheard a group of Legends developers at Starbucks grumbling that management in their infinite stupidity had eliminated the best weapon ever, I hacked into their GitHub account and uncommented the code back in. I created one and only one Muramasa—mine. Just seeing it in my weapons cache gave me confidence. I couldn't give it up, certainly not to this goof; it was my secret superpower.

"Yeah, that's what I thought." Buzzcut started dialing again.

Did I want to find Ryu, or did I want to play games? I handed him my phone to show him the impossible sword in my arsenal. It should have glowed like the Holy Grail in a medieval painting, but it just sat there, another weapon in my cache, only its power set at infinite, its strength set at infinite, its durability set at infinite, marking it as anything other than a regular sword you could buy for a BiteCoin or two.

"My oh my," Buzzcut said, fondling my screen. He looked at me differently now, a gaming god come to earth. "You really do have a Muramasa. And you're giving it to me? Just for letting you in? Must be a Chinese spy." He picked up the phone again.

"Wait," I pleaded. I explained that my friend Ryu who worked here for SüprDüpr was missing.

"Take it to the police."

I grabbed my phone out of his twitchy hands and dialed Mayeda, afraid he wouldn't answer this late. It rang and rang until finally an annoyed cop answered, his voice scratchy with sleep. "Whaddaya want, shrimp? It's two fucking thirty in the morning. No, I don't have any fucking updates on Satoshi. Now can I go back to sleep?"

I was never so relieved to hear that dipshit's voice. I had him confirm my story, cop to gate guard. When he was done, Buzzcut handed me back my phone. "You should've come with a search warrant."

"The cops don't care," I said. "I've got to find out what Ryu was doing here and take them the evidence."

"You should have gotten Dr. Deauville to put you on the list."

"I think she's covering up something."

"Oooh," he said, suddenly excited. "You think she's involved? Wouldn't that be crazy—everyone here is in love with her. Did she kill him, you think? Was it poison or a sword?"

"Good questions, Detective Pikachu. Are you going to help me or not? All you have to do is walk over there with me."

"Nope," he said, folding his arms over his chest. "Not 'til you set me up with that Muramasa you promised."

I parked the car by the side of the road and squeezed into the shack with Buzzcut. Once the impossible sword was transferred into his account, he sat up straight, glowing with pride. I felt two inches shorter, unmasked and alone. I wanted a drink then, but the best he could offer was a Red Bull.

"No, thanks," I said, refusing the can from the cooler. "That shit's really bad for you."

He shrugged. "To each his own." He slammed an entire Bull in one gulp.

"Did you ever see Ryu come or go from the facility?"

"Nah," he said. "I'm on the graveyard shift. Hardly see anyone but the cleaning crew. I wouldn't recognize him anyway. No way to know without checking his badge."

The badge. I pointed at the clunky old Windows computer on the desk. "Do you have a log of everyone coming and going?" When he looked at me like I was stupid, I gave him Ryu's name to check. He searched through the records. "Last entrance was a week ago. Sunday at 10:07 a.m."

That was the morning after he met Satoshi, the day he drove away. "When did he leave?"

Buzzcut leaned towards the screen, his head cocked in confusion. "Well…this is weird. He never signed out."

Something must have happened that morning. Buzzcut checked the incident reports, but there were no alerts that day—no fire or explosion that might have killed Ryu, at least nothing that warranted the security team leaving the safety of their hut.

I asked him to check if Katie was there that day, too. A long list of dates and times scrolled up the screen. He searched the page until he found the entry. She'd checked in at 7:53 a.m. Then he whistled in surprise. "She didn't sign out either. What the fuck's going on around here?"

Buzzcut didn't understand, but I did. The SüprPorter worked, just as Ramesh described. It teleported Katie and Ryu somewhere. Katie was still alive. Ryu was gone, never to be seen again.

While waiting for his replacement to arrive, Buzzcut and I pawed through the entry logs. Ryu had been to the lab twice without checking out; Katie had done it nearly a dozen times. Since she was teleporting regularly, Ramesh had to be wrong about one of the two travelers arriving dead. But then why hadn't it worked for Ryu?

Or had he teleported himself to India or to a beach in the Caribbean? The logs of the teleporter control system would tell me everything I needed to know.

When the second guard arrived clutching a styrofoam cup of coffee and a half-eaten sandwich, he looked at me with raised eyebrows. "Old friend from Iowa," Buzzcut said to explain my presence. "Look what he gave me." He showed Sandwich the Muramasa sword in his arsenal and they ooh'ed and aah'ed over it together.

When they were done palling around, Buzzcut asked his partner, "Okay if I take him with me on my rounds?"

"Yeah, sure," Sandwich mumbled through a mouthful of food, his hands already on the controller, firing up his own game. Buzzcut stepped out of the shack and motioned me to follow.

The moon filtering through the trees lighted the deserted parking lot. We cut between two buildings, following the ellipse on the ground in front of us from Buzzcut's flashlight, arriving at an open quad that was a squishy mess of mud. In the center of the clearing was a small square shack, its wood siding and corrugated aluminum roof resembling a backyard toolshed.

"Is that it?" I'd expected the world's first teleporter to be a science-fiction monstrosity, full of tubes and wires and glowing Tesla coils, not an unlit, windowless shed from Home Depot.

Security cameras hung off the edge of roof, red LEDs blinking through the darkness. There were no markings anywhere on the building, not even a SüprDüpr logo, nothing except a no trespassing sign tacked to the wall. The door, I was surprised to find, was secured with a simple, old-fashioned padlock, probably bought at the same hardware store. We tried every one of the keys on Buzzcut's ring, but none of them opened the lock. I pulled on it and banged on the door with no effect other than scraping my fingers raw. That hurt far less than the mental pain from kicking myself for thinking I could get inside. I'd given up my Muramasa for nothing but a glimpse of the exterior of a garden shed. No wonder Buzzcut had agreed.

"Got a pair of bolt cutters?" I asked, already knowing the answer.

"Nope," Buzzcut replied grinning, and not even the Sword of Muramasa could cut through this simple metal lock. I'd need to find another way to get inside to find out where Ryu and Katie had gone.

Chapter 23
Hair of the Dog

If I could grab the teleporter's log file for the Sunday morning when Ryu disappeared, I'd know exactly where he went. It was unlikely that the teleporter itself was connected to the internet, but Katie must've done the mapping calculations somewhere to load into the system. All I had to do was find it.

Although I had my own login now to the company network, my account was limited to a tight workspace. I didn't have access to anything other than Slack, email, and my own calendar. I spent the remainder of the night trying every trick I knew to break out of the sandbox and into Katie's files, and when those didn't work, I searched for new vulnerabilities on the dark web. But no matter what I did, I kept hitting my head on the same impenetrable firewall. Whoever set up SüprDüpr's security really knew what they were doing.

Hoping for inspiration, I poured a cup of Mu and stared out over the empty streets. But no matter how hard I gazed through the window, no new ideas came to me. Even the trusty Mu only made my head swim.

As the sky began to lighten and the stars faded away, the quiet of the night shattered into the cacophony of early morning—delivery men dumping crates of frozen fish in front of the sushi joints, garbage trucks banging dumpsters in the alley, cars racing down Jackson on emergency caffeine runs. When the sun reflected off the windows of the shopfronts across the street, filling my room with light, it was time to screw the cap back on the bottle of Mu and return my friend to the fridge. From the cabinet, I took out the small tin of matcha to brew a thick cup of green tea. The verdant smell of a lush field of grass spreading through the room meant it was time for my parents' visit.

From the *butsudan* shrine atop the tea cabinet, the bridal pair watched over me from inside the frame of a wedding photo. Kaa-chan was a princess in a red silk kimono embroidered with gold cranes, Tou-san a lord in a black tuxedo with tails that stretched to his feet. The photo was flanked by a matching pair of white urns. I placed a shot of Johnnie Black in front of Tou-san's urn, then prepared a bowl of matcha for Kaa-chan. Two white votive candles flickered their yellow flames, two separate trails of black smoke tangled and fought silently as they curled upwards into the air. I hit the small gong with its wooden rod, the clear hum resonating from this world into the next calling the spirits of my parents to me. Bowing in apology, I begged for their forgiveness and wished them the peace they'd never found in this life, whether together or separate now, and asked them to watch over and protect me.

Next came the ritual cleaning without which Kaa-chan's spirit could never rest. From inside the closet, her five wise vacuums stared out into the room. The workhorse blue canister, its long hose resembling an elephant's trunk, sat beside a squat shopvac that Kaa-chan insisted could only clean outside dirt. Then there was the heavy red upright for hoovering up the rugs. And the fancy, handheld cordless she'd received as a return gift at a funeral, the weirdest swag ever, that she only used to clean the grit out of other vacuums. And then there was her favorite, the matte pink Panasonic, quiet and ultra light, that she'd hand-carried back from Japan and loved, apparently, more than life itself. She ran it over every surface of the house each day though there was never a speck of dust anywhere. Now it sat in the closet like a sad, pink puppy awaiting her return. To use it myself would be sacrilege, so I patted its side and took the blue elephant from the closet.

While Kaa-chan's spirit watched to make sure I dusted every bowl and pot and lacquered caddy inside her tea ceremony cabinet, my mind drifted to Ryu. How far had he been willing to go to please Katie and where could he be now? When I was done with the cabinet, I switched the attachment and ran the vacuum over the couch, sucking up the drips of food and drabs of lint, thinking about the teleporter and dead rats and whatever else was locked in that shack.

Then I snapped on the roller head and ran it over the carpet as I rehashed the critical question: Ramesh claimed that one of the two people teleported would live and the other die, but if so, the odds of Katie surviving a dozen teleportations was too improbable to consider. Either Ramesh was completely wrong, or I was missing something important, some way Katie had solved the dilemma. Then the vacuum head jammed and became as stuck as my mind. I flipped the head over to find the roller wrapped tight with strands of fiber. I thought they were from the carpet, but pulling one off, it turned out to be a black hair. Too long to be mine, it had to be Sumire's. And then my own head unjammed.

"*meet at ryu's apt after work*" I texted Sumire. Then I tucked the vacuum back into the closet and flopped onto my clean couch to sleep.

"Why are we here?" Sumire asked as soon as I hopped off the Bird. "And why aren't you wearing a helmet?"

She was dressed in a Pretty Rhythm t-shirt instead of her usual lawyer clothes. I laughed. "Why aren't you wearing a pink wig?"

She looked down at her shirt—a drawing of three bubble-eyed girls—and grinned. She'd dug up an old manga t-shirt she'd worn back in high school. It only made my stomach churn when it reminded me what I'd promised Mayeda.

"Did you find something?" she asked.

"We'll see," was all I said.

When we entered the apartment again, there was no smell, no sound, no hint of Ryu, only the soft scent of Sumire's chamomile spreading from her wake.

"What are you looking for?" she asked.

Instead of answering, I headed straight to the linen closet to grab the purple Dyson. Kaa-chan, the vacuum connoisseur, called it the glamour doll of vacuums—sleek and expensive, designed to impress rather than for doing real housework. I carried it into the bathroom to dump its canister onto the white tile floor.

"What are you doing?" Sumire screeched as dust billowed into the air. She held her t-shirt over her nose and grabbed the vacuum out of my hands.

I waved the dancing motes from my eyes and coughed the grit out of my mouth. When the dust settled, a gray cone sat on the floor like the sands of time mixed with balls of lint. Slivers of pistachio shells stuck out from the pile along with fibers of white carpet. Sumire gasped when I shoved my hands into the mess and pulled out a strand in triumph.

"What's that?" she asked. I held it close to her glasses. "Hair?"

"Yup," I said, unable to conceal my grin. "Long hair."

"Could be anyone's."

Holding it up to the window, the hair shimmered copper in the light. "Know anyone with red hair?"

"We'd need a DNA test to be sure."

"I'm sure. It's the hair of the dog that bit him."

I tried to hand the strand to Sumire, but she jumped away and let it fall to the ground. "Was she here? With Ryu? We checked the security video. We never saw her come in."

"That's not how she got here."

"Then what? Did Ryu give her a key? We still would've seen her on the video."

There was no way to explain without letting Katie's cats out of the bag. "She teleported here."

"Get serious, Ted. How did she get in?"

"I am serious. That's what Ryu was working on. Nobody is supposed to know."

"Come on, cut the crap."

"It doesn't matter. We can take this to the cops. We've got evidence now—Katie's hair in Ryu's apartment. They can use this to get a search warrant and find out what Katie was up to. All they need to do is get the teleporter logs and we'll know exactly where Ryu went."

Sumire's hands were on her hips, the skeptical lawyer again. "What are the police going to do? Just imagine us in court—'Yes, your honor, this strand of hair is evidence that the suspect teleported into the missing person's apartment.' Come on, Ted, they'll laugh us out the room."

"Okay, forget about the teleporter. Katie was here. We have evidence. Isn't that enough?"

"So what? Katie's his boss. The fact that she was here proves nothing."

She was probably right. But we had to get a search warrant. There was another way—the one I'd been dreading. "Give this to Mayeda," I said. "Get him to push his buddies to investigate."

She looked at me with narrowed eyes. "I don't understand how he can help. I can call Mike and see if he'll meet us, but I already know what he's going to say."

"Not us," I said. "You."

She cocked her head.

"Just you, Bunny," I repeated. "Alone."

"Why do you still hate him so much? That was a long time ago, Ted."

"It was a couple days ago."

"What was?"

"When I talked with him."

"You talked to Mike? Why didn't you tell me? What did he say?"

"He said—" I started. Then stopped. "He said, well…he said he kind of likes you."

"I like him, too."

"And maybe he's not so bad," I choked out. That was the best I could do.

"He seems like a decent guy now, even if I did have to beat him up once."

I couldn't help reminding her, "You broke his nose."

She giggled. "Yeah, well…I warned him. And if he couldn't defend himself from a girl half his size, what kind of cop would he make?"

"The kind that's in love with you."

Her draw dropped. "L-l-love?" she stuttered. "In love with *me*? Mikey? That Mikey?"

I nodded. At least she wasn't jumping up and down with glee. I wanted to tell her to stay away, that she should stick with me. But that would be selfish. And pointless. "He wants to see you. You know, like a date."

I thought she'd be happy, but she only glared at me. "What are you, his pimp?"

"He could help you find Ryu. Better than me. Is that such a bad idea?"

"Really, Ted? Is that what you want—pawn me off on him? Get me out of your hair so you can go back to your stupid video games? Do you really want to get rid of me that bad?"

Despite being heartened by her resistance, it still seemed the best plan. "You could meet him for drinks."

"I don't drink."

"Get an iced tea. Or a shave ice." Anything but a cherry *kakigori* at Shuei-Do. "Just show him the hair and tell him you need a search warrant."

"You want me to use him?"

I was tempted to ask if this was different from how she'd been using me. But Ryu was my friend and I'd volunteered for the job. And that would make her angrier. With her nostrils already flaring as she stared at me, I was afraid she'd smash my nose, or whatever they do in aikido. "Just say you need his help to find your brother."

"That's a bad idea."

"If you want to find Ryu, we need the cops to help us. Just one drink. A cup of tea."

"Noodles," she snapped. "I'll meet him for noodles. And he'd better not get the wrong idea or I'll beat him up again."

I was glad to see Broomhead, the Chinese kid, at the concierge desk of Ryu's building again. He wasn't so glad to see us. He ducked as Sumire made a beeline for his desk, a fierce scowl on her face.

"Can't help you," he said, holding his textbook as a shield.

"We need another look at those security logs."

"I got in trouble last time."

"Get out of my way."

Broomhead knew there's nothing to do but run away when confronted by a furious dragon. Sumire elbowed him aside and took the controls of the security video.

"What time?" she grunted.

Ryu had arrived at SLAC on Sunday at 10:07 a.m. I told her to start searching from 10:15.

"Come on, Ted, we've already checked these tapes. There's nothing here."

"We were looking for Ryu," I reminded her. "Looking for someone arriving."

She insisted we were wasting our time but played the video anyway. Only a few people passed through the front door on Sunday morning. We paused a few times when someone with long hair passed the camera, but all turned out to be false alarms.

"See? Nothing here. Let's go."

I stood dejected as the video kept rolling. Was it possible I was wrong? There was no doubt the hair in Ryu's apartment was Katie's, but it could have been from long ago, left in the vacuum for ages. I hung my head. "I'm sorry."

"No, it's me who's sorry. I had no right to drag you into this. I'll leave you alone so you can climb back into your stupid hole. Sorry for the inconvenience."

I didn't know what to say to Sumire, so I said nothing. I stood there unsure why I felt so dejected. I was only doing what was best for her, and one day she'd realize it and thank me. Or not. Either way, she was right—there was nothing here. I'd been sure Katie and Ryu teleported somewhere that Sunday morning, but if so, it wasn't here.

I was about to give up when a flash of emerald caught my eye. A tall woman in a green sundress popped into view.

"Stop!" I said.

We backed up to watch frame by frame. The woman was toting a TJ's shopping bag. Her head was ducked low, her hair tucked inside a blue and gold baseball cap. A thin silver chain on the back of her bare neck glinted in the light. She looked like any other SJSU student off for a morning stroll. But though we couldn't see her face, there was no mistaking those long legs as they strode past the camera and out to the street.

Chapter 24
Dinner of Champions

Sumire refused my invitation to come back to my apartment, storming off instead. I felt bad but convinced myself it was better this way anyway—I suspected that as soon as I dove into the maps, I'd uncover bad news. I'd rather not have to answer Sumire's questions until I could make sense of it myself.

If I was right, Katie had teleported from SLAC directly into Ryu's apartment. That was how she got in. That meant someone else, presumably Ryu, had teleported the same distance in the opposite direction from SLAC.

Opening MeMaps on my computer and zooming in as far as it would go, I pinned the spot where the teleporter sat in a locked hut on a muddy field at SLAC. I extended a line south from there to Ryu's apartment in San Jose. Without adjusting for the curvature of the earth, it was a little over nineteen miles. Not exactly accurate to the millimeter, but extending the line nineteen miles north of the teleporter, accuracy didn't matter. I gasped in horror at the screen. The opposite spot was in the ocean, five miles off the rocky coast north of Half Moon Bay.

I zoomed in to look for an island or shoal to land on; the closest were the Farallones, more than twenty miles further out. If Katie had sent Ryu into the sea when she'd teleported to his apartment, that was no accident—that was cold-blooded murder.

I closed the blinds and poured myself a Johnnie; I had some heavy thinking to do. The only evidence I had was a strand of Katie's hair in Ryu's apartment and a video showing long legs walking out the lobby of his building. If the police actually wanted to investigate, that might be enough to bring her in for questioning, but it was clear they had no interest in doing anything, not unless I *habeas*'ed a *corpus* or two.

If I could break into Katie's phone, I'd have real proof she'd been there. I dove down into the depths of the deep web to the Password Pirate supersite. It claimed a billion stolen passwords for sale but had none for Katie. Or Higgs. Or Deauville. Though they did have a few of my own. How embarrassing. I wasted the next hour updating every one of my passwords.

As I kept working, trying anything I could, my stomach started growling. It was too late to pick up a bento now. Balled up in frustration, my mind revving over the red line, I was in no mood for sitting next to a gaggle of gobs inside a noisy restaurant. My freezer, though, was empty except for a bag of blueberries and a box of petrified waffles. The refrigerator wasn't much better. Rooting through the cabinets, I discovered an unopened jar of Soylent I'd bought long ago.

After mixing the chalky powder into a glass of water; it tasted exactly like it looked—gritty and dusty—with a strange aftertaste of asparagus and grapefruit that made me want to gag. As I was dumping the jar into the trash, an idea hit me. I dropped a banana into the blender with three scoops of Soylent, then tossed in the frozen blueberries, filled it with ice, and topped it up with Mu. The whirring blades crunched the concoction to a rancid blue. When I opened the top, the smell of banana toffee wafted through the room. It tasted like a cross between nigori sake and a cheap chu-hi cocktail. Not great, but better than waiting ninety minutes for Postmates to deliver the wrong order.

Dinner done, I returned to the desk, but after staring at the screen for another hour, I ran out of things to try. I retreated to the couch, buried my head in my arms, and screamed long and loud. When I was done, the room fell silent except for a neighbor banging on the wall to be quiet. I realized I'd been avoiding the inevitable. I checked the clock—it was too late to call Mayeda. But I called anyway.

"Hiya, pal," he said, surprisingly friendly. "Can't believe you actually came through."

My heart sank. Sumire must have given up on me and set up a date with Mayeda. When I heard voices shouting behind him, I wanted to hang up. I thought he was with his buddies at the police station until the clatter of dishes erupted over the line. A loud shout of Cheers! in the background. No cheer for me while he was out celebrating.

"Hey, Mayeda," I yelled into the phone. "I need to talk to you tonight. In private. It's urgent. Can you meet me somewhere quiet?"

"Off duty now, pal. How about you come by tomorrow?"

"It's about Sumire," I said, a reminder he owed me big time.

"I'm *busy*, shrimp, if you catch my drift."

I was ready to give up when I heard a woman's voice barely audible over the din. "Is that Ted?" The voice was unmistakable. The voice I missed. The voice sitting next to a cop late at night, drinking together in a loud place.

"Put him on speakerphone," she demanded. The voice that once punched a big Hawaiian kid to protect me.

"Let me just—"

"Give me the phone, Mike." The voice that accepted no dissent from anyone, cops and suitors included.

147

"Ted, is that you?" Sumire asked, the only voice I wanted to hear. "Please don't stalk me. Mikey and I are just having noodles. It's fine. I'm sorry I yelled at you earlier."

"I think I know what happened to Ryu."

Shouts in the background, loud cheering from a TV. "What?" Sumire yelled back, her voice an octave higher.

"Where are you?"

"Yukiko's."

It took me a moment to realize they were two blocks away, eating ramen at the Dandy Lion.

When I poked my head through the narrow doorway, the air heavy with steam and garlic, Yukiko rushed over to block my way in. "Sorry, Ted, full tonight."

I followed her panicked eyes to a table in the back corner. She must have thought I was here to break up Sumire's date. Or worse. "Bring us a bottle of Dassai," I said. The smell of food—real food—made me hungry. "And a bowl of miso ramen," I ordered. "Hold the Soylent."

"Ted, no," she pleaded, grabbing my arm. I squeezed past and headed for their table.

Sumire's back was to me, her hair clipped in a beaded beret. The manga t-shirt she'd worn earlier was replaced with a lacy midi dress, thin straps highlighting her aikido-toned shoulders. A silk scarf around her neck added a dash of color. For someone reluctant to meet the cop for coffee, she sure had dressed up for noodles. Mayeda wore a too-skinny sports jacket, his hair freshly trimmed and oiled. I felt guilty for intruding until Sumire turned to look at me, her smile making me glad I came.

"What are you doing here?" he grunted when he saw me.

I grabbed a chair from another table to sit beside Sumire. "Sorry for the interruption, pal," I said to Mayeda, probably too much of a smirk on my face. I was sure he would have punched me if Sumire wasn't there. All he could do was slouch in his chair and glare at me.

"You've been drinking," Sumire declared, a flash of anger.

I would have turned red if my face wasn't already flushed from the alcohol. "Just a Soylent smoothie," I tried. Unfortunately, Yukiko picked that moment to arrive with the bottle of Dassai. Her eyes darted between us as she set three cups on the table.

"Take it away," Sumire ordered. "Ted doesn't need it."

"I could use some," Mayeda said, holding out his cup in exactly the wrong move.

"Mikey doesn't need it, either." She grabbed the cup out of his hand and handed it to Yukiko. "Could you bring a pot of mugicha?" Her voice was soft and sweet, like a coating of honey over steel rebar.

I caught Mayeda's eyes. He looked defeated, worse than getting his nose broken again. He thought I was taking away his girl, and maybe I was, but we still needed his help. I stuttered and struggled to explain what I suspected without mentioning teleportation. I had to stop every few seconds whenever a cheer erupted for a fresh *kanpai*. I pointed at the door. Mayeda thought I was telling him to go home. I pleaded with him to join us. He shook his head until Sumire asked him to come with us.

We headed up 5th Street in the chilly night, a thin moon lighting the way. Sumire walked beside me, her sandals clip-clopping up the sidewalk, matching me step for step. When we reached the red-tiled roof of the Betsuin temple, we found the heavy door locked. We retreated to the garden in the back where we leaned against the rail of the humped bridge over a Zen river of smooth rocks. A cold wind swirled around us, scattering leaves across the ground. I stood facing Mayeda, Sumire beside me, hidden in the length of his shadow.

Sumire took a baggie from her purse and handed it to Mayeda.

"What's this?" he asked, puzzled, holding it up to the spotlight. Sumire explained it was Katie's hair that we'd found in Ryu's apartment.

Mayeda handed it back to Sumire. "So?"

"She was there," she insisted. "She was in his apartment. After he was gone. She took evidence with her. We found her on the security tapes."

He shrugged. "What do you want from me?"

"Interrogate Dr. Deauville," she demanded.

Mayeda raised his arms in surrender. "I told you, I'm a beat cop, not a detective. I don't get to interrogate anyone."

"All we need is a search warrant for her phone and the company's computers," I said.

He turned to me, angry. "Investigating Katie like a common criminal? Raiding SüprDüpr like they're drug dealers? I guarantee you, shrimp, that's not gonna happen."

Mayeda and I stood staring at each other while Sumire's eyes blazed with anger.

"Come on, pal," I pleaded. "All we need to find Ryu is Katie's GPS coordinates. Or a copy of a log file on a machine in Palo Alto. We just need your buddies to get a search warrant. Can you do us this one favor?"

"Like the favor you did for me?"

I bowed my head. "I'm sorry for intruding," I said. "I really am. I didn't intend to break up your date. I just want to find Ryu. All I'm asking is your help to get a search warrant so we can find her brother."

"Please, Mikey," Sumire begged.

Mayeda's expression softened. "I would if I could, Sue Mary, but there's nothing I can do. Not when Katie has friends around town."

"Jesus," I exclaimed.

"Hey, pal, don't take the chief's name in vain. He's doing a good job. And she's helping. A hundred million dollars to get the homeless off the street, beautify the parks, increase the SAT scores? You think Jesus is gonna bring her in and give her the third degree? Uh-uh. And if you think it's just Jesus—think again. She's got friends all over town who wouldn't take kindly to harassing an important, upstanding citizen."

I finally understood why Katie had donated such a large sum to the city's renovation. It wasn't a real estate scam, it wasn't about charity or even finding jobs for the city's poorest residents. It was buying friends. In their eyes, all the evidence in the world would add up to less than a hundred million dollars.

I gave up begging and screamed at Mayeda about the stupidity of the police protecting Katie. Sumire swatted my arm. "It's not Mikey's fault," she said.

"It is," I shouted into the night. "He could do something. Anything. Throw her in with all the homeless people they drag away from the park. Plant some drugs on her. Just get a search warrant and we'll find out who Katie dropped in the drink off Half Moon Bay. Might be Ryu."

"What!" Sumire yelled.

I put my hand on her shoulders to calm her, but she shoved me away. I told her to wait, I'd explain in a minute, and turned back to Mayeda. "I know where to find a body. I know the exact coordinates. Accurate to the millimeter."

He bellied up to me, chashu pork on his breath. "Look, pal, I'd love to help. But I told you, there's nothing I can do. Half Moon Bay—out of our jurisdiction. If you know where a body is, go find it yourself. If you had a body, there'd be an investigation, then maybe some evidence of a crime. If you can prove she dumped the body, I don't care how much money she gave the city, nothing's going to protect her."

"He's right," Sumire said. "Let's go." She grabbed my arm to pull me away. "Come on, Ted, I'm getting cold."

"What are we supposed to do?" I asked Mayeda. "Rent scuba gear and go hunting on the sea floor?"

"Nah," he said, ignoring my sarcasm. "Currents there are rough. You'll end up dead yourself. If I was you, shrimp, I'd start with the coroner's office. Come to think of it, I might've heard something about a John Doe or two washing up on the beach around there."

Sumire gasped. I thanked Mayeda.

"Yeah, well, thanks for nothing, pal." He turned to Sumire and took her small hand in his. "It started as a nice evening, Sue Mary," he said. He pecked her cheek, buttoned his too-tight jacket and sulked off into the darkness.

Watching him go, I felt a twinge of guilt. I'd gotten his hopes up before smashing them against the rocks of the Zen river.

"You can be a real jerk," she said when we were alone.

I nodded. "I'm sorry."

"At least you mean well. Even if you are kind of clueless." She sniffled. "Now tell me everything you know."

I placed my hands on her bare shoulders and explained what I suspected.

"Ryu?" she asked, eyes tearing up. "You think she killed him? Just like that? With teleportation? That doesn't make any sense."

"It's the only thing that adds up."

"That seems so crazy."

A cold breeze rustled through the maple trees, causing Sumire to shiver. I pulled her close against me. She leaned her head on my shoulder. "Can she really be that evil?"

A good question I had no answer to. We stood swaying in silence.

She sniffled, wiping away a tear. "How do you know it was Ryu?" she asked. "Maybe it wasn't him. Maybe she teleported him to Russia and he just needs to find his way back?"

"It's possible," I answered.

"Then what do we do?"

As much as I hated admitting it, Mayeda had a good idea. The next stop had to be the coroner for Half Moon Bay, especially if a body or two had washed up recently.

We stood there in the cold holding each other. "Thank you for caring about Ryu," she whispered.

"Not just Ryu," I said so quietly I wasn't sure if she heard. She said nothing as I ran a hand through her hair.

Another cold gust caused her to shiver again. "We should go."

"It's late," I agreed.

But neither of us moved. We stayed swaying in the warmth of each other's arms atop the vermillion bridge.

My lips reached out to touch hers. She turned her head away. "Don't ruin everything, Ted." She buried her cheek against my shoulder, her body tight against mine.

Instead, I kissed the tip of her ear, sticking out through her hair.

We continued holding each other while the cicadas chirped their own lonely tunes and the wind swirled dead leaves onto the banks of the Zen river.

Chapter 25
Cold Hands of the Coroner

"I'm looking for my brother," Sumire said to the receptionist of the San Mateo County Coroner's Office when we arrived as soon as they opened the next morning.

The sad-looking girl behind the counter was dressed in a dull blue blouse. "I'm so sorry," Bluegirl whispered, barely able to look up from her desk. "Did someone call you?" Bouncy doo-wop music streamed from a tinny speaker atop the credenza behind her.

"He's missing," Sumire said.

"We think he drowned off the coast here," I added. I pulled up a map and zoomed in on a spot between Montara and Miramar, two towns on Route 1 along the coast I'd never heard of. "Have any bodies been found in that area in the past couple of weeks?"

"Oh yes," Bluegirl said, red eyes perking up. "We had a wash-up."

Sumire gasped. Bluegirl shuffled through a door to the back, then a minute later, waved us over.

I held Sumire's hand, cold with sweat, as Bluegirl led us into a room that resembled a doctor's office. A wall of shelves was filled with stacks of folders in disorganized piles. I was disappointed there were no glass specimen jars, no row of brains pickled in formaldehyde. The man behind the desk stood up to greet us. Wearing a plaid shirt and sporting a close-cropped beard, he looked more like a coder than a coroner. A white lab coat hung from a hook on the door, not a speck of blood on it.

"Well, hello there," he said to Sumire sounding like a friendly pediatrician. I wouldn't have been surprised if he'd handed her a lollypop. Bluegirl glared at him. He rubbed the sad girl's shoulders as he escorted her from the room, whispering something in her ear and patting her behind before shutting the door. He offered a chair to Sumire, ignoring me, and sat across the desk to face her. "I understand you're here about a John Doe?"

Sumire showed him a photo of Ryu.

"I don't know how to put this, Miss Yamashita." He placed his manicured hands atop hers, his eyes devouring her. "After a few days in the water, a corpse can become difficult to recognize. Besides the putrefaction, we have a considerable population of sharks in this area. Did he have any distinguishing features we can use for identification?"

She pulled her hands away from the coroner and pointed at her chin. "Ryu had a scar on his cheek. The bone was broken here."

The coroner frowned. "I don't think that's going to help in this case. Is there anything else? If not, would you be able to obtain a copy of his dental records?"

Sumire patted her arm. "He had a tattoo of a cross."

"When was that?" I asked. That left me as the only man in town who didn't have at least one tattoo. I envied Ryu that he had something to believe in enough to deface his body, even if it was nonsense. The lecherous coroner undoubtedly had a tattoo of the hypocritical oath on his ass to impress bereaved women. I once thought of etching a bottle of Johnny on one arm, a bowl of tea on the other, but decided I didn't need yet another reminder of Kaa-chan or free advertising for a billion-dollar brand.

The coroner stood and paced around the room, stopping behind Sumire. "I don't know how to ask this," he said, placing a hand on her shoulder. "Did your brother have any trouble with drugs?"

Sumire shook her head as she squirmed away from his fingers.

"Did he sleep on the street?" he asked, his hand grazing her hair. "Have a history of schizophrenia? Mental illness?"

I jumped up and pushed myself in front of the coroner. "Her brother was fine."

"Then I'm sorry, I can't help you." He retreated to dig through the stack of folders on the shelf and opened one. "The John Doe that washed up near Pillar Point had traces of fentanyl and methamphetamines in his bloodstream. We also found evidence of diabetes and bacterial infection. That's a strong indicator of long-term homelessness. The police assume he's from one of the transient encampments along the highway." He snapped the folder shut and dropped it back atop the pile. "Unfortunately, we have no other way to ID the body, so we're stuck with him taking up space here forever. If there's any chance the John Doe could be your brother, please take a look." His eyes roamed over Sumire again, a ghoulish grin exposing sharp teeth. "I have to warn you, though, the cadaver is pretty badly decomposed."

"No thanks," Sumire said. "I'm sure that's not Ryu."

The coroner looked at me for the first time. "How about you, kid?"

The thought of looking at a pickled corpse made my stomach churn, but the coroner's stupid grin, daring me in front of Sumire, left me no choice. "Sure," I said. "Let's take a look. Just in case."

Exiting the office, the coroner followed behind us, a hand on the small of Sumire's back. She stopped, eyes narrowed behind her glasses, and elbowed him in the gut. He grunted, doubled over, clutching his chest as we scurried out of the room.

In the hallway, an intern led us to the chiller in the back. The room was frigid. He pulled open a stainless-steel drawer, a puff of air escaping. Inside was a body bag. He unzipped the front to expose a body badly mangled, the face half eaten away. He was short. And old. Sumire closed her eyes in relief—it wasn't Ryu.

Despite the mottled, sloughing skin streaked with mud, I recognized the narrow eyes and stringy, gray hair, and most of all, the shreds of an army jacket—Azaz. He must have gotten that ride to the beach he'd wanted, but that's as far as he'd gotten. Unless…after the police had taken Azaz away, had he been brought to the teleporter to be zapped to the bottom of the sea?

Chapter 26
Downtown Resurrection

When we arrived at St. Jimmy's, looking for anyone who knew Azaz, we were shocked to discover the park clean. The tents of all the homeless people had been swept away overnight, the two blocks once again a leafy oasis of grass and trees. Gardeners were busy sprucing up the park with rows of spruce saplings; wooden benches sported a coat of shiny green paint. The only smell of weed was the clover and dandelions sprouting from the freshly-laid grass. A large billboard in the middle of the park declared the downtown revitalization in progress, thanks to Mayor Gadh and the City Council and the largesse of SüprDüpr and BiteCoin Ventures.

I thought the homeless people must have been shooed away onto nearby streets. But walking around, we found the entire neighborhood clean, the sidewalks spotless, all the trash and tents and shopping carts cleared away. Kaa-chan would have been ecstatic. The platoon of blueboys patrolling the park were reduced to sipping Frappuccinos.

I spotted the two cops who'd taken Azaz away, Doughboy and the Viking, standing in front of Trinity Cathedral. As we approached, the hulking Viking leered at Sumire, then elbowed his rotund partner. "Hey, isn't that the lawyer chick that's got Mikey in a lather?"

"Shut up," I said. "Her name is Sumire, and she's with me."

I caught Sumire's surprise as she pulled my arm to leave.

"Yeah, Sue Mary," the Viking sneered. "That's Mikey's girl for sure." He grabbed her, smothering her in his muscles, while Doughboy shot a photo. "Radio in a complaint for lewd public conduct," the Viking told his partner. "Get Mikey dispatched here."

Doughboy chuckled. "Looks more like child molestation to me."

"Get off her," I yelled. Sumire kicked his shin to escape from his grasp.

"Ooh, a feisty one," he snickered. "Ditch Mikey, babe. You need a real man like me."

I planted myself in front of the Viking, his abs straining against the starched fabric of his uniform, and stared up into the cave-like darkness of his nostrils.

"Relax, twerp," he said, shoving me backwards as if I weighed nothing. "We're just having a little fun."

Sumire grabbed my arm before I did something stupid. "Let's go," she ordered, pulling me away.

But I'd come here for a reason and I wasn't leaving. I planted my feet and stood to face the two cops. "Where are all the people who were living here?"

"Those fucking tents? The city finally grew a pair and kicked 'em out. They're gone now and we're not letting them back."

"Gone where?" I asked. "That guy you hauled away a few days ago turned up dead in Half Moon Bay. Any idea what happened to him?"

"None at all," the Viking said. "Now get lost, twerp, we're busy here." He reached out a hand for Sumire. "But the cutie can stay. I could use a feisty little lawyer."

"Let's go, Ted," she said, backing away. "Now." This time I didn't argue.

I followed Sumire until she stopped under the shade of a crepe myrtle. Smooth branches stretched their canopy overhead, the ground carpeted in coral pink petals. She brushed the flowers off a wooden bench in front of the tree and sat, patting the slats for me to join her.

"What are we doing?" I asked.

"Just watch," she said, a finger over her lips. "And listen."

Across from us, the white marble of the Corinthian gleamed in the sunshine, cops standing guard in front. Behind us, the light rail screeched to a stop, a bell clanging as it disgorged its passengers. In the distance, sirens screamed. Traffic rolled past, an occasional honk. From the corner where the old apartment building was being converted into SüprDüpr's homeless shelter came the humming of activity—indistinct voices, an occasional shout, the movement of vehicles, but we couldn't see anything over the ten-foot-high barrier in front. On the other side of 3rd Street, a rhythmic metal banging rang out, people shouting to each other in Spanish. The engine of a flatbed truck groaned as it backed through a gate beside the arm of a crane sticking up over the barricade.

The breeze set the branches of the crepe myrtle swaying, petals the size of pennies raining over us. One landed on Sumire's head where it glimmered against the blackness of her hair. I picked it off, my fingers brushing the side of her ear.

"Stop it," she said, slapping my hand away. She brushed the flowers out of her hair, cute ears sticking out.

A young couple walked past holding hands, a squat bulldog waddling behind, sniffing everything in its path. The dog stopped to poke its head in my lap. While I squirmed away, Sumire reached over to scratch its ears.

"Come on, Mack," the woman said, exchanging a friendly glance with Sumire.

Sumire turned to me. "We should get a dog," she declared.

"Sure," I said without much enthusiasm. But what was this *we* and where did I fit in with this dog?

Sumire pointed down the street at the red brick tower, the only high-rise on the square, the building where SüprDüpr had its secure office that I'd visited only once. "Let's go up there."

I thought she was taking me to confront Katie inside the MeWork on the fourth floor. In the elevator, my heart beat hard, my palms turned sweaty, but Sumire pressed the button for the top floor. I followed her down the corridor, past doctors' and lawyers' and accountants' offices, until we reached a dentist at the end of the hall.

The lobby was filled with white plastic chairs and soft, insipid music. Sumire poked her head through the reception window and asked, "Would you mind if I took a photo of the park from up here?"

The receptionist led us into an unoccupied torture chamber while gushing about the sudden revitalization. She handed us each a free toothbrush and floss before shutting the door behind her.

We stepped around the chair of horrors to a wide window of thick glass. Below us was the verdant park, trees raising their limbs up towards us. Down the street, we could see the shelter under construction behind the barricade, metal scaffolding already being erected, its parking lot a beehive of activity. Cars and vans flowed through a driveway in the back guarded by a covey of cops. More cops were pulling homeless people out of police vans and marching them to a row of white canopies. There a crew was sorting them, sending some into the shelter and the rest to the old armory next door. Standing in the middle of this organized chaos directing operations was the old woman I recognized from police headquarters—Doom Lady—the same woman who'd warned me about losing my nose if I didn't stop poking around the encampments.

Across the street at a separate construction site, a crane reached onto the flatbed of the truck we'd seen backing in, picking up a pallet of metal tubes that glinted in the sun. The crane lifted the pallet while workmen in blue shirts and orange vests guided it through the air and set it down on the ground.

"Scaffolding?" Sumire asked.

I shook my head. The pipes were too big for construction.

"An outdoor prison?"

"Cyclotron tubing." I was in the middle of showing Sumire the teleporter ring when the door squeaked open and the receptionist peeked inside.

"Sorry, guys, we need the room. So unless you want your teeth cleaned..." She pointed at the chair of horrors. I escaped out to the hallway where I waited for Sumire to finish thanking the woman.

Back on the street, we walked past the Corinthian to the corner of St. James where the flatbed truck was maneuvering out through the gate again. Sumire and I looked at each other when we saw the name on the door—Clifton Circus Supply.

Sumire laughed. "Is that where you buy your cyclotron tubing?"

I hurried over to a trio of workers getting ready to leave in a beat-up pick-up truck. "What are you building?" I hollered over the rhythmic clanging.

"*Jaula*," one yelled back.

"Cage," a second translated for me.

"A big fucking cage," the driver said from the other side.

Sumire was right. An outdoor prison. "For all the homeless people?" Was Katie planning to keep them outdoors in a giant metal cage until she needed them for teleportation? That was even crueler than I'd imagined.

The three glanced at each other and burst out laughing. "For *elefantes*," the first said, requiring no translation.

"Two elephants," the driver added, holding his hands far apart. "Two really big fucking elephants."

Chapter 27
The Lies of a Pizza Pie

My stomach in knots, I slid in beside Katie, our knees barely inches apart in the absurd little phone booth in the back of the MeWork office. The cross—Ryu's cross—was dangling from her neck, its rubies glowing. When she turned her head, her hair swiped my face—the same hair we found in Ryu's apartment.

"Show me how the mapping works," Katie demanded, a fog of onions around her.

When she'd ordered me to come to the office today to demonstrate my software, I knew this could be my last chance to find out what was going on. Once the mapping was integrated into the system, she might not need me anymore.

Despite my hesitation to complete the project, I'd worked through the night until I typed the final `return(void)`. But when I'd tested the system in the morning with photos I'd scraped off MeMaps, I noticed something that made me wonder how the teleporter could work at all.

I typed a command to start the software running. A map popped up to set the spot for the teleportation origin. When I asked Katie where it was, she pointed down the street. "The first SüprPorter is inside the Corinthian. I thought you knew that."

I knew the teleporter was inside the Corinthian, but not where inside. To calculate the destination to the millimeter, the starting point had to be equally precise. I zoomed the map as far as it would go. "Where exactly?"

Katie tapped the screen with a painted nail. "Here," she said. "In the basement."

With the Corinthian built on raised ground, the basement was at street level rather than hidden underground. Not an obvious place to fill with industrial machinery. The basement had been a senior fitness center until a week ago when SüprDüpr took over the building. More importantly, Katie had promised the basement would be reserved for something far more important than a teleporter. "You said we were putting a Gianni's there."

Katie shrugged as if that were unimportant, as if her promises weren't meant to be believed. "We had to make compromises," was all she offered, not even an apology.

A Gianni's in the basement was always too good to be true, but she'd lied to my face from the start, smiling all the while. I wondered what else she'd lied about.

"Show me what happens next," she said. I asked for the destination. "Satoshi's place. I promised to demonstrate the teleporter to him. It seems you know where he lives."

Eventually, we'd have millions of people sharing their photo archives with us. But for now, I only had my own photos and whatever I could scrape off MeMaps. There weren't any photos of Satoshi's palace online, but I'd taken a selfie in front of the tea house when I'd gone to visit him. I added the photo, setting the destination to the center of the tatami mat above his secret passage. "How's that?"

Katie was thrilled. When I set the software running, it pinned the exact location inside the tea house and calculated its opposite location—an empty culvert beside Calaveras Creek, deep in the Diablo mountains. I told Katie we couldn't identify the exact spot until we had photos of the area.

"Oh, I have some," she said, surprising me. She showed me an image of a wooded hillside beside a small, meandering stream. "I sent our Chief Location Officer to scout the area last week."

When I suggested she install my app on her phone to try the software herself, she eyed me skeptically. "What about security?"

The public blockchain that selected the photos was connected to dedicated cloud servers that did the complex number crunching. The server then passed the map coordinates to the teleporter over a VPN. "Bank-level security," I said. "Two-factor authentication so only you can log into the teleporter."

Katie declined to connect her own phone, slacking me the photos and ordering me to add them myself. Once they were indexed, I set the software running. It identified the landing spot, accurate to the millimeter, on a small patch of grass at the edge of a wooded hill.

Katie clapped her hands. "This is magnificent, Ted, exactly what we need. I'm so glad I convinced you to join us. Truly fantastic work. And in such a short amount of time. I'm doubling the amount of your stock options—what do you think of that?"

A beautiful woman gushing over my genius while promising to make me rich was a dream I never wanted to end. But I still didn't understand how the teleporter could work, even with my magnificent software.

"Well…there might be a tiny problem."

She pulled back, suddenly suspicious. "What kind of problem?"

No matter how awful the traffic on the 280, I didn't expect many customers to come to the Corinthian just to be teleported across the Valley. The value of a teleporter was zapping cross-country for a lunch meeting and returning in time for dinner.

I opened a map of Boston and zoomed into the MIT campus, dropping in an old selfie on the steps of the Great Dome. When I pinned the spot in front of my feet, the opposite location popped up on the map. It was in the middle of a wide expanse of Pacific Ocean. No land, no islands, only a curved grid over empty blue. For a trip from San Jose to Boston, I showed her, the opposite location was in the middle of the sea, three hundred miles southwest of Waikiki.

"So?" was all Katie said, not the gasp I'd made when I'd noticed the problem testing the system this morning.

"There's nothing here but water." I zoomed out and out and out until a few atolls appeared, pinpricks scattered over the blankness. "Boston, New York, Washington—all the places people want to go—the opposite spots are in the ocean. There's nowhere for anyone to land." I ignored the cold stare as I asked, "How can the teleporter possibly work?" I was sure that's what had happened to Azaz.

"Ships," she said through clenched jaw. "We're leasing a fleet of ships for people to land on."

"Ships?" I stammered. Ships would work. I hadn't thought of that. I bowed my head, feeling stupider than I'd ever felt before. I wished I could teleport myself right now onto a ship in the middle of the ocean.

"I've spent my entire life working on this, Hara. Do you understand?" I could only nod. "Do you think I wouldn't have noticed something so fucking obvious?"

"No," I mumbled. "Probably not."

"Then stick to your own fucking job and don't ever question me again."

Even as I apologized, I wondered: if ships were so important, why hadn't she mentioned them before? Ships would solve the problem, that was true, but was that really her plan? They'd take days to get into position and she'd said the military had only minutes. A fleet of ships to cover all the world's oceans would be outrageously expensive. It was a good story, though. If I didn't know better, I might have even believed her. But someone who would lie about a pizza pie would lie about anything.

"Homeless people are washing up on the shore," I said quietly. "What happened—did they miss the boat?"

She snapped her head, hair whipping my face. "What did you say?" Her face turned bright red, nearly matching her hair.

"A body was found on the beach near Half Moon Bay," I stated, my heart racing. "A homeless man. Named Azaz. I knew him—he was a vet. He lived out there in the park."

She stared at me, eyes aglow with anger. "Then everyone should be thankful we're building shelters to get the vagrants the help they need."

"When you teleported yourself into Ryu's apartment, you didn't teleport Azaz into the water?"

She slammed her laptop shut. "I don't know what you're talking about," she said, and stood to leave. "It's time to test your software on the actual teleporter. I'll prove it's perfectly safe. Come to SLAC tomorrow to hook it up to the prototype," she ordered. "Be there at 11 a.m."

As she strode away through the buzzing door, I closed my eyes to hold back the panic. Ryu had met her at the prototype. He'd never returned. Did she really expect me to follow in his missing footsteps?

Chapter 28
Backdoor Through the Front Door

My first thought was to delete my software and get the hell out of town, head back to Boston or slip away to Cancun. On second thought, I agreed with my first thought. I could relax on the beach with a margarita in hand, leaving Katie in the lurch without the software to run the teleporter. That would be the safe thing to do. The smart choice, too. But my third thought was that I'd be running away. Again. And it wouldn't help find Ryu. I'd disappoint Sumire, and worse, I'd disappoint myself. My fourth thought was that now that I'd shown Katie how the software worked, she could get Satoshi's team of blockchain developers to build it without me. At worst, it would cause a few weeks' delay. When the margaritas ran dry, there would be nothing but the deep blue sea in front of me, filling up with the bodies of all the sad people that lived at St. James Park.

I called Sumire and told her everything despite the NDA; or nearly everything—I didn't want to alarm her. But she was alarmed anyway. She ordered me to quit the company and stop searching for Ryu. She forbade me from even thinking of driving up to SLAC in the morning. "Please, Ted, promise you won't go. I'd never forgive myself if something happened to you," she said. "And I'd never forgive you, either."

I turned off the lights, closed the blinds, and sipped at a Yamazaki until an idea pinged into my head. It was simple. With my mapping calculations running on the MeCan cloud connected to the SüprPorter control system, I'd have an easy way to hack in. Then I could grab the log file off the teleporter and see where it had zapped Ryu. All I had to do was add a secret backdoor into the teleporter controller. There was only one problem: to add the software to the teleporter and connect it to the cloud, I'd have to go to SLAC tomorrow.

The thought was terrifying. I poured another Yamazaki to give me confidence, then another to give me courage, and a last one for my nerves. This was my best chance to find out what happened to Ryu, the Yamazaki urged, the only way to stop Katie.

I spent the rest of the night hiding a secret login deep in the software where nobody would ever find it. When I was done, it was 4:30 a.m. and my head was throbbing. I texted Sumire: "*have 2 go 2 teleporter tmrw. if i don't come back pls forgive me. teddybear.*" Then I went to sleep. Only to be awoken before 8 a.m. by Sumire banging on my door.

As the pony galloped up the Valley, the industrial suburbia faded to dusty trees and scrub, the mountains of Mountain View hidden behind tall pines. The lush green lawns of Los Altos slid past as the traffic thinned, until I exited the highway to climb the Sand Hill again. The big venture capital firms filled row after row of low-slung buildings on the left. Even bigger venture capital firms were a wall of money on the right. Then I reached the concrete slab that marked the entrance to SLAC.

I was hoping to find the game-playing guard, Buzzcut, at the gatehouse—he still owed me change on the payment of the Muramasa—but he only worked the nightshift. The guard there now looked past retirement age. I was sure he had no interest in Muramasa swords and was too busy processing the line of cars at the entrance to play games. I tried to think of ways to sneak in, but this time it was easy— my name was on the visitors' list. "You're over at the SüprDüpr shed." He handed me a guest badge and pointed to the parking lot. "Hey, love your 'Stang."

I revved the engine in appreciation and squealed the tires as I pulled onto the loop around the facility. "You okay?" I said to the lump of blankets stretched across the back seat.

"It stinks of oil," came the muffled voice.

"At least it's not onions," I joked.

Instead of a titter of amusement, I heard only a faint grunt of annoyance as the blankets slid to the floor. Sumire's tousled hair looked back at me through the rear-view mirror. She looked nervous, more nervous than me, but the set of her jaw made it clear she was angry, too.

I left Sumire by the car in the visitors' lot and slipped past the brick buildings to reach the shed. Red LEDs of the security cameras hanging from the roof eaves blinked their warnings. But the padlock that had kept me out last time was gone.

Even before I had a chance to knock, the hinges squeaked as the door swung open. Katie stood in the doorway, rays of the sun striking her hair and turning into a ball of flame. The silver cross hung around her neck, rubies sparkling. A white cat dashed out through her legs, rushing across the field.

"Schrödinger," she called, whistling at the cat. "Get back here now!" But it kept running until it hid out of sight. "Oh, well," she sighed. "He'll come back when he's hungry." She pointed into the darkness behind her. "Come on in."

I hesitated, curiosity fighting against caution. "Let's get cracking, Hara," Katie said. "We don't have time to waste."

Even from the doorway, the stink of onions was overwhelming. It almost covered the odor of unwashed flesh of a homeless encampment. Had Katie brought Azaz here to use in the teleporter herself? It was hard to imagine her driving him in her red Porsche convertible, the passenger seat reserved for her dog. That must have been Ryu's job, the reason he'd been trolling the park. Until he'd realized the unsheltered people he was bringing here weren't coming home.

I was startled by angry barking as the pint-sized dog rushed at me. "Oh, Higgsy, it's just Hara." Katie swooped him up in her arms and thrust him at my face. He snarled, saliva glistening from crooked teeth as he clawed the air in front of me. When I stepped back, Katie laughed and pulled the dog to her face, rubbing his wet nose with her perfect one. "Let's get to work," she said, leading me into the room.

In the back were two steel chambers that resembled submarine hulls. They had heavy doors and were covered in a mesh of fine wire. Three-inch-thick cables snaked across the concrete floor. From the corner I heard a strange squealing. I looked over to see a row of cages filled with white rats. Each one had a number marked on its side.

Against the wall was a rack of servers, LEDs winking green and amber. Katie logged onto one of the computers, shielding her password with her body before handing me the keyboard. She watched every keystroke I made while I installed the module to connect the teleporter to the MeCan cloud servers crunching the map coordinates. As I was working, she reached up to a shelf of cleaning materials and grabbed a brown glass bottle.

To Katie's annoyance, I hummed as I worked, but it helped keep me calm. "Done," I said a few minutes later. The backdoor inside the software module was awaiting my secret command.

Katie opened the heavy, stainless-steel door of the chamber. "Ready to try out the teleporter?" She motioned for me to crawl inside.

I shook my head. There was no way I was getting in. My work was done—my software was running. Now that I could break into the teleporter using the backdoor from the safety of my couch, it was time to get the hell out through the front door.

Whistling loudly, I backed up towards the exit. I saw Katie's arm move, even caught a pungent whiff, but didn't have time to duck before the fluid splashed my face. The world spun. I collapsed to the floor. I caught a glimpse of a wet handkerchief as I slipped into darkness.

When my eyes fluttered open again, my head was still swimming. The bottom half of my body was inside the teleporter; the rest of me was soaking up the cold of the concrete floor. Sumire kneeled over me, one hand touching my forehead, the other pointing at Katie, a small pistol in her hand. That wasn't the plan. She was only supposed to get me out of here, summoning security if needed. Katie stood with her arms folded, uncowed by a tiny gun that looked like a toy.

Sumire helped me up. I was woozy and had difficulty standing, but the scent of chamomile made me feel safe. She held me around the waist while I braced myself against the steel chamber to stop the world from spinning.

"Who in the hell is she?" Katie yelled.

"I'm his lawyer, Sumire Yamashita." She introduced herself as if this was a client meeting, waving the gun instead of shaking her hand.

"Yamashita?" Katie repeated. She looked down at short Sumire with a condescending glare.

"You remember my brother—Ryu?"

"Ray? You mean the flake who ran away? When you see your brother, tell him he's fired."

Sumire pointed at the chain around Katie's neck. "You're still wearing the cross he gave you. He was in love with you. So you used him, didn't you?"

"Get rid of her," Katie yelled at me. As if she were the one holding the gun.

I stood upright, legs wobbling. "Let's go."

Sumire didn't move. "Ryu was here with you when he disappeared. What happened to him?"

Katie shrugged. "I have no idea."

"The evidence suggests otherwise."

"Evidence? What evidence? Ray broke in and teleported himself somewhere, maybe Geneva, maybe Mars, I don't know. Said he was consulting with experts, wouldn't say where, and took all our blueprints with him. I assume he's setting up a competitor."

I considered demanding to see the teleporter log to find out where Ryu went and prove she was a liar. But I didn't want to tip her off and give her the chance to delete the file before I could grab a copy. I'd see the truth as soon as I got home.

But Sumire wasn't done cross-examining Katie. "What were you doing in his apartment after he disappeared?"

"I don't need to tell you anything," Katie said, then decided to tell us anyway. "When he took off, I went to his apartment to find out what he stole. The answer, unfortunately, was everything. Your brother is trying to destroy my business and you third-rate Nancy Drews are accusing me of what?"

I stood beside Sumire, leaning on her arm, my head starting to clear. "Did something go wrong with the prototype that you covered up? Or did you just kill him, ballast for the teleporter, like Azaz who washed up on the shore?"

"You don't know shit, Hara."

Sumire grabbed the silver cross hanging from Katie's neck. "Tell us what happened to Ryu."

"He's gone," she choked out, then pushed Sumire away. "And good riddance." She ripped the chain over her head and threw it at Sumire. It hit her chest and dropped to the floor. "Now get the hell out of here, both of you, or I'm calling security." She punched numbers into her phone.

Sumire bent over to pick up the cross, holding it in a balled fist. I saw trouble brewing. "Let's go," I whispered to Sumire, nudging her towards the door. "We already have what we need."

Once we were outside in the fresh air, I had to shield my eyes against the sunlight. Katie stood at the doorway. As we stumbled across lawn, she yelled after Sumire, "I'm filing charges for assault and battery. I'll get you disbarred."

I looked over my shoulder and laughed. "If you do that, I'll put in a complaint to the labor board that you promised pizza to your employees and never delivered."

Katie slammed the shed door shut behind us. I took the gun from Sumire's hand. It was lighter than I expected—plastic—nothing but a toy. She shrugged, a guilty grin. "It was all I had."

I hugged her in relief, then we scurried away to find the pony. When we reached the parking lot, a security team intercepted us, real guns drawn, and escorted us out of the facility, warning us never to return.

Chapter 29
Sweeney Todd Ridge

When Sumire pulled my car into the parking lot of her law office, I assured her my head had cleared enough from whatever Katie had drugged me with to drive myself home from here. She looked skeptical even as she handed me back my keys. I was still a little woozy, but nothing a shot of coffee and an aspirin on the way home wouldn't cure.

Standing beside the burbling car, Sumire hugged me tight, the warmth of her body relaxing me while the smell of chamomile calmed my jitters. I kissed the tip of her ear. She pecked me on the cheek. We stood that way until a partner sauntered past with a golf bag and reminded her he needed his brief finished by this afternoon.

"Don't do anything stupid," she warned me. "I know you, Theodore Tatsu, maybe better than you know yourself. Go home and stay home. Go back to your usual otaku self. Do your hacking or whatever, but don't even think of leaving until I come over after work. If you find out anything about Ryu, text me—we'll get Mikey to take it to the detectives."

Uh-huh. I nodded. There was nothing for me to say.

On the short ride home, I thought of Katie and how she had attempted to teleport me somewhere, presumably the same place as Ryu. If I'd gone alone to SLAC as planned, I would never have returned. I owed my life to Sumire, but rather than feeling bound in a straitjacket of debt and obligation, I felt only a warm glow of appreciation.

My thoughts were interrupted by the buzz of the phone. I glanced over where it was wedged in the ashtray, expecting a text from Sumire putting her orders in writing. Instead, it was an urgent summons from Satoshi: "*Come to tea house now. Need to talk. Very important.*"

Did Satoshi know Katie had tried to teleport me to nowhere? Had he given his permission or ordered her to get rid of me? As much as I wanted to hear what he had to say, I had to get home and grab the log file off the teleporter before Katie realized what I was doing.

Back at my apartment, I cracked my knuckles and dove in. My backdoor worked exactly as planned, giving me remote access to the computers controlling the teleporter at SLAC. I raised my fist in triumph. In the game of wits, I'd outsmarted Katie, turning her own need against her.

After downloading a copy of the log file, I superimposed every set of coordinates onto a MeMap. I found the blue pin in San Jose just south of the 280—Ryu's apartment. And the pin for its opposite off the coast of Half Moon Bay. There was another pin in downtown San Francisco, two more near Satoshi's palace, and a cluster on top of each other in Los Gatos. Zooming in, all the Los Gatos pins were inside Katie's condo—she'd teleported home a half dozen times. I sat staring at the map. The teleporter worked, not just once but every time. She was right—this would change everything. No more cars, trains, or airplanes. Ramesh had to be wrong about a fifty-fifty chance of arriving dead or she couldn't have survived so many trips. Katie must have found a solution. But if so, what happened to Ryu?

On the Sunday when Ryu disappeared, there was only one teleportation in the log—one person sent to Ryu's apartment, the other into the sea. That had to be Ryu. But it was Azaz's body that had washed up on the shore. And I'd met Azaz in the park days after Ryu had disappeared. So the pin in the water couldn't be him.

Zooming in, I realized a second pin I'd thought was on the coast was actually just offshore at Pillar Point Harbor, close to where Azaz had been found. Checking the log details, that teleportation took place late Thursday afternoon, the day Azaz was hauled away by the cops. The opposite location was inside City Hall. When I'd confronted Katie in the parking garage that morning, she'd rushed off, claiming to be late for a demo for investors and then a meeting with the mayor. She must've driven to SLAC, and for her demo to the investors, teleported herself back to City Hall to meet the mayor. Or maybe the mayor was at SLAC, too, and she'd teleported him back to his office. Either way, someone had saved an hour in traffic; Azaz had lost his life.

I zoomed back out to examine the map again. Most of the pins were inside Katie's condo. The opposite spot was a cluster of pins on the peninsula a few miles south of South San Francisco, on a strip of wilderness in the Santa Cruz Mountains known as Sweeney Ridge. There were no homes there, no roads except a dirt fire trail, just scrub and grasslands and a strange concrete bunker that was once a Nike missile silo. Had Katie set up a landing pad at that spot? I had to see what was there. I considered telling Sumire where I was headed, but she'd order me not to go. It would be impossible to hike into the wilderness after dark and there was no way I was waiting until tomorrow.

I left the pony at the trailhead in Millbrae and walked towards San Andreas Lake. Already late in the afternoon, the loop around the lake was filled with joggers, speed walkers, bikers, birders, skateboarders, electric wheelchairs, and dogs. Lots of dogs: big huskies, small poodles, ugly bulldogs, silly shibas, and fluffballs in racing strollers, their tongues lolling in the wind. Not the deserted wilderness I was expecting. But as the path curved around the backside of the lake, the crowd thinned to the serious joggers.

A chain-link fence ran beside the trail, bare scrubland on the other side. I kept walking until I found the dirt fire road that led to the rocky hillside. A locked gate blocked the way up the path, a no trespassing sign strapped to the pole. I waited, fiddling with my phone, until the coast was clear. Hooking my fingers onto the rusty metal, I struggled to pull myself over. In video games, my avatar was always nimble and athletic, able to scale any barrier with ease; in real life, I was better at video games. As my feet flopped around on the chain link mesh, an angry pit bull bounded towards me. I barely reached the top before the dog lunged at my legs, sharp claws pawing just out of reach. The prongs of protruding metal scraped the skin off my arms as I scrambled over the top and fell to the ground. I landed on the hard dirt with a bang, a cloud of dust rising around me.

A man, his snarling face matching that of his pit bull, jerked the dog away. Although I was safe on the other side of the fence, he eyed me suspiciously. I worried he might report me to whoever ran the park. "Dropped my phone," I told him, pretending to hunt through the scrub for it. The man grunted and yanked the dog's leash to lead him off to terrorize a pair of joggers.

I rubbed my bruised hip as I limped up the dirt path. I kept my head ducked low, hoping nobody would see me, until the trail led into a line of evergreens and curved deep into the woods. After a few minutes trudging uphill, I heard rustling in the brush beside me. I stopped.

A white rat poked its head out from behind a rock and sniffed around. After dashing across the dirt trail in front of my feet, it skirted through a crack in the hillside. Another rat appeared, its beady red eyes watching me, the number 12 drawn on its side. It followed the first rat and disappeared into the hillside. More rats, all numbered, popped out from behind the weeds. When a cat jumped out, a mirror image of Katie's white cat, Schrödinger, the rats scattered in fear. These weren't field mice, I realized—they were lab rats, the same as the ones at SLAC, bred to solve mazes, not hunt for food while hiding from predators. That's how Katie had solved the mapping problem without my software—simple trial and error. She'd teleported rats to see where they arrived. I had to be in the right place.

Around the bend, I came to a clearing where tall weeds grew over the boulder-strewn ground. Water trickled down the stony hillside, ant-sized waterfalls turning the trail to mud. Along the ridge above me, scraggy pines rooted into the rock. The air was filled with the scent of evergreen and decaying leaves. Then I caught a whiff of something more sickening than onions. I had to pull my shirt over my nose. When I heard the sound of gacking behind me, I turned to see a pair of buzzards fighting over a root protruding from the rock. More buzzards around them were digging their claws into the dirt. Another pair were fighting over a stick. Their friends watched perched on tree branches while the rest of the flock circled overhead.

I tossed a rock at the two buzzards fighting over the stick. They turned their curved necks to stare at me. "Shoo!" I yelled, but they only hopped a few steps back. I ran at them, waving my arms wildly, until they buzzed away. I rushed around the clearing shouting until the entire flock cleared off to higher ground.

Picking up the stick the birds had left behind, it felt strangely heavy. Not wood—bone, I realized, sinews still attached, strips of muscle and skin hanging off. I dropped it on the ground and grabbed my throat to avoid throwing up.

I found the rest of the hand sticking out of the rock, skin torn from its fingers, the muscles ripped away, the exposed bone darkened to a woody brown. Around it were more body parts—arms, legs, pieces of a skull protruding from the rock. Strips of clothing strewn over the ground. When I pushed away the branches of a bush growing from the ridge, I found the face of the Prophet, another homeless man the cops had taken away, staring out from inside the rock. He was locked in an expression of horror, eye sockets wriggling with maggots, hands embedded in the hillside over his head, pleading to the heavens. I jumped back screaming.

I checked the map again. This rocky ridge was exactly opposite Katie's bedroom in Los Gatos. To teleport herself home, Katie had zapped the Prophet here. From the cluster of pins, there had to be at least a half-dozen more people embedded in the hillside. They were all dead and she was alive. Every time.

I finally understood what Ramesh hadn't figured out. His theory was right—for one person to live another had to die. Katie swore the teleporter didn't harm anyone, but she was a red-haired liar. She'd survived every time because she'd teleported the second person straight into the rock. Or the ocean—for the teleporter, water was no different from solid stone. They were dead the instant they arrived, which meant Katie stayed alive—a solution as ingenious as it was monstrous. Satoshi had said there'd been some compromises in the teleporter design. But it was perfectly safe for one person, as long as the mapping worked—my mapping—and the second person was teleported somewhere guaranteed to be dead on arrival. She needed my software not to find a safe landing site but to ensure the second person couldn't survive.

I marveled at her brilliance even as I gasped at the horror. No wonder she needed to keep everything secret. Ryu must have found out and gone to Satoshi. But instead of stopping Katie, he'd told her what Ryu had figured out. She'd lured Ryu to the teleporter and killed him there, too.

My first thought was to call Sumire, but I wasn't ready to tell her what I'd found; there was no doubt now that Ryu was dead. I dialed 911. When the harried dispatcher asked what was my emergency, I struggled to find the words to explain the body parts embedded in the rock around me.

Chapter 30
Starbursts

A black and white police helicopter hovered over the treetops, scaring away the buzzards, the loud thwack-thwack of the rotors hurting my ears until it darted down to the blue waters of the lake and lowered itself onto the blacktop of a maintenance yard. From up on the hillside, I watched the cops scramble out of the belly of the dragonfly. After cutting the lock on the gate, they started up the fire road as a second cop-chopper flew in from the south, San Jose Police in blue lettering across the side, landing beside the first. While I waited for the cops to make it up the hill, I snapped photos of the Prophet's face, of the bits and bones of all the other bodies scattered over the ground. I finally had the evidence we needed so Jesus could no longer ignore SüprDüpr's crimes.

Two cops clomped into the clearing—a man in his fifties in a striped tie and brown corduroy jacket, and a younger woman in a crisp blue uniform, eyes hidden behind mirrored sunglasses. The insignia on the side of her arm showed they were from San Francisco. I asked why the big city cops had come this far down the peninsula.

"That's the city's water supply down there," the corduroy cop said, pointing at the lake. "And this land you're trespassing on is owned by the San Francisco Public Utilities Commission. In other words, son, this is our jurisdiction."

Sunglasses waited on the edge of the clearing while Corduroy reconnoitered the site. I followed Corduroy to point out the Prophet's face embedded in the hillside. He slipped on a pair of half-moon glasses and leaned in to examine the rock. He whistled in surprise, then swore under his breath. "Make sure this creep doesn't go anywhere," he yelled back to his partner.

Sunglasses snapped to attention, a hand on her holster, her expression a menacing glower.

"I found them," I said.

Corduroy eyed me suspiciously. "That so?"

"There's more." I rushed over to show him another body embedded in the rock.

"Halt!" Sunglasses yelled, whipping the gun from her holster. "Don't move."

I stopped. Put my hands up. "I know who did this."

Corduroy chuckled. "That right?"

Sunglasses trained her gun on me as she asked her partner, "You think he had something to do with it?"

"No!" I insisted.

"Maybe he did, maybe he didn't," he said to Sunglasses, ignoring me. "You work homicide in San Francisco fifteen years, you see a lot of weird shit. And half the time the person who calls it in is the same person who did it." He held up a small bone with tweezers to examine it in the light. "They're so proud of their handiwork, it drives them crazy when nobody sees it." He dropped the bone into an evidence bag and turned back to me. "And this kid looks like the kind of fucked-up creep who'd do some fucked-up shit like this."

Corduroy thrust the baggie in my face. "I've been in homicide a very long time, son. Seen more than my share of serial killers and psychopaths. Seen bodies cut up. Bodies dumped in the garbage. Bodies dissolved in acid. Bodies buried in concrete. I thought I'd seen it all, I really did. But I've got to hand it to you—in all my years on the force, I've never seen anything like this."

"It wasn't me," I protested.

"Yeah, yeah. You just happened to hop the fence, hike up a hill, and end up in right here for no reason?"

"I was looking for my friend."

"Sure, sure. And is that your *friend*?" He pointed at the face peering out the rock.

"No. That's the Prophet."

"The *Prophet*? Really? A prophet like Jeramiah? Or perhaps Ezekiel?"

"He's a homeless man. He lives in St. James Park in San Jose."

"Then tell me, son, how did this prophet from San Jose get stuck in the rock here."

I had to say something. And there was nothing else I could say that would explain the bodies. "He was teleported."

Corduroy chuckled. "That so? Like Star Trek?"

"That's how the teleporter works. One body has to—"

"Cuff him," he ordered Sunglasses. "We got a 5150—no telling what he might do."

Sunglasses slammed me face-first into the ground and dug a knee into my spine. Pulling my arms behind my back, she tied my wrists with a plastic strap that cut into the skin. She looked over to Corduroy, proud of her work, asking him what to do next.

"Call for backup. Get forensics here. And check if we've got a geologist on staff. If not, have them call the archeology department at Stanford and get someone here pronto."

Behind me I heard the crunching of footsteps on the ground. "No need," said a phlegmy voice, as ancient as these hills. It sounded familiar. "We'll take it from here."

"That so?" said Corduroy. "And who the hell are you?"

"Joseph Martin. San Jose P.D."

When I twisted to look up to see who he was, the knee dug deeper into my spine. As the old cop walked past me, I caught a glimpse of a herringbone sleeve— Jesus' chief of staff.

"This is our jurisdiction," Corduroy declared.

Herringbone cleared his throat. "This kid give you some crazy story about a teleporter?"

"Yeah. How did you know?"

"Escaped from Emergency Psychiatric Services. Stole some corpses from the coroner's office. A whacko, no doubt, but he's our whacko. So hand him over."

"We're arresting him anyway."

"Call it in," Herringbone said.

Sunglasses barked into the radio strapped to her uniform. "Officer requesting immediate backup at San Andreas Reservoir. Multiple 187s. Suspect apprehended and under detention."

The radio crackled to life. "Officer Robertson? Detective Howley with you?"

"Yes, ma'am."

"Request for him to contact Captain Dixon immediately."

Sunglasses glanced over to Corduroy. "10-4 that. Can you confirm backup being dispatched?"

"Negative on backup pending Captain Dixon's orders."

Corduroy stomped off behind a clump of trees, his phone to his ear. His voice grew loud and agitated. After a long silence, he said, "Yes, sir," a few times, saluted the tree in front of him, and trudged back to where Herringbone stood grinning. "I don't know what the fuck you guys pulled, but you can have the little shit. Just make sure you get every scrap of those corpses out of here, because if any of this crap pollutes our drinking water, we're sending an invasion force to commandeer your reservoir."

Sunglasses jerked me to my feet and pushed me at Herringbone. He placed a shaky hand on my shoulder.

"I figured it out," I said, excited to tell him about Katie and Ryu and the homeless. "They're from St. James Park. I—"

Herringbone yanked my arm hard. "Don't say a fucking word."

The San Francisco cops started down the hill just as the hazmat crew arrived in white space suits to collect the body parts. Instead of marking chalk outlines, shooting photos, and collecting DNA, they simply tossed the bodies into orange highway litter bags like any other trash.

"This is murder! Aren't you going to investigate?"

Herringbone shrugged. "Just some missing body parts. Let's get out of here. Jesus wants a chat."

We hiked down the hill in silence, slowed by Herringbone's arthritic knees. When we reached the parking lot, I was excited to fly in a helicopter for the first time in my life, but Herringbone pulled me to the patrol car. "I know what happened to Ryu," I said once we were on the highway. "I've got photos I can show you."

I tried to reach for my phone, but my hands were cuffed behind my back. It didn't matter, though, because Herringbone wasn't interested. "Show them to Jesus," he said.

We rode the entire way back to San Jose without speaking another word. I listened to the chatter on the squawky police radio, surprised to hear nothing about a murder investigation or even dispatching officers to Sweeny Ridge. When we arrived at police headquarters, Herringbone led me to the confession room and pushed me inside.

"Can I explain now?" I asked.

"Keep your fucking mouth shut until Jesus gets here."

He left the room, leaving me alone. I waited, worried what would happen now that Jesus had me in his clutches. Then the door burst open and Herringbone returned. Jesus stormed in behind him snorting like a bull. He slammed the door, rattling the window frame.

"Do you know what a fucking mess you made, you little prick?"

"It was Katie," I protested.

He grabbed me by the collar and lifted me out of the chair to slam his fist into my ribs.

"Oof," I grunted as I fell back into the seat. "I found the bodies," I coughed, struggling to catch my breath. "I didn't kill them. That was—"

"Don't say another fucking word."

Jesus reached over to press a button on the back of the table. A speaker overhead crackled to life. "Yes, Chief?"

"Shut off the recording."

"Sure thing, Chief." The static cut off and the room fell silent.

Jesus stood in front of me, hands balled into fists. I didn't understand why. I'd solved the mystery for him. I'd found the bodies. I'd identified the murderer. Did he really think I murdered the people I'd found? "Katie killed them," I tried to explain.

"She teleported them into the hillside. I can show you the photos." With my hands still cuffed, I pointed with my chin to the phone in my pocket.

I never saw it coming, just an explosion of stars before everything went black. When I came to, the entire Milky Way swirled in front of me, my consciousness focused on the screaming pain in my jaw.

"Take it easy, Chief," Herringbone chuckled.

"Little sack of shit."

"Ow," I yelled.

"Awake now?"

I said nothing.

"Forget how to talk?"

I hummed a tune, "King of Pain," the first song that popped into my head even though I hated The Police. Jesus didn't like it either—he smashed a boot into my shin, shooting another wave of pain up my leg.

He leaned in, his face inches from mine, garlicy breath blowing over me. "Who told you where to find the bodies?"

"Nobody," I said, wondering why he asked.

"Was it Satoshi?"

"Satoshi?"

"Did that rich prick tell you where to look?"

"It's how the teleporter works. Katie teleported them there, into the rock."

Another explosion of a white-hot sun, an instant of searing pain. When my vision flickered back on again, I could barely catch my breath.

"Be careful, Chief. We don't need another corpse on our hands."

"Fuck." Jesus let go with a final shove. "Send this prick to the shelter. Let Dr. Deauville have him."

The shelter? Next to the Corinthian? Where a teleporter was being built in the basement instead of a pizza parlor. A teleporter that needed two bodies to operate—one to live, one to die.

I jumped up, my legs and ribs screaming with pain. Jesus shoved me back into the chair. Despite the futility, I tried standing again. Jesus grabbed my collar and pinned my head against the wall. "Relax, kid," he sneered. "They'll take good care of you at the shelter. The preacher there is a personal friend of mine."

I looked over at Herringbone, my eyes pleading with him to save me.

"What do you want me to do, Chief?"

"Get Lilac in here."

"Sure thing," he said and strode out of the room.

It was just Jesus and me alone now. "Why?" I asked.

"SAT scores, kid. Don't ever forget the SAT scores."

"By killing the homeless people?"

He slammed me against the wall and dropped me back into the chair. Something warm and sticky ran down the back of my head. "You think decent people want to live in the middle of their shit? In case you haven't noticed, we've got a crisis on our hands. You want honest citizens to stay, you got to put a stop to the drugs and crime. That's our job. That's *my* responsibility. They destroy our parks, shit on our streets, take our tax dollars in handouts. Money that ought to pay for more teachers, better schools, more police. If we can't kick them out or lock them up, then God help us because we have to do something. Anything that gets those bums off the street sounds like a winner to me. You got a better idea, kid?"

I had plenty. Like public bathrooms and showers for a start. Help with mental health and addiction for another. But I'd have to debate the best use of our tax dollars another time. First, I had to escape.

I lunged forward in a head-butt, knocking him backwards, more in surprise than pain. But that gave me enough room to jump up and dash for the exit. With my hands cuffed behind me, I struggled to turn the doorknob to escape. Then the door burst open, knocking me over. I lay sprawled on the floor.

Herringbone stepped into the room. Behind him was old Doom Lady who'd warned me about losing my nose, pink medical gloves on her hands. Was she actually going to cut it off? Jesus held me with a chokehold as Doom lunged at me with a syringe. I tried to shake loose from his grasp, but he was too strong. Doom jabbed the needle into my arm. Coldness radiated through the muscle, pain dissolving as euphoria spread. My limbs went limp and the light in the room darkened to stars flickering in a midnight sky.

"Shame about kids these days," Jesus chuckled, the last thing I heard. "Just can't seem to keep themselves clean. Hope he enjoys his dreams."

Chapter 31
The Apple Tree

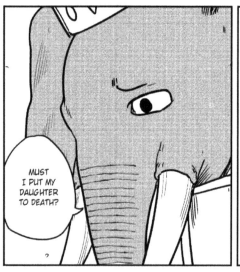

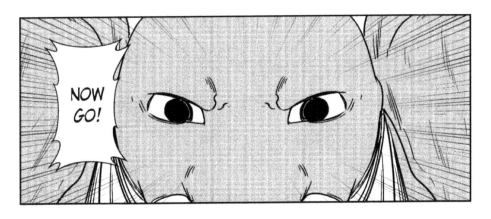

193

Chapter 32
Something Complicated

My eyes were lost in the crisscross pattern of the ceiling tiles, my body enveloped in a warm glow. Sometime later, maybe minutes, maybe hours, the chiseled face of the Viking, the muscled cop from St. Jimmy's, stood over me, grunting in disdain. Strong arms hoisted me into the air, slung me over his shoulder like a sack of rice and carried me from the room. He hauled me down the corridor and banged through the door into the bright light. I felt the radiance of the sun on my face. I loved the sun, and it loved me back.

Tossed into the cruiser, I landed face down in the dark. The seat smelled of rubber, grease, and cleaning chemicals. At least my nose seemed intact. I tried to sit up, but down was better. I ran my fingers across the vinyl, heard the door slam and another open. A head peered through the wire barrier. A bad haircut on a Japanese-Hawaiian. "Hiya, pal," he said.

I remembered I didn't like the cop but couldn't remember why. Something complicated, too complicated to remember now.

"Let's get out of here," he ordered the Viking.

The engine rumbled to life. The seat cushion yielded gentle pressure as we pulled away. Through the slant of the rear window, I watched the trees, the traffic lights, the tall buildings slide past in front of a pastel blue sky. I listened to the street noise, the whine of the car, the crackle of the police radio; hummed along to the oscillations of the universe until Mayeda spoke again. "Take the 101."

The car screeched to a halt. I nearly slipped to the floor.

"The shelter's that way."

"We're taking a detour."

"But that's—"

"We're not going to the shelter."

"Jesus said—"

"Fuck what Jesus said. Get on the 101."

"I hope you know what you're doing."

"Yeah, me too."

The car jerked forward again, the engine whining. I wondered where we were going, and if there were any elephants there. I wanted to go to the park and visit the elephants in the circus tent. I'd ride an elephant down St. James Street, past a carousel playing a happy tune on the calliope. I hummed a carousel song, or maybe it was Mr. Kite, until I broke up laughing.

"What the fuck's with him?" the Viking asked his partner. That only made me laugh harder.

"Lilac shot him up with chinatown."

"Hope he's enjoying the ride."

"Get off here."

"Where are we going?"

"We're going where I tell you."

"Jesus is not gonna be happy about this."

"Jesus is not gonna know about this, got it?"

The car stopped, then started again, turned, then turned again. Then stopped. A window slid down, cool air rushing in.

"Thank God." I heard a woman's voice. A voice I recognized. A voice I loved. "Is he okay?"

"Depends on what you mean by okay."

I pulled myself upright for a glimpse of Sumire's beautiful face through the window before gravity dragged me back down. Her ears were sticking out like an elephant's. "You can fly!" I laughed. I was so happy to see her. But I had to pretend not to be. I couldn't remember why. Something complicated. "Su-mi-re," I sang, then sang it again.

"Shut up, twerp," the Viking yelled. I continued singing.

"You got another way in?" Mayeda asked. "Better nobody sees him."

"Through the garage. I'll open the gate."

A few minutes later, I was dragged from the car between the two cops. My legs were like jelly, strong hands around my waist, the hard steel of a gun digging into my hip.

"Stand up," the Viking ordered. I laughed.

A hand caressed my back. My legs suddenly found strength.

"You forgot this, pal," Mayeda said. A red baseball hat slipped onto my head—my remembrance cap. I felt the hands of my father and my grandfather and the rest of my family stretching back for generations giving me strength. I stood straight and started walking.

Kind of. Half dragged to the elevator. Then down a hallway, feet tripping over the carpet. Through a door that opened to a small room bright with sunshine. I sunk deep onto a quilt as soft as a cloud.

"We'll drop off someone else at the shelter under his name," Mayeda said. "If anyone notices, they'll come looking, so get him somewhere safe. And keep him hidden. Jesus has eyes everywhere."

"Thanks, Michael. I don't know how I can repay you."

"I'll think of something."

My eyes fluttered open to see her kiss his cheek. I tried to protest, but I was so sleepy that all that came out was, "Heeeeeey, donduuuzaaaa—" And somewhere in the middle of the last "a," the elephants arrived to carry me back to their magical land.

🐘   🐘

Clack clack clack. Sounds invaded my head as the elephants faded away. I raced after them, trying to catch them, but more clacks chased them off for good. I cracked open one eye, afraid of the burning light, but the room was dark. I took a deep breath. A dull throbbing in my head. A sharper pain in my ribs. My jaw was stiff. My back unbending. My body felt broken into a million pieces like the corpses in the woods, picked over by the birds. Was I at the shelter? No—not cold metal and cinderblock; the aroma of chamomile on clean, silky sheets, wrapped in a blanket of air. My eyes adjusted to the yellowish light radiating into the room. Sumire's bedroom. The phantasmagoria of earlier began trickling back. I felt sick. Not like a hangover. Buried under two feet of dirt, no strength to claw my way out.

Clack clack. The sounds landed on my head like a silver hammer. Maxwell's equations banged through my head. *Clack clack.* I yawned. The noise stopped. Warmth on my neck. Fingers touching me. When I reached up, the throbbing in my side burst into an inferno of pain. I grunted. A hand soothed me.

"Awake now?" Sumire's voice, filled with concern.

I tried to answer, but nothing came out. My mouth was cracked, my tongue pasted shut. She ran her fingers through my hair. I closed my eyes and listened to our breathing. I'd never been in this apartment before, but it felt like the home I'd always wanted.

She set her laptop to the side and folded her arms over her chest. "What the hell were you thinking, Ted? You nearly got yourself killed."

I held my side and rolled over to look at her. Everything was fuzzy. Sumire handed me my glasses, helped me put them on. Everything was still fuzzy, just in a different way. She was wearing pink cotton pajamas, legs under the blanket, sitting up against the wooden headboard. Her face was devoid of makeup, a few dark blemishes washed by the laptop glare. The light reflecting off her glasses made her look bug-eyed, not the teen girl I once knew—older, in control. But the tips of her ears still stuck out from her hair like a bunny rabbit.

"Coffee?" I croaked.

She looked at me like a sick child deserving of sympathy but not indulgence. "Please, Bunny?"

"I'd tell you to make it yourself," she said. I was surprised by the anger in her voice. "But I can see that's impossible. So just this once, Theodore Hara. Then you've got some explaining to do."

Explaining. Yeah, there was a lot of that. Like how I came to be wearing penguin print pajamas with lacey cuffs, my own clothes folded neatly on the desk. I reached out for them, but my arm fell back onto the bed, landing on a plush hedgehog. It had a pointed face with a black nose and a silly grin, its body covered with fuchsia fur. I pressed it tight against my chest.

When Sumire returned, her stern expression dissolved into laughter. "You look so cute in penguins."

I tossed the hedgehog at her, or more like pushed it across the bed in her direction. She picked it up, held it to her face, its long snout against her pert nose, and petted the top of its head. "I see you met Tatsu," she said, holding up the stuffed animal. "Kind of looks like you, don't you think? Tries so hard to be prickly, but really, he's soft and kind of cuddly."

She set the stuffed animal on top of the pile of clothes, his round, glittery eyes watching us, his expression naïve and stupid. I didn't like being compared to a hedgehog doll, but at least I wasn't the plush pig wedged against a pillow. I didn't want to know his name. Or which one she kept next to her on the bed.

She helped me sit up and handed me a mug of steaming coffee. I held it carefully in a shaky arm, knowing there'd be hell to pay if I spilled even a single drop on her blanket. I downed a large gulp, singeing my throat. I drank the rest in a long, burning swallow then held out the empty mug, begging for more. She huffed but returned with the carafe. I drank a second cup, then a third, finishing the entire pot before handing the mug back, my heart banging uncomfortably in my ribcage.

"Better now?"

I really wanted some water and some aspirin, but I wasn't about to ask. I nodded meekly. She folded her arms over her chest. "So what the frick, Ted?"

"What?" I said, ducking my head.

"What were you doing out there alone? You knew it was dangerous. And you don't exactly have the best judgment."

"What was I supposed to do?"

She just glared at me.

"What?" I said. "I couldn't take you."

"Why not? I want to find my brother as much as you do."

Couldn't she see I was protecting her? "We'd both be dead now."

"I told you not to do anything, didn't I? I told you to wait for me. You should've at least told me where you were going. You should've called me when you found the bodies."

"But—"

"I ought to kill you myself. Thank God Mayeda heard you'd been brought in. And he called me."

"You kissed him," I blurted out. "I saw it."

Sumire threw the plush doll at me. "Is that all you can think about, Ted? You think you're so smart, but you're a complete idiot. You ought to kiss him yourself. He saved your life."

"If he's so great, why won't he arrest Katie?"

"How?"

"I found the bodies. She killed them. All of them. I've got evidence. I've got the logs from the teleporter. She teleported the homeless people from St. Jimmy's straight into the rock. I found them. I've got photos."

"And Ryu?" she gasped. "Did you find Ryu?"

I shook my head. "He's not there," I said, and felt guilty when she sighed with relief. I'd have to break it to her that Ryu was at the bottom of the ocean. But neither of us was ready for that.

I felt around for my phone. It wasn't on the bed next to me, wasn't on the floor charging. I searched the pile of clothes on the desk, but it wasn't there, either. I started to panic. "Where's my phone?"

"You didn't have it when you got here."

My wallet was missing, too, but my phone was my life. In my befuddled state, I could have dropped it on the seat of the patrol car. Or it might have fallen out of my pocket while Jesus slammed me around. What would I do without it? The photos, at least, would have been uploaded to the cloud. I pointed to Sumire's laptop.

With a shaking hand, I tried to navigate to my photo archive. My password didn't work. I tried again carefully, one letter at a time, but the red error box didn't go away. I hit the password reset button.

Username not found, came the response.

I tried once more with the same results, and again, and again, and again. "Fuck," I said, panic rising.

"What?"

"I've been deleted."

Sumire closed her eyes. "I'd better warn Michael. Then we've got to get you out of here."

Chapter 33
The Motel on Cemetery Lane

Even the ghosts in the old cemetery along the darkened road were asleep, only the beacons of the motels lighting our way. We parked in the back and walked past air conditioners buzzing like cicadas despite the cool air prickling my arms. Sumire stopped in front of a door, the curtains drawn, no light seeping out. She knocked. When the door cracked open, I was surprised to see Kenta peering out from inside.

"Hey, bruh," he whispered. Behind him, two double beds filled the room, their maroon quilts unrumpled. In the back, the light from the bathroom cast a harsh glow. I looked at Sumire, confused.

"It's safer," she said. "I thought it would be better not to register with our own names or credit cards. Just in case."

"Is this okay?" Kenta asked as we stepped inside. I assured him it was better than my own apartment—it even had a bed instead of a lumpy couch to sleep on.

I had no bags to unpack, no laptop or phone to connect to the free Wi-Fi, no toiletries to stow in the bathroom, not even a pair of slippers. I felt disconnected. Kenta put one hand on the doorknob and waved goodnight. I hoped Sumire would stay to keep the ghosts at bay, but she turned to leave, too.

"When are you coming back?"

"It's better if I stay away. Until we get this sorted out. In case anyone is watching."

When I asked how we'd keep in contact, she pointed at a bulky plastic thing next to the television attached to the wall by a cable. Instructions printed on the side explained how to use it.

"We need burner phones," I said. I looked over to Kenta waiting at the door, but he didn't understand. I grabbed the phone out of his hand and opened the Best Buy site to search for a prepaid MePhone. "One of these." I hearted the image of the newest model, an XXL with a kickass CPU in blackhole black, then marked a matching device in wormhole white for Sumire. But I'd need more than a phone to survive in a hotel room. I needed a computer, too, a fast one. I searched through dozens of crap offerings until I found one suitable for running multiple virtual machines simultaneously.

Sumire yanked the phone away. "Uh-uh," she said. "No way, Theodore Tatsu. You stay out of trouble."

"What am I supposed to do here?" I asked. There was nothing in the room but the phone and a television.

"You can read a book. I'll get you a Kindle." She scrolled down the page.

"How about a video game?"

Sumire rolled her eyes but didn't object. I found the latest PlayStation and dropped it into the cart. It wasn't great for hacking, but it would have to do. It had an eight core CPU that could run multiple copies of Linux and a high-end GPU that I could use for blockchain calculations. I looked over at Kenta. "How about a bottle of Dassai?" I asked with a grin. "To help with the pain." I grabbed my side in semi-mock discomfort, the real pain flaring as I moved.

"No way," Sumire said and turned to Kenta. "Don't you dare," she warned. "That's the last thing he needs." Kenta nodded meekly.

While she ranted, I slipped a prepaid debit card into the cart before handing him back the phone. There had to be a liquor store somewhere in the area if I had money.

At the door, she hugged me tight. I hardly noticed the pain despite my bruised ribs. "Don't do anything stupid," she said. "In fact, don't do anything at all. Just wait here until we get this sorted out."

Right. Like that was going to happen.

All night while the Valley slept, I was wide awake. With nothing to do. I clicked on the news. Politics, wars, a small earthquake in Indonesia—there was no shortage of news. Nothing about the body parts in the woods, though, that should have dominated the headlines. The local news was full of fires, shootings, and traffic accidents, an outbreak of typhus among the people living on the streets of San Francisco, plus weather and sports, the Giants losing again, the last wild-card spot fading out of reach. And then in the final segment, there was Katie in a red satin gown cut high up her legs, a rope of diamonds sparkling around her neck, hosting a charity benefit under a white canopy on the lawn of St. Jimmy's Park.

"I want to thank all the wonderful people who came out tonight to give the most amazing support to our new homeless shelter," she said into the microphone. The bright lights of the cameras captured her megawatt smile. "I hope everyone will join us for SüprDüpr's super spectacular demonstration. Come see the elephant and the greatest revolution in transportation ever. Next Tuesday at noon, right here in St. James Park."

I shut off the TV. I had three days left to stop her.

Chapter 34
Fistful of Dollars

I dreamt of woodpeckers growing louder and louder as if the birds were hammering my own skull. When I opened my eyes and saw the maroon quilt and powder blue walls, I remembered where I was. "Kenta?" I yelled towards the knocking, but when I tried to move, my body exploded in pain.

I hobbled to the door to find Kenta standing outside with two large bags in his arms. The one with a Best Buy logo he handed to me, and the other, he carried into the room. When he unzipped the top of the insulated bag, steam wafted up smelling of pork and garlic and sesame oil. My stomach gurgled in anticipation; I hadn't eaten in nearly a day. Kenta placed containers of chashu and broth on the desk, and handed me a tray of gyoza and a carton of fried rice. I peeked inside the Best Buy bag— burner phones, gaming console, credit card. Check, check, check. But that was all. "You didn't bring anything else?"

Grinning, he reached into his pocket and tossed me a bottle of extra-strength ibuprofen. "Thought you might need this, bruh."

"Thanks," I grumbled, not nearly as thankful as he deserved.

He grabbed the insulated bag and laughed. "Oh, forgot this." He handed me a fist-sized, olive-green bottle, black calligraphy on the cottony white label. "Whatever you do, don't tell Yukiko." It wasn't big, it wasn't chilled, but it was Dassai 39. I was so happy I hugged him despite the pain. My best friend ever.

"Join me?" I cracked open the bottle. I made it a point not to drink during the day, but this wasn't drinking—this was medicine.

"Nah. Got to run. Have to prep for lunch."

I wasn't as disappointed as I should have been; it was an awfully small bottle to share. As he headed out the door, I lifted the sake in a salute and brought it to my lips, a sweet sip of heaven filling my mouth.

"Thought you might need this, too." From the doorway, he tossed me a small ceramic cup, the cobalt blue bullseye staring out from the bottom.

After slurping down the noodles and scarfing the entire carton of rice, my stomach rumbled in appreciation. With the ibuprofen and sake coursing through my veins, I could finally breathe again. My fingers tingled with the alcohol and I could move my arms without grunting. I dumped the empties in the trashcan under the bathroom sink, then cracked all my knuckles. It was time to get to work.

It only took a few minutes to set up the burner phone with an anonymous MeCan account. Converting a gaming console into a Linux server took longer. While waiting for yet another reboot, I headed into the bathroom. Standing in front of the toilet, the green bottle of Dassai peeking out from the trashcan caught my eye. I was glad I noticed it before Sumire returned. Having her mad at me was bad enough, but I couldn't get Kenta in trouble. I rearranged the trash, hiding the bottle under the styrofoam bowl, but knew she'd sniff it out anyway. I had to get rid of the evidence.

Stepping out of the darkened hotel room felt like being teleported into a different world. The day was hot and dry, a dusty wind blowing in from the desert. I lifted a hand to shield my face from the blinding noontime sun as I walked around the motel looking for the dumpster. I found it in the back of the parking lot, a pair of tents spread out on a small strip of grass beside it. Two men sat on the curb, a younger one smoking weed, an older one clutching a brown paper bag. The older one called out, "Hey, you done with that?"

"Sorry," I said, holding up the bottle. "It's empty."

"That's recyclable!" He pointed at a shopping cart behind him overflowing with bottles and cans.

After dropping the dead soldier into the cart, I started back towards my room. I wondered how long they'd been camped in the motel parking lot, and how long before management called the cops. If the police came, they'd be taken away. To Katie's shelter.

I walked back to warn them. "What's your names?"

"Everyone calls me Finchy," the older one said.

"I'm Boo," said the younger one.

I held out my hand. "Tatsu."

Finchy laughed. "'Tots'? Ha-ha, that's a stupid name."

He had a point. I asked them where they came from and how they ended up here. Finchy had done three tours in Iraq, then bounced around when the war ended. "Nobody needs an old soldier," he said. I thanked him for his service. "Yeah, that's what everyone says. But nobody pays for retraining. Or PTSD therapy." He took another gulp from his bottle.

Boo had grown up in San Jose, a couple miles from me. "Dropped out of college, man—too expensive." I realized I was lucky—the prune orchards had paid for six years of tuition and two degrees. "All the jobs around here pay shit, you know, unless you're a programmer. This is all I can afford." He pointed at his tent. He was right about real estate prices—my crappy apartment gobbled up most of my paycheck. And I was a highly-paid mathematician. At least Boo's tent was clean. And neater than my apartment. He even had a vacuum cleaner. But that wouldn't help him when the cops arrived.

"Listen, guys," I said. "You gotta get out of town."

Boo took that the wrong way. "Fuck you, man. We're not bothering nobody."

I had to make them understand. "Seriously, guys, it's dangerous here. The cops are rounding up everyone and taking them downtown."

"New shelter there." He turned to Finchy. "Wanna check it out?"

"Nah, downtown sucks. It's all chinatown there. Rather stay here where it's nice and peaceful."

"Chinatown?" I asked.

Boo took another toke. "Yeah, man, that shit will fuck you up something bad."

"What's chinatown?"

He pantomimed a syringe being injected into his arm, then fell over onto the grass. Whatever I'd been injected with, probably heroin or fentanyl.

"Look guys, you can't stay here. It's not safe."

"Not safe anywhere for us."

"They're killing people at that shelter. If the police take you there, you're dead. Understand? You gotta get out of town quick."

Finchy laughed. "How you suppose we do that? Take one of them Ubers?"

"Hey," Boo said, "I used to drive an Uber."

"No shit?"

"Damn straight. Until my old lady took off with the car."

I had to do something. "Stay here," I told them.

They looked at each other and laughed. "We're not going nowhere."

I found an ATM in the motel lobby that accepted the prepaid card, then returned to thrust a fistful of twenties at them. "Get on a train, bus, whatever. Just get the hell out of here."

"Fuck you, man. I thought you were cool."

I pointed at the sign attached to the light pole. "Private property. Beat it." It was for their own good. They didn't move. "Soylent!" I yelled. "They're turning people into Soylent at that shelter."

That got their attention. "No shit, man?"

"That's what happened to my friend, Azaz."

206

Finchy looked up at me. "You know Azaz?"

"He's dead. And you'll be, too, if you don't get out of here quick."

They grumbled but folded their tents and loaded them into the shopping carts. I watched as they trundled toward the street. At that rate it would take them days to reach the border of Morgan Hill where they'd be safe. I rushed after them and used Finchy's phone to order an Uber to Half Moon Bay. "You'll like it there," I said. "Nice and peaceful. Just make sure to stay out of the water."

As I was heading back to my room, I heard a low-pitched, whoop-whoop sound at the street. I turned to see a cop car pulling up in front of the pair. The cops jumped out, pushed the carts into the weeds, and shoved the two into the back seat.

"Hey!" I yelled, racing to catch up. "Where are you taking them?"

"New shelter downtown," a cop said through the window. "They'll get help there."

"Stop!" I shouted, but they zoomed away, siren screaming, gumballs sweeping the air.

I stomped back to my room and slammed the door. It was up to me to save them before it was too late.

I searched the entire internet, checked Reddit and Medium and Quora, read police logs and Twitter feeds of people transcribing police radio chatter, but found no mention of the body parts I'd discovered, no news about SüprDüpr or Katie. I considered ubering to the lake and hiking back to the clearing, but I was sure the area had been sanitized by now. Worse, there were probably cops there watching for me, especially if anyone noticed I wasn't at the shelter. I thought of contacting Corduroy with the San Francisco Police, but decided it was too risky—he'd probably call Herringbone.

After writing up a description of how SüprDüpr's teleporter was killing homeless residents, I sent it to the tip lines of a national newspaper, a cable news network, and a tech news magazine, offering the first to publish a Pulitzer-worthy exclusive. I was sure they'd fight over the chance to expose Katie and blow the story wide open. I daydreamed of the headlines tomorrow, a medal from the President, a standing ovation from Congress. I held my breath when the first reply arrived from the cable news organization.

"In the considered opinion of our science editor," it started, "teleportation is impossible." Reading further, the health and wellness editor recommended I seek professional care. "Don't despair, David," the template read. "There are effective treatments available for a wide range of mental illnesses." It went on to list the toll-free number of a suicide prevention hotline if I needed someone to talk to.

The thought that they confused me with one of the Davids who sent them tips every day did make me despair. But that didn't prevent me from shooting back a snippy reply: "Tell your science editor to watch the SüprDüpr demo on Tuesday at noon. That's when she'll realize she just lost a Pulitzer. Because teleportation is real. Then get yourself a better science editor after she kills herself."

I was still hopeful when the inbox buzzed again, this time from the Amazon Post. I skimmed through the form letter opening, democracy only works with engaged citizens like me, whistleblowers are critical to effectuate positive change, blah, blah, blah.

"In attempting to confirm these grave allegations regarding the activities of SüprDüpr, out staff reached out to the San Jose Police Department which granted us a phone interview with the Chief of Police, Jesus Raguel. Chief Raguel stated that his department has recently investigated allegations of criminal activity by the company and found them to be 'not only unequivocally baseless but totally absurd.' He indicated that the department has concluded that a disgruntled former employee by the name of Theodore Hara is the source of these malicious rumors intended to disparage the company. Chief Raguel also indicated that this same individual has outstanding warrants for his arrest for unauthorized computer access with malicious intent, wire fraud, and trafficking in passwords. Consequently, if you are Mr. Hara, we urge you to desist in your smear campaign and turn yourself in to the local authorities."

I banged the delete key with malicious intent and slumped my head on the table. Nobody would believe me, not with Jesus covering for Katie. Nobody would expose SüprDüpr. There was only one way—I'd have to get Katie herself to show everyone the horror of her invention. In front of the entire world. On live television. The demo.

Chapter 35
The Unbearable Sadness of Apple

My first stop was the Best Buy on Steven's Creek, in the shadow of the Tangerine Tower. I was glad Kenta had put a thousand dollars on the prepaid card because after the $300 I'd given the two homeless guys, I needed most of the rest for the quadcopter. There were plenty of crappy toy drones on the shelves, but one with a high-resolution camera, 2 km range, thirty-minute flying time, and low noise rotors didn't come cheap. That left little money for a disguise, so I birded to the Goodwill down the street. After searching rack after rack of old clothes not much different from what I was already wearing, I found the perfect way to blend into the background—a pizza delivery uniform.

In the bathroom, I changed into the blue shirt with red collar and black polyester pants, and for the topping, donned a cap adorned with a smiling pizza emoji. When I looked in the mirror, the camouflage was perfect; I could hardly see myself standing there. I even felt strangely compelled to pay myself a tip. The smell of grease and pepperoni oozed around me, generating a fog of invisibility even as it made me hungry. There was no choice but to make a detour to Gianni's for a ramen-top special, even though it was twenty minutes out of the way.

At the counter, a pot-bellied man with a round face was bossing around a crew of kids. "I need to talk to Gianni," I said.

"I'm Yuehan." He shook my hand with fingers covered in wet flour. "Everyone call me Johnnie." He handed me a waxy napkin that did little to wipe away the slimy mess.

"Anyone talk to you about building a shop in downtown San Jose?"

He didn't seem to understand.

"I heard you were opening a franchise across from St. Jimmy's."

He looked at me confused. "Bad location," he said. "Too many homeless, too far from highway for delivery."

I wasn't surprised. I should have known Katie was a liar from the start. "The park is fixed up now," I said. "You should see it—full of foot traffic. Perfect for a pizza joint selling by the slice."

"No slice. Whole pizza ten dollar. You want?"

"Yeah, give me two." I needed the pizzas anyway to complete the disguise.

I directed the Uber to drop me off a couple blocks behind the Corinthian, away from the park and its swarm of cops. Standing beside a banged-up Corolla that was easy to mistake for a pizza junker, I unpacked the drone and sent it flying. It rose over the street to float high above one of the apartment buildings Katie had purchased. I pushed the drone forward, zooming up St. James Street, past the Corinthian, to peer down over the shelter.

Police cars streamed in and out of the parking lot, even more today than when we watched from the dentist's office. A bigger crowd of unhoused people were lined up in front of the white canopies, waiting to be led to either the shelter or the armory. I slid the drone down to the construction site on the other corner. The work was complete, the trucks, stacks of pallets, and construction crew gone, a giant steel cage standing empty, waiting for elephants.

Panning the camera wider, I caught a glimpse of something festive in the parking lot behind the Corinthian. I maneuvered the drone overhead and watched a crew of workers putting up a circus tent, a huge canvas of red stripes hoisted high in the middle. I circled around until I spotted the open flap in the back and maneuvered to peer inside. Despite the 4K resolution of the cameras, it was too dark inside the tent to see what was hiding there. I dropped the drone low over the parking lot, barely off the ground, trying to stay away from the workers, but one of the food crew spotted it and yelled to the others. As I lifted the drone back up out of reach, I saw them scurrying to close up the tent. There had to be something important inside and this was my only chance to see it.

I shot the drone forward as fast as it would go, dodging a gauntlet of flailing arms, to zip through the flap as it was closing. Inside was nothing but a covered space over the parking lot, a massive steel pole in the center. The last thing I saw before the transmission cut off was a broomstick swinging straight at the camera.

I replayed the video, pausing where the drone had been high over the big top. I wondered why the small tent needed such a thick pole. Rewinding, I noticed the white outline of an elephant painted onto the street in front of the Corinthian. Then it hit me. Of course. The teleporter inside the building was exactly halfway between the tent pole in the parking lot behind the Corinthian and the spot where the elephant would materialize out front. One elephant would be impaled behind the building while the other would arrive at the head of a parade before a cheering crowd.

I took off the pizza cap, breaking the camouflage, and bowed my head in sadness. To stop Katie, to save all the people in the homeless shelter, an elephant would have to die. There was no other way.

🐘   🐘

"What did you do with the thousand dollars I already gave you?" Kenta asked when I called for a fill up.

"Pizza," I joked. He didn't laugh. "It's for Ryu," I added, begging for more. I hated asking, but I knew Kenta would have no choice. He moaned and complained, but finally agreed to load another five hundred onto the card. "Thanks," I said when I saw the balance increase. "Any chance you could not mention this to Yukiko?"

If Yukiko found out, she would tell Sumire and that would be almost as bad as the sake. At some point I'd have to tell Sumire what I was doing, but I needed to be far enough along that my plan would make sense instead of sounding insane.

"Don't worry, bruh," he grumbled. "Yukiko would kill me if she found out I was giving you money. With the baby, you know, things are kind of tight now."

I suddenly felt like a jerk. I'd never considered whether Kenta could afford it. But what else could I do without access to my own bank account? I promised to pay him back as soon as I could.

Summoning the Uber, I expected the driver to be pleased with what had to be the largest fare of his career, but instead he complained the entire trip that it would take two hours to drive back from this godforsaken wasteland. When we pulled into the gravel parking lot, I jumped out to escape his final tirade. No five-star rating from me, I thought, as the car peeled away in a trail of dust that led all the way back to the highway. But I'd need a way to get home—the nearest Uber was an hour away. I imagined myself riding into town on an elephant like a maharajah, but that would take too long. I wished I had a teleporter to zap me back in seconds.

At the top of the hill that led to the preserve, a crew of trainers were guiding the two elephants down the path towards the parking lot. I'd arrived just in time. Two trucks waited at the base of the hill, metal cages built into the trailers. Then I saw the woman in a white dress billowing in the gusty breeze—Angelica—waving her arms to block the path while screaming at the trainers.

When I rushed up the hill, the elephants saw me and flapped their ears. Google raised his trunk in a salute. Apple trumpeted a greeting.

"You!" Angelica yelled when she spotted me. "It's all your fault! It was you who convinced the chairman of the foundation to take our elephants away."

Katie must have worked her charm on the monied old fart who owned this place. "I'm sorry," I said though it wasn't my fault.

"Sorry? Don't say you're sorry. Do something! Call your boss and tell her the elephants can't come to your parade."

"Sorry," I said again. "I can't."

"Then what the hell are you here for?"

"I came to say goodbye."

She didn't understand and I wasn't about to explain. I closed my ears to her entreaties as I stepped around her and started up the hill.

No matter how hard the trainers in front yanked the ropes tied to the elephants' necks and the trainers behind them swatted their butts, the two elephants refused to budge. A man in a white lab coat strode past me wielding a pachyderm-sized needle.

"Stop," I called as he approached Apple.

"Stay back," Labcoat ordered me, eying Apple warily.

"Don't you dare harm them," Angelica yelled.

"These animals are dangerous. They need to be sedated."

"They'll come with me," I said to hoots of derision from everyone.

Ignoring Labcoat's demands to keep away, I approached Apple with bated breath, my heart beating hard, afraid she'd swipe me left off the hillside to send me crashing into oblivion. Instead, she brushed my cheek with her trunk, caressing me with the little finger on the end. Then she turned and nudged me towards Google behind her.

Google rested his trunk on my shoulder while Apple tapped the flat crown of her head against my chest. I should have felt their immense weight, been terrified of being crushed by the smallest misstep, but I had no fear at all. It was like my dream and I was their baby elephant. I kissed Google's dusty trunk, then spread my arms wide around Apple's massive head. She smelled of grass and dust and summer. Flies buzzed around us. People were yelling, but I barely heard them. My head pressed tight against hers, bones like steel plates beneath leathery skin, I felt her sadness overwhelm me. "Kaa-chan," I sniffled. "I miss you." I sensed her pain as I blinked away the welling tears. "Why did you have to kill yourself? Why did you have to leave me?"

She grunted in reply, but it meant nothing to me, nothing I could understand. She was an elephant, after all; just an old elephant, nearing the end of her long life.

"Enough already," Labcoat said, preparing to stab Apple with his needle.

"No," I shouted, slapping the needle away.

Angelica cheered. "Tell them to stop."

"They need to be sedated," Labcoat warned again.

"They'll come with me," I said, grabbing the rope out of the trainer's hand. Holding it loosely, I began humming *Norwegian Wood* out of tune. Apple swung her trunk to the beat and stamped a heavy foot on the ground. They followed me down the hill to the beat, crunching over the gravel until we reached the parking lot. I left Apple beside the first truck and guided Google to the second, leading him up the ramp into the cage. I rubbed his trunk then stood on tiptoes to kiss the side of his face. After shutting the gate, I returned to Apple and led her onto the other truck, locking the cage behind us.

"Let's go," I hollered to the drivers.

Two drivers headed for their cabs when the foreman told them to stop. "Un-uh. Against regulations. He can't be in there."

"I'm staying."

"Come up front with me," the driver offered.

A trainer unfurled the blue tarp over the bars of Google's cage like a curtain, hiding him inside. He stamped his feet in fear. "It's okay," I cooed, but the stamping turned to banging against the steel bars, rocking the trailer. I was afraid he'd tip over. "Relax," I soothed to no effect.

I started humming *Let It Be*, the same Beatles song Tou-san whistled while we washed his Mustang together. The trainers and drivers and foreman, even Angelica looked at me like I was crazy. Labcoat brandished his foot-long needle. I hummed louder. To everyone's surprise, including mine, the banging slowed and softened. Angelica began singing along and the others whistled to the long-forgotten words. The cage grew silent, the swaying eased to a final stanza. Labcoat stood on the sidewalk, his mouth hanging open. When the song was over, I stood with my hand on Apple, and pointed at the tarp on the roof.

"Close it up, boys," I yelled. "It's time to roll."

The trainer looked to the driver who pointed at the foreman. He waved an arm in disgust and walked away. The driver shrugged. "It's his funeral." The engine shuddered to life.

When the trainer released the clamps and the tarp fell over the cage, total darkness descended. I gripped Apple's trunk as the truck lurched forward, leaned into her as we turned onto the road, held tight to her leg as we bounced over potholes until we reached the highway.

Two hours later, when the truck stopped at a traffic light, I pushed the tarp back to see where we were. A thin line of sunlight illuminated the cage, falling over a tool chest in the back. I had Apple smash it open with her foot. Inside were screwdrivers, a drill, crowbar, tire jack, emergency lights, and a can of black spray paint. I considered spraying "Katie is a killer," but that would just be crude. And ineffective. I had a better idea. Using the phone to light Apple's side, I painted an S, the ends curled into an upright infinity, and added the umlauts on top—the SüprDüpr logo— onto the flank of the elephant.

When I was done, I kissed the crown of Apple's head and waited for the truck to stop. "I love you," I whispered. Then I pushed the canvas back, sunlight exploding in my face, and clambered down to the street. When the truck jerked forward, Apple trumpeted a sad farewell. I hummed *Norwegian Wood* to myself as she rumbled away, tears streaming down my cheek, already sad for what I had to do next.

Chapter 36
Throw Mama from the Teleporter

The solution was simple—just move the spot for the two elephants to materialize by a few feet each. That should have been easy. But when I tried to get into the teleporter through my backdoor again, an error message filled the screen: "All your base are gone!"

Damn. One of Satoshi's programmers must've discovered my backdoor. I probably would've liked the taunting bastard if I didn't hate him so much.

I swore at my incompetence. I was locked out, my backdoor deleted, my *persona non grata*'ed. The front door worked no better—Katie had changed her password. Now I was stuck, back to square one. I'd have to find another way in. I spent all night searching for any bug to exploit until my head fell onto the keyboard. In the morning, there was still nothing. My code was rock solid. I swore at my competence.

I lay on the bed to think, but without my friend Johnnie, my thoughts swirled with no focus, hopping from one useless idea to another. I needed serious inspiration. This was an emergency. With the last of my money, I bought a bottle at the MiniMart down the street, the most expensive one they had—Suntory Hibiki—its amber liquid refracted inside a twenty-four-sided crystal bottle.

As soon as I inhaled its aroma of oak and cedar, the solution banged me on the head—a 51% attack. Rather than changing the spot that Katie set for the elephants to appear, I could change the map instead.

All I had to do was get the blockchain to pass a fake map to the calculation software, which would send the wrong coordinates to the teleporter. The blockchain validated the correct local map to use by a vote of all the computers. I just had to supply a map with fake coordinates and convince the blockchain it was legit. And that only required 51% of the computing power to agree. I couldn't change the existing computers, but I could bring a lot of my own friends to the election.

MeCan's DeepThought cloud service offered instant computers for use, hundreds of thousands of state-of-the-art machines, enough to overwhelm the blockchain, for rent at pennies to the gigaflop. Stringing together a few petaflops, though, added up to real money. Kenta's prepaid card had only a few dollars remaining.

I called Kenta, feeling guilty to beg again. "Any way you can help me out with a little more cash?"

Silence. Plates clattering. People talking in the background. I waited. He sighed. "How much?"

How much did I need? More than a thousand, for sure. Probably closer to ten thousand. That was asking a lot. But there was nobody else I could ask. I wished I had more friends. I told him I could probably get by with five thousand dollars.

When I heard the sharp intake of breath, I added, "It's just for a couple days." Once the demo was over and the world knew the truth about SüprDüpr, I could come out of hiding. "It's for Ryu," I added, piling on the guilt.

"Yukiko's not going to...the baby expenses and all...I can't...you gotta understand."

So much for my best friend ever. "How about four thousand?" I tried. That might be just enough. "I'll pay you back. With interest. You can tell Yukiko it's an investment."

But it was impossible to squeeze blood from a turnip. "Sorry, bruh. I would if I could—you know that. I just don't have that kind of cash."

I stared at the useless phone.

"What about Sumire?" he asked, as if that were some brilliant idea. "I'm sure she'd be willing to help."

"I can't."

"I can't either. I'm really sorry, bruh. Maybe I can dig up another five hundred. Would that help?"

I knew what I needed to do, even if I didn't want to do it. At least it wouldn't be from pity. I thanked him and hung up before he could apologize again.

Sumire picked up her burner phone on the second ring, the first time I called it. "What is it?" she whispered, panic in her voice. "Is everything okay?"

"I'm fine," I said. "I need money."

"Ha," she grunted, all panic gone. "For what?"

"Hashing power. I need at least 1.21 gigahashes per second."

Technobabble always worked with the clueless scrubs in the office, but Sumire was too smart for that. "Why do you need 1.21 *jigahashes*, Ted? Whatever that is."

"I'm bored. I want to download porn. Lots of it."

She didn't laugh. "You're hacking."

"It's not hacking," I said. It wasn't hacking, not really—it was a blockchain attack. But the difference was difficult to explain. And wouldn't matter anyway. "I figured out how to stop Katie."

"You'll get caught. And I don't want you to end up like Ryu. They're looking for you, you know. You'll only make it easy for them to find you."

"There's no way anyone can trace me," I insisted. "Not even the NSA." Well, maybe the NSA since they invented the Tor browser and the dark web itself, but nobody else.

"Just stay there," she ordered. "I'll come over later and we can discuss it. Besides, I may have something to show you." When I asked what, she said, "Can't talk about it over the phone. I'll show you later. Don't do anything until then."

When Kaa-chan put her foot down, the only argument Tou-san ever made was to grab the Johnnie and watch her stew while he sipped at his cup, neither of them saying anything. Japanese people fought with silence. I didn't want to fight now. But I didn't want to be my father, either.

"I need to do this," I said. "One way or another. I have to stop Katie and there isn't much time left. If I can't get the money for a blockchain attack, I'll have to break into the Corinthian to reprogram the system. And that really would be Mission Impossible. So will you help me or not?"

A pause on the line. She knew I was bluffing. Finally, she sighed. "How much?"

"Ten thousand," I said, expecting a gasp and a list of reasons why that wasn't going to happen.

"Fine," she said, surprising me. "Under one condition."

I cringed. "What?"

"I'm paying for it. It's not a loan."

In other words, I was working for her. On her terms. And I had no choice but to agree.

"And you promise to be absolutely careful?"

"You said one condition."

"Stop screwing around and promise you won't do anything dangerous. Because I can't lose you, too. You understand that, don't you?"

No, I didn't understand. Lose me from what? What were we, after all? Not lovers, not investigator and client. But neither were we just friends or childhood sweethearts. I'd always been drawn to math because it was never ambiguous; there was always a right answer, even if finding it was a puzzle. But at least I knew the right answer to tell Sumire now. "Yeah, I promise." I had no intention of putting myself in any more danger than I had to, not before I could find out what she needed me for besides looking for her brother.

I read the digits of the credit card to her and a couple minutes later, had my anonymous DeepThought account running through a VPN from Moldova loaded with ten thousand dollars.

Chapter 37
Nevermore

I was deep in the code when a tapping noise broke me out of my trance. I blinked and realized the glowing frame of light around the blackout curtains had faded away; four hours had passed while I'd built my army of zombie blockchain miners. Now they were nearly ready. I returned to working on the last routine when I heard the tapping again. The door, I finally realized.

"Ted? Are you in there?" came Sumire's voice from outside, sounding simultaneously worried and annoyed.

The Suntory bottle beside me glowed a golden hue. I stuffed it into a drawer. I downed the rest of the glass, then dashed to the bathroom to hide the cup.

The knocking grew more insistent. "Ted? I know you're in there."

"Just a sec," I hollered. I dropped in a toothbrush for disguise, then rinsed out my mouth to be sure.

When I opened the door, Sumire was wearing a coral-colored dress and stood two inches taller in heels. She had a red ribbon in her hair and thick mascara and fake eyelashes that made her resemble a middle-aged woman trying hard to look Sumire's age. Eyes narrowed, she peered into the room behind me. "What are you up to in there?"

I pointed at the repurposed PlayStation wired to the TV. "Just gaming." I took the bags of groceries from her arms.

After stepping inside and shutting the door behind her, she grimaced as she slipped out of the shoes. She sniffed at the air. "You've been drinking," she said.

"Just a few sips," I admitted. I hadn't drank much of the Suntory yet.

"Come on, Ted. Your face is red." She fanned the air. "And I can smell it on your breath."

Jeez. She'd never objected to a nip or two from the bullets I'd brought to the river, had even been partial to vodka herself. But there was no point in arguing. I raised my hands in surrender. She was about to say something more, so I changed the subject, "Did you bring something to show me?"

She pulled out a document. "SüprDüpr's cap table," she said, holding it up in triumph.

I grabbed the list of the company's shareholders out of her hands. Katie's name was on top, Satoshi's right below. "How did you get this?"

"Sorry, NDA," she said, grinning.

"Don't forget—you're my lawyer."

"Let's just say I had a pleasant dinner with their lead investor. I told him I represented an ultra-high-net-worth individual considering putting money into their fund."

In other words, she'd gone out with some balding fart from Sam Hill Ventures, leering over her while he devoured a $300 steak. That's why she was so dolled up. I felt a stab of jealousy as I imagined her flirting with the baldie all evening. At least he'd come through with the cap table.

The spreadsheet of investors continued on for three pages. Below Katie and Satoshi and Sam Hill Ventures was Jesus and Evgeni—the CEO of MeCan—filling out the board of directors, Mayor Gadh and the entire city council as special advisors, the publisher of a local newspaper, the mayors of other cities around the Valley, and eleven of the twelve postdocs, too. It was there in black and white—all of them owned shares in SüprDüpr that would be worth millions if the company succeeded. No wonder they were happy to do Katie a favor or two, whatever she wanted to help out. I scanned down the page until I found Ryu's shares crossed out, marked forfeit. I flipped the page and looked over the rest: big-time politicians, a former Secretary of Defense, newspaper owners on both the right and the left, a fresh chunk for the owner of the elephant preserve. And there at the very bottom was my own name, my shares marked as forfeit, too.

"Holy shit," I said, my mouth hanging open.

"I told you she was a scammer."

"How could you know?"

"It was obvious just looking at her. But you men keep falling for it. I wasn't surprised you were attracted to that trashy glamour like a moth to a blowtorch, but Ryu? I still don't understand why he quit a good job to work at that crazy place."

"It's Unicorn Valley," I said sarcastically. "We're building the future. Reinventing the world. At least that's what everyone in this town says. Nobody with any ambition stays at Intel or MeCan, not when you can get crazy rich at a startup. I think Ryu was attracted to the glory when teleportation changed the world."

"And you?"

"I just want to make a difference, like what I do actually matters."

She looked at me, head cocked. "You do matter," she said.

"For what? To spend all day writing software that nobody needs?"

Sumire took my hand in hers. "Don't be an idiot, Teddybear. You matter to me."

"Oh," was all this idiot could say. If I wasn't an idiot, I would have pulled her tight and kissed her. That's what I wanted to do. That's what I should have done. But instead, I was an idiot and said, "Matter for what? To help you find your brother?"

"Is that all you think you mean to me?" she snapped, pulling her arm away. "Honestly, Ted? Tell me that's what you really believe and I'll leave right now."

I stared into her wide, chocolate eyes and she stared right back at me. The hero worship that had once made me feel tall with her gaze was gone, replaced with concern and warmth and even anger now, all mixed together, and maybe that was real love.

"God, you can be so dense. You know that? You're really smart, and you're even more stupid."

I couldn't deny she was right. "I try," I protested.

"Yeah, that's why I love you, I think."

The words hit me like a slap across the face, a blow more than a caress. "You love me? After everything that's happened?"

"Wrong answer, Ted."

I leaned toward her, lips searching for hers.

Two hands pushed me back. "Even more wrong, Teddy."

"I don't understand."

"That's the problem."

"Then tell me."

She sighed. "You're not ready, Ted. Not for me. Not for anybody. Not even after all this time."

"Why?" I asked, motioning my complete incomprehension.

"This," she said, opening the drawer hiding the bottle of Suntory. "I can smell it on you. On your breath. On your skin. It's worse than another woman."

We were having *this* argument. "I like sake. An occasional whiskey—what's wrong with that? I'm not an alcoholic," I insisted. "I only drink at night. I'm a social drinker."

"You don't have a social bone in your body."

"It helps me concentrate. Some people drink coffee. Some people take Ritalin. I have a drink or two. What's the big deal?"

"You drink because it helps you forget your crazy mother. The same reason your father drank. And it'll kill you as surely as it killed him. Can't you see that? I won't be there for that again, Ted, believe me, I won't. You have to straighten yourself out before it's too late because I can't do it for you."

"You might be in for a long wait."

"I've waited eight years, Teddybear. Your time is up."

Despite my ineffable charm, it was hard to believe she'd waited for me when I disappeared across the country without even following me on Insta. The complete opposite of a stalker. "You're saying you've had no other boyfriends since we broke up? I find that hard to believe."

"You're not listening, Ted. As usual. I never said I didn't have any other boyfriends. I've had plenty of boyfriends. I traveled a whole summer with Alex. We made love on the beach in Santorini. Yeah, I know you don't want to hear that. And worse, he was tall and strong, which I know you want to hear even less. He said he loved me, until he said he loved someone else more. I had an affair with a law school professor, the most brilliant man I ever met, yes, more brilliant than you, and almost as stupid, too. It was like a dream, until it was a nightmare. So no, Ted, you're not the only person who's made me suffer."

"I didn't—" I started, but Sumire wasn't finished.

"Typical male. You think I sat around pining for you when you left town in that crappy car you scraped together in some weird monument to your father? Well, I've got news for you, Ted—there were classmates at Princeton and friends at Berkeley, and I'm embarrassed to say, a quick fling or two that ended as soon as it started."

"Stop," I pleaded. I didn't want to hear about her flings.

"Stop?" she said. "Just when I'm getting to the good part? Because you see, Ted, none of those romances felt right. They were fun, and maybe I was even in love once or twice, but we didn't fit together, not like you and I did long ago, not like you and I do now. I didn't realize what I was missing until I walked into your sad little apartment and knew right away you needed me as much as I needed you. When I saw that dog-eared old manga there, all I wanted to do was sit with you on the riverside reading the rest of that stupid manga together for the rest of our stupid lives."

"Really?"

"It was a strange feeling that I thought would go away, but it never did. It just felt comfortable, beside you, even as my world was crumbling. And then, Ted, you stupid idiot, you told me to go out on a date with Mayeda. You almost broke my heart again. I was ready to kill you myself this time, you know."

I didn't know. I was oblivious. To everything. "Sorry."

"Yeah. I know. You really are. But that's not enough. Every time I'm ready to give up on you, you do something to redeem yourself. You've lost your job, you've risked your life to find Ryu. I know there's a good person in there, but the drinking, Ted, it's got to stop. For your own sake. You may think it's a bit of fun now, but it'll destroy you just like it destroyed your father."

"I'm not an alcoholic," I repeated.

"So prove it. Stop now. Right now. Today. I'll stay here with you if you need help."

I didn't need help. Not to stop drinking, if that's what I ever wanted to do. Not to stop Katie, and that's what I needed to do today. "The demo's tomorrow," I said. "I'm busy now."

She kissed me on the cheek. "Sayonara, Ted," she said. "And good luck." She turned and opened the door, a cool breeze fluttering the curtains.

"It all ends tomorrow," I yelled from the doorway as she stormed out into the night. "SüprDüpr dies. Come by and see the show—St. Jimmy's at noon."

But she didn't even turn around. The sound of the door slamming echoed around the room. It was the loneliest sound I'd ever heard.

I grabbed the bottle out of the drawer and stared at the label, black calligraphy down the front of the crystal. Distilled and barreled ages ago when Ryu, Kenta, and I were still the fearless threesome, long before Sumire and I had ever kissed, while she was still the fierce girl in a Hello Kitty t-shirt. I needed a jolt to finish my coding; I needed an eraser to get Sumire out of my head; I needed a drink, now more than ever.

I carried the bottle by the neck into the bathroom to grab my glass, a streak of toothpaste down the side. I filled the glass halfway, wishing I had some ice.

Tou-san would have poured three fingers and cradled it in his hands, swirling the liquid to open the flavors. He'd sit at the dining table for hours staring into the glass while Kaa-chan focused her anger, scrubbing the pots to a mirror finish until there was nothing left to clean, nothing more to vacuum. Then she'd yell at me in Japanese while I sat doing my homework, telling me not to become a good-for-nothing like my father who couldn't even understand what she was saying. I'd get up and leave, head to my room or out to Ryu's house to avoid hearing more. When I returned home late in the evening, Tou-san was usually out at the Dandy Lion, Kaa-chan locked in her bedroom crying, *Norwegian Wood* playing in a loop in her ears.

I dumped the glass into the sink, staining the porcelain reddish yellow. I unscrewed the cap and poured the liquid gold out, gurgling down the drain. When the room was silent again, the bottle clunked against the bottom of the trashcan, its echo never ending. I picked up my toothbrush and brushed my teeth, then sat at the desk and cracked every knuckle twice. It was time to show the world how teleportation worked.

🐘   🐘

My fingers were stuck on the keyboard, page after page of the letter j filling the screen, when I was awakened by a loud rumbling. I jumped up and snapped open the curtains as a flash of lightning split the sky, lighting up the oaks and jacaranda in the cemetery across the street. A loud crash of thunder rattled the windows. Headlights speared through the pouring rain, the drumbeat on the pavement a waterfall. The demo would have to be postponed, I thought with relief—I'd fallen asleep before I could finish testing. But even as the lightning continued splintering the sky like angry fingers from heaven, patches of dusty blue opened on the horizon.

When the storm's tantrum rolled off towards the desert, damp air floated into the room. Sparrows lined up on the telephone wires, chirping a happy tune. There was little time left to finish.

Without the whiskey, my head pounded worse than any hangover. I fired up the Keurig and downed a double dose of ibuprofen. Once the synapses returned to ready state, I resumed debugging. It would take at least three days to test everything; I only had three hours. I worked as fast as I could, shot after shot of coffee to help me concentrate. My fingers jittery, my heart pounding, my brain abuzz with flies, I made too many mistakes. I needed a drink to slow down and think. I was tempted to bird over to the MiniMart to pick up a bullet of Johnnie. But I told myself no—I didn't need it, and this was the time to prove it, right now when I needed it the most.

I guzzled water instead, glass after glass of it, waiting for the caffeine jitters to subside. Then I fired up my army of fake blockchain voters and armed them with my fake maps. I didn't even erase my tracks. There wasn't time, and it didn't matter—everyone would soon know what I'd done.

I stood at the window and took a deep breath, watching the swaying oak trees behind the cemetery wall. I clapped my hands twice and bowed as I called Ryu's name. "Help me today," I begged him. "I'm sorry for everything that happened between us. I hope we can be friends again." I knew it was pointless—Ryu was a Christian. So I crossed myself and prayed to Jesus, asking for his help, too. And then to God, and Allah, and the Buddha, and Douglas Adams, and finally to Ganesh, the elephant god, praying for his forgiveness. I hoped at least one of them was listening.

A raven swooped down to land on the slick blacktop outside my door, its feathers glistening iridescent purple in the morning sunshine. It turned its head sideways to look straight at me, its eye a perfect circle, and squawked three times to tell me something I couldn't begin to comprehend. Then it jumped up, flapped its wings, and soared away to the heavens.

Time was up. I donned my remembrance cap and locked the door behind me.

Chapter 38
Forty-Two Shades of Elephant

It was nearly high noon as I fought through the mass of humanity converging on St. Jimmy's. The entire world, or at least all of Unicorn Valley, was here to see Katie's demo. The plaza was overflowing with parents and children out of school for the day, bankers and lawyers down from their high-rises, even the flunkies from City Hall joining the curious and inquisitive from every corner of the world, thousands of feet trampling the freshly replanted grass to witness history in the making.

On the corner, the new shelter stared blankly over the square, its windows boarded and barred, police guarding the door in front. I pulled my remembrance cap low, then turned it backwards in case the cops were looking for me, but there was no chance they'd notice me amidst this mass of humanity. For the first time in my life, I was grateful to be short.

Cottony clouds sashayed high over the boxy towers that lined Santa Clara Street. On the horizon, I could just make out the Tangerine Tower against the outline of the hazy mountains, imagined Evgeni in his dome looking down over us while Satoshi sat in his Zen teahouse, sipping a bowl of matcha. I wished I could be there to see his expression when his billion-dollar investment evaporated into a worthless record on his blockchain. For a moment, I considered sneaking into the SüprPorter in the chaos that was about to ensue and teleport myself to Satoshi's tea house to deliver the news in person. Then I remembered that to zap myself there, someone would have to die for my sin.

I pushed my way to the barricades that lined 3rd Street and found the elm at the curb, the same tree that Azaz claimed as his home. It was a fitting tribute to the vet Katie murdered that his spot was about to become ground zero in her downfall.

Across the street, the white marble of the Corinthian shimmered like Cinderella's palace. When the tall doors swung open, the gathered masses erupted in cheer. Katie emerged in a chestnut-colored gown, her hair fluttering in the breeze. She waved to the cameras broadcasting the event to every corner of the world, then saluted the mayor, the city council, and all the luminaries awaiting their turn to congratulate her on ushering in a new era in transportation.

Descending the marble staircase in stiletto heels, when she spotted me at the front of the crowd, she nearly stumbled. Her smile froze, her teeth bared in hatred for the blink of an eye. Then she blew a kiss in my direction. Thinking the kiss was for them, the multitudes roared with delight and returned her kiss ten thousand-fold. She strode into the middle of the blocked-off street, her ugly chihuahua at her heels, and stood before an outline of an elephant painted on the street. Raising her arms high overhead, she motioned for the marching band to play.

When the clock ticked over to exactly twelve o'clock, the music stopped mid-thump; silence fell over the square. A sharp wolf whistle pierced the air, demanding action, then another, and another. Overhead, a pair of police drones circled, surveying the asphalt below. Everyone was waiting for an elephant to appear, but there was none yet, not a live one, not a corpse, not even a Beanie Baby.

I closed my eyes and hummed a tune until the explosion split open the world. A shock wave knocked the crowd back on its heels, toppling children off fathers' shoulders. A sphere of white light seared my eyelids as it expanded from the center of the elm tree, then imploded into itself before disappearing in a flash of light as bright as a million suns. A collective oooh trilled out of every mouth; then the screaming began.

Twelve thousand pounds of flesh materialized out of nowhere, not at the front of the parade as Katie intended but speared through the middle of the elm. Her forty-two shades of gray, from the ashen gray of her drooping trunk to the silvered gray of her floppy ears and the dusky gray of her wrinkled hide was marred only by the perfect blackness of the SüprDüpr logo painted across her side. A canopy of branches hung over her, golden leaves falling like rain. Her head slumped, eyes wide in shock; she hung motionless in the tree. Apple was dead.

Over the screams that filled the park, I heard a wild trumpeting from behind the white marble building. The second elephant—the one Katie had intended to impale inside the circus tent away from view of the crowd—was alive. I cheered when I caught a glimpse of gray in the distance as Google galloped off towards the highway.

The panicked crowd scattered all around me while I petted the rough hide of the dead elephant. "I'm sorry," I repeated over and over, while humming the sad Beatles tune. Sirens dopplered towards us from every direction; a police helicopter flew overhead, its slow thwop-thwop filling my ears until a cop car raced into the intersection and pulled to a stop at the curb. Its siren still screaming, Mayeda jumped out and jabbed his nightstick in my chest.

"I warned you, shrimp," he yelled over the din. "There's nothing I can do for you now."

"There was no other way," I said. "Your buddies were all in on it."

The Viking nearly ripped my arms off snapping handcuffs on my wrists. "Let's go, twerp," he said. He pointed up at a drone hovering low overhead, its camera watching me. "Jesus wants a word with you."

He was about to shove me into the cruiser when sharp nails dug into my neck. I turned to find Katie behind me, her face contorted with rage. "Why, Ted?" she demanded, as if she didn't know the answer.

When I said the world needed to know how the teleporter worked, she screamed, "You murdered a unicorn!"

SüprDüpr, her billion-dollar unicorn, R.I.P. "Can I get its head mounted?"

Her face turned as red as her hair. She kicked me with a pointed shoe. I gritted my teeth through the sharp sting and laughed. "Sorry, Katie, it's over."

"We would have been billionaires," she insisted. She stabbed a long finger towards the homeless shelter. "And we would have helped all the ones who could be saved, don't you understand?"

I looked at her again—the perfect face, the statuesque body, the sharpest mind in a town overflowing with geniuses. She had no idea how much of a monster she was. "You're even crazier than my mother."

The pint-sized chihuahua bit deep into my ankle, shooting pain up my leg. I escaped into the back of the cruiser where I stared at the white marble palace gleaming in the sun. Then the door slammed shut and the car rolled through the chaos, leaving the dog and Katie standing beside the murdered elephant, barking their obscenities at me.

Chapter 39
The Teleporting Bodies of Calaveras Creek

A girl in a crop t-shirt and canvas hi-tops came rushing at Katie as she stomped back up the stairs. It wasn't until I noticed her ears sticking out that I realized it wasn't just any girl.

"Stop!" I yelled to the front seat. The Viking only laughed.

"It's Sumire!" I said to Mayeda, pointing my chin towards the sidewalk.

Mayeda tapped the Viking on his bulging arm. "Hold up," he said. The Viking groaned, but the car jerked to a stop.

"Let me out," I begged. Though I couldn't see her face, I could see trouble brewing. She was poised in a crouch, legs parted, determined and unstoppable. Whatever happened next wouldn't be good. I needed to stop her, or at least take the heat. "We've got to help her," I said. The front seat ignored me.

Katie's face turned bright red, her arm pointing at the elephant pinned in the tree as she screamed at Sumire.

"Get her before she does something crazy," I told Mayeda.

"What do you want me to do, arrest her?"

"She's my lawyer. Just get her in the car."

But it was too late. When Katie jabbed a finger straight in my direction, Sumire grabbed her arm and tossed her face-down on the ground.

"Oof," Mayeda winced in sympathy.

"Get her," I demanded.

The Viking turned to sneer at me. "We're not your minions, twerp."

Katie lay on the concrete, blood spurting from her nose. Two cops grabbed Sumire's arms. Mayeda jumped out of the car, saluted the drone overhead, and sauntered into the crowd.

A coterie of cops huddled around Katie, offering their assistance. When Mayeda reached them, he took Sumire from the two cops holding her. She hugged him tight; he enveloped her in his arms.

"You gotta let me out," I implored the Viking.

"I don't have to do nothing for you, twerp."

An ambulance screamed through the crowd and pulled up at the curb. While the cops lifted Katie to her feet and escorted her to the paramedics, Mayeda snuck Sumire back to the patrol car. I melted with joy when I noticed Sumire's t-shirt—the cover of *One Piece*, the manga we always read together.

When she saw me inside the back seat, she broke into a wide smile. "Hello, Ted," she said, as if she hadn't walked out on me forever the previous day. "Thought I might run into you here."

She slid in beside me and rested her head on my shoulder. Mayeda hopped into the front. The Viking turned on the siren and the car rolled forward again.

"Nice move," I said.

Sumire blushed. "You saw that?"

My hands cuffed behind me, I leaned awkwardly to kiss her cheek.

"Mmmm," she purred. "No alcohol. But you need a shower, Ted. You smell like an elephant."

I started to say I was proud to smell like an elephant when she kissed me on the lips. Electricity zapped through me. For the first time in years, I knew everything would be okay.

"Hey!" the Viking yelled from the front. "None of that in here! Save it for when you get out of jail. In ten years."

As he guffawed at his joke, I worried everything might not be okay. I needed to figure out what to do. We only had a few minutes until we arrived at the police station where I'd face Jesus' wrath again.

What would Katie do now that her plans were in shreds? Go home to cry? No way. Take whatever money was left in the bank and run away? For Katie, even a hundred million was petty cash. She'd insist she was right about teleportation and make fresh plans for SüprDüpr. But she'd need Satoshi's help.

"We gotta go to Satoshi's place," I told Mayeda. "We can nab both of them there."

"Sorry, shrimp. Out of our jurisdiction."

"You're the one under arrest," the Viking added, as if I needed reminding.

How would Katie get there? Of course—she'd use the SüprPorter. She'd even had me configure a trip to the tea house when I demonstrated my software. I was sure she'd already teleported there at least once to show Satoshi, maybe convinced him to try it as well.

"Give me your phone," I said to Sumire.

She tried handing it to me, but my wrists were still cuffed behind me. I instructed her to open a map and trace a line from the Corinthian to the tea house.

It was just over ten miles, almost exactly to the south-west. Extending the line the same distance to the north-east landed in a wooded valley deep in the mountains beside Calaveras Creek. A place nobody would ever visit. Except Katie, who had already scoped out the site, even taken pictures. "Pin it," I said. It wasn't accurate to the millimeter, maybe not even to the meter, but it was close enough. I hoped.

I glanced up to the front seat. The cops were listening. Mayeda might be okay, but there was no doubt the Viking would rat us out to Jesus. I leaned towards Sumire, my mouth against her ear. "Hike to that spot," I whispered. "Bring reporters. And a camera crew."

Though the reporters had ignored me, they'd believe a lawyer like Sumire. Now that the SüprDüpr demo had failed so spectacularly, they'd be desperate for an inside scoop. Even the science editor who'd insisted teleportation was impossible would kill for the story. If he hadn't already killed himself.

"What's there?" Sumire asked.

"Dead bodies," I whispered. She gasped. "Be careful." I kissed the tip of her ear. She nodded. "I will."

"And Bunny-chan?"

"Yes, Ted?"

"*Aishiteru.*" The one word of Japanese I knew she understood because I'd told her that before, many times, many years ago, when we sat under the purple jacaranda trees reading manga together and watching the river flow by.

"I know, Teddybear."

Chapter 40
Hello.World

Herringbone was waiting for us at the perp entrance at the back of the police station, flanked by a blueboy on each side. When we pulled to a halt in front of the security gate, a sunburned cop rushed over to help Sumire out of the back seat while the other stood with a sneer on his face, hand on his holster, waiting for someone to make his day.

"Ma'am," Sunburn said, smiling as he tipped his cap to Sumire. Make My Day jerked me to my feet and slammed me against the car door. I gasped for air while an elbow dug into my back.

"Don't touch him!" Sumire yelled, shoving Make My Day off me.

"Do what she says," Mayeda laughed, a hand shielding his face, "unless you want your nose broken."

"She's a lawyer," Herringbone warned the crew. "Just bring the perp in and book him. Gently." He turned to Sumire. "And you," he said, "you stick around the lobby until Dr. Deauville decides if she wants to press charges for battery. Jesus would be thrilled to see you disbarred."

Sumire turned to me. "Guess I'll see you inside."

"Go," I whispered. "Get out of here. As fast as you can."

After kissing me on the cheek, she took my remembrance cap and placed it on her head, ears sticking out the side. I was about to tell her how cute she looked when Make My Day pulled me away, not so gently, and shoved me towards the gate.

"Follow the map," I yelled as the uniformed cop pushed me through the door, Herringbone right behind.

They led me into a small room for photographs and fingerprints, then dragged me into the chaos of the bullpen. Herringbone typed up a bunch of forms on a computer older than me, charging me with felony animal cruelty, then spat the pages out on a printer that still zipped back and forth like the classic frogger game. When the paperwork was done, Make My Day pushed me down the hallway to a holding cell in the back that reeked of alcohol. He swung the cage open and shoved me inside, then glanced about to make sure nobody was watching. The only person inside the cell was a drunk passed out on the bench.

"Elephant killer," Make My Day spat at me, kicking me with his steel-toed boots. I yelped in pain. "That's for my son," he snarled. "He loves elephants. He's been crying all day because of you." Then he kicked me on the other leg. "That's for my daughter. She loves parades and wanted to be in a marching band. Now she's traumatized for life." Then he punched me in ribs, the same spot Jesus had already pummeled. "And that's from all of us here for fucking up everything and making our town go to shit."

"Ow," I grunted, doubled over in pain.

"Asswipe," he muttered. He slammed the grated door and stomped away.

I could barely breathe for the throbbing in my side while bolts of pain shot up both legs. I held my ribs and staggered to the far corner to slump against the graywashed cinderblock. A cockroach peeked its head out from a crack to wave a friendly antenna at me. The drunk on the bench snored loudly. Even from the opposite side of the cell, the smell of alcohol and body odor was overwhelming.

Alone with my thoughts, I worried Sumire wouldn't find anything in the hills. Without the bodies, Jesus would try to pin Ryu's murder on me. I grew depressed thinking about what would happen. When a rat darted across the floor, I whistled at it to stop so I could ask it the meaning of life. It ignored me, too busy with its own problems to give a rat's ass about mine.

The whistle didn't stop the rat, but it did awaken the dead. The drunk choked a couple times before struggling upright in a fit of coughing. When he finally caught his breath, he saw me hunched over in the corner and narrowed his eyes to slits. "Who are you?" he croaked.

"Ted Hara," I introduced myself. "Unicorn killer."

He looked around the pen, confused. "Where are we?"

"Police station," I said. He grunted, surprised. "Holding cell," I added.

"At least it's not that shelter downtown. Turn you into Soylent there."

"Oh, it's worse than that. You can't even imagine."

He erupted in a fit of coughing until it subsided and he spat on the floor. Then he looked me over. "What's a nice boy like you doing here?"

"Pachycide," I answered.

He spat on the floor again. "That like patricide?"

"Same thing," I said. "Only bigger."

He laughed, loud and happy, though I was sure he had no idea what he was laughing at. I guessed him to be about Tou-san's age, but it was impossible to tell; his once pale skin was sunburned to a mottled brown, his dark hair streaked with gray, matching his bushy beard. He waved his hands to shoo away an imaginary fly buzzing around his head.

Graybeard declared, "I'm here for robbing a liquor store."

That figured. "Pretty stupid, don't you think?"

"Nah," he said, proud of himself, or at least happy to relate his story. "Bank robbers rob banks cause that's where the money's at, right? I robbed the liquor store cause that's where the hooch is at."

"And you got caught?"

"No, I got the drink just fine. It's when I went back later to buy some Soylent that they nabbed me."

Right. "Why not get a job? Employers around here will give you all the Soylent you want for free. Beer and whiskey, too."

"Already got a job," he said enigmatically.

"Liquor store thief?"

He laughed again, his eyes dazed. "Liquor store thief. Ha-ha, that's good. Maybe I can find one of those jobs on Indeed. Not very good at it though. Nah, I'm a writer. Surprise you, huh? Got a master's degree in writing, for what that's worth, which isn't much anymore. Cause nobody reads, at least not anything worth reading. Used to drink to help me write just like Hemingway and Fitzgerald. Now I drink so I can dream about what I'd write if I wasn't drunk."

That sounded too familiar.

Greybeard seemed intelligent, if lost, not unlike my father, a few years further gone. He asked what I was doing here. Without a computer or a phone or a video game, I had nothing better to do, so I told him my story.

When I was done, he chuckled. "Too crazy to make into a novel—nobody'd ever believe that."

That gave me an idea—if he could write novels, he could write HTML. Or do software testing. Companies were so desperate for employees, they were recruiting housewives in Bulgaria to build WordPress sites in their spare time. It didn't require an advanced degree in mathematics or even the ability to add. I could teach him. Of course, he'd have to sober up first. And quit robbing liquor stores.

I yelled at the cops long enough that they stopped ignoring me. When Sunburn came to shut me up, I begged him for pen and paper.

"What for?"

I pointed to Greybeard sitting on the bench looking sick. "Teach him how to program."

"Him?" the cop scoffed. "This I gotta see." He returned with a cop's spiral notebook and stood outside the cell. I sat beside Greybeard, flies both real and imagined buzzing around us, and explained how to print text to screen. Greybeard didn't get it.

"Show me," the cop said, handing me his antique MeCan JR phone. Fortunately, it still worked, even if the screen was too small for Greybeard's aging eyes. I typed the commands and hit go. "`Hello, World`," popped up on the screen.

"What's your name?" I asked.

"DC," he said. I wasn't one to make fun of someone's weird name. "`Hello, D.C.`," I made the program write on the screen.

The cop came into the cell to watch. Greybeard grabbed the phone out of my hand and had it display, "`Hi, Copper!`" He laughed as he held it up to the officer.

I showed them how to adjust the font's size and color, then made the big leap—turning the text into a string variable. Greybeard got it immediately, even explained it to the confused cop.

I spent the afternoon teaching both of them HTML and CSS, even a bit of rudimentary JavaScript until the steel bars of the door swung open. The Viking stood over us, arms folded, a thick ring of keys in his hand. Mayeda entered behind him. I was glad to see him, like a long-lost friend. "Hiya, pal," I said.

"Your lucky day, shrimp," Mayeda said. "You're out." The Viking scowled his disappointment.

I hadn't even had a bail hearing yet. "Did Sumire find the bodies?"

"Don't ask me. Someone called somebody, that's all I heard. They didn't tell me nothing except to get you the hell out of here."

I was suspicious. "Who?"

Mayeda lifted his eyes upwards.

"Jesus?" I asked. "Why would Jesus want me free?"

He pointed his finger upwards. "Higher."

Who was higher than Jesus? "Mayor Gadh?" That made no sense.

But Mayeda nodded. "You didn't hear nothing from me, pal."

Why would Gadh spring me from hell? He was implicated, too, owning shares in SüprDüpr like the rest of them, expecting Katie to teleport the city's SAT scores into the stratosphere and his own political aspirations to the moon.

"The mayor works in mysterious ways," Mayeda chuckled as he crossed himself. "Best not to ask."

I shook hands with Greybeard and promised to help him after he got out. Sunburn begged me to continue teaching him. Since there was no way I was coming back to the police station, the three of us agreed to meet at Greybeard's tent on the freshly planted lawn of St. Jimmy's. Sunburn promised to bring the coffee.

As I was walking out, the cockroach peeked out from the crack in the wall and dipped his antenna at me. I waved a fond farewell. Then I limped out through the open gate, hands clutching my side, to follow Mayeda down the long corridor, a free and confused man.

Chapter 41
Voice of Gadh

Sumire didn't answer her phone or reply to my messages. I was worried. I hoped she was still in the wilderness with no cell coverage, not dead in the woods with the other bodies. There was nothing I could do at the police station, though, and no reason to continue hiding in the motel. It was time to go home.

Birding down the streets of Japantown, I shouted a greeting to Mrs. Okada sweeping the sidewalk around her optometry shop before skidding to a stop at the Nijiya. I hadn't eaten all day.

As I walked down the refrigerator aisle to grab a bento, the bottles of sake called out to me: the Hakkaisan whispered my name from the peaks of its eight snowcapped mountains, the Kikusui sweet-talked me to come closer, the overwhelming silence of the Mu waited patiently, while the sparkling Dassai sisters bowed demurely, each more seductive than the other. My mouth watered, my heart raced, my hands shook as I reached out. They promised to help me find Sumire, or comfort me if she didn't return.

No, I told myself, I needed to be clearheaded. I needed to be ready for Sumire. I needed to be ready for myself.

I picked out a salmon bento, grabbed a big jug of electrolyte drink to wash down the ibuprofen, then crossed the street to Shuei-do for an assortment of *mochi* to celebrate when Sumire returned.

Climbing the creaking staircase back to my apartment, I was surprised to find my door ajar. Inside, the file cabinet had been ransacked, papers strewn over the moldy carpet. All my computers were gone, their cables left snaking across the floor. The empty bottles from the recycling lay dead on the counter, making a mockery of what had already been a perfectly disgraceful mess. I rushed over to Kaa-chan's tea cabinet, relieved to find unmolested the collection of priceless implements that nobody would ever use.

I reached inside for Kaa-chan's favorite tea bowl, hand-thrown and unsymmetrical. Turning it over, I stared at the signature on the bottom, ten strokes that meant enlightenment—Satoshi. As I traced the character with my finger, I had my own moment of enlightenment. Instead of peace and harmony, though, it filled me with anger for Kaa-chan's selfishness at leaving me alone in this world.

I smashed the bowl onto the floor where it landed with a clunk. I stamped on it with my bare foot, breaking it into pieces, smashing it into smaller and smaller shards until there was nothing remaining but gray dust. I took out the bowl Kaa-chan had made with Satoshi and smashed it to bits, too. Next was my favorite—blue and white and perfect—and ground it into the carpet. Then the next. And the next. Until every bowl in the cabinet was reduced to ash. When I surveyed the destruction around me, I thought I heard Tou-san cheering.

There was still no word from Sumire. I brewed a cup of tea with a teabag and set it in front of Kaa-chan's urn, then offered tap water in a shot glass to Tou-san. Not what they wanted, but from now on what they'd get. I lit two candles and bowed my head as I rang the bell to summon them, begging for their forgiveness. I asked them to watch over me, but this time, I asked them to watch over Sumire, too. Then I picked up the wedding photo, kissed it once, and put it away inside the cabinet.

The carpet was a mess, the whole room covered in gray dust. The five vacuums gasped at the disaster in front of them when I opened the closet door. I grabbed the pink Panasonic, Kaa-chan's pet, and ran it back and forth over the ground, whining as it sucked up the ceramic dust to restore the carpet to its original moldy green color. I continued cleaning for what felt like hours until the pain in my side overpowered the ibuprofen. Only when the high-pitched whine faded to its last echoes did I realize the phone had been vibrating. There were a dozen messages lined up waiting. All of them from Sumire.

"Where are you?" I asked when I called her. "I was worried."

"Where were *you*?" she replied. "You didn't answer."

"I was cleaning."

That surprised her. "I was sure something had happened to you."

"Something did." It was difficult to explain.

"Get over to the Dandy Lion," she said. "Hurry!"

A million thoughts rushed through my head as I ran to the ramen joint, the innumerable ways my plan could have gone awry and placed Sumire in danger. When I rolled the wooden door open on its rail, I was surprised to see a large crowd standing inside facing the television in back. For the first time ever, the TV was tuned to something other than a baseball game or highlights of the sumo match. Sumire was standing under the TV, still in her manga t-shirt and hi-tops. I shouted her name.

Half of Japantown—from the golf farts who spent every night drinking here to the robed priests from the temple who wouldn't be caught dead in a noodle bar—turned to look at me.

"Teddybear!" she yelled. Despite the tittering at my nickname as the crowd parted to let me through, I couldn't imagine anything she could have said that would've made me happier.

I put my arms around her waist and pulled her tight. "Thank God you're safe," I said. But when I leaned in to kiss her, she turned to squirm away.

"Um, you kind of need a shower."

I started to tell her everything that had happened, but she shushed me and pointed at the screen. On the television, a news conference was starting, a man approaching a podium in front of a crowd of reporters. It wasn't until I noticed the post-modern monstrosity behind him that I recognized the round face, the squat body, the watermelon belly of Mayor Gadh. He flashed a smile of the whitest teeth before speaking into the bank of microphones.

"I'd like to give an update on reports of bodies discovered in the Diablo Mountains," declared the voice of Gadh as cameras flashed around him. "The bodies are being extracted now and are undergoing DNA identification. While we are aware of rumors that the bodies may have been members of the displaced community of San Jose, that has not been determined conclusively so I will refrain from comment at this time. However, as a proactive measure, the San Jose Police Department has opened an investigation into whether these deaths are connected in any way to the activities of a local startup named SüprDüpr, of which everyone I'm sure is aware of their elephant disaster earlier today which is under separate investigation."

"I found them," Sumire told me as the mayor droned on. "Right where you pinned it. It was awful. Body parts all over the place. And rats. White rats. Everywhere. I got the hell out of there as quick as I could."

"Are you okay?" I asked. Instead of replying, she snuggled against me, holding her nose from the smell. "How did Gadh find out so quickly?"

"He's omniscient," she joked, pointing up to the heavens. "Satellite phone. One of the reporters called him while we were still out there."

"Before I take questions," Gadh continued, "I'd like to salute the efforts of a courageous young woman named Sue Mary Yamaha."

"It's 'Su-mi-re!'" I yelled at the TV. I didn't even bother correcting the mangled last name.

"There are never many heroes in a tragedy like this, but today we have one—a young lawyer and citizen of San Jose whose search for her missing brother prompted her to discover these bodies. We owe her a tremendous debt of gratitude. On behalf of the entire city, I'd like to offer her our sincerest thanks."

The crowd inside the noodle joint erupted in cheers. Hands reached out to pat Sumire's back. It was me who figured it out, I wanted to scream. But Sumire grabbed my hand and kissed my cheek and I realized it didn't matter.

When Gadh left the podium to congratulations all around, I balled my fists, "Is he going to get away with this? Him and Jesus, too?"

"Don't worry, Teddybear. I sent a copy of SüprDüpr's cap table to everyone in the press. You can post it on Reddit, too, or write up the story on Medium."

The cap table. Listing all the shareholdings, Gadh's as well as Jesus' and the entire crew of Katie's angels. "You're brilliant," I said.

"I know," she answered, smiling.

When the press conference ended, we said our goodbyes and followed the crowd though the narrow doorway. As soon as we stepped outside, I was blinded by flashes from hundreds of cameras, reporters fighting for space on the sidewalk shouting questions at Sumire. I ducked through the crowd and stood on tiptoes to wave at Sumire a last time. Then I headed home. There was a box of *mochi* calling me from the refrigerator, and I was getting hungry.

Chapter 42
Life, the Universe, and Elephants

Ryu's second funeral was at Betsuin Temple. After skipping the first at his church, there was no avoiding this one. With both of my parents' funerals in this same sanctuary, there was no place I less wanted to be. I waited until the rest of the crowd had headed inside and the chanting of the priests began floating over the lawn before I climbed the stairs and stepped over the threshold into the chapel.

The hall was packed. All of Japantown was here. Mayeda and his buddies in crisp blue uniforms sat together in the back. Politicians in sharp haircuts perched together near the front. Mrs. Okada, the optometrist, sat beside Mr. Nishida, the dentist, just as their shops had sat side-by-side on Jackson Street since the beginning of time. The crew from Nijiya filled an entire row. The sweet girls from Shuei-do sat behind them, next to the manicured women from the Shiseido shop. The dayglow pink hair of the waitresses from the sushi joint added a dash of color to the inky sea of black.

Sumire was in the front row between her divorced parents, her head craned scanning the door all the way in the back. When she saw me, she waved for me to join her. I'd planned to hide in the last row and duck out as soon as the ceremony was over. Sumire had different plans. She pointed at the bench beside her. I pointed at my clothes.

I was dressed in a black hoodie and jeans, the only dark clothes I owned. I couldn't bring myself to buy a black suit, not after tossing my last one in the dumpster after Kaa-chan's funeral. There was no way I could sit in the front row with Sumire looking like a bad avatar of Zuck.

I could almost hear Sumire sigh from across the room. I was hoping she'd let me hide in the back and castigate me later. But with all of Japantown watching, she strode down the aisle to escort me to the front.

Sumire's father stood to shake my hand. I smelled the tang of alcohol on his breath. Before I finished offering him my condolences, Sumire's mother, short and gaunt, wrapped me in a bearhug and planted a wet kiss on my cheek.

"Thank you, Tatsu-kun," she whispered. "You were a real friend to Ryu."

I wished she was right. Her words made me feel guilty for abandoning him, not staying in touch, not keeping him out of Katie's clutches. "I'm sorry," I said, bowing my head in shame.

"Don't be. You brought him back to us. Without you, he'd be lost forever."

When she let go of me, I tried slipping away to the back. I didn't belong here—I wasn't family. But the two women grabbed my shoulders and sat me on the bench between them. Her mother gripped my arm on one side, Sumire clenched my hand on the other. And somehow, being trapped between these two women felt exactly where I belonged.

A poster-sized photograph of Ryu looking proud and handsome in his high school baseball uniform stood behind the casket of inlaid mahogany. The casket was sealed, of course. I wondered what was left of Ryu's body when it was recovered from the depths of the ocean.

The casket was surrounded by wreathes of white carnations donated by every organization across Japantown, even the police department and the mayor's office. Against the wall, the five golden Buddhas sat staring outward, silently chanting their message that this world was but an illusion, our lives of suffering nothing but a trifle to be endured.

When a gong rang out, the chanting ceased and a hush fell over the room. The minister stepped to the podium and began singing hymns in English and Japanese. Sumire's hand tightened on mine. I squeezed hers back. On the other side, her mother leaned in closer. I wrapped an arm around each and pulled them against me. Sumire buried her head in my shoulder and started crying. Hot tears streaked her mascara, puddling against my neck.

When the prayers stopped, Sumire took a handkerchief from her purse. Instead of dabbing around her eyes, she wiped the cloth under my glasses. "You're crying, Ted," she said, stating the obvious.

I didn't know if I was crying for Ryu, or for my mother, or for Apple the Elephant, or for the family I'd suddenly found.

As we took our turn at the casket dropping incense powder into the flame to wish Ryu a safe journey, above the casket I saw an elephant floating. Apple's spirit still needed my help to find the peace of the next world.

The pony galloped into the parking lot in a crunch of gravel; a cloud of white dust billowed as I pulled up alongside the lemon Prius.

"You're late," Sumire said, waving the grit away from her face.

I checked the time. It was three minutes before 6 p.m., which made me two minutes late. "Sorry," I said. "First day of work."

When I climbed out of the car, a yippy little dog growled at my ankles.

"Come, Higgs," Sumire said, clapping her hands. The dog didn't move.

"Higgs?" I looked down at the ugly mutt. He snarled at me through crooked teeth.

"Isn't he a little cutey? We always wanted a dog, didn't we?"

I didn't know what she meant by 'we' because there wasn't a we, not yet, though I aimed to change that today. Still, I didn't care much for dogs in general and this one in particular. And he didn't like me either. "You wanted a dog," I said. "Not me."

"And you wanted me. So *we* wanted a dog. Simple math, Ted."

"But why him?"

"Someone had to take care of him now that Katie's gone." She started up the path. "Come," she said, though it wasn't clear if she was calling to the dog or me. Higgs growled at me before trotting off after Sumire's ankles.

As soon as she left the hospital, a bandage over her broken nose, the wig and sunglasses less of a disguise against the waiting cameras than the 49ers jersey and flip-flops she'd borrowed from a nurse, Katie had headed straight to the Corinthian to teleport herself to St. Kitts—a small island in the Caribbean with beautiful beaches and no extradition treaty—leaving the dog behind.

"Too bad about the nose," I said. I imagined Katie's pretty face marred forever with a crooked beak.

"I wouldn't worry," Sumire said. "She'll get a better one. That wasn't her first, anyway."

The day Katie disappeared, the federal government had classified teleportation research top secret as a weapon and sent a platoon of Marines to guard the Corinthian until the SüprPorter could be dismantled and trucked to Los Alamos National Lab. Around the same time, seventeen billion dollars of BiteCoins disappeared into a new anonymous wallet. The police assumed that Satoshi was holed up with Katie on their island paradise. I took one glance at the map and knew they were wrong; Katie had teleported herself from San Jose to St. Kitts, so Satoshi had gone in the opposite direction—to the bottom of the Pacific.

Sumire noticed a bandage on my arm and looked at me with concern. "What happened?"

I peeled away the white gauze to show her a fresh tattoo—the face of an elephant wearing an Asahi baseball cap. "Pretty cool, huh?" I was proud of it. My elephant.

Sumire rolled her eyes, unimpressed, and started up the hill. The dog jumped around in front of her while I trailed a step behind lugging a shovel and a shopping bag. Behind us, the door of the trailer slammed.

"You!" a voice screamed. I turned to see a finger pointed at me like a gun. "You stay away from here." Angelica rushed up the hill and planted herself in front of us, glowering as she blocked our way.

"The court granted him visitation rights," Sumire explained. "And he's paying for Google's upkeep."

That was the deal Sumire had negotiated to keep me out of jail—a guilty plea to misdemeanor cruelty to animals, the other charges dropped. How I would pay Sumire back the million dollars for Google's upkeep I owed as restitution, I had no idea. Not with my new job.

"You killed Apple," she spat at me.

"Sorry," I said quietly. "I loved her like my mother."

"Murderer!" she screamed and ran away. Higgs chased after her until Sumire whistled him back.

When we reached the top of the berm, I hollered into the hills. As the echo bounced around the forest, a loud trumpeting returned in reply. Google lifted his trunk in greeting and trotted over to the fence. We clambered down the hill to meet him.

Higgs slipped under the fence and bounded around the elephant's thick legs, unafraid of being stomped on. Google reached out to place his trunk on my shoulder. Sumire fed him an apple from her bag. He popped it into his mouth and gestured for another.

Taking out a bag of carrots, Sumire's idea of a healthy elephant snack, she asked why I brought the shovel.

From the top of the ridge, Angelica was watching us. We'd have to move fast. I grabbed Sumire's hand and ducked through the fence, pulling her along.

"What are you doing?" she screamed.

"Hurry!" Angelica was already dialing security.

Sumire grabbed my arm as we dashed across the open ground. Higgs yapped as he danced around our feet while Google loped behind. Halfway to the forest, I had to stop to catch my breath. Google reached out to take the heavy shopping bag and shovel in his trunk. My load lightened, we raced for the woods, ignoring Angelica's exhortations to stop.

After reaching the trees, we hid behind a thick stand of bamboo. I took the bag from Google's trunk and opened it up to show him. Inside was a collection of bones and ash. From the sad glaze over Google's eyes, I could see he understood.

"Where did you get that?" Sumire asked.

I told her about the head zookeeper at Happy Hollow who'd been given the unhappy task of disposing of the remains of an impaled elephant. I'd helped him with the cremation, taking a bag full of bones with me when we were done.

After digging a hole in the loamy soil, I reached into the shopping bag and pulled out long metal chopsticks. I handed a set to Sumire and kept another for myself. Together we gripped a bone between us as the Buddhist ceremony required, lifting it out of the bag and depositing it into the ground. As we held a second bone, Google took it from us. He lifted it high in the air and trumpeted so loud it felt like my ears would explode. A flock of birds rose from the trees and scattered across the sky. Google stamped his front feet, shaking the ground with the force of an earthquake, then set the bone in the hole beside the first one. Overhead, a raven circled, cawing down at us.

We held the next bone out to Google, but he didn't take it. Sumire and I looked at each other. Holding the bone between us, we lifted it high into the air. I whistled as loud as I could and Sumire yodeled. Overhead, the raven answered with a caw. Then we stamped the ground and set the bone down beside the others.

Before we could get the next bone out, Google lifted the entire bag with his trunk and dropped it into the hole. As he swept loose dirt over it, Sumire and I joined in with our hands to cover the hole. Then Google tamped it with a foot and Higgs jumped around on top.

We petted Google's rough hide while he trumpeted one last time. I was sure he was saying goodbye. The sad sound echoed off the distant mountains and dissipated into the air. The raven flapped its wings, cawed once more, and flew away.

While walking back towards the fence, Sumire asked, "When are you going to tell me about your new job?"

The headhunters had begun calling within minutes of the news about SüprDüpr. A startup in its death throws meant coders looking for work, managers with full teams ready to jump ship, even Harvard MBAs willing to take jobs at less than exorbitant pay. Headhunters lived for the day a unicorn imploded, sending them into a feeding frenzy. But other than Katie, the only employee of SüprDüpr the headhunters could find was me. So they'd begged for introductions to the rest of the team, offering a big commission for every hire. I laughed and hung up.

I told Sumire about the lowly intern in MeCan's HR department who'd called asking if I was looking for a new career. I'd told her I enjoyed being unfairly fired from MeCan so much the first time, I'd love to try it again. Then I hung up. I'd put the kettle on to make tea, but the water wasn't even boiling when the phone rang again, this time from the vice president of HR, the same woman who'd stripped me of my badge. She wouldn't stop apologizing for the misunderstanding. I'd told her to talk to my lawyer before hanging up on her. The tea was still brewing when Evgeni, the CEO himself, called from the 44th floor of his Tangerine Tower to offer me a promotion to manage their new blockchain group. I'd get a private office with a mountain view, plus all the kale-frosted gluten-free pizza I could eat. I didn't laugh and didn't hang up. Instead, I convinced him to invest in my startup.

Sumire eyed me suspiciously. "You're building a startup? You?"

"The next unicorn," I said with a straight face.

"Doing what? And you'd better not say you're revolutionizing transportation."

"Better," I laughed. "Coding schools. We're teaching people how to program. Basic stuff—HTML and CSS, WordPress maintenance. Some JavaScript for the advanced students."

Sumire knit her eyebrows. "Aren't there plenty of coding classes already?"

But mine would be different, I told her—no tuition. Free food and housing. We'd take the homeless, the displaced, anyone without a job. Even cops, if they want to be rehabilitated. We'd teach them a skill. They'd live in our dorms during training—no drugs, no alcohol, free medical care. When they graduated, they'd have a job waiting.

"Employers are desperate," I explained. "MeCan already signed up. And guess who's financing it—Sam Hill Ventures, the guys who funded SüprDüpr. The guilt card helped. Promising not to expose their role in SüprDüpr helped even more."

"That's evil," she laughed. "And legally, that's extortion."

"It's for their own good. They'll make billions from this investment."

"How can you afford to build training centers?"

That was the best part. I'd negotiated a deal with the mayor to take over the SüprDüpr shelter. And I was converting the Corinthian to classrooms now that the teleporter was gone. No bars on the windows, no cops, no guards. Doctors instead of pastors. All the Soylent they could drink. And job training.

"Katie actually had a good idea," I said, "even if it was only so she could kill them. Mayor Gadh is promoting it. And Gianni's is putting a pizza shop in the basement. Best spot in town now that St. Jimmy's is full of tourists."

Google stamped his feet in support.

Was I deluded, infected with *unicornitis*? Probably—but so was every founder of every startup. It came with the territory. Most crashed and burned while a rare few succeeded. But with Gadh tweeting about it, mayors all over the country were begging me to open a school in their city. The VCs were fighting each other for the right to hand me millions of dollars.

Of course, I wasn't so deluded that I thought this would help everyone. But it was a start. Once we had the first schools running, we'd open more inside prisons so people would have a job when they got out. The opportunity was massive.

"I need to hire a lawyer," I said. "Someone who understands real estate. We're going to replicate Teddybear Code Shelters in every city. We'll help people, really help them, and make money, too." I took Sumire's hand in mine. "Join me," I pleaded. "I need you."

I looked at Sumire hoping she'd be excited. But she only sighed. "Teddy, Teddy, Teddy. Why couldn't you get a regular job?"

"This is the job we were waiting for, Bunny."

"You mean this is the job you were waiting for?"

"And you were waiting for me. So we were waiting to do something useful. Together. It's simple math. Join me. One plus one equals a billion dollars. This'll be the next unicorn. You'll have your own office. With a view of the park. And all the Gianni's you can eat."

Sumire laughed. Then she wrapped her arms around me and kissed me. "Okay, Ted," she said. "On one condition."

"What's that?" I asked, holding my breath.

"I get to be Chief Elephant Officer."

As I hugged her tight, Google wrapped his trunk around our shoulders and Higgs yapped at our feet.

"I'm never letting you go again," I whispered.

"I know, Teddybear."

Goodbye!

Acknowledgments

In Haruki Murakami's short story, *The Elephant Vanishes*, the narrator tries to figure out how an elderly elephant could disappear from its cage. Anyone who studies magic knows making an elephant disappear is the easy part; the real trick is making it reappear. But if a hulking elephant suddenly materialized out of nowhere on the streets of San Jose, what would that mean? Being the heart of Silicon Valley, someone had just become a billionaire for inventing a better form of transportation.

When the first words of what eventually turned into *To Kill a Unicorn* were written more than six years ago, the story was about an angry toaster, an evil dog, and a magically appearing elephant. That draft went up in flames. Version two, where Ted and Katie made their first appearances, sank into the swamp. I thought I was making progress, but version three fell over and burned down before also disappearing into the swamp. What followed were weeks and months tearing up outlines and tearing out my hair. I became the caricature of a writer—crumpling up sheets of paper and throwing them onto the floor.

Then one day, it hit me—I had to let go of the story I wanted to write and write the story that wanted to be written. It was tough to let my angry little toaster go, but once I did, everything fell into place.

By coincidence, *Bad Blood*, John Carreyrou's exposé of Theranos had just come out. The details of how Elizabeth Holmes' idea for a better blood testing machine turned into a billion dollar fraud provided the missing details for how Katie would keep the horrific downsides of her teleporter secret from the public. As the denizens of Silicon Valley are fond of repeating: there are no problems, only opportunities. Even murder can be a solution for the creative entrepreneur who finds the right problem.

So I owe a huge debt to both John Carreyrou and Elizabeth Holmes. And to Haruki Murakami. And, of course, to Douglas Adams, Salmon Rushdie, and the writers of the screenplay of Chinatown.

Over the more than half decade it took to bring this book to fruition, there were so many people who lent a hand, offered useful advice, or provided encouragement. To everyone, a huge thanks.

To my illustrator, the manga artist, Ardee Arollado, who somehow knew exactly what I wanted.

To my professors in the MFA program in Creative Writing program at Otis College: Peter Gadol, Guy Bennett, Marisa Matarazzo, and Paul Vangelisti. Paul's class on the mystery novel was especially helpful, particularly his advice to always follow the money.

To the Pandamoon Publishing team who did their magic to turn a rough manuscript into a book. Zara Kramer, the CEO and Publisher, who runs a publishing company like a startup. Alan Kramer who gets everything done. Elgon Williams and Christine Gabriel leading the marketing charge. And especially, Rachel Schoenbauer, editor extraordinaire, who pointed out the little things on every page that needed improvement.

To the team at Beamlink, who taught me what it means to be young and smart. If some of the characters' banter sounds familiar, well, I owe you a bottle of sake. And especially to Mateo Abascal who showed me how Ted should act and sound.

To early readers, Rebecca Copeland and Jackie Fuchs who provided essential feedback.

To all the startup founders who give me daily inspiration. The challenge of writing a novel is nothing compared to what it takes to build a company from scratch.

And most importantly, to my wife Satsuki, who stands by me and encourages me, my reason for getting up every morning, who teaches me the secrets of tea ceremony and vacuums, who leaves me to work in peace on the novel, ignoring the screams from my office, and only interrupts my writing for emergencies once every few minutes.

Lastly, to you, for reading my crazy story all the way to the very last line of the acknowledgements. A big *arigatou*!

About the Author

DC Palter is a startup founder and CEO, with twenty-five years experience leading tech companies. As a venture investor and startup advisor, he's guided dozens more. His weekly articles on business strategy and venture capital are followed by tens of thousands of readers throughout the startup community.

Beginning his career as a research engineer in Japan, DC developed a deep appreciation for Japanese culture. He's the editor-in-chief of *Japonica*, a journal of Japanese culture, and the author of *Colloquial Kansai Japanese*, a guide to the Osaka-Kyoto dialect. He's also published two textbooks on satellite communications. His articles on technology and investing have appeared in over 100 industry publications and journals. To Kill a Unicorn is his first novel.

DC holds an MFA in creative writing along with degrees in engineering, marketing, and law. He currently resides in the Silicon Beach area of Los Angeles together with his wife.

Your purchase of *To Kill A Unicorn* by **DC Palter** supports our growing community of talented authors. If you enjoyed this book, please let the author know by posting your review at https://www.pandamoonpub.com and register today to receive advance notice of new book releases, special bundles, and discounts.

pandamoon
publishing

Growing good ideas into great reads…one book at a time.

Visit http://www.pandamoonpublishing.com to learn about other works by our talented authors.

Mystery/Thriller/Suspense

- *A Flash of Red* by Sarah K. Stephens
- A Rocky Series of Mysteries Book 1: *A Rocky Divorce* by Matt Coleman
- Ballpark Mysteries Book 1: *Murder at First Pitch* by Nicole Asselin
- Ballpark Mysteries Book 2: *Concession Stand Crimes* by Nicole Asselin
- Bodie Anderson Series Book 1: *Code Gray* by Benny Sims
- David Knight Thrillers Book 1: *The Amsterdam Deception* by Tony Ollivier
- Dee Rommel Mysteries Book 1: *10 DAYS* by Jule Selbo
- Dee Rommel Mysteries Book 2: *9 Days* by Jule Selbo
- *Fate's Past* by Jason Huebinger
- *Graffiti Creek* by Matt Coleman
- *Juggling Kittens* by Matt Coleman
- *Killer Secrets* by Sherrie Orvik
- *Knights of the Shield* by Jeff Messick
- *Kricket* by Penni Jones
- *Looking into the Sun* by Todd Tavolazzi
- *Mile Marker Zero by Benny Sims*
- *On the Bricks* by Penni Jones
- *Project 137* by Seth Augenstein
- *Rogue Alliance* by Michelle Bellon
- *Sinai Unhinged* by Joanna Evans
- *Southbound* by Jason Beem
- *Suicide Souls* by Penni Jones
- *The Juliet* by Laura Ellen Scott

- *The Last Detective* by Brian Cohn
- The Moses Winter Mysteries Book 1: *Made Safe* by Francis Sparks
- The New Royal Mysteries Book 1: *The Mean Bone in Her Body* by Laura Ellen Scott
- The New Royal Mysteries Book 2: *Crybaby Lane* by Laura Ellen Scott
- The New Royal Mysteries Book 3: *Blue Billy* by Laura Ellen Scott
- *The Ramadan Drummer* by Randolph Splitter
- The Teratologist Series Book 1: *The Teratologist* by Ward Parker
- *The Unraveling of Brendan Meeks* by Brian Cohn
- The Zeke Adams Series Book 1: *Pariah* by Ward Parker
- The Zeke Adams Series Book 2: *Fur* by Ward Parker
- *This Darkness Got to Give* by Dave Housley
- *To Kill a Unicorn* by DC Palter

Science Fiction/Fantasy
- Children of Colonodona Book 1: *The Wizard's Apprentice* by Alisse Lee Goldenberg
- Children of Colonodona Book 2: *The Island of Mystics* by Alisse Lee Goldenberg
- Dybbuk Scrolls Trilogy Book 1: *The Song of Hadariah* by Alisse Lee Goldenberg
- Dybbuk Scrolls Trilogy Book 2: *The Song of Vengeance* by Alisse Lee Goldenberg
- Dybbuk Scrolls Trilogy Book 3: *The Song of War* by Alisse Lee Goldenberg
- Everly Series Book 1: *Everly* by Meg Bonney
- Everly Series Book 2: *Rosewood Burning* by Meg Bonney
- Finder Series Book 1: *Chimera Catalyst* by Susan Kuchinskas
- Finder Series Book 2: *Singularity Syndrome* by Susan Kuchinskas
- Fried Windows Series Book 1: *Fried Windows (In a Light White Sauce)* by Elgon Williams
- Fried Windows Series Book 2: *Ninja Bread Castles* by Elgon Williams
- *Humanity Devolved* by Greyson Ferguson
- Magehunter Saga Book 1: *Magehunter* by Jeff Messick
- Magehunter Saga Book 2: *Priesthunter* by Jeff Messick
- *The Bath Salts Journals Volume One* by Alisse Lee Goldenberg and An Tran
- The Crimson Chronicles Book 1: *Crimson Forest* by Christine Gabriel
- The Crimson Chronicles Book 2: *Crimson Moon* by Christine Gabriel
- *The Grays* by Dave Housley and Becky Barnard
- The Phaethon Series Book 1: *Phaethon* by Rachel Sharp
- The Phaethon Series Book 2: *Pharos* by Rachel Sharp
- The Sitnalta Series Book 1: *Sitnalta* by Alisse Lee Goldenberg
- The Sitnalta Series Book 2: *The Kingdom Thief* by Alisse Lee Goldenberg
- The Sitnalta Series Book 3: *The City of Arches* by Alisse Lee Goldenberg

- The Sitnalta Series Book 4: *The Hedgewitch's Charm* by Alisse Lee Goldenberg
- The Sitnalta Series Book 5: *The False Princess* by Alisse Lee Goldenberg
- The Thuperman Trilogy Book 1: *Becoming Thuperman* by Elgon Williams
- The Thuperman Trilogy Book 2: *Homer Underby* by Elgon Williams
- The Thuperman Trilogy Book 3: *Thuperheros* by Elgon Williams
- The Wolfcat Chronicles Book 1: *Dammerwald* by Elgon Williams

Women's Fiction
- *Beautiful Secret* by Dana Faletti
- *Find Me in Florence* by Jule Selbo
- *The Long Way Home* by Regina West
- *The Shape of the Atmosphere* by Jessica Dainty

Non-Fiction
- *Marketing for Freelance Writers* by Robyn Roste
- *The Writer's Zen* by Jessica Reino

Printed in the USA
CPSIA information can be obtained
at www.ICGtesting.com
LVHW021040051223
765518LV00086B/2789